ALSO BY SUSAN CRANDALL

*Back Roads*

4-4-04

# *The* ROAD HOME

## SUSAN CRANDALL

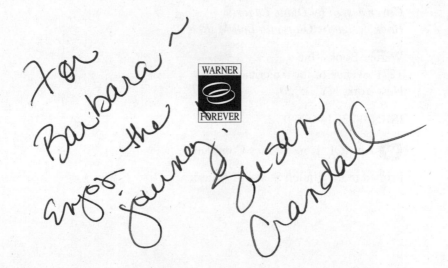

For Barbara ~
Enjoy the journey!

Susan Crandall

WARNER
FOREVER

*For Reid and Allison,*
*my touchstones to the ways of the youthful heart.*

# Acknowledgments

My thanks to the ladies of WITTS, Alicia, Betty, Brenda, Esther, Garthia, Laurie, and Pam, for picking me up when I was down and pushing me ever forward. To Karen Kosztolnyik, for keeping me pointed in the right direction—even when my own compass went haywire. To Vicky Harden for the keen eye in the final read through. To Linda Kruger, who dug me out of the sand and saw what I could be. To my husband, Bill, and my children, Reid and Allison, who had to learn to live under the same roof with a writer and newly imposed deadlines.

It's strange how a single event can alter the course of your entire life. Of course, some are obvious: winning the lottery, getting hit by a car when you're riding your bicycle, saving a kid from drowning in the lake, or your momma running off with a liquor salesman. But it's those more secret things, the ones that keep quiet and don't reveal themselves until the fall of events has completed itself, that seem to make the most significant changes. You know something started you on the path from there to here, but only by backtracking can the source be found. Follow the trail of toppled dominoes and pretty soon, there you are, staring squarely at the reason your life took a left turn onto a gravel road filled with potholes instead of a right turn onto the sweetly paved blacktop with clear shoulder markings.

For Lily Holt, that event was finding a single cigarette butt.

# *Prologue*

There were things in this world that just didn't make sense. Like how it was just fine and dandy for eleven-year-old Lily Boudreau to walk around in the family's apartment over the Crossing House Tavern, do her homework over the beer cooler, cook dinner over the jukebox and even go to bed right over the pool table in the back, but it was against the law for her to set foot on the first floor. They had moved to this apartment shortly after Lily's mom left to start a new life, so Dad could take care of them while he worked. He was the owner and tended bar, but she couldn't even go down and kiss him goodnight. If she had something to tell him during working hours, she had to call him on the phone. Like he worked miles away instead of right beneath her feet.

As her dad got ready to go down to work, she flopped on the couch next to him, grumbling once again about that stupid law. "Why can't we just ignore it? Who would know?"

Dad looked at her with his do-we-have-to-do-this-again? face. "We might think it's silly, but it's still the law." He paused, right where he always did, and rubbed his hand over his face—like he always did. "It wouldn't be right to just follow the laws we like—you can't just pick and choose. What if someone thought it wasn't fair that they couldn't drive when they were three sheets to the wind? Just think of the things that could happen."

Well, that didn't seem nearly the same at all. Lily knew her dad never let anyone leave the Crossing House after they'd had too much to drink. He'd call Mr. Mills's cab company to take them home. Oh, they *did* think it was a stupid law then—she'd heard them cuss a blue streak at her dad. Their drunk tongues had a hard time getting the words out, but their loud voices made up for that. It was always the same. *"Benny,"* they'd say, *"give me my goddamn keys!"* And she'd hear a pause during which her dad must have been talking. *"I ain't too drunk! Just look at my hands—steady as a rock!"*

"But that law makes sense," Lily said. She'd seen the accident out on the curve on Quarry Road. The one everybody still talked about in real quiet voices. The one that killed two little kids and their mom.

Dad ruffled her hair. "Just the same, it's all in the way a person looks at it. A law's a law. Like it or not. So"—he kissed her on the forehead—"you just pick up that phone and call if you need anything." Then he put on his white apron and headed downstairs. She heard him call back over his shoulder, "Don't forget your homework."

"Better be hunting down Luke if you're worried about somebody's homework!" Her older brother was in serious danger of repeating eighth grade—all because of math. Well, English and social studies were pretty iffy, too. Tomorrow was D-day. She laughed; that was a good one! Luke'd be *lucky* if it was D-day and not F-day.

Dad's laugh echoed up the stairwell that led to the bar's

kitchen. Then she heard him holler hello to Henry Calverson, the cook. He had to holler, because Henry was about as close to deaf as a person could be and still hear a freight train pass through his living room.

"Evenin', Benny. Kiddos okay?" Henry asked—well, shouted—his usual question.

The comforting sounds of business getting under way downstairs drifted up to the apartment. Once the bar started to fill up, Dad would shut the door at the bottom of the staircase. Until then, Lily went about getting dinner ready for Luke and their little sister, Molly, listening to Henry sing too loud and way off-key.

She liked to hear Henry sing.

As she set the macaroni and cheese on the table, her mind hurried on toward evening. She and Luke had serious business to attend to.

It was twilight when she finally locked the door behind them and they headed down the outside stairs. Instead of taking the road, they slipped down to Blackwater Creek and followed it to the dam. On the other side of the tall spillway was Forrester Lake, which, up until a handful of Chicago people bought up all the land on the far side, had been Forrester Reservoir. Funny how money can change everything, even the name of a body of water.

It was dark enough in the woods that they needed their flashlights. As Lily started to switch hers on, Luke put a hand out to stop her. "If you're right," he whispered, "we don't want to let anyone know we're coming,"

It was still spring, so the water was high enough to roll over the spillway, creating a noise that sounded a little bit like rain falling on leaves—enough noise to mask their movements. "I'm right. Somebody's been here."

They moved toward the rocky limestone outcropping a few yards to the left of the creek bed, not far from the bottom of the dam.

From the first day she and Luke had stumbled upon it, Lily had loved the place—which is exactly what they called it, only with capital letters. The Place. It was nice to slip into the cool shadows of the overhanging rock and sit on the logs they'd dragged there for seats. She liked the way everything sounded more clear in the deep ravine—the birds, the trickle of the water over the stones in the creek bed, the rustle of a rabbit in the brush, the sharp chatter of an angry squirrel.

It was when she'd come earlier today that she'd found it. A cigarette butt. Evidence that someone had invaded their private hideout.

They ducked behind a large honeysuckle bush, still unable to see anyone. Night had fallen and The Place had a host of its own shadows.

Suddenly a match flared under the outcropping. Two boys sat on the logs, lighting cigarettes. One was tall and skinny, about Luke's size. The other one was a little bigger—broader.

"Well, shit," Luke whispered. "At least they're kids."

Lily didn't know if that made it better or not. Adults might be here a couple of times, then forget about it. Kids—well, they'd probably fight for it.

Lily leaned close to her brother's ear. "What are we going to do?"

Luke smiled; his teeth shone blue in the darkness. She recognized the smile. It was a declaration of war. Lily felt a thrill go through her. She didn't normally like to fight, but when someone takes something that's yours—you just have no choice.

She said, "Shouldn't we try asking them to leave first?"

Ignoring her, he shot to his feet, crashing loudly through the bushes and snapping his flashlight on. He held it at shoulder height and shone it right in the faces of the two boys.

"Hey!" Luke could have a really deep voice when he worked at it. "You kids!" He was working at it.

Immediately the two glowing ends of the cigarettes disappeared.

Luke kept the boys blinded with his flashlight.

"We weren't doing anything, Officer."

Lily crouched lower and stifled her laughter with her hand. They thought Luke was the sheriff!

"Where you boys from?" Luke had to keep his sentences short. He couldn't use the deep voice for too long at a stretch without it cracking on him.

The skinny one with the light hair said, "Cottage over on Mill Run Road."

*Cottage?* Those places on Mill Run Road were bigger than most of the houses in town. And what were these richy summer kids doing poking around on this side of the lake? Their side had the marina and the ice cream place.

"What're your names?"

After a long hesitation, while Lily imagined the kid was weighing the possibility of getting caught if he lied, the skinny one said, "Peter Holt." His voice squeaked slightly.

Lily was pretty sure he told the truth. Who would *choose* to be a Peter?

The bigger one stepped forward, more into the light. When he did, Lily's breath caught in her throat. It was the kid who had helped her little sister Molly late last summer when she fell off her bike at the park. When Lily had found the two of them, he'd already gotten Molly to stop crying. In fact, he had her laughing a little bit.

"Clay Winters," he said.

His voice was deeper than last year. Deep enough to make Lily wonder how long they were going to buy Luke's impersonation.

"Your folks let you smoke?" Luke used just the right tinge of adult-sounding sarcasm.

"We just wanted to try it. We don't even like cigarettes. We won't be doing it anymore," Peter, the skinny one, said.

God, even Molly wouldn't believe that line.

Luke grunted, just the way she'd heard Sheriff Hayes do when he didn't buy a kid's story. "Get on home. Don't let me catch you back here."

"Yes, sir," both voices chimed together.

When they were almost out of the range of the flashlight beam and Lily was about to burst out of her hiding spot, Luke called out, "Hold it!"

The boys froze. Clay turned to face him.

"Be at my office at four o'clock tomorrow. Bring your parents."

One of the boys said, "Shit!" under his breath.

Luke said, "What was that?"

Clay said, "We'll be there, sir, but my father's in Chicago."

"That's fine, son. He can call my office at four."

*Don't push your luck. Just let them go,* Lily pleaded silently.

"Go on," Luke finally said. He kept his flashlight shining from his shoulder until the sounds of their flight disappeared. Then he burst out laughing.

Lily exploded from behind the bush. "You should have stopped while you were ahead. Once they go to the sheriff, they'll know they were tricked."

"Yeah, but by then they'll have had to tell their parents."

"But they'll come back here looking for us!"

He rubbed her hair, just like Dad did. "That's right. We'll be ready."

She and Luke took to the field of battle as though their very lives depended upon it. They warred with Peter and Clay through the early weeks of summer—water balloons and booby traps, tit for tat, attack and retaliation. It had been all-consuming, the reason they got out of bed each morning, the subject of their quiet conversations at night.

The Fourth of July dawned and Lily felt a charge in the air.

"The only way to gain the upper hand," Luke said, winking at Lily, "is to stake your territory first." He loaded a paper grocery bag with fireworks.

Lily didn't like the idea of missing the Fourth of July parade and picnic in the park. But if Luke said it had to be done, it had to be done. So just as the sun was coming up— Luke assured her that rich kids never got up until nine—she and her brother left a note for their dad and headed to The Place. They each held a brown grocery bag. One was packed with snacks and a couple of bottles of Coke. The other, ammunition—firecrackers and some illegal M-80s, bottle rockets and even a few real aerial fireworks.

That was another law Lily never fully understood. It fit right up there with not being able to go downstairs to talk to her dad at the Crossing House. You could buy illegal "out-of-state" fireworks if you told the man you bought them from that you weren't going to set them off in Indiana. Every year the same beer-bellied man, who called himself Firecracker Bill, came to Glens Crossing from Tennessee and set up a tent in the parking lot of Kingston's Market. Of course, Dad didn't have any idea that they pooled their allowance and visited Firecracker Bill. If he had, there would have been no more allowance or Fourth of July for either of them.

As the day wore on and boredom was replaced by severe boredom, Lily's regret over missing the festivities grew. She'd never noticed how little there was to do at The Place. Of course, she'd never been stranded here like a castaway on a desert island. Man, if it could be so boring here, why did they care if someone else used it every once in a while?

She'd just bet those kids, Peter and Clay, were at the watermelon-eating contest at the park right now. And Dad would have Molly's bike all decorated with red, white and blue streamers for her to ride in the parade.

Sighing as loud as she could without getting light-headed, she was disappointed when Luke didn't stir from where he was dozing with his head on a big rock.

For a while, she sat next to him and amused herself by tickling his nose with a jack-in-the-pulpit she'd picked near the big sycamore. After the fourth or fifth time she got him to scrunch up his face and scratch, that used up all its amusement.

Sighing again, she leaned back on her elbows and closed her eyes. The sunlight flickered through the leaves and she watched it play in pink patterns on the insides of her eyelids.

Something small hit the ground nearby. Lily figured it was an acorn or walnut knocked loose by a squirrel, so she didn't open her eyes.

The snap of the firecracker brought her directly to her knees. The sharp acrid smell of gunpowder stung her nose and a puff of blue smoke clouded her vision. Luke was at her side before she'd drawn a breath. He got his arm around her shoulder and knocked her back to the ground.

"Bastards," he whispered through his teeth. "I knew I shouldn't have gone to sleep."

"It's *them*?" As she whispered it, she strained to see any telltale movement in the bushes.

Luke looked at her like she didn't have a brain in her head. "Who else, Einstein?" He crawled over to their fireworks bag and dug around in it for a minute. When he crawled back to where she was crouched behind a log, he shoved a bunch of firecrackers into her hands. "You just hold this stuff." He opened a box of kitchen matches. "I'll light and throw."

She looked at the firecrackers she held. "Could these hurt someone?"

"Only if they go off in your hand."

Lily felt her eyes widen.

"Don't worry. They're not going to be lit in *your* hand."

She just about said he might want to be concerned about his own fingers, but she didn't want him to think she was a wuss.

Just about the time Luke struck the first match, another firecracker came flying from the shrubbery to their left. Lily drew herself into a ball and squeezed her eyes closed, waiting for the *pop*.

Instead, she heard a loud hiss.

Luke launched his first round.

Lily looked behind them. A smoke bomb was spewing a red cloud.

"Peeeewwwww."

"Give me another one." Luke poked at her closed fist.

Handing it over, Lily still couldn't actually see the enemy. She heard something land back near the limestone outcropping—far enough away that she stood her ground and waited for the explosion without flinching.

When it came, it was much louder than she expected. She

ducked her head close to her shoulders. Luke was trying to pry another firecracker out of her clenched fist. "No!"

"Gimme!"

"It's too danger—"

The rapid succession of explosions made them both spin around.

The paper sack jumped as if it were filled with popping corn. It smoked, then burst into flames. Lily's copy of *Little Women* was right next to the bag—as was the blanket. She started for them and Luke jerked her back.

He jumped over to the bag and tried kicking the flames out. But it was too late, the bottle rockets and fireworks had started to take off.

Lily ran toward him, but something big came crashing past her. She lost her balance and teetered to the left.

Clay skidded to a stop beside Luke, seemingly oblivious to the rockets taking off in every direction, and scooped up fistfuls of dirt, throwing them onto the burning blanket.

Once she regained her balance, Lily started toward the fire again. The pops and hissing kept going and a rocket whizzed past her ear. If she hadn't ducked, she was certain her hair would have been on fire. She was almost to Luke when something hit her leg.

She screamed, falling to the ground. It felt worse than the time she was accidentally shot by a BB gun.

Looking down, she saw the long launching stick of the firework protruding from her thigh. The fuse snapped and hissed as it burned closer to the rocket filled with explosives.

Clay was there before she could react. He pulled the rocket from her thigh and hurled it a good ten yards away before it exploded. He bent over her, shielding her from the worst of the burning spray of color that showered them.

The rocket was deep. In her brief look, Lily had seen that nearly half of the shell was buried in her leg.

Luke was still trying to spread the arsenal and get the burning fuses stamped out. Clay picked Lily up. "She's bleeding pretty bad. I'm taking her for help."

The pops sounded farther away. The searing pain in Lily's leg occupied most of her attention, but she heard Luke yell, "Wait! She's my sister. I'll take her."

"Put out the fire, then catch up," Clay called back. Then he yelled, "Peter! Help him!"

They reached the path, where Peter stood staring at Lily's bloody leg for a moment before he took off in the opposite direction. The terror she saw in his eyes told her she was in serious trouble. She started to shake.

Clay kept moving. He murmured softly in her ear, "Take it easy. I'll get you to a doctor. It'll stop hurting soon."

Lily let her head fall against Clay's shoulder and pressed her lips together to keep from crying out. Her leg felt like it was on fire. She hadn't looked at it after he had pulled the rocket out. She was too afraid of what she might see. He had said she was bleeding. She couldn't tell. It just hurt.

The trek through the rough woods seemed to take forever. Normally, it took Lily and Luke fifteen minutes to get to The Place. But Clay was moving slowly, his footing sometimes faltering. His breathing sounded like he'd been running a mile. At one point she heard Luke say he'd carry her for a while, but Clay kept moving.

Then she heard another voice. This one sounded as scared as Lily felt. And that really got her worried—this was a grown-up voice. Lily landed in the back seat of a car. Doors slammed closed. Then they were moving again. A woman with blond hair was driving. She kept asking Clay where Peter was.

After the fifth time, he nearly shouted, "I don't know!" Then he added, more quietly, "He's okay."

Clay kept turning around in the front seat and looking at Lily. Luke was in the back next to her, holding a towel against her leg.

Once they pulled up at the emergency room of Henderson County Hospital, other people crowded around her. She lost track of Luke and Clay and the woman who drove the car.

Lily felt all floaty, like she was a kite bobbing on the breeze. She heard her dad's voice, felt his hand on the top of her head.

"How are you feeling, sweetie?"

The pain in her leg was still there, but much more dull. She hesitated opening her eyes. Dad was going to be really mad. Right now he was talking to her like he did when she was sick. Once he knew she was better, it was going to hit the fan.

She opened her eyes. She was in a hospital room.

Dad smiled.

That made her more worried. Was she going to be crippled?

Then he said, "There's someone here to see you."

He stepped away. Lily was surprised when the face that appeared next wasn't her brother's, but Clay's. His eyes moved restlessly back and forth from her leg and her face. Finally, he looked her in the eye.

He had the most incredible golden brown eyes with a darker brown ring around the irises. Lily almost forgot how much her leg hurt when he looked at her like that. It was as if she were the only person in the world that mattered.

"I—I'm sorry. We didn't mean for anyone to get hurt."

She shook her head and the room swam for a moment. "You carried me all the way home. You could have run."

The startled look in his eyes told her he was shocked she'd even think such a thing.

She said, "Besides, it was an accident." She looked around his shoulder to see if her dad was listening. He'd left the room. She said, more quietly, in case Dad was just outside the door, "We shouldn't have had those rockets in the first place." She paused. "I suppose Luke's grounded." For a moment she almost wished she *would* be crippled—that way Dad couldn't be too mad at her.

Clay smiled. "Let's just say none of us are going to that spot by the creek anytime soon."

It was then that Lily noticed the bandage on his right hand. "You're hurt?"

He quickly tucked the hand behind his back. "Just a little burn."

The events of that horrible moment began to take on definition in her mind. "The fuse on the rocket burned your hand when you pulled it out of my leg."

He looked away. "It's not bad."

"But if you hadn't pulled it out . . ." Lily realized that what felt like a vast burning crater in her leg would have been exactly that. With a sense of sickness in her stomach, her close call became crystal clear. "Oh, my gosh, it could have blown my leg completely off!"

Clay laughed, but it was a nervous laugh that said he was just trying to make her feel better. "Oh, it wasn't that dramatic. You're gonna be okay. Don't think about it anymore."

At that moment, looking into his eyes, she decided she could trust Clay Winters with all of her eleven-year-old heart. And Lily Boudreau didn't give her trust easily.

*Twenty-one years later*

# *Chapter 1*

For the past twelve years of her marriage, Lily had fought against the cyclone working to tear her world apart. She'd frantically snatched and grabbed the pieces, as the winds whipped and whorled, ripping them away more quickly than she could reassemble them.

Maybe she shouldn't have tried so hard. Maybe at sight of the first black thunderhead on the horizon she should have simply thrown her body over her son, covered her head and waited to see where things settled after the storm. Maybe then her ex-husband, Peter, wouldn't be in alcohol rehab right now. Then the divorce would have been over before Riley was old enough to react with so much antagonistic belligerence and bad behavior. Even if he had, he would have been young enough to control—and it would all be just a distant memory by now.

Exhausted from the past days' emotional events and the five-hour drive from Chicago, Lily pulled up in front of the southern Indiana lake cottage and shut off the engine, telling herself she *was not* running away. She was putting necessary space between Riley and his grandparents, herself and her ex-husband. She was taking the first step toward a new life.

After a long and bumpy struggle, she and Peter had surrendered the fight for their marriage. And for some inexplicable reason, with the ending of her present, Lily had a sudden, irrepressible urge to review her past. That past was deeply rooted in Glens Crossing, the catalysts for its changing course embedded in this cottage on Forrester Lake.

She rested her chin on the steering wheel and studied the house. It was still the same forest green with white trim it had been since it was built by Peter's grandparents. Two tall stories, it had deep, open eaves, multipaned windows and a foundation made of river rock. The lower half of the front porch pillars were river rock, too, topped with square wooden supports that were wider at the base than at the top. A symbol of tradition, of familial stability.

She hadn't been back here since she and Peter eloped fourteen years ago. The lake house was Peter's now, deeded to him by his grandparents on his twenty-fifth birthday. That was one of the few things his parents couldn't circumvent. Lily had no doubt that Peter's father would have given his right eye to have prevented that transfer of control.

Although the ownership was Peter's, they had never returned here as a family, she, Peter and Riley. It seemed best to let the specters that dwelt on this quiet lake rest undisturbed. The past had caused enough unrest in their lives from three hundred miles away.

The mere mention of Forrester Lake always brought doubt to Peter's eyes, a pain born of wondering if Lily would have been his had things unfolded differently. In his most unhappy moments, he always posed the same question: *"If Clay walked through the door today, would you leave with him?"*

The question, no matter how often she heard it, no matter how she steeled herself against it, made her heart trip a little faster. Clay had abandoned her, discarded her love with no more thought than he'd give yesterday's paper. And she hated him for it. But it was an odd sort of hatred, one that fueled angry fires in her soul and flirted with the edges of her heart at the same time. When she thought of him, she wanted to strangle him with her bare hands; she wanted to throw herself into his arms for one more embrace. Both feelings brought self-loathing. She was so weak. Weak enough to have damaged Peter's life while trying to save her own.

She *had* loved Peter, she supposed for nearly as long as she'd been *in love* with Clay. But it had been a different kind of love, a safer love, than what she'd felt for Clay. Clay set off volcanic upheavals deep in her soul. Peter calmed her spirit, warmed her with security. Clay was passion. Peter was family.

Throughout their marriage, her reassurances had done nothing to erase Peter's doubt. It had grown and expanded, becoming the strongest link and, at the same time, the thickest wall between Lily and her husband.

Now, as she looked at the house, a sense of *déjà vu* settled over her, draped itself weightlessly about her shoulders, wrapped tightly around her chest and sent far-reaching roots directly to her soul. So easily did the years of adulthood slip away, leaving the heart of a girl exposed and bleeding. A girl who had trusted completely, without reservation—and paid the price.

What would she have done, if Peter hadn't been there to pick up the pieces when Clay left?

And now she was alone, really and truly, alone. There was no one to pick up the pieces except Lily. And she would do it. She had to, for her son.

The press of tears was strong. But she would no more let them fall now than she did fourteen years ago. Forge ahead. Take care of business. Deal. That's what had sustained her for most of her life. No sense in ignoring the tried and true at this point.

She glanced at Riley leaning against the passenger door, asleep. He didn't stir. His head remained propped on his hand, his dark hair tousled over his closed eyes. The tinny beat from his headphones was the only sound in the car.

Every time she saw him sleeping, her heart broke. He looked the same as he had when he was three, sweet and open and loving. When he was sleeping, there was no trace of the wary tension and defensive attitude that dominated his waking features.

He'd been "excused" from the last week of seventh grade for "conduct unbecoming." That's what went in the official record. What really happened was Riley's friend had come to Carrigan Park Prep School with some pills he bought at a party. The exact type of drug had yet to be determined. That's what frightened Lily the most—he took something without any idea what it was.

After swallowing the pills, Riley and two friends flushed cherry bombs down three of the toilets in the boys' bathroom. They'd been too stoned to even have the sense to run. They just sat there in an inch of water, watching the plumbing spew.

Riley had insisted this was his first experience with drugs. Lily wanted to believe him. She wanted that with all of her heart. There had certainly been no indication of his using prior to this.

Anyone else might have been expelled from school, but Peter's parents stepped in and softened the blow—again. Being on the board did have its perks. But this had to stop,

before Riley got into something with permanent consequences. When she'd called Peter at the Sheldon Center to
tell him about Riley's latest, they'd agreed the boy needed to
be away from his current environment, at least for a little
while. He'd urged her to use the cottage. As her options
were currently limited by expediency and a tight budget,
she'd agreed. Although Peter came from a wealthy family,
their own financial situation ranged in the comfortable
middle class—and with the dissolution of the marriage, the
money had been spread thin.

Reluctantly, she shook Riley awake, got out of the car
and climbed onto the front porch. As she put the key in the
front door lock, Lily thought she heard a shout from the
lake. She jerked her gaze in that direction and saw the empty
water glinting in the late afternoon sun. It had been Clay's
voice, calling from a distant memory. The four of them,
Peter, Clay, Luke and Lily, had raced from the shore to the
diving island nearly every day. Clay always reached the
dock first, pulled himself out of the water and urged Lily on.
The day she actually beat the other two boys Clay had
grabbed her against his wet chest and twirled them in a
circle.

The old sadness and anger mingled in her heart as she
thought of it. Maybe reviewing the past was going to be
more difficult than she'd anticipated.

"Mom?" Riley's voice made her jump. He was right
behind her, weighted down with his duffel and backpack.
"We going in, or what?"

She didn't look at him, afraid he'd see how shaken she
was. Throwing open the door, she tried to sound cheerful.
"Here we are." She didn't want him to view this trip as punishment, exactly, but as an opportunity, a chance to start
over. She'd lectured for the first hour of their trip south,

trying to drive home the fact that he was being given a chance that few in his situation were allowed. He seemed to listen, nodding his head in agreement, but Lily thought it was entirely for her benefit. Riley didn't have a clue.

In her hastily thrown together plan, she had decided not to see anyone until tomorrow. She needed a few hours to mentally adjust. Once word of her return was out, she would be bombarded with a thousand questions, most from people who felt they had a right to details of her life just because she'd been born in this town.

So she stuck to her plan, stowing away the feeling that she was sneaking into town like a thief. Once the car was emptied, she went about settling into the cottage. She turned on the water, uncovered furniture, washed linens, chased cobwebs and nagged Riley to unpack his duffel.

The sun set and the night turned chilly. She was tempted to have Riley bring in some firewood from the rack beside the boathouse. Even though the cottage was seldom used, there had always been a handyman to keep the grass cut, the windows clean and the firewood stocked—Peter wouldn't think of breaking such a tradition. For years she'd worried over the unnecessary expense. Now she was grateful. But who knew how long it had been since the huge rock fireplace had been used? It wouldn't do at all to call Peter and tell him she'd burned down the family cottage. She passed on the fire.

Before they'd left Chicago, she'd packed a cooler and enough groceries to get them through the first night. After a makeshift meal of summer sausage, cheese, crackers, fruit and almost a full bag of Oreos—which Riley still twisted apart and ate the center of first—they sat on the leather club sofa in the living room. Through his earphones, Riley immersed himself in a hard-core CD, all driving metal and screaming voices. Lily stared into space, wondering exactly where she was going to go from here.

The decision to leave Chicago had been easy. Riley couldn't go on thinking his grandparents could undo his missteps. Talking to Peter's parents rarely availed anything beyond empty promises to be less meddling. Something had to be done before Riley took a step that couldn't be undone. She hoped a full summer with the stability of her own father's loving discipline would set a good paternal example. But after that? Her future was a blank slate. The only thing she knew for certain was that she had no intention of settling here permanently—not in a town that knew each and every bone of the skeleton in a person's closet.

She sighed and told herself to take one day at a time, she had three whole months to figure out what was to come next. If she was careful, she had enough money to make it through until fall. Then she would have to land somewhere permanently and find a job. She had no idea what job that would be. She had no marketable skills. During her marriage to Peter, she'd spent her spare hours on her hobby, pottery. She'd taught several ceramics classes at the community center in the inner city, but that hardly counted as work experience.

She glanced at Riley. Where they ended up depended a great deal upon how he managed himself over the summer. She didn't really think that returning to the same private school in Chicago would be the answer. He needed to live in a world where everyone was accountable for their actions. A lesson that had taken Peter thirty-four years to begin to learn. Not that Peter was a bad person. He just couldn't face the things he perceived as failures. And those failures had piled up until they tumbled him like an avalanche. The final snowflake that set his most recent decline into motion came from errors in judgment that cost his company—his father's company—a fortune. Of course, his father's reaction hadn't been much help. Publicly he'd defended Peter and the company position. Privately he'd made sure his son knew exactly where the finger of blame was pointing.

Lily finally lifted Riley's earphones and slid them off his head. The angry, powerful beat of the music became louder in the silent room. "Why don't you go upstairs and pick out a bedroom?" She raised her voice over the music.

His hazel eyes narrowed and he gave her a sidelong look. "Doesn't matter." He started to put the headphones back on.

She interrupted the action by putting her hand on his head and brushing back his hair. He pulled away, as she knew he would. Sometimes it was hard for her to realize the distance that had grown between them over the past year. "You might want your dad's old room." She waited for some reaction. She didn't get one. "Or the guest room—it gets lots of morning sun."

"I don't care," he said through tight lips, nipping the words into a staccato beat. Then he seemed to back off just a bit and said more softly, "You pick."

It was moments like this, when he showed her that he knew he was being a prick and actually tried to make amends for it, that let her know he wasn't yet lost.

"Okay," she said, "I'll put the sheets on in Dad's old room. It's the one to the left at the top of the stairs." It seemed odd that a place that had been so familiar to both her and Peter was totally alien to their son.

Riley actually managed a half-smile. "All right."

Lily picked up the sheets from the dining room table and started for the stairs, uneasy with the knowledge that she was sharing the house with a child who was quickly becoming a stranger. Where had her happy little boy gone?

The one who picked wild violets and dandelions and delivered them with the eagerness and pride befitting two dozen white roses. The apple-cheeked child who'd broken her heart when he made her cinnamon toast and brought it to her in bed when she had the flu.

His voice stopped her halfway up the stairs. "Mom?"

She stopped, her heart jumping to conclusions. "Yes."

"When's the cable coming?"

Her shoulders sagged. "Tomorrow morning."

"Good."

Lily heard the music as he turned it back on. She was about to go back and do what she knew she should—tell him the cable, and all other privileges, would come when he earned them. But tonight she was just too tired for the argument.

She climbed the rest of the stairs, bone-weary and sick at heart. *God, give me the strength to pull him back and the wisdom to know how to start.*

The next afternoon, after the cable guy left, Lily forced herself to get on with it. She stood just outside the screen door that opened into the kitchen of the Crossing House Tavern. It was nearly four o'clock and preparations for the evening trade were getting under way. She heard the sounds of pots clanking and dishes rattling as someone pulled them from the dishwasher and stacked them on the shelf over the stainless steel worktable. There was the muffled clatter of glassware being carried out to the bar in their plastic dishwasher trays. A warm comfort bloomed in Lily's chest. It was as if she'd never left.

In her mind, she could see the heavy black iron skillets and the no-frills white stoneware, gray-marked from years of knives and forks scraping across their surfaces, the frosted beer mugs and stainless steel bowls filled with peanuts.

"Evening, Henry!" Her dad's voice carried out the door.

Lily smiled when she heard the once-familiar booming greeting. Henry Calverson was still the cook—and apparently still without a hearing aid.

Henry was one of those fixtures from childhood that was always there but never really thought about, like running water and electricity. Something that would be sorely missed if taken away. Lily was taken by surprise at the flood of happiness she felt knowing he was still here.

She waited, listening a few moments longer, unwilling to interrupt the soothing sounds of routine with her arrival. She had spent so many years closing her mind to this place, shutting this town out of her life, that she was startled to realize that coming home could feel so good. She savored the moment, the warmth of reminiscence, before the barbs and stings of reality set in.

"Why, lookee here!" Henry shouted—his normal speaking voice. He never had adjusted to the fact that he couldn't hear but everyone else still could. "Benny!" he called to her father as he threw the screen door open and pulled Lily inside. "Lily's here. By God, Lily's come home!" He threw his sinewy arms around her and hugged her close.

Lily was surprised at his strength. Henry had to be seventy-five, a man of average height and way below average weight—from the feel of his grip he was nothing but bone and gristly muscle.

He held her at arm's length and looked her over. "Still pretty as a picture. Now, where's that baby? Benny said he didn't get your blue eyes, but has that hair of yours. Brown sugar sprinkled with cinnamon."

She pushed her hair behind her ear, a reaction of self-consciousness left over from a childhood in which everyone commented about her having her mother's hair. Any connection with the woman who'd abandoned her family made Lily wiggle beneath her skin. Leaning closer to Henry so she didn't have to shout quite so loud, she said, "That baby is thirteen years old! He's at home watching MTV."

Henry shook his head and muttered something about time slipping away. Then he said, "Home? You didn't bring him to Glens Crossing, then?" He frowned.

"Oh, no. I mean he's at the lake house—where we're staying. Peter's family's place."

Henry nodded. Something flashed in his eyes, a question unasked, an opinion unuttered. After her mother ran off with a liquor salesman when Lily was eight, Henry had stepped up his protective attitude, especially about Lily and her little sister, Molly. Since he'd had no children of his own, she supposed she and Henry pretty much looked at each other as surrogate family. She didn't like to be the cause of the uneasiness she saw in his face at the moment and was glad when her dad came crashing through the swinging door.

"There's my girl!" He moved quickly toward her and Lily found herself lost in the bulk of his embrace. "Why didn't you tell me you were coming?" Then he stilled. "Something's wrong." A statement, not a question. Her dad always did have the best emotional radar in the county.

She didn't know if she was relieved that he sensed it, or more on edge because she couldn't skate through this initial homecoming with the pretense of carefree happiness. What she did know was that she couldn't find her voice at the moment, so she simply shook her head.

Her dad didn't push, he just stood there, arms around her,

rocking her gently side to side. God, it felt good to be the child again, if only for a few moments.

Finally, she felt she had the strength to stand on her own again. "I'm fine." As she said this, she found herself swiping at a tear.

Dad just stared at her with those big brown eyes. Had his hair been completely silver the last time she'd seen him? It shamed her that she couldn't remember.

"It's a long story, Dad. I promise to tell you the whole thing, but right now you've got customers." She nodded toward the swinging door, where one of the waitresses stood with an order in her hand and a look on her face that was a cross between annoyance and complete confusion.

"Faye, this is my daughter, Lily."

Some of the confusion cleared from the woman's face— none of the annoyance.

Lily said, "Nice to meet you, Faye."

Faye nodded and stuck her pen behind her ear. It immediately became lost in the cloud of russet hair. "Benny, the beer tap's out." She clipped her order on the end of the stainless worktable.

"All right." He turned back to Lily.

Apparently, Faye wasn't satisfied. "It's Friday night, won't be long 'til we'll be overrun."

Benny cut a sharp look her way. "I said, all right."

Faye disappeared back through the swinging door. She hit it hard enough that it swung back and forth three times before stopping.

Benny said, "Faye's been here so long, she forgets who owns the place." He put an arm around Lily and moved toward the door. "Come sit at the bar while I change that keg."

As he led her from the kitchen, she realized this was the

first time she'd been inside the bar/dining room during operating hours. When she'd married Peter she was only
eighteen—Dad had stuck to his guns about twenty-one
means twenty-one until the day she left. The closest she'd
ever been to the bar was the kitchen door, and that hadn't
been until she was almost eleven. By then, considering the
years of being denied a glimpse, her imagination had taken
on all sorts of ideas about the mysterious interior.

One day, one of the waitresses had noticed her straining
to see through the swinging door and stopped. She looked at
Lily and said, "No sense in breakin' your neck. Here, take a
good look." And she held the door fully open.

Of course, the bar was closed, otherwise she wouldn't
have been allowed on the first floor at all. So Lily had to
imagine what it was like filled with people and music and
cigarette smoke. As she'd looked around, there was none of
the mystique she'd envisioned. It was just a big room with
short windows high on the wall opposite the bar.

The wall with the windows was lined with red vinyl
booths over which hung stained-glass lamps. Then there was
a row of six square tables set at an angle to the corners of the
room, a jukebox and an old walnut bar lined with backless
stools, also in red vinyl. Behind the bar was a large plate-
glass mirror and shelves filled with bottles of liquor. On the
far end, to one side of the front door, was a dartboard. The
pool table was tucked out of her range of sight, in the back
beside the kitchen.

As Lily now looked at it with her thirty-two-year-old
eyes, she realized the place looked just the same, maybe a
little more worn. She couldn't help but hesitate as she
crossed the threshold, feeling she was breaking the rules.

Benny stopped and looked at her. "What's wrong?"

She smiled and shrugged. "Just seems weird. I've never been in the bar before."

He gave her one of his low-key laughs and hugged her against his side. "It has been a long time. But you're legal now, kiddo." They went through the door.

Benny went behind the bar, Lily walked beside the stools. She settled on one as he bent to change the beer keg.

He said, "Molly called yesterday." His head was out of sight, stuck under the bar, muffling his voice. "Said she's going to try to make it home for a week this summer. Not sure when, said med school is really wearing her out."

Lily warmed with pride. Molly was going to be a pediatrician. "I hope she makes it before I leave."

Benny's head popped up, his eyes peering over the walnut edge of the bar. "Leave? You just got here. I figured you'd stay through Riley's summer vacation—with his dad in the hospital and all."

*Oh, boy.* "Dad, our divorce was final two weeks ago."

He came to his feet and leaned over the bar. "Is that why you're back here? I thought you were trying to work things out."

"That's partly why I'm here." She decided to leave their discussion about Riley to a more private moment.

Benny straightened and narrowed his eyes. "He got a girlfriend?"

Lily smiled sadly. If only it were that cut-and-dried. "No, Dad."

"Now, Lily, tell me true, I know he's got a drinking problem. Did he hit you?"

"Peter's getting help for the drinking. I wouldn't leave him because of an illness. And no, he was never a violent drunk—just the opposite. He got quiet—depressed." She sighed, suddenly feeling very, very tired. "We're still friends—that was what we always did best anyhow, be friends. Peter needs to get himself straightened out. But I'm not sure we were ever good for each other married." Her voice drifted lower.

Benny's gaze sharpened on her. "You belong here, Lily. Maybe if you and Peter had settled in at the lake house . . ."

Lily shook her head. "I can't see that would have helped anything." She couldn't think of anything more detrimental to her marriage than being face to face with memories of Clay Winters every day. But, of course, her dad didn't know about her and Clay. "Besides, you know how people are around here. It's always been sort of a love-hate relationship with the lake people. Can't see how my switching teams would have worked out."

Benny waved a hand in the air. "Pffft. You always made too much of that sort of thing. You just gotta give people a chance to show you their true nature."

"Hmmm." Lily didn't venture into that territory. It was an old discussion. "I'd better get back to Riley. Can you come for lunch tomorrow?"

The smile on her dad's face made her regret all of the missed lunches over the past years. "That'd be great."

She slid off the stool and headed toward the kitchen to say goodbye to Henry. Just as she went through the swinging door, she turned back around and waved to her dad. Out of the corner of her eye, she caught sight of a man coming through the front door. He was silhouetted against the bright light behind him. But there was something in the tilt of his head that shot a flash of familiarity through her. As she was turning to get a better look, Faye pushed her the rest of the way through the door. Lily tried to get another glimpse as the door swung back, but it didn't swing wide enough.

"Comin' through!" Faye maneuvered Lily out of the way as she passed back through the door with a tray full of salads.

"Watch out, Lily, she'll knock you over. I got the bruises to prove it." Henry had Lily by the elbow.

It occurred to Lily that if she was going down, Henry's hundred pounds wouldn't be nearly enough to counter the fall, but she smiled and thanked him.

She was tempted to go back into the bar, just to satisfy her curiosity about the man coming through the door. But she really needed to get back to Riley. She hated leaving him alone for too long, unable to shake the fear that he'd fall into some trouble while her back was turned.

Besides, it could have been anybody. After all, she'd lived in this town for eighteen years. There were a hundred people who might trigger such a reaction. She brushed it off and climbed into her car.

Still, as she drove home, the vague familiarity of the man entering the bar niggled at her memory, refusing to let her be.

# Chapter 2

**B**enny had a difficult time concentrating on his business. Lucky for him, most everybody in the Friday night crowd wanted nothing more complicated than draft beer. That was part of what he loved about this town, its simplicity. Oh, there were a few folks who liked to put on like they were sophisticated city people, ordering martinis and white Russians. But for the most part, Glens Crossing was made up of honest, hardworking people who wanted nothing more than a cold beer to finish out the work week.

His daughter plagued his mind. Lily had always been so dependable, so steady. That child had never given him a minute's worry. From the time she was a little girl, she had a balanced determination about her—had her head on straight. Even when her mother left, Lily didn't miss a beat, stepped right in and helped with her little sister, held their family together. But something in her eyes tonight, something he'd never seen there, had him bothered.

For a moment he wished Luke were here, and not off in some godforsaken country, spying on people who wanted to blow the US of A completely off the planet. Luke had always been able to squeeze the troubles out of Lily, the things she kept to herself and worked through on her own. But Luke wasn't here—in fact, Benny didn't even know *where* he was. So it was going to be up to him to help Lily.

"Hey, Benny?"

"Yeah?" Benny blinked and looked at the man seated across from him at the bar. Benny had known him by sight since he was a teenager, as he summered here and ran a bit with Luke. Benny never could keep any of those summer kids' names straight. But this past year the fella showed back up here and took over the marina at Forrester Lake, so Benny started calling him Bud, same nickname as the previous manager of the marina. Came in once a week, on Friday. Two beers and he'd leave. Quiet guy. Benny liked him.

"Just checking to see if you were still in there," Bud said.

"Preoccupied, I guess." Benny gave a shake of his head. "Got a couple things on my mind."

Bud pushed his beer away, leaned his elbows on the bar and grunted. The nod of his head said he knew the feeling. "Anything you want to tell?"

Benny smiled and drew another beer. "Thanks. But this is something you couldn't help with. Hell, I don't even know what the problem is."

Bud picked up his beer and took a drink. "Well, don't let it fester. Bad for your soul."

After a minute, Benny said, "My daughter's in town." He didn't really know what to say beyond that. After all, this guy knew Lily. Besides, he couldn't really define those troubles to himself. Lily's worried eyes told him it was more than she was sharing at the moment.

"Ahh, the soon-to-be doctor?"

"No. The other one." He started to draw another round for the table in the corner. "You remember, the one who learned the hard way not to play with fireworks." After a brief pause, he added, "She and her husband, Peter—you knew him, didn't you?" Without waiting for an answer, he said, "Well, they're divorced."

Bud slid off his stool, a jerky motion that drew Benny's gaze from his work. The cold beer foam on his hand told him to shut off the tap. "Something wrong?"

Bud shook his head and fished a few bills from his pocket. He laid them on the counter as he started to back away. "Better go. Tomorrow's a busy day at the lake."

Benny nodded. He might never get that fella figured out. Kept to himself for the most part. He did seem to take a shine to Benny. But talking about fishing and the weather was one thing, letting someone in was another matter entirely. Far as he could tell, nobody got in with Bud.

Faye hustled to the bar and rattled off an order. By the time Benny had it filled, his thoughts were back to Lily. He hated the care lines creasing her brow and the way her eyes clouded with worry. Maybe tomorrow's lunch would clear things up.

Clay shoved his way out the door, a cold sweat pricking his forehead and his beer lying like lead in his stomach.

Lily was here.

Did she know he was in Glens Crossing? He quickly dismissed the possibility. Most everyone around here knew him by the nickname Benny had given him.

As he crossed the parking lot, the crushed stone felt particularly cruel, trying to twist his ankles. He ignored the two or three greetings tossed his way, hunching himself deeper into his shirt collar. Once he reached his motorcycle, he got on, but didn't trust himself to take it out on the road just yet. It felt like he'd been told someone he loved had died. Even though nearly the opposite was true. Of course, he'd known Lily was alive, but now he discovered their worlds just might be on a collision course.

When he'd run into Luke eighteen months ago in Madrid, of course the subject of Lily and Peter had come up. There had been no way to avoid it. Luke hadn't known about his sister and Clay, nobody had—Lily had made certain of that. So Clay had listened, with his hand threatening to shatter the beer mug it cradled, while Luke filled him in on their married life.

Lily never stayed in Glens Crossing. Luke said it. Never in the years since she'd married Peter. Why was she here now?

It was Luke's final statement on the subject that rang in Clay's ears to this day. *"Funny, I always sorta thought she'd end up with you."*

"Yeah, buddy," Clay said, as he finally started his motorcycle, "so did I."

Lily called Riley from her cell phone. Once she established that he was still lying on the couch in front of the TV, she decided to take the long way home. She circled around the north side of the lake on the narrow, winding road that had been replaced long before Lily left Henderson County with a faster, straighter two-lane just a little farther north. She passed through the scarred section of forest that had burned a year ago. There was something haunting about the blackened, limbless tree trunks sticking up from the just-recovering ground growth. Here and there, a tiny new sapling had been planted and staked. Someone had long-reaching faith. At the moment, she couldn't imagine such tremendous optimism.

If it had been earlier, and if she'd been in a more solid

frame of mind, she might have driven to the dam instead, and taken the trail to The Place. She wondered if it had changed over the years. Was the trail even still there? Had the vegetation masked the spot she had been willing to go to war over? Would she be able to find it again? Those were questions that she would leave for another day—or another lifetime.

The afternoon easily slid into early evening by the time she got back home. In the purpling light of the waning day, Lily walked around the deserted first floor of the cottage. Riley's duffel no longer sat just inside the front door. The early evening stillness seemed intensified by the echoey interior and long shadows. The house seemed more empty than when they'd first arrived.

A horrible thought seized her. Had Riley taken off? She pushed down the panic and finished her search of the house. On the kitchen counter were the crumbs and dirty knife from a peanut butter and jelly sandwich and a half-full glass of milk. She wrapped her hand around the glass—warm. Then she looked out the window at the dock and boathouse. No sign of Riley.

Her heartbeat seemed to resonate in her ears as she climbed the stairs. The door to Peter's old room was closed, but not latched. She slowly pushed it open. The second she saw Riley sprawled asleep on his father's old plaid bedspread, she breathed a sigh of relief. In that instant she realized how desperate things had truly become, by what a fragile string her control over her son was held. She truly felt this was her last chance to pull him back. If she failed here, she feared she would lose him forever.

She lingered near his bed for a long moment, listening to his breathing. He seemed so calm now. If only he could find that same peace in his waking moments. With one finger, she brushed the hair off his forehead. Then she took the quilt that was thrown over the footboard of the bed and laid it gently over him.

He didn't stir, so she decided to leave him sleeping. She went out to the dock. The weathered boards creaked under her weight as she walked to the end. The sun was no more than a memory behind the tree line, the surface of the lake smooth and black. The tree frogs had begun their evening song and an owl hooted in the treetops.

She stood at the end of the dock, closed her eyes and drew a deep breath. The scents were the same as she remembered—blossoming lilacs, fresh-cut grass and the moist fragrance of lakeside woodlands. Slipping her shoes off, she sat down and dangled her feet in the water. The season was early, the water still cold, making an ache shoot up from her ankles to her knees. But she welcomed the sensation, recalling all of the years when she, Luke, Peter and Clay had come out of the water with blue lips, insisting to Peter's mother it wasn't too early to swim.

God, could it really be fourteen years since she'd spent a night in Henderson County? Now she was settling on the "other side" of the lake—the money side. She wasn't sure she liked it.

Everyone thought she'd married Peter Holt for his money. But that wasn't it at all. She'd married him in spite of his money. At the time, however, she didn't know he'd married her, at least in part, to spite his parents. What had begun as a complicated web of emotions had quickly unraveled to reveal there was nothing of substance holding the two of them together.

Staring out upon the still, black surface of the lake, she heard a fish jump. Lily allowed herself to be lulled into memory by the smells and sounds around her in the gathering darkness. The years dropped away like wilted petals from a rose. For the briefest moment she was a girl again, a girl whose only real worry was how to run a couple of intruders away from The Place.

Not for the first time in the past months, she wondered how different her life would have been if she just hadn't found that cigarette butt.

At the time, it seemed the most important event in their limited lives. Someone had invaded their territory. Worse yet, it had been summer kids. But their war ended on the Fourth of July, during the same summer in which it began. Short-lived as wars go, even for children. The truce didn't come in small measures, in peace summits and negotiations. It came of necessity, in a moment of absolute terror.

Lily now thought it was a bizarre irony that their conflict had begun with a cigarette butt and ended with fire. Maybe she should have paid more heed to the symbolism of ember to flame—but, of course, she was only eleven. What had she known of symbolism?

After several minutes, she tore her gaze from the dark surface of the lake, where the past played like a movie on a screen. She pushed her shorts higher on her leg and laid her hand on the puckered scar on her upper thigh. It was no longer pink, but had blended with her skin as old scars do. It may have happened long ago, in another lifetime, but every time she touched it, it made her feel connected to Clay. It was as if, no matter where he was, even though he'd erased her from his mind, when she touched that scar, she touched him.

From the day of the accident, they'd been close. Clay had always said, as they compared their scars, his palm and her thigh, that they were linked forever by the brand of that rocket. And it was true.

For years she'd not allowed herself to even look at it. She'd managed to change the focus of her entire life, everything around and about her. But no matter how much time passed, how much things changed, that scar would always be his.

The next morning, as Lily prepared lunch, she rubbed her aching temples. Two nights in this place filled with secrets and memories had only made her sleeplessness worse. She hadn't expected to rest well away from her own bed; never had she captured a good night's sleep away from home. But in this house, fragmented dreams cut even into that twilight place where she lingered between wakefulness and sleep, robbing her of any rest.

She drew in a deep breath, rotating her tense shoulders, and looked out the window toward the lake. Riley was lying in the sun on the end of the dock. His shirt was off, his hands were folded behind his head. She relaxed a bit. A little sunshine had to be good for him—a break from angry music and mind-blurring video games. A step in the right direction. Time alone with nature always helped her sort through her problems. Maybe Riley would discover the same elixir.

By the time she had lunch ready, her dad was pulling in the driveway.

Riley was polite, in a strained way, and quiet, all through the meal. He made a hasty exit the second his sandwich was gone. As he headed toward the door, he said he was going to take a walk around the lake.

"Wait," Lily called after him.

He stopped and looked back at her from the kitchen door.

"Where, exactly, are you going?"

He huffed. "Just around the lake. Jeez, Mom, it's not like I know anybody around here."

Lily heard her dad clear his throat softly. He thought she was being overprotective. But he didn't yet know what had happened. And while she wanted to demand Riley remain in plain sight every minute, she knew that was as unproductive as it was impractical. She had to give him his freedom in small increments. As he proved himself worthy of her trust, she could expand his range. "All right. But stay on the path. And don't be gone longer than forty-five minutes."

Riley rolled his eyes and started for the door with a grunt.

"You have your watch?" she called.

Without turning back around, he raised his arm, holding his wrist where she could see it.

The whole purpose of this lunch was to talk to her dad alone. But as soon as Riley walked out the door, the words dried up in her throat.

Her dad spoke first. "The boy's in trouble."

For a moment, Lily rearranged her napkin in her lap. She'd planned on working up to what had happened with Riley, laying a foundation that might help explain his recent behavior. But she should have known better. Her dad never did beat around the bush.

"Yes." She raised her eyes to meet his. "I really can't blame him for being angry. I just don't know how to help him get around it."

"What's he done?"

Lily searched for the place to begin, the moment when Riley had started to change. She sighed and twisted her hands in her lap. "He's just spiraling out of control. At first I thought this behavior was a passing thing, a response to the divorce. But it's getting worse. I'm afraid he'll do something that'll be completely off the deep end if I don't figure out how to reach him."

"You didn't answer me. What's he done?" Her dad's

brown eyes held that steady bead on her, in that way that had always drawn confessions from her lips as a kid.

She kept her gaze diverted when she said, "He blew up a toilet in his school with a cherry bomb."

"And?"

She looked up. "That's not enough?"

He kept his gaze fixed on her, making her squirm. "That's not all."

No sense in drawing this out. If her dad was going to be able to help her, he had to know everything. "Pills. A buddy of his brought them to school. They took them, then blew up the plumbing."

Benny made a harrumphing sound deep in his throat, but didn't say anything.

"Dad, he didn't even know what those pills were—and he took them. They could have killed him." Fear strangled the last of her words. She drew a deep breath and forced back the threatening tears. "He said it was the only time he'd used drugs of any kind." She looked into her dad's eyes, seeking a nod of reassurance that she should believe Riley. She didn't get one.

"I guess I should be grateful to Peter's dad," she said. "Riley could have ended up in jail." The very thought of her son caged with *real* criminals made her lunch churn in her stomach. She just couldn't see that putting him in jail would do anything but exacerbate his self-destruction. She had to find another way.

She went on. "I guess what scares me most is his attitude. None of this is a big deal." She started to shake so hard her teeth nearly rattled. "He's blowing this off—my God, he could have died!"

Benny waited a long while before he said anything. Lily was glad for the time to gather her composure.

When he finally spoke, it was with the same pragmatic approach he used for everything. "So there were no police charges, no questioning, no reports filed? Nothing to really send a message to the boy?" He raised one black eyebrow, as if he already knew the answer.

"Of course not. That would look bad for the school. Aside from some strong lecturing, dismissal from the last week of classes—like Riley isn't happy to be missing final exams—there is no punishment."

"Then it's up to you."

She let out a long breath, and her shoulders sagged. "I know. I want to do the right thing. But I'm a big source of his anger. I'm afraid I'll just push him further away—so far that I'll never get him back. Dad, he's so fragile right now." Lily buried her face in her hands, so very, very tired.

"That's just what he wants you to believe. That anything you might do to punish him will result in disaster. But I'll bet my life, at the same time, inside he's begging to be stopped. To have someone save him from himself."

Lily's eyes stung with unshed tears. "There's that, too. The saving from himself. Dad, Peter has never dealt with responsibility for his own choices. It's always some outside influence that's bent on sabotaging him, nothing is ever the result of *his* actions. I don't want Riley to grow up and never be able to face up to the things he's responsible for."

As soon as she said this, her hand went to the scar on her leg and rested there. After the Fourth of July accident, Clay had stepped up, taken the blame and dealt with the aftermath. Peter had disappeared.

Benny got up and walked to her side of the table. He put both of his hands on her shoulders and squeezed. "This summer can be a new start. We'll just have to make him see that everything he does has consequences. Once he sees you mean business, he'll come around." He kissed the top of her head. "Hell, maybe just getting him out of that city will be enough."

Lily put a hand over her father's where it rested on her shoulders, feeling for the first time in days that she'd found a life raft on a stormy sea. "Maybe you're right. God, I hope you're right."

The following Wednesday, Riley was caught sinking the neighbor's boat.

"All right," Sheriff Steve Clyde said, "Mr. Willit has agreed not to press charges if you pay for the damages to the boat and follow the rules of your probation." He looked pointedly at Riley Holt. "And I set those rules."

The sheriff knew this "probation" was nothing of the sort. He wasn't a judge and it had no legal binding. But he wanted the kid to know he was on thin ice. Probation was a word they all understood. "From this point forward, consider yourself an ant under a magnifying glass. Everywhere you go, everything you do, I'm gonna know, your mom's gonna know, and if need be, the prosecutor will know. You screw up, it's juvenile hall for you. This is no free pass. Here in Henderson County, you take responsibility for what you do. You understand?"

Riley nodded, slumped lower in his seat and folded his hands in his lap. The sheriff could see the defiance rippling under the surface, but the boy managed to keep it in check. He took that as a good sign. With seven kids of his own, he sympathized with Lily. It had to be hard to be dealing with this on her own. He'd never thought much of Peter Holt, typical summer kid—fast cars, fast boats, no responsibility. From what he had gathered, back in the day when they were all teenagers vying for summer territory, Peter was a carefully controlled accessory for his wealthy parents. They barked, Peter jumped through hoops. The guy never went out on a limb for anything. The most defiant thing he'd done, to Steve's knowledge, was marry Lily. Obviously, that hadn't worked out too well.

But Steve held hope; Lily had insisted there be some way for Riley to pay for the damages. Not just by dipping into the account fattened by birthday and Christmas checks—really work for it. It was Benny who'd come up with the logical solution.

Benny had raised three kids on his own and managed to keep them out of trouble. Grown up fine. The little one, Molly, was in med school out East. And Luke was off in the Army Rangers.

Deep down, Steve wanted to tell Lily that she should move back here permanently. There wasn't a better place to raise kids than Glens Crossing. Kids grew up at a normal pace, not shoved into adult situations before they were mature enough to understand the consequences. He just couldn't understand why anyone would choose to raise their child in a dirty city.

"Okay," Steve said, "go get your mom."

He could see how slowly Riley moved, dread hampering his movements. That was good. That meant Lily had a chance. The kid still wanted to please her—or at least not disappoint her.

Lily followed her son back into his office. Her face held the same strained look he'd seen on his own wife occasionally when he got home from work. Tired eyes, tense brow and tight lips. A look that said for half a dollar they'd sell their children and run away with a gypsy caravan. Only his wife had seven kids pulling her strings and pushing her buttons. It looked like Lily had her hands full with just one.

"Have a seat." He tried to offer her support in his gaze without softening his expression in front of Riley. "Okay, Riley, I want you to explain to your mother what we've discussed here this afternoon."

Riley leaned forward in his chair, rested his elbows on his knees and kept his eyes on his twisting hands when he spoke. "I'm on probation."

This wasn't news to Lily. She, Steve and Benny had had a long discussion about the best course of action while they let Riley get a good taste of a jail cell. Up until ten minutes ago, Riley had no idea his mom or his grandpa had arrived at the station.

Steve crossed his arms over his chest and leaned against his desk. "That's just fine, son, now tell *your mother*. I think your hands have the idea by now."

It was a long moment before the boy raised his eyes and turned his head to look at Lily. Steve saw the effort it took to hold his temper. He mentally commended the kid—thirteen was an ugly age, filled with ugly thoughts and unbearable frustration.

"I'm on probation." Riley said it softly, shame edging his voice.

It was the shame that made Steve give him a break. Had he mouthed off or acted as if it were no big deal, he would have let the kid squirm. But Riley seemed to be owning up to what he'd done. So Steve took the floor and explained the rest of what was expected of Riley as if it were news to Lily, too.

"That's it," Steve concluded. "Any trouble and you're back in jail and will have to go before the judge. Got it?"

Riley nodded, this time looking Steve directly in the eye.

"Mrs. Holt?"

Lily took a minute to respond, as if her mind had been numbed by stress. "Um, yes. Yes, I understand."

"All right." He motioned toward the door.

Riley got up and moved quickly, a trapped animal given an avenue of escape. Lily moved a little more slowly. As she passed she silently mouthed the words, *Thank you.*

Watching from his office window as they got in their car, he sent up a little prayer for Lily—and Riley, too. What Benny had arranged for the boy was, in Steve's estimation, much harsher than anything the court system could have dredged up. That boy was going to learn the hard way.

Lily slipped her sunglasses on against the glare of the rising sun. Riley sat staring blankly ahead, not completely shed of sleep. She wondered if he'd spent as restless a night as she. They hadn't talked much about what transpired yesterday afternoon in the sheriff's office. It didn't seem to make sense to beat a dead horse. Riley knew he'd screwed up, but she didn't think the reality of what he was facing had sunk in. She'd wait until he'd spent his first day working before she drove the point home. Maybe she wouldn't have to, maybe he'd learn something on his own.

But there was a lingering question she had to ask. There had been so much commotion yesterday, she hadn't voiced it. "Why'd you do it?"

Riley kept his gaze fastened on the road ahead and shrugged.

"Come on, Riley!" She nearly flinched at the hard edge in her own voice. "What made you pick Mr. Willit? He's known your dad since he was a kid."

She saw him take a deep breath and let it out. "The old

geezer yelled at me—all I was doing was walking through his stupid yard. I wasn't hurting anything."

Lily supposed in his pubescent point of view, that made sense to Riley. She just bit her tongue. Her point would be better made after he'd spent the day in the sun scrubbing algae off of boat hulls.

"Call me when you're ready to be picked up this afternoon."

Riley shifted in his seat and rolled his eyes toward the passing woods.

"Maybe you'd like to walk home." Her fingers tightened on the wheel to keep from smacking him.

"Fine."

"Fine."

After another mile, she started to feel badly about snapping at him. He was in a terrible situation and she had a big hand in getting him there. She patted his knee. "Call me. I'll pick you up."

He didn't respond.

Turning into the marina, she was struck with how little it had changed. The old gas pump was the same, as was the bait shop. The only difference she could see was the old bottle-dispensing Coke machine had been replaced by one with a lighted front that sold cans. Lily parked right in front of the open office door. In the confusion yesterday, she hadn't asked, but as things appeared unchanged, she assumed the marina was still a one-man show with Cecil "Bud" Grissom at the helm.

As she turned off the engine, she wondered if Bud's brother Ed was still making noises about flying saucers bothering his cows.

Her thoughts of the old days quickly disappeared when she stepped out of the car and heard raised voices coming from the office.

"I promise it won't happen again—" The voice was young—and pleading.

"You're damn right it won't. Now get on outta here—and take that damn cat you've been feeding with you."

Lily stopped in midstep. That voice . . . Not Cecil.

"But I need this jo—"

"You used up your second chance. Don't bother saying another thing, just go."

Lily's heart lodged in her throat. Her ears began to ring and she stood frozen, watching a boy of about sixteen emerge, slump-shouldered, from the office. He was freckle-faced and looked underfed—and about as harmless as a newborn puppy. She couldn't imagine what he'd done to deserve what had just happened.

The man inside couldn't possibly be who it sounded like.

Just as she began to draw an unfettered breath, assured it had been a trick of her imagination, like that moment on the front porch when she'd thought she heard Clay calling her from the lake, he stepped out of the office and into the sunlight.

Her breath froze in her throat. She stared stupidly as he walked past her, toward her son.

Clay Winters didn't seem surprised to see her. Not that he gave her more than a quick glance as he passed.

She stared mutely at him, trying to make order in her mind, to stop the mad whirling of past and present and fashion it into something that made sense. A peculiar buzzing feeling came from just beneath her skin.

He stopped directly in front of Riley. "Sheriff says I have to put up with you for a few weeks." Clay stood there with his hands on his hips and stared at Riley until Riley lowered his gaze to look down at his feet. "Damn stupid thing, sinking a boat." Then he turned around and started toward the dock.

Riley shifted restlessly, but didn't follow. He finally gave Lily a questioning look.

She couldn't begin to find her voice. There was no air in her lungs to pass her vocal chords. Clay Winters. Impossible.

Clay barked over his shoulder, "Hurry up. We got work to do."

Lily stood, feeling as if she'd been slammed in the midsection with a baseball bat, and watched them go, Riley moving slowly behind Clay.

When Clay was about halfway to the dock, he picked up a hose that was lying on the ground and sprayed a fat yellow tabby cat who was napping on a large rock in the sun. "Get!"

Dread coiled in Lily's stomach. She fought the maternal urge to protect her child, to grab Riley and run away from the multifaceted dangers that lay within Clay Winters.

Just before they got to the dock, she managed to find her voice.

"Hey!" She searched for something to say that wouldn't sound like whining.

Clay stopped. It was a long moment before he turned around to look at her. "What?"

Lily walked closer, determined to stop this before it got any worse.

Riley took a step back when she got close. The satisfied look on his face made her rethink what she was about to do. If she intervened, just because she was *afraid* something unpleasant was going to happen, would it be any different than what the in-laws had been doing for years? What Riley had done had *earned* a little unpleasantness.

As soon as she looked Clay in the eye, she realized she'd made a mistake. But it was too late, too late to tear her gaze away. He held her silent and paralyzed, as if the past years had never happened. A storm of memories and emotions swirled violently in her chest.

At one time, those light brown eyes had made her heart stop, her good sense slide silently away, made it so nothing else mattered but him. There were tattered fragments of all of those things in the wild wind whipping her soul—and it pissed her off. How could he, after all these years, after he'd hurt her so deeply, still stir such feelings inside her?

She was such a stupid fool.

She glanced back at Riley. The pleased anticipation she saw on his face made her put everything else aside and do what was right. She had to let him go. She had to trust that her dad knew what he was doing.

"When should I plan to come and get him?"

Clay squinted slightly and she saw how much the years had altered him. He was harder, more rugged-looking than she remembered. But it was more than looks. It went much deeper. His speech was different. He used to talk to her for hours. He could paint a picture or rise a tide of passion in her with no more than the tone of his voice. She'd loved to just listen to him. But now his sentences were clipped, with no wasted words. His entire demeanor had changed. The wealth and city had been wiped cleanly away. No one would ever guess he hadn't lived on this lake his entire life.

"Depends on the day. He leaves when I leave." He turned around and walked down the dock, the boards squeaking under his weight.

Riley looked stunned. She could feel the anger coming off of him like heat from a roaring fire when he passed her and followed Clay. He didn't look at her. He didn't say goodbye.

The deep throaty rumble of the inboard engine started

before Riley even climbed into the boat. They were swinging away from the dock before he'd taken a seat. She saw him stagger slightly and grab on to the windshield to steady himself and hoped with all of her heart she hadn't made a mistake by not taking him back and turning him over to the sheriff instead of leaving him here.

For a long minute, she remained standing where she was, unable to command her limbs to carry her back to her car. What on earth was Clay Winters doing in Glens Crossing? And what in God's name had happened to him that turned him into such a coldhearted bastard?

# *Chapter 3*

The boat cut across the churning wake of another craft, bouncing hard enough to make Clay's teeth rattle and casting a cool spray of water across his heated face. Now that he'd made such a production of getting in the speedboat and tearing away from the dock, he'd better figure out where he was going. He didn't know why he couldn't overcome the urge to run. Hell, he'd been face to face with death and had less of a visceral reaction than what had grabbed him when he set eyes on Lily.

The thing that struck him the strongest was how little she had changed. Over the years, he'd imagined she'd aged as much as he had. He'd expected a fuller face with eyes lined at the edges, perhaps the easy life adding a few pounds. That thought sent a bitter edge of jealousy slashing through him. Why did she deserve a better life than he? Why had betrayal given her the rewards of love, marriage, family, when he'd been denied?

His eyes remained focused on the green water in front of him. His mind, however, slipped to a time past—a single summer he thought he'd blocked from his memory. He thought he was prepared. Had convinced himself that seeing her wouldn't make any difference. The past was over. Lily had been effectively locked out of his soul. She was a part of something as far removed from his current life as Camelot. A fairy tale with an unhappy ending. She had no power over the Clay Winters that lived in his body today.

He was wrong.

Luke had said Lily never returned to Glens Crossing. Clay had been a fool to believe. He'd come here because it was the only refuge he could think of in this tired, ugly, manipulative world. It was a place without pretense, a place of childhood dreams, a place that had brought out the best in him. The only place he had loved—and been loved. Maybe that part of him was as dead as the giant walleye mounted inside the marina office. Nothing left but glass eyes and a plastic-coated shell, completely empty of decency. Maybe he'd spent the last year running, only to find himself back in the place where he started. Maybe he'd taken the risk of coming back here for nothing.

His palm itched. As he rolled his fingertips inward to scratch it, he felt the smooth scar and stopped. He slapped his palm against the leg of his jeans to calm the itching. It only set off a stinging that demanded even more attention. Leaning over the side, he showered his hand in the cold spray from the bow of the speeding boat. Through all of his turmoil, all of his thoughts since he'd gotten the call from Benny, he had managed to not once look at the scar that branded him more deeply than flesh.

There must be something twisted deep inside him to have agreed to this situation. Something akin to not being able to tear your eyes away from mangled wreckage and flashing lights on the interstate. When Benny had called, Clay's answer was out before his mind had fully wrapped around the far-reaching implications.

Why, after all of these years, would he open himself to the person whose betrayal cut the deepest? Why expose himself to the very thing he was trying to expunge from his soul—that bleakness, the surety that nothing pure existed in this world, the black anger that seemed to be consuming him an inch at a time?

He glanced out of the corner of his eye at the boy. He already disliked Riley Holt. Probably had before he even laid eyes on him. He was man enough to admit that to himself.

Suddenly he caught himself searching for a resemblance to Peter and tore his gaze away. Was his decision based on perverse curiosity? Or was he really looking for a way to hurt Peter through his son? That thought only confirmed what he already knew about himself. Something dark had taken over his soul.

They hit a big chop in the water. Clay's feet bounced and he fought to retain his balance. He was going dangerously fast, but couldn't bring himself to pull back on the throttle.

Riley was jolted off his seat and landed half under the dash.

Clay pretended not to notice.

"You know anything about boats?" he asked over the wind and deep rumble of the engine. "Aside from how to sink them, that is."

The boy looked at him for a brief second, then pulled himself back onto the seat and faced ahead once again. He shrugged. "Grandpa has one."

"But do you *know* anything? Other than how to have your ass hauled behind it on skis?"

This time the boy's eyes cut to him and stayed there,

narrowed with the urge to say more than he did. "I know about boats."

Clay just held the kid's gaze, daring him to let loose the riptide of anger he saw churning just beneath the surface.

After a long moment, Riley turned away.

Clay spun the boat around and headed back to the marina, no longer worried about pretense. Lily would be gone by now, and the kid wasn't about to ask questions at this point.

He cut the engine so quickly when he hit the no-wake zone of the marina that Riley rocked forward in his seat. Coasting up to the dock, he said, "Jump out and tie us up."

Riley moved, albeit slowly. Clay watched him tie up the boat with admirable skill. *Well, let's just see how far that knowledge goes.* Most likely beyond filling the tank with gas and charging it to Daddy's—or Grandpa's—credit card, the boy would be in no-man's-land.

Stepping onto the dock, he made a show of inspecting the knot and checking the play in the line. As Riley looked up at him with a look of smug satisfaction on his face, Clay grunted. "It'll do." Then he headed back to the large pole barn used for storage and boat repair.

Once he reached the wide sliding doors, he stopped and waited with his hands on his hips for Riley to catch up. "It won't do you any good to poke along around here. You don't leave until the work is done."

Riley stopped directly in front of him. "I've got the money to pay for that friggin' boat. I don't need to work here."

"Is that right? You think money makes you who you are? Well, money don't mean squat, kid. Time you learn that." He shoved a gallon of muriatic acid and a Scotch-Brite pad into the boy's hands and pointed toward a boat sitting on a trailer inside the fenced lot. "That hull is to be clean by day's end."

Riley looked at the boat, then back at Clay. "You've got to be kidding, dude."

Clay shook his head. That twenty-six-foot hull had two years' worth of algae on it. It'd take a grown man from sunup 'til sundown to get it down to the fiberglass. "Nope. Better get started."

As he headed toward the office, he heard Riley mutter, "Bastard."

"That's right, *dude*," he called across the lot. "Better get used to it."


Lily wanted a drink. Two drinks. Maybe a washtub filled with margaritas. She had new empathy for Peter's need to drown his tribulations in alcohol. There was something almost magical about the way one little bottle had the power to shave the edges off the pain—at least for the moment. That's what kept her driving past the liquor store at the edge of town: the knowledge that no matter how you pickled it, your trouble would be there sitting on your chest, staring you in the face the moment you pried open your hung-over, bloodshot eyes. If nothing else, Peter had taught her that.

Why hadn't her dad mentioned Bud was gone and Clay was the person he'd set Riley up with? If she'd been fore-warned, she might have stood a chance, might have been able to do more than stand there with her mouth hanging open and her heart thumping so strongly against her chest that her T-shirt vibrated.

God, she hated being blindsided. She didn't make a habit of running from her problems, but she did like to meet them with the proper preparation. She knew her dad hadn't done it on purpose. She held this conviction wholeheartedly simply because he had no idea she and Clay had ever been more than summer friends. Still, she couldn't help feeling she'd had the rug ripped out from under her and her dad could have at least softened the landing.

After the way Clay had reamed that poor kid who sounded like he needed the job more than he needed air and water, Riley, who was there expressly for punishment, was doomed. An ache started somewhere deep in her chest, a tightening that threatened to surge into a full-blown crying fit.

Then she realized that she didn't know who she wanted to cry for, herself or Riley. What kind of selfish mother was she?

She rolled down the window and let the cool morning air blow against her hot cheeks. Breathing deeply, she was amazed at how even the air here felt different than Chicago—and it was more than the number of idling cars and belching smokestacks. Take away that and Chicago still felt . . . populated. Too much concrete holding heat, too many hormones colliding in the air, too much hurrying. Here, even on the courthouse square, the air spoke more of flora than fauna, of open space and deep shadowy woods.

Shadowy woods.

The Place.

Suddenly everything in her universe was coming back to that one spot. As much as it beckoned her, she'd faced enough of the past this morning. She certainly wasn't going to prod her already seeping wounds by going there.

She headed down the main drag in Glens Crossing, pulling into an angled parking spot in front of the Dew Drop Inn. Since liquor was out, coffee at the little café was going to have to do. And, deep down, somewhere buried beneath the foundation that Clay had so recently shaken, there was a tiny voice that cried out for company. It was a voice she had taught herself to ignore. Long ago she'd developed a whole host of white noise to cover it. Suddenly it was louder than it had been in years, rising above the busy mental racket she'd concocted to drown it out—and she didn't know why.

As she started to pull open the glass door, a tall man pushed against it from the other side. He gave her a nod as he passed, rolling the toothpick from one side of his mouth to the other. Then he was gone. It felt like she should know him. But she couldn't make the connection that had a fourteen-year break in it.

Lily told herself she was bound to have a whole lot of moments like that during her first days back in town and walked on into the restaurant.

Like her father's tavern, the Dew Drop had changed little in her absence. The same embossed turquoise vinyl booths lined one side, the same knotty pine paneling covered the walls. The rest of the room was filled with wood-grained Formica-topped tables sided by chrome and vinyl chairs (these brown, not turquoise). Slices of fresh pie filled a glass case that sat on the end of the counter.

All of the booths and tables were filled. Lily took a seat on a stool at the counter, near the pedestaled cake dome filled with doughnuts.

The waitress set a cup of coffee in front of Lily. "Hope Tad didn't knock you on your derriere on his way out. Bulls his way around everywhere. We're all just supposed to jump out of the way. Don't take it personal." She was about Lily's age, and very attractive. Suddenly Lily was self-conscious of the baseball cap she'd put on when she'd not had time to get a shower before taking Riley to the marina. "Hope regular's okay. Fresh pot. We don't serve much decaf in the morning."

Lily could do no more than blink at the waterfall of words tumbling from the glossy lips. She was certain the waitress didn't draw a single breath between her sentences. "Thanks."

The woman nodded. "Special this morning's the western omelet, side of bacon or sausage, and toast. Course, I prefer the French toast. Willie, he's our cook, makes the best French toast in the state—no exaggeration. Been selling a lot of the omelets today, though. On Wednesday, we have blueberry pancakes. Not the canned or frozen kind. Real blueberries. You should be sure and stop in on Wednesday. You want cream with that coffee?"

It took Lily a minute to realize the woman had actually paused for an answer. "Oh. Yes, please."

The waitress set a small pitcher of cream beside the coffee cup. As Lily creamed her coffee, she said, "Did you say that man's name was Tad?"

"Well, yeah. Figured you knew him, since you went to school together. Class of '89, right?" She didn't pause for confirmation. "You probably don't remember me. Cassie. Cassie Edmunds. I was two years behind. Class of '91."

She was right, Lily didn't remember Cassie. However, she'd never forget Tad Fulton: basketball star, homecoming king, most popular guy in school, and, in Lily's book, number one asshole. The mere mention of his name made the hairs stand up on the back of her neck. Now that she thought about it, that guy did look a little like Tad, blond hair a little darker, another thirty pounds on his athletic frame. Had she known it was him, she just might have punched him in the nose.

"We took the state championship in basketball my senior year. Did you know that?" Cassie hadn't paused for a response, steamrolling right on into her next comment. She settled her elbow on the counter and propped her chin on her fist, apparently ready for a long walk down memory lane. "It made all of the Midwest papers. We were the 'Cinderella' team. Tiny little Glens Crossing High over all of those city schools. Town practically closed down during the final game, everybody went to Indy to see it. Sorta like that movie, *Hoosiers*. Course now they have class division basketball. No more Cinderellas." The nostalgic look faded a bit from her eyes and she straightened back up when Mildred, the waitress that had been in the Dew Drop as long as Lily could remember, passed, giving her a pointed look and pursed lips. Cassie made a slight smacking sound with her tongue and said, "Bet Tad wishes he could have been on *that* team. What can I get you?"

"Ah, nothing. Coffee's fine." Lily was having trouble adapting to Cassie's way of sliding a question on the end of a totally unrelated statement.

"'Kay, then." Cassie patted the counter with her palm. "Call me if you change your mind. Really oughta try the French toast."

Mildred came up beside Cassie and bodily nudged her into motion. Then she lowered her voice to Lily. "Sorry, 'bout that. Cassie's real wound up today. She's got a date with Bud tonight, you'd think she's got bees in her underwear." She paused. "Glad to have you back in town, Lily. Your dad's gotta be on cloud nine."

Lily somehow doubted, considering all of the trouble she'd brought along with her, that her dad was anywhere near the heavens at this moment in time.

All of these years and not once had she considered how her absence affected her father. It had never crossed her mind. But these past few days, everyone in town seemed to be making one pointed comment or another about how her dad had missed her. She tucked away the niggle of guilt playing with her senses.

Then Lily's mind skipped back a beat in the conversation. "Cassie has a date with Bud—the guy at the marina?"

"Yep. Been after him since he came to town. I told her she didn't know what she was biting off, but you can't tell Cassie anything. I told her not to marry that husband of hers, but do you think she listened?"

"Cassie's married—and dating?"

Mildred laughed. "Oh, no. That man is long gone. Too bad she's barking up that same tree again."

"What do you mean?" The question was out before Lily could censor the words.

"I've seen the type a hundred times. Good-looking devil—quiet, remote, not about to let anyone inside that body armor he wears. Every woman thinks she can save him. No woman's safe around him. Cassie's been mooning over him for months. Girl's bound to get a broken heart. There's something . . . dark about him." She fluttered her hands in the air. "I don't mean criminal or anything. Just—closed off, you know, sad."

"Mean," Lily added.

Mildred's gaze shifted over Lily's shoulder, toward a customer seated in a booth across the room. "Oh, no. Not Bud. Not a mean bone in his body," she said distractedly as she picked up the coffeepot and moved away.

"Bullshit," Lily muttered under her breath. Clay . . . Bud . . . had grown a mean streak as wide as the street out front. Was mean to cats. Chewed up scrawny teenage boys and spit them out just for fun.

She cradled her head in her hands. Her son was next.

*       *       *

Before she returned to the lake, Lily took care of some errands in town. She needed some paint from the hardware store for the avocado bathroom she couldn't tolerate one more day, and a coffeemaker, a couple of power strips, and extension cords. That old cottage offered one outlet per room, with the exception of the kitchen. It had two. Also, she wanted to pick up a pair of swim trunks for Riley, as he'd been responsible for his own packing and left his in Chicago.

The JC Penney store still sat on the alley across from the courthouse and Duckwall's Hardware appeared to have the same window display she remembered from high school—a red Radio Flyer wagon, a wide snow shovel and a bag of ice-melt, a spread of little seed packets, a tan and blue two-gallon lemonade crock, an assortment of rakes and shovels, and a barbeque grill. Mr. Duckwall obviously didn't like fussing with changing the display with the progression of seasons. As backward as this all was, it brought a strange sense of comfort to Lily as she made her rounds.

Walking around the courthouse square, she studied the mix of storefronts and law offices, some new, many the same. When she'd left Glens Crossing there had been only two lawyers in town, one of whom served as judge; both had to be nearing their hundredth birthdays. Now she noticed several plate-glass windows with the names of attorneys-at-law lettered on them—attorney, not lawyer, not counselor. Each of the new attorney offices noted their specialties: divorce, personal financial and estate planning, personal injury claims, court litigation. Didn't seem to be anyone admitting to criminal defense. Well, some things had kept up with the times, she thought.

The courthouse itself hadn't changed. It was three stories, a mix of red brick and limestone, showing tall double-hung windows and topped with a clock tower you could see all the way from Forrester Lake when the leaves were off the trees. She remembered coming here as a youngster with her dad to pay the taxes each May and November. They'd stand in line at the treasurer's office sometimes for a half an hour before their turn at the window. Always when they were finished, Dad took her and Molly to the drugstore on the corner for ice cream sundaes. Lily had loved tax day.

She was standing there smiling absently at the courthouse when she heard someone call her name.

Turning toward the voice, she was surprised to see Karen Kimball moving toward her with a grin on her face. "I heard you were back in town, I just couldn't believe it." When she got close enough, she gave Lily a brief hug. "We missed you at the ten-year reunion. How long are you going to be in town?"

Lily kept a polite smile on her face. She couldn't imagine anyone had noticed when she ignored the invitation to the reunion, least of all head cheerleader, prom queen and class secretary Karen Kimball.

"Through the summer." Lily didn't elaborate further. If Karen had heard she was in town, she undoubtedly knew about Riley's incident, and probably about Peter's hospitalization, too. Besides, Karen had been in an entirely different social strata than Lily in high school; this friendly overture took her completely off guard. Lily let her gaze travel to the girl standing just behind Karen.

Karen reached behind her and pulled the girl forward. "This is my daughter, Michaeline. Honey, this is an old school friend of mine, Lily . . . Mrs. Holt."

*Ah-ha!* Maybe that was it. Lily was no longer Lily Boudreau, daughter of the local tavern owner, she was Lily

Holt, of the Chicago Holts, currently living on the "right" side of Forrester Lake.

The girl had a hard time keeping her eyes off the ground when she offered Lily a handshake. "I like to be called Mickey."

"Nice to meet you, Mickey." Lily took the girl's tentative handshake and smiled.

Karen cleared her throat. "We've discussed this, *Michaeline,* time and again. It's time to put away that childish nickname. You have a beautiful name. Use it."

Mickey's jaw tensed and she looked away. Her hands fidgeted in front of her.

Karen said to Lily, "It's so hard to make them see what's best for them." Then she leaned closer and lowered her voice. "I know you understand my frustration."

Lily didn't bother to explain the difference between a teenager wanting to exert her independence by being called what she wants and one who is a runaway train, breaking laws and his parents' hearts at the same time.

Her sympathy went out to this girl, so unlike her mother. If there was a prom queen under that string-mop of straight blond hair, she was deeply hidden. None of her mother's self-assurance was evident in the shy smile and downcast eyes. Lily said to Mickey, as if the whole name conversation hadn't come up, "I have a son about your age. Thirteen?"

Mickey smiled, revealing a mouth full of plastic braces and purple rubber bands. "Thirteen next week."

"Well, happy birthday early."

"Now," Karen said, "we'll have to get together. My number's in the book under Fulton."

That didn't really come as any surprise. "You married Tad?"

"Married *and* divorced. But that's a long story for

another time. We'll have lunch. 'Bye, now." She took a step in the direction from which she'd come. Mickey lingered, looking like she wanted to say something. "Come along, Michaeline, your brother should be done at basketball practice."

"'Bye," Lily said. Then, as it just seemed Mickey could use the support, she called, "'Bye, Mickey."

The girl looked over her shoulder and smiled.

Unwilling to coop herself up inside painting on such a beautiful afternoon, Lily filled her day by cleaning out the boathouse. If she didn't keep moving, she was going to spend all day thinking and worrying about Clay Winters. And, she decided within the last hour, he just wasn't worth that much energy. Obviously, she'd been completely misled by him during his summer visits. Not once had she seen the indication that he was capable of being such a bastard. It just went to prove, love *is* blind—and deaf, and completely without gumption.

She gritted her teeth and batted away those thoughts. Here she was, thinking about not thinking about him. Dammit.

With a concentrated effort, she threw herself into her current project. At first she'd thought she'd set up her potter's wheel on the back porch. It offered enough space and plenty of natural light. But the boathouse provided more isolation, something she preferred while working. She gave an inward flinch; Peter had always laughed when she called her pottery "work." He'd considered it an acceptable hobby for a Holt wife, something to fill her hours once Riley had started school, nothing more. She knew she wasn't good enough to sell. But when she put her hands in the wet clay, all else fell away. Something about taking a lump of mud and turning it

into something useful, or simply ornamental, brought satisfaction to her soul. It was enough just to create. It didn't
really matter if anyone else appreciated it or not.

The process of organizing a new work space did keep her
body moving throughout the afternoon, but her mind refused
to keep on the task. Time and again she found herself
walking out of the wide double door with something in her
hand and no idea what she intended to do with it. She would
pause in the blazing sun, blink at the object, which ranged
from fishing poles and bait pails to cartons of old sporting
magazines, then glance back into the comparative dimness
of the shed, then back at the thing in her hand again. It made
for inefficient work, but the purpose was truly more that of
having activity than accomplishing a goal.

And, even though she'd put her faith in her dad's judgment, occasionally her stomach would flip as she worried
about Riley at the marina.

In the late afternoon, in anticipation of his call to be
picked up, Lily took a shower and spent an hour deciding
what to wear. At first she selected an expensive designer
sportswear set, slacks and a knit shirt, topped with a cotton
sweater tied about her shoulders. Looking at herself in the
mirror, she was completely disgusted by what she saw—
someone trying to make an impression, as if she were going
on a first date. Or, she thought sadly, someone trying to
make a show of how much Clay had so carelessly thrown
away.

She ripped off the clothes and tossed them on the bed.

Then she took the opposite approach, sneakers with holes
in the toe and baggy coveralls with paint splattered on the
legs. She stepped back in front of the tall mirror.

Well, that just looked ridiculous, all she needed was

pouffed bangs, some huge earrings and slouch socks and she could jet right back to the eighties.

Off came the coveralls, out came her favorite pair of faded jeans and an old blue heather-tone T-shirt from the Gap. She scrubbed off all of the makeup she'd applied to go with the designer outfit and slapped on a little mascara and lightly powdered her nose. The last thing she wanted Clay Winters thinking was that she was in any way trying to impress him.

Nonchalant indifference, that was the ticket.

She put her hair up in a bobbed ponytail and left the bedroom.

After that, time moved with impossible slowness, each second digging in its nails, clinging to the day, moving on only when reluctantly shoved aside by the next second. The shadows didn't seem to move across the kitchen floor, appearing as permanent markings instead of passing time. Lily paced and fidgeted, fussing with a salad she was making for dinner, arranging and rearranging the cherry tomatoes and cucumber slices.

Soon the sunlight was masked by sporadic clouds, making the kitchen look aged and depressing. This room could really use her attention next.

Then she caught herself. This wasn't her house. It was Peter's. She had no rights here. Yet, strangely, she didn't feel like a visitor. She felt like she belonged, like she was a part of this house she'd pointedly avoided for fourteen years. Now that she was surrounded by these familiar walls, she realized this house held more childhood happiness than youthful misery and confusion. She supposed it was that poignant combination that made it feel like home.

Six o'clock came and went with no call from Riley. Twice since that hour, Lily had picked up the telephone.

Twice she'd hung up without making a call. She didn't want to embarrass Riley. Nor, if she was totally honest with herself—something that she'd noticed was becoming increasingly harder to find, self-honesty—did she want Clay to think she was a mollycoddling mother who couldn't let her son out of her grasp for a full workday.

That thought only brought about more frustration. Against her will, she'd spent the entire day alternately dreading and craving the moment she would see Clay again. When she caught herself imagining him falling on bended knee, begging her forgiveness, admitting that leaving her had been the worst mistake of his life, she wanted to kick her own ass. That was the furthest thing from what she wanted. Her life was complicated enough without introducing another challenge. One rebellious teenager on the brink of starting himself a criminal record and one alcoholic ex-husband who still depended solely upon her (Peter's parents had yet to admit he had a problem) should be enough to keep any woman's emotions fully occupied.

But somehow, a short time would pass, and she'd find herself back at that very mental scene once again.

She tried to focus on the fact that she had to keep Peter's recovery in mind. What would he do if he knew Clay was living in Glens Crossing? How would it affect him to know Riley was spending every day with the man? At the best of times, Peter couldn't overcome his jealousy of Clay—even before Lily had been thrown into the mix. It was something he concealed well—at least as long as Clay was around. Once Clay disappeared, that jealousy swelled as Peter chewed on it until it nearly choked him.

Now she and Clay and Riley were bound together by a circumstance Peter wouldn't see as coincidental. The entire scenario, as unlikely as it was, would sing betrayal in Peter's ears.

There was only one logical answer. Peter couldn't know. There was no reason for him to find out. Even if Riley mentioned Clay (which he couldn't do without admitting he was in trouble again), he knew him only as Bud. Peter would make the same assumption she had—Cecil "Bud" Grissom was still running the marina. This was definitely a case of what Peter didn't know, couldn't hurt him.

As for herself, perhaps no amount of forewarning would have prepared her for this reunion, one she had foolishly assumed would never come about. Early on, she'd created an impenetrable capsule around the part of her that had belonged to Clay. Now those walls were dissolving, leaking emotions so toxic she wondered if she could tolerate them. If only she could call poison control and get an antidote for desertion and betrayal.

The phone rang and Lily nearly jumped out of her skin. The balloon of her emotions exploded. She snatched the phone from its cradle so quickly it fell from her grasp and she had to chase it across the kitchen counter.

Her voice sounded breathless to her own ears when she answered.

"Come get me." There was something just short of tears in Riley's voice.

Her heart stumbled in its beat. "What's wrong?"

The phone went dead in her hand.

*Chapter 4*

Lily's nervous fingers had a difficult time getting the key in the ignition. All of her apprehension over seeing Clay again had flown out the window the instant she'd heard distress in her son's voice. A million disastrous scenarios flashed through her mind as the key finally slid home.

As she started the car, she heard the first rumble of thunder. Glancing at the western sky, she saw towering black thunderheads moving quickly in her direction. By the time she turned from the long unpaved driveway onto the road, the first fat drops of rain hit the windshield, sounding like the car was being pelted with overripe grapes. The wind whipped the trees, sending a shower of seeds and spring-green leaves skittering across the rain-dotted pavement in front of her.

Lightning forked across the darkened sky and the clouds let loose. Lily had to slow nearly to a crawl because the windshield wipers, even on high speed, couldn't keep the windshield clear enough for her to be certain of the road. This narrow old blacktop had no shoulder, the weeds coming right up to the driving lane. Those weeds were quickly followed by a ditch. Lily knew from experience, once she had her car off the edge, the only way back was with the assistance of Hank Brown's tow truck.

Her stomach was knotted and sour by the time she turned into the marina. There were no cars left in the parking lot. Through the slashing rain, she caught sight of a form huddled under the tiny awning over the door to the office. That form unfolded and made a dash for the passenger door before Lily had time to realize it was Riley.

"My God, you're drenched! Why on earth were you waiting outside?" she asked as she brushed the dripping hair back from Riley's forehead.

"The door's locked." He swiped the water from his face.

Lily grabbed his hand and looked at it. His skin had the look of a second-degree burn. "What happened to your hands?"

"Had to use acid on the boat—he made me do it all day."

"No gloves?"

Riley shook his head.

"Where's Cl . . . Bud?"

"Gone."

"Gone? He left you here alone?" Lily flashed hot.

"Had a dinner to go to. Come on, Mom. I'm freezing. Let's get home."

As Lily turned the car around, she bit back the words of anger she wanted to unleash against Clay. Riley was already hostile enough, he didn't need any fuel from her. She opted instead to probe a little more and see if there was more to this story.

"Did you like the dessert I packed in your lunch?"

He shrugged. "Didn't eat."

"Why not?"

"Didn't have time. Man, my hands hurt. Mom, I can't go

back there again tomorrow." His voice cracked. He finished just short of a sob. "It was the worst day of my life."

There was a sharp stabbing pain in the center of Lily's chest, in the place where panic always centered when Riley had been hurt. She gritted her teeth against it. "Well, you don't have a choice. But I'm going to set a few things straight with Bud. Don't you worry about that. Tomorrow, things are going to be much more reasonable."

Riley sniffed and wiped his nose on the back of his reddened hand.

*That bastard. Left a kid out in a storm alone, all because he had a hot date with the* chica *from the café.* Lucky for Clay she needed to get Riley home, fed and dried out; she'd most likely strangle him on sight.

Clay sat in the single upholstered chair in his apartment on the second floor of a hundred-year-old house near the center of town. He was trying not to be ashamed of himself for making Cassie wait. He'd used the storm to justify his delay when he called her. Truth was, he wished he could take back the hastily said words that agreed to go to this church supper in the first place.

He didn't attend church on a regular basis. Hell, last Sunday had been the first time in years that he'd even set foot inside one. The last time he'd looked up at a cross over a church altar had been seven years ago, inside a bombed-out shell of a building near the border of Bosnia. That's where he'd found the dead boy. That's where he'd discovered there was no God.

With a shiver, he shook off the memory. He would not allow himself to go there in the light of day, when he had control.

Instead, he brought Jason McGuire to mind, a living,

breathing boy, one Clay *could* help. He had only gone to church last week because Jason had invited him when he and his dad had been fishing at the marina the Saturday before. Jason was going to say a special piece during the service and wanted everyone he knew to be there to hear it. One look at those slanted blue eyes and that sweet, innocent smile had made the lame excuse dry up in Clay's throat.

So, there he'd been last Sunday, uncomfortable as hell, waiting on the front steps of the Methodist church to tell Jason what a good job he'd done, when Cassie nabbed him. Clay didn't think for a single minute her timing was coincidental when she asked if he'd go with her to the benefit supper right when Jason came up and took Clay's hand. Cassie had tried just about every avenue of attack in her campaign to get him to go out with her. She just didn't seem to see that he wasn't worth the effort.

His original intention had been to make a cash donation and skip the dinner. The proceeds were to send Jason to a special-needs camp for Down's kids. But, at that moment, there had been no way out. He knew it was better to hurt Cassie's feelings now than later. Cassie had . . . expectations. He knew it. She knew it. What she didn't know was that he was in no way capable of meeting them. But, damn, he just couldn't disappoint Jason.

Besides, in this little town there would be no casual sex, no one-night stands—not when the woman wanted it otherwise. And Cassie wanted otherwise, he could read it in her eyes. Damned if he knew why. He'd done nothing to encourage her, had bordered on rude most of the time just to warn her away.

Clay rubbed his temples. The storm was obviously not going to blow out anytime soon. Might as well get on with it. He reached for his shirt. The sooner he picked Cassie up, the sooner he'd be dropping her back home. And the sooner she'd begin to get over the idea that he was what she wanted.

Just as he was headed to the door, his telephone rang. He let the machine pick up; it was probably a telemarketer. In the year he'd been in Glens Crossing, nobody ever called him at home. Nobody knew Clay Winters. They only knew Bud at the marina, the grouch who took care of business and never made a friend. Only Jason had been impervious to his indifference, but Jason never looked upon anyone with derision. He obviously couldn't see Clay for the ugly, unbefriendable soul he was.

Clay hadn't bothered recording his own greeting on the machine. It picked up and an impersonal, electronic voice asked the caller to leave a message.

It beeped. After a short pause, a voice stopped him halfway out the door. "This is Lily," she paused, "Holt." As if he wouldn't recognize that voice if it echoed across a thousand miles of barren desert. "I just picked Riley up. He's drenched and starved. How could you leave him out there in a storm like that? I don't think this is what the sheriff had in mind." There was a pause, as if she were looking over her shoulder to confirm she was alone. "He's in the shower now. I don't want him to overhear what I have to say to you, so call me back after elev—"

A blinding blue-white light and a loud crack of thunder cut off her voice and the power at the same moment. Clay stumbled toward the phone, unwilling to let the sound of her voice go. The answering machine clicked off. He felt around for the phone, picked it up, unsure if he was going to say anything or not. He didn't have to make the decision. The phone was dead.

For a long moment, he stood there gripping the receiver.

The gloomy darkness seemed to hold an unnatural weight of its own, making it difficult for him to breathe. On a normal day, it wouldn't yet be dark. But with the storm, his living room looked as if night had fallen. He hated night, endless with its darkness, its torment . . . its memories. Never did he allow his place to fall into full darkness. The TV, sound muted, always kept the dark away while he tried to sleep.

Slowly, he replaced the receiver. Lightning continued to flash, giving his movements a jerky appearance, like a strobe light in a funhouse. His hand lingered on the phone.

Once he pulled in a full breath, the wonder of her voice began to dissipate and the meaning of her words sank in. What on earth she was talking about? The kid in the rain? He had to admit, that thought held some appeal. Wouldn't hurt the kid to toughen up some. But he sure as hell didn't leave the kid locked out. Riley had said his mom was on her way. Clay had left him inside the marina office, with instructions to just pull the door closed behind him when he left, it would lock automatically.

He recalled the surprised look on Riley's face when he told him he was leaving him alone. Clay knew it was a risk, but he wanted to start things off right. Riley had to know he wasn't his jailer. He had to know that until Riley did something to make him do otherwise, Clay was going to trust him.

The day had gone pretty much as Clay had expected. Riley had moved sulkily about his work, casting hateful glances Clay's way when he thought Clay wasn't looking. A couple of times Clay saw him swipe his eyes, but he concealed his frustrated tears behind a veneer of silent attitude.

Riley Holt hadn't lived a life that bred toughness. It was a stretch for him to manufacture it. By the end of this summer, Clay hoped to forge a little strength to the boy's mettle. Clay had seen what weakness could do to a person. Better Riley learn early on what it really takes to be a man. But it wasn't going to be easy if Lily was going to make a habit of playing mother lion each time the kid got a little shook up.

Just for a moment, Clay thought the family life of his childhood, the one he'd always considered cold and disappointing, might have been for the best. If his mother had lived, had his father been the kind of warm and nurturing man Clay had always wished for, perhaps he wouldn't have had the strength he needed to survive the life he'd led. Maybe his father had done him a favor. Then a little voice popped up from the back of his mind, *And maybe you wouldn't have led* this *life at all.*

Immediately he cut off that avenue of thought. Perfectly fruitless. No sense in rehashing what could never be.

He left his house dreading the evening even more than before. Lily's voice had slipped under his skin and was making him feel like his bones were itching, a profound discomfort that there was no way to scratch.

By the time he reached Cassie's apartment, situated over the garage of one of the biggest houses in town, he was in no mood for small talk—or any talk, for that matter. He felt like a heel when she ran out with an umbrella before he could get out of his truck. She slipped in the passenger side, pulling the folded umbrella in after her.

"Whew! That's some storm. Raining ponies and elephants. That's what my grandma used to say . . . much worse than when it rains cats and dogs." She gave a nervous little laugh. Before Clay could say anything, she went on, "I didn't see any need for both of us to get drenched. My power flickered a minute ago. I hope the power is still on at the church. Jason is such a sweet kid. I hope the weather doesn't keep people away. I really want to thank you for coming with me."

Clay mustered a smile. Ponies and elephants. That pretty much described the stampede of words from Cassie's mouth. At least if she was chattering along, that meant he didn't have to come up with anything to say himself. God, he wished this was over.

As they got closer to the church, the streets fell into darkness. No street lamps, no house lights. Clay's hopes inched higher.

Then shame crept up his cheeks when he heard the genuine concern in Cassie's voice. "Oh, no. Please let the church have lights. Jason is going to be soooo disappointed."

The parking lot at the Methodist church was full—and dark.

"Well, no sense in getting drenched," he said. "Looks like the party's over." He pointed to the group huddled under umbrellas headed toward their cars.

"Maybe the power will come back on," Cassie said. "Maybe we should just sit here for a bit and see. You know, it usually doesn't stay off too long. Except when we have ice storms. Then sometimes it takes days to get things back up and running."

Clay interrupted her before she gave the entire history of the electric company in Henderson County. "Like you said, no sense in risking life and limb in this storm." As if to punctuate his comment, a loud clap of thunder shook the truck. "I'll just get you back home where it's safe."

She started to open her mouth, but he was quicker. "Don't worry about Jason. Looks like they had a good crowd already." Besides, he planned on making whatever donation was needed to get the kid to camp. Didn't have anything better to do with his money.

"It's just that he wants to go to this camp so badly. You can just see it when he talks about it. Last week, I ran into him and his mom down at Kingston's Market. He couldn't talk about anything else.

"I remember when I went to camp. Well, I went to camp lots of times. But the first year, let's see, I was seven . . ."

And as she went on to list all of the camp activities she'd ever participated in over the course of her entire life, Clay thanked the raging storm for knocking out the power.

He was a horrible human being.

After he declined Cassie's effusive invitation to come inside so she could make him dinner, Clay started driving. He was much too restless to go home and listen to the silence of four bare walls. If not for the rain, he'd go home and exchange the aging truck for his motorcycle. Speed always had a way of untangling his troubles. A year ago the rain would have made no difference. He would have climbed on the bike and ridden until he was soaked to his bones. But this past year, living in the comfort of clean sheets and regular hot meals had softened him.

He headed out of town, to lose himself in the darkness on unfamiliar roads. After taking several turns, an astonishing realization hit him. No matter how far he drove, none of the roads were alien to him. For the first time in his adult life, he'd been somewhere long enough to make it his. That thought irritated his consciousness like a grain of sand in the eye. Was that what he wanted? To be a part of something permanent? He'd never thought so. At least, he mentally chided himself, he never admitted it, even in his dreams.

The storm continued and he let himself fall to the hyp-notic rhythm of thunder and lightning and the steady thump of his windshield wipers. Not as calming as an eighty-mile-an-hour wind in his face, but it finally began to soothe the sharp edges of his thoughts. When he once again focused on his surroundings, he realized he'd driven to Peter's old lake house—Lily's house.

Just as he neared the lane that led through the woods to the house, a car pulled out onto the road without its lights on. If it hadn't been for a flash of lightning, he wouldn't have seen it at all. When it got about a hundred yards away from the drive, the taillights came on.

Clay wasn't close enough to tell what kind of car it was, but it wasn't the one Lily had driven that morning. She'd been in a champagne-colored Toyota Camry, three or four years old with a four-inch scrape on the driver's-side rear quarter panel. He remembered because he always remembered details, even when he wasn't concentrating on them. A holdover from his past.

The car that pulled out of the drive was dark, low and fast.

He glanced at his watch. Eleven.

Stopping his truck at the end of the drive, he sat there for a few seconds, debating. He rested both hands on the steering wheel and laid his temple on them, looking down the lane to see if there were lights on in the house. The heavy foliage prevented even the slightest flicker from reaching the road.

If the car belonged to someone Lily had been entertaining, why keep the headlights off until it was away from the house?

He pulled his truck off the road and got out. Something just didn't feel right about that car. He started down the lane. He'd just take a quick look and assure himself everything was all right. It was something he'd do for anyone, he told himself, out here, relatively isolated.

Reaching the point where the woods thinned enough to see the house, he stopped. Not because he didn't want to be seen, but because he simply could not make himself go one step closer. He'd avoided this side of the lakeshore as much as possible. He'd always taken care not to look at the Holt cottage and its well-maintained emptiness in his comings and goings along the lake. It took a concentrated effort, considering he serviced all of the boats currently sitting on expensive lifts all up and down this stretch of water.

Now here he was, face to face with it, and it robbed him of his breath. The old sting of humiliation and pain colored all of his memories here. Damn Lily for taking that one precious sliver of peace away from him.

The rain picked up in intensity again, plastering his hair to his head. He let the cool drops run down his face and slide inside his shirt collar. Finally, he moved. There were no lights on, on the first floor. He circled around the house. On the lake side, a weak light shone from Peter's parents' old bedroom. All of the first-floor windows were intact. With practiced stealth from another lifetime, he carefully checked both the front and back doors. Locked.

Satisfied, he walked back to his truck.

Who in the hell had been sneaking around here at this hour? Another thought bloomed. Perhaps Lily had a lover and didn't want her son to know. The guy had to resort to sneaking in and out.

Somewhere deep in his chest, he felt a twinge of deep-seated pain. It came and went like a flash of lightning overhead.

Well, hell, why should he care about how she was carrying on?

He didn't.

All the way back to his truck, he told himself that over and over.

* * *

After Riley went to bed at nine, Lily laid down in the master bedroom, the telephone within arm's reach on the nightstand. The storm continued to slash away at the trees, scraping and tapping like skeletal fingers against the siding. The lightning came in increasing and receding waves. The only lamp in the room was a low-wattage Tiffany (she was certain it was the real thing) on the dresser. As much as she wanted to retain her angry edge, the only thing she felt would protect her when she spoke to Clay, the steady beat of the rain against the window lulled her into a half sleep.

The phone rang at nine forty-five.

With a startled gasp, Lily jerked up onto her elbow. With a hammering heart, she picked it up.

"Hi, you all settled in?"

Peter. Lily let out a breath. "Yes. Everything's in good order with the house. Riley's sleeping in your old room." She didn't know why she offered that information, unless it was a way to offer Peter a connection, a compensation for bringing Riley to a place that brought him into contact with Clay Winters.

"Bet he's loving the lake."

She made a noncommittal noise in the back of her throat. "It's as lovely as ever here. When you get out, you should spend some time here." God, why on earth had she suggested that? Over the past fourteen years, Peter had dealt with the lake cottage with an inexplicable mix of protectiveness and resolute avoidance.

"That'd be great. I'd love for the three of us to explore our old haunts. Lily . . ." He paused. "I'm really trying. And I think I'll be able to come home soon."

She bit her tongue when she wanted to blurt out that he'd taken her suggestion all wrong. But Dr. Burtron had cautioned her to be careful these first weeks of Peter's treatment. So she said, "Just take one day at a time. You shouldn't rush things. The house will be here whenever you're ready."

And maybe he would—be ready, that is. Finally ready to face the past and deal with the future. The more she thought about it, the more she thought it probably would be a good step forward if he came back here and looked at the past face to face. But not with her here. She didn't want to find herself drawn back into the old position of constant crutch. That wouldn't help her or Peter. And, she had to admit, it would be risky. She didn't know if he'd ever be strong enough to see Clay again. If she was present, it was bound to go badly.

"You're right," he said. "I can't rush things." She could hear the disappointment in his voice. That told her just how fragile he still was. When he spoke again, she could hear the manufactured brightness in his voice. "How's my boy? Can I talk to him?"

"I'm sorry, he's already in bed." Thank heaven. She didn't think she could cope with one more trauma today. Riley was always shaken up after talking with Peter. She hadn't been able to sort out exactly why. He always seemed eager to talk to his dad, but after . . . there was always a dark cloud that followed.

"At ten o'clock? All that outdoor activity must really be wearing him out. I remember how tired I'd be after a day in the sun and the water. Zonk right out after dinner. . . ." His voice trailed off.

Lily heard nostalgia coloring his tone for the first time in years. Maybe he was making progress. "Do you want me to get him up?" *Say no. Please say no.* She knew Peter was allowed only one telephone call a week at this point in his treatment. It seemed cruel beyond words to deny him the chance to talk to Riley. However, she thought selfishly, that would just add another layer to the lie of omission she was building.

There was a long pause, then he said, "Nah. He wouldn't remember talking to me anyhow if you woke him. I've never seen anyone who sleeps as soundly as that kid."

"I'll tell him you called in the morning. He'll be sorry he missed you. What time will you call next week? I'll make sure he's here and awake."

"I'll make it earlier, say nine. That way he won't have to come in too early." He sighed. "God, Lily, remember how we used to hang out by the dam until dark when I was his age? Mom was always red hot when I got home late for dinner."

"Yeah," she said softly, "I remember." She remembered that and so much more. It made her heart ache to think about it.

"Well." He blew out a breath that told Lily he was fighting tears. "I'd better go."

"Okay. Riley will be waiting for your call next week."

"Thanks. 'Bye."

"'Bye."

Just as she started to take the phone from her ear, he said, "Lily!"

"Yes?"

"I—I just want to thank you for . . . being here for me. There's nobody else. It means a lot."

The connection was broken before she could respond.

*Lily struggled against the current. The harder she kicked, the more effort she put into her strokes, the farther away from shore she drifted. It was night, and raining. The winds churned the water of the lake into small whitecaps that slapped her in the face.*

*She fought the panic that she knew would drown her, unable to understand where the current had come from. She'd swum this lake all of her life and there had never been the slightest pull in the water.*

*Her arms burned. Her eyes stung. She choked on a mouthful of water and could not regain her breath.*

*Another wave crested over her head. She opened her eyes wider, unable to see anything in the dark, churning water. Her fingers snatched wildly for anything to grab on to. She knew it was futile. She was in the middle of the lake, there was nothing to grasp but more water.*

*Panic slipped away.*

*She was so tired. So tired of fighting.*

*A sense of calm began to radiate from the center of her body.*

*This was it.*

*The end.*

*She didn't care.*

*She welcomed it.*

The shrill ring of the telephone jerked her awake. Her heart hammered. She gasped in a breath. Fear bloomed anew. Not because she had been drowning, but because she seemed to accept death so easily.

The phone rang again.

As she picked it up, she looked at the clock. Three forty-five. Damn, Clay! She didn't mean he should call her in the wee hours when he was done wining and dining his date.

"Yes." It was more of an annoyed bark than a greeting.

"Lily, it's Brownie."

Lily's mind fought the confusion of sleep and fear to

make sense. Brownie? As he continued, it slid into place, Hank Brown from the local garage.

"I think you should get out here to the Crossing House. There's a fire. Your dad needs you."

"Oh, my God! Is Dad okay?" Her mind was shuffling horrors as quickly as the flipping pages of a thumbed book.

"We got him out. Won't go to the hospital. Maybe you can talk hi—"

"I'm on my way."

# Chapter 5

Lily slammed the phone down as she hopped off the bed and slid into her tennis shoes, not bothering to tie them.

Riley. Should she take the time to shake Riley out of a dead sleep? She paused at his door. No. No time.

She dashed off a note and stuck it on the fridge before she rushed out the door.

The rain had slackened. The lightning now flashed in the distant east. Twice on the way to the Crossing House, her car slid through stop signs. She was no longer so familiar with these back roads and it was slick. By the time she saw the signs and hit the brakes, she was too close. Luckily, no one was out at this time of night.

At the third sign, she didn't even hit the brakes.

As she rounded the curve that brought the Crossing House into sight, she was relieved not to see a huge ball of orange fire licking into the night sky. In fact, she could see no flames at all. The flashing lights from the fire truck, ambulance and sheriff's vehicle were the only illumination. The sodium vapor lamp on the side of the building that normally lit the parking lot was out.

She slammed the car into park before it stopped. That threw her forward, jerking her seat belt tight across her chest. It took three tries before she could unlatch the damn thing. All the while, she was scanning the area for her father.

The ambulance, she thought, he had to be there.

Once out of the car, she sprinted through puddles, wet shoelaces whipping around her ankles, toward the ambulance. The front bumper faced her. Light spilled out of the open rear doors. Lily grabbed the handle and swung herself around the open door, her feet skidding on the loose crushed stone that covered the lot.

She looked inside.

Empty. Except for the gurney, which had a sooty gray-black imprint of a body on its white covering. Her stomach dropped to her toes. The breath left her body and her lungs refused to pull in another.

*Please, please, let him be all right.*

A hand fell on her shoulder.

Instantly, she recognized the feel of it, knew who it belonged to.

"Daddy." She spun and threw her arms around her father's thick neck. He smelled of smoke and sweat. His pajama shirt was damp under her hands.

She pulled back for a second to look at his face, assure herself he wasn't badly injured. His brown eyes were so bloodshot it was painful to look at them. She'd never seen him look so miserable. Unable to bear looking into his eyes, she did the only other thing she could, held him close and hung on for dear life.

Finally, she was able to speak. "Are you all right? They said you wouldn't go to the hospital."

"Fine." He coughed. "Be right as rain once I get these lungs cleared out."

"Then you should go to the hospital, get them checked. You could have damage." She took him by the elbow and tried to move him toward the ambulance.

He didn't budge.

"Dad. You have to go."

"Don't think a slip of a girl is going to do what two grown men couldn't." He nodded toward the big smudge on the gurney. "Once I came to my senses, I set them straight. I need to be here." He turned toward the bar. "To see what's salvageable."

There was the slightest break in his voice. Lily couldn't decide if it was simply the result of breathing so much smoke or if he was as choked on emotion. Her gaze followed his.

Other than his children, this bar was all he had in this world. It was his livelihood, his social center, his connection to the town, the hub of his universe.

All of the exterior walls appeared sound. However, there wasn't much light. The first-floor windows were shattered; black smoke trails ran above each one, fanning to the upper floor.

She slipped her arm around him. "Dad, they aren't going to let you in there tonight. There's no power. They'll need daylight to be sure it's safe for you to go in. The floors—"

Benny set his mouth firmly and creased his sooty brow. "I don't reckon I need anybody to tell me when I can and when I can't go into my own place. I know to be careful. I've got to get this place back up and running."

"But Dad—"

He jerked his gaze back to her face. "I *said,* I'll be careful." His tone was sharp. He turned from her, looking once again at the bar. "I'm not an idiot, Lily."

"Then don't act like one! Use the good sense God gave you and let a doctor check you out."

His startled gaze whipped from the smoldering building back to Lily. He pinned her motionless with his dark eyes, reasserting his position as parent.

Lily's ears started to burn.

She ignored them and pushed on while she could continue to ride on the momentum of her frustration. "Damn it, Dad, I'm just asking you to do what you'd make anyone else do. Go, and as soon as you've been checked and released, I'll come back here with you—"

He raised a beefy hand and pointed at the tavern. "Don't think for a single minute I'm letting *you* in there. It's not safe."

Lily cocked her head, pinched her lips together and put her hands on her hips. She held him with the same determined gaze he'd just used on her. She was a parent, too, by God. She knew how to use "the look."

For what seemed an eternity, they remained faced off, staring at each other. Lily felt herself begin to waiver, but managed to keep her expression resolute.

Benny burst into laughter. Which set off a ragged coughing fit. He put an arm around her shoulder and barked out between coughs, "I know . . . when I . . . I'm b-beat." He stepped into the ambulance. "You're coming, aren't you?"

Lily couldn't remember ever winning an argument with her dad. Not once in her entire life. He could be as unbendable as an iron I-beam—logic be damned. A strict disciplinarian, he would hear all arguments, but never could Lily remember being able to change his mind.

And now it had happened. It was both a marvelous and frightening thing. Somewhere in the past few minutes, her position as the protected just got overturned. She was the protector. The tides were changing. Someday, perhaps in the not-too-distant future, her dad would rely on her, just as she had relied on him. The safety net that she always assumed would be there had just received its first nip and fray. Soon there would be holes. Someday it would be gone, nothing left but ragged knots at its anchor points.

For the first time in her adult life, she really felt like she was on her own.

From his first week in Glens Crossing, Clay had been on the volunteer fire department. The town had a couple of genuine firefighters, only enough to put out trash fires and organize everyone else when a real fire came along. This was the first "real" fire since Clay had returned.

When the beeper had gone off, his blood immediately charged, his body remembered and yearned for the all-powerful adrenaline rush. As much as he tried to force himself into the mold of small-town guy, he couldn't deny his deep-seated need for a challenge—danger.

Now the excitement was over.

He waited until he saw Lily climb into her car and follow the ambulance out of the parking lot. Then he stepped out of the shadows behind the tavern. A sickening mix of emotions pulsed through his veins. He'd wanted to take pleasure in the panic he saw on her face when she ran to the ambulance. He'd wanted to know she was finally feeling just a hint of the pain she'd dealt him.

On the day he had come back to Glens Crossing he'd sorted out his life into clearly defined segments. Each related, yet wholly separate from the other. First was the cold and lonely time before he'd met Peter. At that time his life had consisted solely of paid professional care. His mother had died and his father had chosen the hands-off approach to parenting. Once he and Peter had become friends, Phase II began.

Phase II was an aberration. A time that gave him false hope for his life. He'd been ensconced in the warmth of Peter's family and summers in Glens Crossing. He fell in love with Lily. He'd foolishly believed she loved him. He'd planned a life with her. But his plans had been temporarily interrupted and Lily immediately betrayed him by marrying his best friend.

Once Lily married Peter, Phase III, one he'd dubbed "fool to trust," began. This phase taught him costly lessons, ones he vowed never to forget. After that, he put his most valuable asset, his complete lack of need for other human beings, to work. He bartered other peoples' loyalties, played the unsuspecting, ferreted out and used people's weaknesses. He'd become an intelligence operative—a spy. And he'd excelled at it.

That in itself should have told him something about himself.

But he'd held on to the foolish notion that he could, by coming back, recover some fraction of what he had had here in Glens Crossing. Thus began his current phase. And, for a short time, he believed it might work.

That belief was rapidly slipping away. He had yet to name this fourth phase, but something like "biggest fucking mistake of my life" was catching on. Which really said something, because he'd made some real FUBARs—all of which always boiled down to putting trust in the wrong people.

Now Lily was working herself back into his life. The stark terror he'd seen in her face hadn't brought the satisfaction he'd waited so long for. Instead it dredged up unwanted feelings. He'd wanted to rush to her, take her in his arms and reassure her that everything was going to be all right.

He now realized she was his weakness, his only weakness. And it frightened him. For years, he'd hammered his body and his mind to ensure there were no weak spots, no chink in his armor, no point of vulnerability.

He felt naked. Naked and alone. Damn her for making him feel that way.

Drawing his shoulders straight, he vowed to close himself to her. If that was his weak spot, he would reinforce it. She was the most dangerous enemy he'd ever faced. He wouldn't let her hurt him again.

For a long moment, he allowed himself to stand there with his heart aching. Just this once, then he'd let her go.

Brownie came up from behind and slapped him on the shoulder. "You did a good thing tonight. Hell of a good thing."

Clay turned and looked at him. The kindness that showed in Brownie's lanky face made him ashamed. He didn't deserve it.

When it had become apparent that somebody needed to go in and get Benny, he'd been through the door before anyone else could volunteer.

He'd heard Chief Jeffers yelling for him to stop. He didn't. He'd been like a junkie too long without a fix. The response to risk pulsed through his veins, reviving that edgy instinct that had kept him alive for so long.

The rush was short-lived. It had taken him less than a minute to find Benny on the floor at the top of the staircase and get him out. When it was over, a terrible ugly part of him wished it had lasted longer.

Maybe he hadn't been as thorough as he'd imagined

when he left his old life behind and started searching for a new one.

Clay watched Brownie and the others finish rewinding the hoses on the fire truck and loading their gear into pickup trucks and SUVs. As they'd fought the fire side by side, he'd felt like he was one of them. And he couldn't deny that he liked it. But it was all an illusion. He'd never belong anywhere.

"Oh, my God, oh my God, ohmyGod!" Faye swept into the curtained cubicle in the emergency room in a flutter of red fingernails and a streak of copper hair. She threw herself onto the hospital bed, across Benny's chest, arms circling his neck, forcing Lily to take a step back or be knocked down. "Are you all right?" Faye raised up and framed his face with her hands. "Let me look at you. Dear God, look at your eyes, your beautiful eyes!"

*Beautiful eyes?*

Lily stood watching from the corner of the room with her mouth hanging slightly open. She waited for her dad to give a terse response, as he had when Faye had tried to boss him in the bar, but it didn't come. To her amazement, his hand came up and touched the woman tenderly on her shoulder.

"No need to carry on. I'm fine."

Tears slipped from Faye's eyes. "Brownie called. Damn man, waited 'til *now* to call me! You could be dead!" She swiped the tears away. "I just don't know what I'd do if anything happened to you."

"Nothing's happened. Nothing's gonna happen." Now even her dad didn't seem to notice Lily was in the room.

She felt like an intruder, like she was the one who didn't belong. She slipped out of the cubicle and went in search of some coffee. When she stopped at the hospital cafeteria, she ran into Fire Chief Jeffers.

"How's your dad doing?" he asked as he filled a paper cup of coffee for her. "Take anything in it?"

She shook her head. Her mouth was dry. She didn't want to talk about coffee, or the weather, or even how her dad was faring medically. She wanted to ask him if he knew about her dad and Faye. In fact, the words were ready on her tongue when she realized how that would look. The daughter asking the local fire chief about her dad's love life.

"He's okay," she finally said. "They'll probably let him go after one more inhalation therapy. They said he was lucky to have been exposed for such a short time."

"Well, there's one man to thank for that. Bud went in and got him before any of us could get organized. Against all procedures, of course, but it got the job done." He shook his head, as if to marvel at the bravery. "With a lightning strike like that, Benny should have had plenty of time to get out. He called the fire in. Dispatch told him to get out. But you know your dad, he thought he could fight the thing himself. Bud found him on the floor at the top of the stairs."

"Bud . . . Winters? He was there?" Would the surprises of this day never end?

"Yes, ma'am. He's the best volunteer we've got. The man's not scared of the devil himself."

Lily's world slipped another notch on its well-organized axis. In this whole drama, it seemed she was the only one who didn't have a vital role, who didn't belong.

Jeffers went on, "Course that can play havoc sometimes. Lucky for me he's not a hotshot hero looking for headlines. The guy really knows how to handle himself. Said he never had any firefighter training. Must just come natural to him.

Some men are like that." His voice reflected the admiration that showed on his face.

She closed her eyes for a second and rested the paper cup of hot coffee against her temple, hoping to reduce the throbbing there.

He noticed her distress, even though he couldn't begin to imagine the far-reaching reason for it. "You should head on home. I imagine Faye'll insist on taking Benny home with her when they cut him loose. The woman can be bossy as an old hen, Benny won't stand a chance. She's so protective of him you'd think they'd been married for fifty years."

Lily's eyes widened. "They're not, are they?"

He raised his eyebrows, causing dark creases in his forehead where the grime from the fire still clung. "What?"

"Married?" She could barely get the word out. It couldn't be. But then again, all of her conversations with her dad in the few days since she'd been home had been centered around Riley. And apparently she was as receptive as a stone not to have picked up any indication whatsoever that there was anything between Faye and her dad.

"Well, not to my knowledge—but then, I'm not always in on what goes on around here." He chuckled as if she were in on the joke, but it just made her feel stupid. Stupid and self-centered.

Lily looked back toward the emergency room. Part of her wanted to go in and give her dad the third degree, find out just what was going on. Another part of her wanted to slink out the door and slip into the first hiding spot she came across.

The chief put a hand on her shoulder. "Go home. He's in good hands." He looked out the window. "It's almost morning, your son will wonder what happened to you."

Lily followed his gaze. The eastern sky was streaked

with pink and orange. "You're right. I'll just go and say goodbye, make sure he doesn't need anything."

Chief Jeffers nodded. "Tell him I'll be along shortly."

Walking back to the emergency room, she felt like she was ready to rip the curtain aside and discover there really was no Wizard of Oz. Once she went back inside that cubicle, she'd have to acknowledge Faye—and she wasn't sure she was ready to do that just yet.

*She* should be the one taking her father home. It was the right thing to do. She hadn't figured on this little kink in her world. Well, that was really the crux of it, wasn't it? she asked herself. She hadn't figured on anything. Not on how differently people of this town were going to look at her. Not on how her infrequent, abbreviated visits affected her father. Nor had she even considered that *his* life might have changed in these past years. She hadn't imagined that Riley would end up in trouble before the car engine cooled from the trip from Chicago. And she certainly hadn't figured on the complication of seeing Clay Winters again.

God, her head hurt.

When Lily pulled into the marina to drop Riley off for work, it was eight-fifteen. Clay was standing in front of the office, feet apart, arms crossed over his chest. He looked pissed.

The little groan that accompanied Riley's indrawn breath made Lily cringe.

"Don't worry. He knows about Gramps's fire," she said. "I'm sure he expected you to be late."

Clay honed his narrowed gaze in on Riley as he got out of the car, and she began to doubt. She lowered her window and made like she was looking for something in her purse. She'd planned on doing the adult thing and getting out, thanking him for saving her father, but the look on his face made her hesitate.

"Work here starts at seven. You're late."

"Mom was at the hospital with Gramps."

"Were you?"

"Was I what?" Riley's words were more quiet than Clay's; he had his back to the car.

"At the hospital?"

"No. I was home in bed, Mom didn't wake me."

"Got an alarm clock?"

"Huh?"

"An alarm clock. You're old enough to get your own ass out of bed."

"Jeez, get off my back." Now Riley's voice was loud and clear. "It wouldn't have made any difference. She just got home. I didn't have a way here."

"Then you should have gotten up even earlier. A two-mile walk never killed anybody."

Lily jumped out of the car. "It was my fault. He didn't even know I was gone." Then she looked him in the eye. "Were *you* here at seven?" If he'd even gotten two hours of sleep, he couldn't have been here on time himself.

"Six-fifteen. The fish bite early."

"Well, I'm sure you understand this is a special circumstance—"

"My guess is, every day has some 'special circumstance' for Riley. He's to be here, ready to work, at seven. No exceptions." He turned from Lily to Riley. "Better get a move on. You've got two over there beside the shed."

Lily looked at the boats. Both hulls were green-gray with dried algae. Then she looked at Riley's hands, still raw from yesterday's work. When she glanced at his face, he looked ready to cry.

"Maybe he could do something else today," she suggested. It took effort, but she was pleased with herself in managing a sweet tone. "Look at his hands."

Clay took one of Riley's hands in his and Lily's heart stepped right into her throat. Clay's hands were strong-looking, she'd forgotten how strong. Riley's fingers were long, like Clay's; she wondered if they would grow into hands with that kind of strength.

"Bet those babies sting," Clay said.

Riley nodded.

Clay dropped his hand. "Maybe you should forget the acid today, just use soap and water."

"He'll never get through that muck without—"

"Go on," Clay said to Riley.

With slumped shoulders, Riley scuffed toward the shed.

"Well, at least give him some gloves!" Lily kept her voice low enough that Riley couldn't hear, uttering the words between clenched teeth.

"We had the glove discussion yesterday."

"Goddammit, Clay! Don't make his life hell"—she thrust her finger toward her son, now beside the boats—"just because you have issues with me!"

For a moment he looked like he was going to explode. He leaned closer to her face and said, his voice low but trembling with restrained fury, "Issues? . . . Issues? What a nice, bland term. Is that what they call it in your social circle? My, God, woman, you are a piece of work."

For a long moment Lily was speechless. Then she found her voice and her anger. "You bastard! What happened between us was a hundred years ago. It's over and done. I've let it go. Maybe you should, too." It felt surprisingly good to see the pain that flashed in his eyes.

Clay couldn't fight the wild urges inside him. His anger

was a beast too long restrained. He got so close to her face he could see the soft down on her cheeks. His fisted hands shook. "Never."

He spun around and walked away. If he stayed there one more second, looking into those pale blue eyes, he was going to touch her—and he didn't know if it would be to snatch her off her feet and kiss her, or to wrap his hands around her throat.

# Chapter 6

It took all of Lily's willpower to walk away and leave Riley in Clay's unforgiving hands. She felt anything she said would be a further detriment to her son's treatment. So she stopped talking. Besides, Clay's last statement stole the breath from her lungs. The way he'd said "never" sent a chill up her spine. There was something so deep, so dangerous, in his tone that she actually felt a prick of fear. And that was something she would never in a million years have expected. It was clear Clay wasn't the man she remembered, but how changed was he? Could he actually be unstable or violent?

If he showed the slightest indication that he'd use more than words against her son, she'd go to the sheriff and ask for an alternative arrangement. As much as she'd like to avoid seeing Clay ever again in this lifetime, such a thing would be a last-ditch option. The gleam in Riley's eye when he had sensed she was going to intervene spoke volumes about how far the child had to go in his journey toward accepting responsibility.

She drove from the marina toward the hospital, following

the curve of the road around the lake, back toward town. The winding road climbed the hills that ridged the eastern side of the lake. As she finished the S-curve, it came into sight. The fire watch tower on Fiddler's Hill. Her gaze was drawn to it, as if it emitted an unseen yet intense mesmerizing power. How many times had she awakened from dreams and worked to scrub the image of that tower from her mind? Now here it was. Although the years had worn on her, the tower looked as if time had surrendered its hold, leaving it to bask in bygone days.

It sat off the road about a hundred yards, rising a dozen or more feet above the treetops, looking a little like an oil derrick with a tiny house on top. It had been erected long before Lily was born, before they used helicopters to monitor the lands surrounding the Hoosier National Forest. The metal stairs zigzagged back and forth until they reached a roofed platform. That platform was surrounded by a half-wall so a person, or two people—the thought actually caused a hitch in her breath—could be up there, completely hidden from the rest of the world.

Now that Clay had been thrust back into her life, the memories, those she'd managed to keep stored so deeply inside they never saw the light of day, were working their way to the surface. She pulled into the small graveled spot where forestry workers parked when monitoring from the tower. It was so seldom used that weeds sprang up almost as thickly in the gravel as they did on the side of the road, but it provided a level place to park. Shutting off the car, Lily sat back, closed her eyes and let the memory flow over her, washing the present away.

Soon she was there, back on that night that first signaled a change in the wind.

*     *     *

It was Friday night. The whole crew gathered at the edge of town, at the park just beyond Kingston's Market. Lily could hardly believe she'd finally finagled her way in. Luke never allowed her to play "slips" with the high school kids—even though she was fourteen and going into high school herself. Lucky for her, Luke wasn't here tonight. He'd had to drive Great-Aunt Minnie to her sister's in Louisville. He'd griped about it all week long and Lily had pretended to feel sorry for him. Deep inside she was jumping for joy.

Slips was a lot like hide-and-seek, but played at night, spread over a huge area, and you were free to move at will. Once found by the "searcher," you had to join in the hunt for the others. Since not many sixteen-year-olds in Glens Crossing had cars, entertainment without prying adult eyes was hard to come by.

Peter and Clay had laughed at the idea of playing a kids' game, but once they'd started, it became a regular thing for them, too.

Boundaries had been set, and the playing field was the same each week, the woods beyond the park playground, down to the creek that ran in a ravine toward the reservoir. Since the grounds never changed, it was more and more challenging to find an undiscovered hiding spot. Caves were strictly off-limits, as was the fire tower. The very thought of being out there crouched in the darkness while someone was looking for her made Lily's stomach tighten with anticipation.

When it came time to start, Lily was surprised that everyone divided up into pairs. Boy-girl pairs. She hadn't expected this. God, she was such a dummy. She stood uncomfortably at the edge of the group, trying not to make eye contact with anyone. No one was going to want to be her partner. Several couples peeled off without waiting for partners to actually be chosen. Lily noticed these were steadies, kids she knew were "an item."

Peter said he'd take Karen Kimball, who looked pleased as could be when he took her hand and they walked into the darkness.

Three other guys picked girls. The crowd was thinning.

Daring a glance up, she saw Tad Fulton was looking her way. He was the biggest hunk in Luke's class. A couple of times he'd yelled at her from a passing car window. She could never make out what he said; she always assumed it was something she wouldn't want repeated.

Oh, God, was he going to make fun of her? She looked at her tennis shoes and prayed he wouldn't say something to embarrass her in front of all these kids.

If Luke was here, he'd send her home. She almost wished he was. It was okay to be humiliated by your older brother, kids expected that.

She could barely breathe. Why had she come?

Feet scuffed through the grass.

Shit, he was going to come right over here and say it. Insults hurled from twelve feet away had time to lose momentum before they hit their target. But Tad was going to aim from point-blank range. She felt like a cornered rabbit—she was willing to bet she looked like one, too.

If she hadn't been so mortified, she might have spun around and sprinted into the night before he spoke. But it felt like the rubber soles of her shoes had fused to the ground.

She felt Tad stop in front of her.

She didn't look up. She wanted to. She really did. She wanted to be the kind of person Luke was, someone who would look a guy in the eye and *dare* him to insult you. But it just wasn't in her. She guessed Lily was a fitting name for her—*Lily-livered.*

"I'll," Tad began, and Lily's muscles tightened, "take Lily."

Did she hear him right? He wanted her to be his partner?

Her doubt evaporated when he took her hand.

With a mouth too dry to say anything, she allowed herself to be led away.

As they passed a couple of the other basketball players, he said, "Hey, somebody had to take her."

One of the guys gave Tad a manly punch in the shoulder. "Eehhh, you go, man."

Just before they broke away from the rest of the crowd, Clay stepped into their path.

Tad jerked to a stop. Lily, a half step behind, bumped into him.

"Lily goes with me." Clay's voice was quiet, but resounded like a steel sword drawn from a scabbard.

"Back off, Winters. I said I'll take her."

Lily didn't see Clay's feet move, but suddenly he was much closer, leaning right into Tad's face. "I said she goes with me." His voice slid down to a whisper. "Now, you can just let go of her hand and pick another girl, or you can go home with a bloody nose."

Was Clay serious? Her gaze shifted from one shadowed face to the other. The hard line of Clay's square jaw told her he was dead serious.

Her mind screamed for her to speak up and not let these two treat her like she was a toddler who couldn't make decisions for herself. But what would she say? Tad was the coolest guy in school—and he'd picked *her.* It was beyond imagining. Yet, something always pulled her to Clay. Even when they were with Peter and Luke, which they were all of the time, she felt close to him. And sometimes, when he looked at her, she believed he actually thought she was more than a kid sister tagging along. To have Clay all to herself for an entire evening . . .

Tad let go of her hand. He and Clay stood nose to nose. For a long moment neither moved. Tad was a couple of inches taller than Clay, but Clay was broader, solid muscle—basketball guard verses quarterback. It wouldn't be a contest easily decided.

Lily sensed the attention of those behind her swing in their direction. The only sound in her ears was of her own breathing and the night noises from the woods. Clay's statement had been too quiet for the others to hear, they'd all been talking and joking around. But now silence fell.

Half of the basketball team was here. They were sure to side with Tad.

*Say something, stupid! Don't let this happen. Stop it now!*

She was still searching for her voice when Tad took a step backward and said, loud enough for everyone to hear, "Thanks, man, for taking her off my hands. It was gonna be a bitch babysitting all night."

Lily saw red. Babysit! She wanted to jump on his back and beat him on the head with her fists. Tad was at least eight inches taller than she, but she took a step in his direction. At the last second, instead of springing onto his back, she slipped her foot around his ankle.

He stumbled forward, pinwheeling his arms for balance.

Lily didn't get to see if he recovered or landed face-down on the ground. Clay grabbed her arm and took off at a trot into the woods.

After about two minutes, he slowed their pace and said, "Why in the hell did you show up here tonight?"

All of her foolish, romantic notions (Clay had been

willing to fight for her, after all) evaporated. "I didn't hear anyone asking Karen Kimball why she was here!"

"That's different."

Lily stopped moving and put her hands on her hips. "What do you mean, that's different?"

"Karen's different."

"You're not making any sense."

"Jesus, I thought surely you'd figured out why Luke keeps you away from these games." He kept on walking. She was about to lose him in the darkness, so she gave up her defiant pose and hurried after him.

"I have. He doesn't want me to have any fun."

She'd just about caught up with him. He surprised her by spinning around to face her. She nearly jumped out of her skin.

"Dammit, Lily! You know that's a crock. Think about it. He lets you hang with us all of the time."

"I see, so he's ashamed of me. Afraid I'll embarrass him in front of the others."

A loud rustling came from the woods on their right. Clay grabbed her arm and pulled her behind a thick-trunked tree. "Shhh."

Lily held her breath and pressed her back against the rough bark. The trunk was wide, but not wide enough to offer cover if they stood shoulder to shoulder. Clay pressed against Lily, face to face—or face to chest, as it turned out. Lily closed her eyes and secretly breathed in the scent of him while they waited for the searchers to pass. He smelled like suntan lotion and outdoors, with just a trace of fabric softener.

The warmth of his body against hers dulled her senses to anything beyond his presence. An unnatural lightness encompassed her, as if she could easily float off into the dark night. Her fingertips felt electrified and she yearned to rest her hands against his chest.

Clay tensed and she knew the searchers were nearby. His hands settled on her waist to hold her still—which was totally unnecessary, no way would she voluntarily leave this shared closeness. Her skin under his touch tingled, just as she imagined it would. He'd touched her plenty of times before, held her hand to help her along, pulled her out of the water onto the diving platform. But this was different. He was touching her with his whole body, making her stomach wiggle and squirm. And, they were alone—in the dark.

In her most secret dreams, Clay had held her in the darkness, protected her, whispered words of love in her ear. She wished with all of her heart that the searchers would remain in their vicinity for the rest of the night, holding the two of them prisoner.

The footsteps stopped nearby, close enough to penetrate her fixation on Clay's nearness. She heard the searchers whispering.

Then the footfalls moved away from them.

Clay inched backward and looked down at her for a moment. It was much too dark here in the woods for her to read his expression. Her breath remained lodged in her chest while she waited to see what he would do.

Finally, he whispered, "I should walk you home."

Her heart sank. She scrambled for an argument.

"Come on, Clay. I'm with you; I couldn't be any safer if I was with Luke. Besides, everyone will laugh at me. I won't be able to go to town for a week. What Tad said was bad enough . . ."

He put his hands on his hips and looked around. "Where does your dad think you are?"

"In my room, reading. Molly's at a friend's overnight.

Dad won't know the difference. It's Friday night, he won't be back upstairs until at least three."

He didn't say anything else, just took her hand and led her quietly through the woods. Lily was surprised when he stopped at the fire tower.

"Up," he said, and pointed up the stairs.

"I thought the tower was off-limits."

"It is. That's how I know nobody will find us."

Lily had often wondered what it would be like to look out from the top. However, her uncertainty about heights always kept her feet on the ground. Then again, Clay had never asked her to climb it. Right now, she'd go up those stairs if the darn tower itself was on fire.

She concentrated on one step at a time and the sound of Clay climbing right behind her. She didn't know if he suspected she was afraid, but after the first couple of flights he put a steadying hand on the small of her back.

Pretty soon, her anxiety fell away. All she could think about was that he was touching her. She began to move more slowly, certain that once they reached the top, he'd take his hand away.

"You all right?" he asked.

"Yeah." The jig was up. No more slowing down.

When she stepped onto the platform, he let go and her nervousness over the height came back. Instead of looking out over the treetops, Lily slid to her knees and sat down, resting her back against the half-wall. Guess she'd never know what it looked like from up here.

Clay stood, turning slowly in a circle. "Man, even the courthouse clock looks little from here. And you can see clear across the lake. There's the lighted flagpole at Peter's dock. Stand up and look."

If it had been anyone else, even Luke, she would have

admitted she was scared shitless. From the moment Clay had stopped touching her, all she could think about was how was she going to get back down. Her knees had started to feel rubbery and her stomach was tied in knots with the mere prospect of standing up and descending those long stairs. But she was with Clay, not Luke. And she'd already been called a baby once tonight. She didn't want him to think of her that way, not anymore.

She reached up and grabbed the top of the half-wall. Slowly, she pulled herself to her feet. As she did, she kept her gaze fastened on his profile. The moon had risen, silvery and nearly full, casting an interesting light on his features.

He looked at her and laughed softly. He put a hand on the side of her head and gently turned it. "Out there."

He let his hand drop from her head to her shoulder. She feared he'd take it away, but he let it lay there. The touch was innocent, but Lily's reaction to it was anything but. The feelings that swept over her caught her off guard. A hot little fire began in the pit of her stomach.

Pointing with his other hand, he said, "See the courthouse, and out there a little farther, that red flashing light is on the grain elevator, the fairgrounds are just on the far side of that."

Lily did look. With the trees shrouded in darkness below, it looked like Glens Crossing was a collection of fairy lights in an inky sea—almost as if the world had been tipped upside down and she was looking down at the sky.

Suddenly she wasn't afraid. She didn't know if it was because her perception of being so high was distorted by the darkness, or if it was her preoccupation with Clay's touch. But the trembling in her knees ceased and the knots in her stomach unraveled.

Clay said, "Did you ever hear it?"

Turning to look at him again, she said, "Hear what?"

"The ghost and his fiddle."

She tucked her chin and said, "Nooo. Don't tell me *you* believe . . ."

He shifted his gaze to the stars. They reflected as tiny pinpoints of light in his eyes. "I want to. A man who loved a woman so much that when she died, he went insane, wandering the hills playing a song so her spirit would know where to find him. I want to believe loving that much is possible."

For the first time in her life, the legend seemed breathtakingly romantic. When the ghost was talked about around bonfires and at slumber parties, it was creepy and weird. The way Clay talked about it, it was heartbreaking.

She didn't know what to say, so she just kept her mouth shut.

After a few minutes, he sat down, leaning his back against the wall. Lily sat beside him.

"Why don't you want the searchers to find us? We're cheating, so we can't win."

He sighed. "If they find us, we have to join the search. I don't want you anywhere near Tad out there in the dark."

A bubble of laughter climbed Lily's throat. "Why would I be afraid of Tad? *You* pissed him off, not me."

He rubbed his forehead. She heard his breath leave him in a rush. "Come on, Lily. Why do you think everyone pairs off in boy-girl teams?"

She shrugged. "To keep things even, I guess."

"God." It was little more than an exasperated whisper. Raising his knees, he rested his elbows on them and ran a hand through his hair. Lily loved his hair, it was straight and dark, and tended to fall over his forehead no matter how often he brushed it back. "You're kidding, right?"

She tilted her head and looked at him.

"Man, it's Luke's job to tell you stuff like this . . ." He looked out into the night sky.

"Like what?" She looked down, so the moon glow didn't reveal her expression. It was easier to feign innocence with her voice than her eyes.

"Maybe you should just ask Luke tomorrow."

"If I don't know what you're talking about, how do I know what to ask him?"

A guttural groan came from behind clenched teeth. "God, you can't possibly . . ." He took a deep breath.

"What?"

"Okay." He sighed and ran a hand through his hair. "Guys like Tad . . . and every other guy, for that matter, except me and Peter, want to get you—well, girls in general—alone in the dark for one thing."

"What's that?"

He threw his hands in the air. "He just wanted to see how far he could get, okay?" Frustration made his voice crack.

"Far? You lost me."

Clay shot to his feet. "Just stay away from Tad!"

Lily couldn't hold herself together any longer. The noise from her throat erupted at first as a squeal and rolled into breath-grabbing laughter.

"You little shit!" Clay shoved her backward.

She rolled around on her back, fighting to pull in a breath. Tears ran from her eyes.

"I ought to turn you over my knee . . ." He knelt beside her and grappled to get a hold of her wiggling body.

She laughed harder and squirmed to get away.

Before she knew it, he had her pressed into stillness with the weight of his body over hers and her hands pinned against the floor over her head.

Suddenly her laughter dried up, leaving her breathless. She looked up into his eyes. She could feel his heart pounding against hers.

Time seemed to stop progressing. She didn't dare move. She wanted him to kiss her more than she could ever remember wanting anything in her whole life.

For a moment, she thought he was going to. He looked like the guys in movies do, right before they kiss a girl.

Suddenly he rolled off her and sat up. "We should go."

Lily felt like a bright and sparkling world had been snatched from her grasp. "I—" She cleared the squeak from her throat. "I thought you wanted to stay here until everyone was found."

"Just come on, Lily." He got up and started for the stairs.

Lily rested her forehead against the steering wheel of her Toyota, surprised by the size of the ache in her chest. She and Clay never again mentioned that night. They didn't return to the fire tower until—

A sharp rap against the driver's window made her gasp and jerk with a start.

Steve Clyde peered in at her. She felt like she'd been caught in the middle of something criminal.

*For you, Lily, those thoughts are criminal.*

"You okay, Lily?"

She rolled down the window and tried to project a calm she didn't feel. "Yes, I was just reacquainting myself with the tower. You know, a stroll down memory lane." Did she sound as casual as she thought she did?

"Well, I was just heading to the marina, to make my presence known, so to speak, when I saw you slumped over the wheel."

"Sorry. I didn't even think . . ."

He waved a hand in the air. "Don't worry about it. It's my job to assume the worst and check it out." He laughed and started back to his vehicle, which was parked right behind hers. Then he stopped and came back. "Just don't go climbing that thing. I'm not sure it's safe. They've had it fenced off for a few years now."

Lily forced a smile to cover her inner turmoil. "Not a chance in hell I'd climb that thing again."

"Glad to hear it."

Lily sat for a few minutes after Steve left, working on shoving those memories back in the dark where they belonged. It was like trying to stuff a bunch of squirming kittens into a flour sack.

By the time she pulled out and headed for the hospital, she had her priorities organized and felt more like herself again.

Lily stopped at the information desk that sat squarely in front of the double doors to the emergency room. It was manned by an elderly woman in a pink volunteer smock. She looked like she couldn't weigh eighty pounds dripping wet and had a thinning fuzz of white hair—the kind that saw the beauty parlor once a week and a satin pillowcase every night. Her eyes looked owlish behind thick glasses. Her plastic name tag had her photo, in which she resembled a gray Tweetie Bird, next to the hospital logo. It said her name was Bernice.

"I'm here to see Benny Boudreau," Lily said.

The woman smiled a grandmotherly smile and pulled out the keyboard shelf on her desk.

"Oh, yes, the fire. Um, could you spell the last name for me? Is it o-w or e-a-u?"

"B-o-u-d-r-e-a-u."

"Sorry, dear, he's been sent home." Bernice gave Lily a smile full of well-worn teeth.

"Oh. Thank you."

Lily pressed her lips together and went to look for a phone book. That's when she realized she had absolutely no idea what Faye's last name was.

"Miss!" Bernice called her back. "Oh, dear." Her gnarled fingers, tipped with pale pink polished nails, flipped through a stack of papers. "I almost forgot. I think there's a message here for you. You're his daughter, right?"

"Yes. Lily Holt." She stood in front of the desk and waited. The woman finished going through the stack and started again at the top.

"Well, now, I know it's here. That redheaded woman handed it to me." She paused and bit her lip. "Hmmm, let's see, what was I doing when she gave it to me?"

Lily put out her hand. "Maybe if I look through them?"

Gray eyes that were hooded by time snapped up to look at her. That sweet grandmotherly appearance shifted to reveal the pit bull terrier underneath. "That'd be against regulations. Just because I'm a volunteer doesn't mean I don't follow the rules. Everybody thinks 'cause we're old we just sit here with our thumbs in our ears. Might as well put a monkey at this desk, far as some folks are concerned."

"Oh, no." Lily pulled her hand back and stuck it in her pocket, as if hiding it would take away the offense. "I didn't mean anything like that. I was just trying to help. I didn't know about the . . . the rule."

The stiff set of the woman's lips relaxed slightly. "Of course you didn't, dear." The attack dog was gone and the grandmother was back. She pulled open a drawer. "Now, let's see . . . when they came by . . . I was just thinking I needed to check the coffeemaker . . ." She closed the drawer and got up from her desk. "She handed me the message. . . .

"Then, let's see . . . oh, yes, they brought in that little boy with the broken arm . . . I still had the message in my hand . . ." Her hand clasped the imaginary slip of paper in front of her as she looked around. "Then the little boy's father fainted dead away, cracked his head a good one right on the edge of my desk. . . ." Pressing her fingers against her chin, she said, "I don't remember having it in my hand when they wheeled him away. Man had a knot the size of a hen's egg. . . ."

Lily's patience was wearing thin, but she'd already offended the woman—and without the note, she was going to have to ask around to find out where Faye lived. People already looked at her as a negligent and uncaring daughter.

She casually leaned closer to the desk, on the off chance she could see something the volunteer had missed.

Bernice cleared her throat.

Lily raised her gaze to see a very disapproving look. "Sorry."

"Just give me a second . . ." As she turned in a half circle, looking on the credenza behind the desk, she slipped a hand in her pocket. "Well! There it is!" She pulled out a folded slip of paper from her smock pocket and looked at Lily with a victorious smile. Nothing but sweet granny now.

Lily took the paper before it made its way into another pocket: "Thank-you, Bernice." The note was no more than an address. Faye's address.

"Oh, everybody calls me Bea." After a second she added, "I hope your dad is on the mend. Tell him I'm so sorry about the fire." She shook her head. "Terrible storm. Just terrible."

"Yes, it was." Lily waved the note at her. "Thanks, Bea."

There was something special about living in a town

where little old ladies cared about the local tavern keeper. More than likely, Bea had never set foot inside the Crossing House, but her concern was genuine.

As Lily walked back out to the parking lot, mulling such thoughts, an idea began to take root.

# Chapter 7

Lily rolled slowly to a stop in front of Faye's house. It was a complete contradiction to the brusque, world-worn woman she'd met at the bar. It blended much more with the Faye she'd seen at the hospital, a side Lily would bet few people knew.

Dad obviously knew.

That thought set off a cascade of unwanted emotions. Her intellectual side said it was good her father had someone to share his life with. Wonderful, in fact. After all, her mother had left the family well over twenty years ago. No one had heard from her since. Lily and her siblings were scattered on the winds, leaving her father alone. It was perfectly natural for him to take up with . . . a woman.

But the part of Lily that clung to the security of knowing her childhood was there, ready to retrieve undisturbed from her father's house, felt the disruption. Someone else had entered the picture, changing the landscape. The child deep inside Lily wanted nothing more than to send that person away, pretend nothing had changed.

How was she going to handle this? Go in there, acting

like she already knew; that, naturally, she and her dad had discussed his love life? Enter with cold and disapproving looks? Maybe rush in with tearful accusations of secrets and disregard for family?

Of course, she would do none of those things. She'd knock. Faye would answer the door and they'd treat each other like the awkward strangers they were.

Lily got out of the car and paused, unwilling to rush things, clinging for a few precious seconds to the childhood that was about to be forever swept beyond her reach.

Faye lived in a yellow and white clapboard single-story house that looked like it had been built in the thirties, on a quiet tree-lined street near the center of town. A tiny porch with two small white pillars supporting the arched roof led to a round-topped front door. Very *Snow White and the Seven Dwarfs*. On either side of the porch were white benches set behind the pillars, perpendicular to the front of the house. Behind those benches were latticework trellises supporting a bounty of bright red climbing roses.

Lily had tried to grow roses. Really tried. After fighting mildew, aphids and leaf-spot for three seasons, she dug up the pitiful, straggly, yellow-leafed things and put them out with the trash.

She looked at the house again. God, it looked like a postcard from the past. A past where Ozzie and Harriet sat around the dinner table with their boys and happily discussed the events of the day. The only thing missing was a white picket fence around the front yard. A far cry from a four-room apartment over a bar in which the children ate dinner alone night after night.

Lily got out and took a wide path to the front door, enabling her to get a look into the back yard. Well, damn. There it was, on the side of the house—the white picket fence, complete with an arched gate with black wrought-iron hinges.

An odd weight settled on her shoulders as she walked up the brick walk that led to the porch. Taking a deep breath, she knocked on the heavy wood door. There was a tiny leaded-glass window in it, right at eye level. Lily tried to see inside without pressing her nose to the glass, but it was too dark on the other side. She listened for footsteps, any noise that said someone was inside.

Nothing.

She knocked again.

Silence.

She finally did press her nose against the window, centering her right eye inside one of the tiny diamonds of glass. The drapes were closed in the living room, the interior swathed in shadow. She angled her head, trying to see down the hallway that led deeper into the house.

"Nobody home there."

With a gasp, Lily spun around, her hand at her throat, her heart racing. A stoop-shouldered old man stood on the sidewalk with a huge puff of beige fur that had to be a cat tucked under his arm.

"I . . . uh . . . well " Her cheeks heated.

"You Benny's girl?"

Truth or lie? Lies always caught up in this town. "Yes. Do you know where they might be?"

The man rubbed the flat-faced cat under its nonexistent chin. "Second time today Sampson's got out. Found him halfway to the square earlier. This time he was only in the Brookmans' hedges." He lifted the long-haired cat so they were face to face. Rubbing noses, he said in a voice normally reserved for babies, "He's such a bad boy. Yes, he is. He knows better than to run off. Yes, he does." He fussed with the kitty for a few more seconds, settling him on his shoulder like an infant. "I'm next door. Haven't seen Faye today. Know she's gone 'cause her car usually sits in the driveway, see it from my breakfast table. Got that little garage packed with gardening gadgets."

Lily stepped off the porch.

"Might want to wipe that nose print off the glass. Faye's very particular." He turned and strolled toward the house next door.

Lily waited until the old man disappeared inside his own house. She glanced around to make certain no one else was snooping around, then wiped the glass clean. When she turned back around, she caught sight of the old man stepping back from the window that looked onto the alley between the houses. Suddenly Lily was certain that Sampson hadn't escaped at all. It was just an excuse for the old man to nib into his neighbor's business.

*Yep,* she thought, *lies always catch up to a person in Glens Crossing—some lies faster than others.*

There was only one place her father could be. He was just stubborn enough to have gone back to the Crossing House, fire inspectors be damned. Lily only hoped Faye had stayed with him. Someone needed to call 911 when the old fool fell through the floor and ended up in the basement.

As the bar came into sight, Lily's aggravation was quickly swallowed by the sick feeling that rose from the pit of her stomach. Seeing the Crossing House in the light of day made her realize just how lucky her father had been. Pulling into the parking lot, she could see areas of the roof had been burned through. The lighted rectangular sign that stood on the peak of the roof appeared to have been the bull's-eye for the lightning. It had been twisted into a

U-shape and thrown toward the rear of the building, still anchored only by a single set of bolts. The fire appeared to have been most intense right where her dad's bedroom was.

Only one car sat in the lot besides her father's, which was still in its regular spot near the Dumpster. Faye drove a late-model silver mid-sized Buick four-door. A grandma car. Who would have thought?

Lily pulled up next to it, got out and looked around. Faye must have been foolish enough to go inside with her dad.

The first thing Lily noticed was the heavy smell that lingered in the air, charred wood, melted plastic and burned upholstery. Carefully entering through the rear door to the kitchen, she sloshed through about an inch of water on the linoleum floor. Although the fire hadn't burned in the kitchen itself, the white walls were darkened by a film of greasy-looking soot. The light that came in through the single window was hardly enough for her to pick her way safely across the room. She took two more cautious steps and was about to call out for her dad when something touched her arm.

With a scream, she jumped away from the touch.

"It's okay! Lily-girl, it's me."

"Henry!" She put a hand over her racing heart. "What are you doing in here?"

"Gotta get this place back up and running." He pointed behind him to a mop and bucket he'd been using to sop up the water. "Benny thinks we can get it done in a week."

Lily looked around. A month didn't appear to be enough time, even with a crew of *young* men working 24/7. And she hadn't even seen the worst of the damage yet.

"I'm sure the insurance will pay for someone to come in and do the cleanup. You and Dad should leave this to the professionals. It could be dangerous."

"You sound like Faye. Heard her squawkin' all the way

out in the parking lot when I walked up. *'Benny, darlin', you shouldn't . . .' 'Wait for the fire chief . . .' 'I told you it was dangerous . . .'"* Henry did a fine imitation of a nagging woman. "Damn mother hen," he said with disgust. "If you women would just leave me and Benny alone, we'd get this taken care of."

"Where *is* Dad?"

Henry jerked his pointy chin toward the bar. "In there with the hen."

Just about that time, Lily heard a crash, followed by her father's unintelligible shout. She'd made it to the swinging door before she heard Faye's voice, soothing, calming—not at all henlike. "It's gonna be fine. We'll just have to take our time. I bet there'll be plenty of folks to help."

No one around here seemed to understand the concept of how insurance worked.

Lily pushed the door open just a crack. Her father slumped with his elbows on the bar, his head in his hands. The skeleton of a bar stool, its upholstered seat melted away, lay on its side near the front door, where he'd apparently flung it in frustration. Faye hovered just behind him, her hand rubbing his back, her lips pressed close to his ear. Lily could no longer hear what she said, just a soft, singsong cadence.

"Dad?"

His head jerked up and he sniffed. "Damn smoke smell's makin' my eyes water."

Lily swallowed the lump that had formed in her throat. "Mine, too." She walked to him. Faye didn't move away to offer them a moment alone. She remained next to him, a hand possessively on his shoulder. Her mascara had run in puddles under her eyes and long gray streaks down her cheeks. Lily couldn't quite decipher the look Faye gave her. It wasn't hostile, nor was it inviting. It felt more . . . challenging.

Lily was the first to look away. "Have you called the insurance company yet?"

Her dad nodded. The slow, heavy action made Lily's stomach drop.

"What's wrong?" she asked, fearing the answer. "You did have insurance, didn't you?"

"Not enough. Building's paid for. Didn't think I'd ever be faced with this kind of catastrophe. My insurance guy kept nagging me to up the coverage. Told me I was risking my business in a crap shoot." He gave a snort of derisive laughter. "'Til now, I've always had a lot of luck at craps."

Lily put her hands on her hips and looked around. "Well, if there's not enough insurance, we'll just have to be creative." She paused, considering if this was the time to broach the subject that had been picking up steam since she'd spoken to Bea at the hospital. Might as well get it out there and see if she could get the ball rolling. "This could actually be a great opportunity. We just need to look at it in the right light."

Her dad looked sick. Faye looked like she'd like to pinch Lily's head right off.

"Really." Lily forged ahead. "There's a whole lot of business to be had in this town that the Crossing House just isn't getting. Now's the perfect time to change the image, bring in some new clientele."

Faye actually made a move in Lily's direction.

Lily took a sidestep to put her father between them.

"That's just ridiculous." With Lily out of reach, Faye had to resort to a purely verbal attack. "What's wrong with our *'clientele'*?" She said the word as if Lily had tried to dazzle them with a fancy foreign language.

Benny remained silent.

"All I'm saying is that there are a whole lot of people who would come in for dinner—families, elderly ladies, summer people—if we gave it an inviting pub atmosphere. Put a railing, or maybe a half-wall with some leaded glass panes on top, to separate the bar from the dining area to make it legal for minors. And use really rich colors, some thematic framed art and subdued lighting. Or we could go with a more nautical theme, capitalizing on the lake cottage look."

"And what about our regular customers?" Faye said.

"Just because you update your business doesn't mean you're going to lose your regulars."

"Our folks like the Crossing House just the way it is . . . was," Faye said. "Put in a lot of fancy hoo-ha and they'll go drink their beer at that shithole on Fourth Street."

"Nobody in their right mind would touch a glass in that place," Lily said. "The health department's shut them down once already since I've been back here."

Faye opened her mouth again, but Benny put a hand up to silence her.

"All this chatter is for nothing," he said. "That 'updating' costs money, lots of money. Remember I said I had too little insurance, not too much." There was an apology in his brown eyes, as if he'd let Lily down somehow.

Over her dad's shoulder, Lily caught sight of Faye crossing her arms and lifting her chin in victory.

"Hmmm, it just seems a shame to let this opportunity slip past. The money would surely be made up quickly with increased business. Maybe we can stretch the budget by doing a lot of the work ourselves."

Faye gave a snort that Lily ignored.

"Dad, you said the building's paid for, right? You could get a loan to make up the shortfall from the insurance."

He shook his head. "I can't afford to be shut down long enough for us to poke along doing things ourselves. Besides, there are things we just don't know anything about, electrical, plumbing—"

"Well, of course, we'll have to hire help for things like that. But the cleanup, painting, decorating we could do."

He put a hand on Lily's shoulder. "It's good that you want to help. I appreciate it, I really do. But I just don't see how it could work."

Lily looked around. Right now the place was a hopeless-looking mess. The second floor had to be even worse. "Please don't dismiss it without thinking about it—at least overnight. You could double your business, maybe even triple it."

"We can't handle any more business," Faye piped in. "Henry's cooking fast as he can now."

"Hire another cook to help Henry! For God's sake, don't let something like that—"

"Lily!" He then lowered his voice. "Don't get so wound up. I'll think about it."

"Good. That's all I'm asking." The more *she* thought about it, the more excited she became about the idea. The Crossing House could be a gathering place for the community. Her father would own the most popular place in town. She looked around the room, suddenly feeling like she could set things right with one hand tied behind her back. "Now, where do you want me to start?"

"Who are you calling?"

Riley spun around at the sound of Bud's voice. His heart leapt into his throat. He knew he'd get caught—it was just his luck.

He said quietly into the receiver, "Gotta go." Dropping

the phone back in its cradle, he said to Bud, "I was just checking in with my mom, making sure she can pick me up after work."

Bud stood there, staring him in the eye, until Riley shifted and started toward the door.

"I'd better get back to work." He'd almost made it out the door when Bud called him back.

"We're going to do something different for a while."

Riley's spirits sank even lower. What could be more awful than scraping boat hulls? One thing was for certain: If Bud wanted him to do it, it was sure to somehow be worse. Maybe he had a horse out back and wanted Riley to shovel shit for the rest of the day.

Bud led him out to the gas pump on the dock. "There may be times when I can't get out here to take care of the boaters. I want to make sure you know the procedures."

Was he kidding? Bud thought he needed *instructions* to pump gas. This guy must think he was a complete moron.

Bud acted like he didn't hear Riley's deliberate grunt of annoyance. "Let's see you gas up that inboard there."

Riley went through the steps his grandpa had taught him, casting the occasional glance at Bud to let him know just how stupid he thought this whole exercise was.

Bud didn't seem the least irritated by Riley's pointed glares. He stood there, limp-limbed and relaxed.

When Riley slipped the nozzle back into the pump, he looked at Bud.

"Now start it."

Riley rolled his eyes and sighed. Then he climbed back into the boat and flipped on the blower and waited a few seconds.

Just as he was going for the key, Bud reached down from where he stood on the dock and plucked it from the ignition.

"That's fine." He sounded like it wasn't fine at all. He sounded pissed.

He turned around and walked away without another word.

"Hey!" Riley's temper snapped. He'd taken about all of this crap he was going to. He jumped onto the dock and trotted after Bud, who kept right on walking. "Goddammit, stop!"

Bud turned around. The look on his face told Riley he'd gone from pissed to *really* pissed. For the slightest moment, Riley felt a prick of cold fear deep in his belly. There was something that went beyond just grouchy and rude in Bud, something that made Riley reconsider the stand he was about to take—at least for a second. Then he pulled in a breath and took another step forward. "What in the hell was that all about?" He jerked a finger toward the boat.

"Had to let my last help go because he kept forgetting to turn on the blower first. Damn kid seemed determined to blow himself up." As if that explained everything, Bud started toward the office again.

"So that's it? You were looking for me to blow myself up?" Riley's anger threatened to lash wildly, like an unmanned fire hose.

Bud called over his shoulder, "Guess I can't count on that now, can I?"

That was it. The pressure burst forth. Logic be damned. Riley ran after Bud, throwing himself low, aiming to tackle him at the waist.

Riley had no idea how it happened. There was a blur of movement. Suddenly the jagged crushed stone was digging into the flesh of his back and the air had been knocked from his lungs. Bud knelt over him, his forearm pressed against Riley's neck. That dangerous look had focused into something sharp and deadly.

As he struggled without success to draw in a scrap of air, Riley saw his brief and uneventful life flash before his eyes. This guy was going to kill him.

The breathless seconds stretched on.

The killing look faded from Bud's eyes.

He took his forearm away from Riley's neck, leaning back on his haunches. The guy's hands were shaking.

"Don't ever do anything like that again." The statement was no more than a hoarse whisper.

Then he got up and walked into the marina office, leaving Riley lying on the ground, lungs squeaking for air, wickedly sharp stones cutting his back.

For several minutes, he lay there, tears blurring his vision, wheezing as he looked into the blue sky and hoped no one drove in the lot.

"That son of a bitch is crazy!" Riley rasped the words when he finally recovered his breath. He rolled slowly to his knees, fully expecting Bud to come back out of the office, help him up and apologize.

He didn't.

Riley sat in the middle of the parking lot for a few minutes, thankful that no one drove in. Then he dragged himself to his feet and walked away from the marina. No way in hell was he sticking around here with a crazy man. This was the kind of thing that showed up on the news. Everybody was always so sorry that they didn't see how insane some dude was—"he was such a quiet neighbor," "taught Sunday school," "everybody liked him"—in time to stop him from killing some kid. So sorry.

Lot of good that did the dead kid.

Well, he wasn't going to end up a feature on *20/20*.

He headed out of the parking lot and started down the road.

# Chapter 8

Riley walked blindly for some time, following the old road that hugged the lake. He trudged on, feeling the sting of the scrapes on his back as he started to sweat. For a long time he was fueled by anger. Then he just felt incredibly sad. How had his life gotten so screwed? Why couldn't people just let things be the way they were? He still couldn't understand how, after being married forever, his parents could just split. They were old, for God's sake! Why bother?

Here he was, stuck in Bumpkinville just because his parents had "grown apart." What the hell did that mean? His mom and dad never yelled at each other the way some of his friends' parents did. Skyler's mom even tried to run his dad over with her minivan, and they were still married. What made his mom and dad think things were so bad?

God, he missed his friends. He and Brady and Zach had planned on going to Space Camp and on a backpacking trip in Colorado this summer. That got blown out of the water with Mom's big announcement. Apparently, divorce had dried up all of the money, too. Grandpa said he'd pay. But Mom was acting totally stupid about it and said no.

Riley looked around and saw no sign of another human being. Most of the traffic stayed on the new road; only the people belonging to the lake cottages and the mailman used this one. Occasionally he passed a gravel drive with a mailbox at the end. But the houses were too far back in the woods to see from the road. Since he didn't know the area all that well, he didn't have a destination in mind. He just had to get away—away from that asshole at the marina, away from his mother. Not permanently, that would bring way too much heat on his head. The sheriff had made that clear. But Riley didn't think even the sheriff thought Bud beating the crap out of him was part of the bargain. Maybe, once this whole thing came out in the open, the sheriff would arrest Bud. A grown man can't just go around beating up kids.

If Bud hadn't interrupted his phone call this morning, Grandpa would already have been on his way down here to get things straightened out. As it was, Grandpa didn't know just how bad things really were. Man, when he found out, Bud was going to get his.

A narrow path appeared on the left side of the road, cutting through the woods toward the lake. Riley took it. Not far from the road, the trail cut sharply to the left again, heading down into a ravine. It was steep enough that his shoes skidded through the dirt if he tried to go too slow. In a few places, old tree roots cut across, making a series of natural steps, but mostly it was smooth and straight down. By the time the path leveled out, he was trotting just to keep his feet under him.

Even though he had to keep swatting the flying insects that wanted to swarm and bite, Riley thought it was really cool down here. He could almost believe he was miles from civilization, where he could hike for hours and not come across anything but wild animals and ancient trees. Soon he heard the sound of moving water, which seemed amplified by the woods around him. The wide creek came into view, tumbling over a ledge of limestone in its bed. He took his shoes off and tied the laces together, then hung them over his shoulder. As he waded in, he imagined this would be a good way to keep tracking dogs off his trail. Maybe he *would* just disappear, then his parents would be sorry.

He walked against the current, watching the way the water rolled around his shins. Soon the sound of rushing water intensified and Riley found himself at the foot of the dam's spillway. The water was just a little deeper here, where it pooled before moving on down the creek. He stood still for a moment, watching the tiny fish nibble at the hairs on his legs, feeling calm inside for the first time in months.

After he tossed his shoes to the dry bank, he let himself fall backward with his arms spread. The cold water eased the sting of his scrapes. He floated there, in the knee-deep water, watching the sun wink through the fluttering leaves overhead.

"There's a water moccasin nest over there."

Riley's arms flailed as he folded at the waist and his feet sought solid ground. His gaze shot in the direction of the voice and he saw a blond-haired girl with knobby knees pointing at a spot not twenty feet from him. He spit out the mouthful of water he'd just sucked in. "What?"

"Water moccasins. Cottonmouths. Snakes. They're poisonous."

Every nerve in Riley's body snapped to attention. His mouth went dry and his heart jumped in his chest. Standing slowly, he curled his toes in order to make less of a target for any snake that happened to be swimming by. It took all of his willpower not to run screaming out of the stream.

He managed to stay put. "How do you know?" There, that sounded pretty calm.

She tilted her head to the side. "Everybody knows that water moccasins are poisonous."

"No." Girls always had to make everything so complicated—just to show off. "How do you know there's a nest? I don't see anything."

"My brother told me."

"Oh, and he's a snake expert. Did you ever think he said it just to scare you?"

"Nope." She wrinkled up her nose.

"No, he's not an expert? Or no, he didn't do it to scare you?"

She blew out a frustrated-sounding breath. "Just get out of the water and I'll show you."

He started to say he'd get out of the water when he was good and ready, but the slim chance that there actually were poisonous snakes in here with him kept his lips sealed. Stepping very carefully, he climbed up onto the bank beside her. Now, if there were snakes, they were at least separated from him by the width of the stream.

She bent down and picked up a rock, then looked at him. "Ready?"

He nodded, the water from his hair running in his eyes.

With amazing accuracy coming from a girl, the rock sailed from her hand and landed in the water just short of the far bank, about twenty feet downstream. Immediately the water began to ripple, then it looked like it was boiling.

"Jesus Christ!" Riley couldn't keep the fright out of his voice any longer. "How many are there?"

The girl shrugged. "Dunno. A bunch."

Riley watched the water slowly settle back into stillness with rapt revulsion. "Why doesn't somebody just kill 'em?"

She turned an astonished gaze in his direction. "Du-uh! They're on the state's endangered list."

"Why would anybody want to *keep* poisonous snakes around? Seems like extinct would be just about perfect."

"Well," she said, squaring her shoulders, "what if we got rid of everything that annoyed us? Kill all of the mosquitoes and the bats go hungry. Kill all of the bats and the mosquitoes take over. Mosquitoes take over and people get more diseases. Everything is connected, everything counts. Besides, if we thought that way there wouldn't be any teenage boys left around."

He shot her a nasty look. "Very funny."

Her cheeks started to turn pink and she lowered her gaze.

He said, "I'm Riley. You're the first kid I've met since I've been here. Don't you have kids in this town?"

She giggled, then swallowed it back down. "Of course we have kids . . . I mean, *I* don't have kids . . . myself." She shifted her weight and looked off somewhere across the creek. "The town does . . . a whole schoolful. We don't get out until next Tuesday."

"Then what are you doing here at nine-thirty in the morning?"

"I'm sick."

"Yeah, right."

"Really. I can't go to school because I have conjunctivitis—pink eye. So it counts as being sick, but I feel fine. My eye just itches. I can go back tomorrow, after I've been on the medicine a full day."

"Let me see."

"What?"

"Your eye. Let me see your eye."

"It's gross."

"Yeah, that's why I want to see it." He didn't know why

it suddenly seemed important to make her feel less self-conscious.

His quip worked. She giggled and looked at him, straight on for the first time.

Brown. Her eyes were brown. He saw it right before her gaze skittered away again. "That's not so bad."

"I had to pick the crust off to get it open this morning."

"Cool."

For a few seconds, neither of them said anything more. Riley was wracking his brain, trying to find something to talk about—anything. It was just good to be with another kid. "What do you do out here? Besides stir up snakes?"

"I like to come out here and read. I've got a really cool place set up over here. Wanna see?" She started away from the creek even before he answered.

Riley realized he would have followed her just about anywhere in order to have at least one friend around here. When they made the crook in the path, he saw a clearing in the undergrowth. There was a huge rock ledge sticking out of the side of a hill, making a little roof over the spot where he saw a blanket spread on the ground. There were several books on the blanket.

"Whoa! This could be, like, a *Swiss Family Robinson* kind of place. I mean, this is way cool."

She sat on the blanket. He took a walk around, studying.

"Your parents just let you hang out here all alone?" he finally asked. "Seems kinda dangerous for a girl—with the snakes and all." He gestured toward the creek.

"Hey, I wasn't the one splashing around in the water, just asking to be bitten." When he couldn't produce a good comeback for that one, she went on. "My mom's at work. She thinks I go to the library. Which makes me think she doesn't pay a whole lot of attention," she added, as if it just occurred to her. "I mean, I *buy* all of my books. She complains about it all of the time. She thinks I should be spending my allowance on clothes and stuff."

"What about your dad?"

"He doesn't live with us. Spends all of his 'family time' working with my brother on his basketball skills. He wouldn't notice if I disappeared off the face of the earth."

"Maybe he could give my mom some lessons. I could use a whole lot less of her nose in my business." He plucked a yellow wildflower and sat down on the far corner of the blanket.

She shrugged. "So what are you doing out here? I heard you were in trouble and had to work at the marina."

He jerked his gaze from the flower he was fiddling with. "How'd you know?"

"My mom told me. She said it served your grandpa Boudreau right—he always seems to know everybody else's business. Now everybody knows yours."

Riley suddenly felt sick. "Like . . . the whole town knows?"

She nodded. "Uh-huh."

"Well, it's not like anyone around here matters. I'm going back to Chicago. It's no big deal."

"I wish I could get out of this town." Her words were no more than a weightless sigh.

Riley looked at her stack of books. "Got anything other than girly stuff there?"

She pulled out a thick one. "*Harry Potter.* Have you read it?"

He scoffed. "A kid's book."

"Actually, it's very well done. A lot of adults like reading it." She pushed it across the blanket, closer to him. "You can read it if you want."

"Nah. Too babyish."

She pulled another one from her stack. "How about *Lord of the Rings?*"

"Why do you drag all of these heavy books out here? You can't read them all at once."

"I couldn't decide what I wanted to read today, so I brought a bunch."

"Well, I guess I could read *Lord of the Rings,* just so you don't have to haul it back. I'll be sure and get it back to you before I leave for Chicago." He didn't really plan on reading it, he just needed a place to be until quitting time. She might not like him hanging around unless he read her book.

"Don't worry about it. It's a paperback—I have the hard-cover at home. Besides, I've already read it twice."

"Twice?" He eyed the thick novel. He couldn't imagine actually reading that many pages just for fun once, let alone twice.

"You might as well get started if you're going to stick around." She picked up another book, laid on her back and opened it.

Riley just sat there for a while.

She didn't shoo him off or nag him to pick up the book. Maybe he wouldn't be forced to read. He stretched out on his back and watched the leaves flutter overhead in the breeze.

After a while he started to ask the girl her name, but the second he opened his mouth she said, "Shhh."

He laid there for a bit longer. Boredom inched closer. It was going to be hours and hours before he could go home.

He picked up the book to look at the picture on the cover. It was dark and gloomy—hopeless, just the way he felt.

Then he flipped to the back cover and read the teaser.

Sounded weird. A place called Middle-earth, wizards, a Dark Lord, Elves and Hobbits.

He opened it to the first page. It began with nonsensical things, like Bilbo Baggins's "eleventy-first birthday" party and his favorite cousin, Frodo, who was in his "tweens." They lived at a place called "Bag End."

It all seemed rather silly, but Riley turned the page and read on—just to see if it ever made sense.

Some time later, he was startled when the girl spoke.

"I'd better go," she said. "Maybe I'll see you around."

Riley blinked and worked to clear his mind of Hobbiton, Frodo and Bilbo, and Gandalf, the wizard. "What? What time is it?"

"Two-thirty."

"No way." It seemed he'd just started reading. Somehow he'd been transported from this place in the woods to another world, where the impossible was commonplace and the day had slipped away.

"Yep. I need to be home before my brother gets home from school." She gathered up her books and put them into a canvas tote. "I always leave the blanket here. Just fold it up and shove it in the plastic bag way back under the rock overhang." She pointed to a little cleft in the limestone.

She was setting out on the path before he called out to her. "Hey! What's your name?"

She stopped and half turned back to him. "Mickey."

"No shit?" It came out before he thought.

Luckily, she laughed. "No shit." Then she disappeared into the woods.

The phone was ringing when Lily came through the kitchen door. It was too early for Riley to be calling to be picked up, so her mind automatically jumped to disastrous conclusions. With an indrawn breath she picked up the receiver.

"Lily, I want to know what kind of nonsense is going on down there." Her ex-father-in-law was in his usual boss-of-the-universe form.

She released her breath. "Hello to you, too, Bill."

"Riley called this morning. He was very upset."

"This morning? What time?"

"I don't know. Morning. Before lunch. That's not the point. Apparently he's being mistreated on this job of his. He says you won't let him quit. Now, I know a boy needs to learn to work. But really, Lily, he's only thirteen. And don't you think he has enough to deal with right now? How much more do you want to heap on him?"

There was plenty implied in that statement. In Bill's eyes, Lily was the source of all of their family problems. *Lily* wanted a divorce. *Lily* said Peter had a drinking problem. *Lily* took Riley away from his home, friends and loving grandparents. Riley's complaint fit right in with Bill's view of the Holt world.

She concentrated on keeping her voice even when she said, "I won't let him quit, huh? Did he tell you *why* he's working at the marina?"

"I assume the same reason any kid works: His mother made him."

"It happens to be ordered by the county sheriff. Riley sank Mr. Willit's boat."

"And Willit pressed charges! Why, I ought to call him right now; I can buy him ten damn boats. He knows that. He had no business involv—"

"Bill! Stop! Riley sank his boat—"

"A boyish prank. Nothing to get the law involved in. I'll take care of the repairs."

"And I suppose you consider what happened at school a 'boyish prank,' too."

Bill plowed right on past logic and pressed his point. "Maybe I should drive down in the morning and get this all straightened out. There's no need for Riley to go through this. It's summer. He should be enjoying himself. He's only a boy."

Lily gritted her teeth to keep the explosion of words from bursting forth. "I swear, if you come down here now . . ." She forced herself to stop and take a breath. "Please. Don't come down. I know it's rough on Riley, but I've got a handle on the situation. I'm keeping tabs on what's going on at the marina. He's only been working there for two days. It's going to take a little adjusting on his part. Right now all he's seeing is that it's punishment. I promise, I won't let him be truly mistreated." It galled her to admit it, but she'd accused Clay of mistreatment just this morning. Riley's expectation to be pulled from the fire was the only thing that kept her from calling the sheriff and asking for an alternate arrangement.

"I have a right to see that boy; I'm his grandfather."

"I don't dispute that you have a right to see Riley. You're welcome anytime. But if you come down here, you aren't to interfere with this situation—in any way. Am I clear?"

Lily didn't miss the fact that Bill didn't once question whether Peter knew of Riley's current problem. That was the way to get things done, cut out the middleman. No wonder Peter was such a mess. He couldn't deal because he'd never been given the opportunity to develop such adult skills. William Holt was in charge. William Holt *always* knew what was best.

"You don't know—"

"Don't push me, Bill." She was actually proud of the steel in her voice.

There was a long pause on the line. Lily could just see him twisting the rubber band he liked to stretch and roll between his fingers when he was thinking. She could sit there and let the silence spin just as easily as he. She knew from experience he expected her to be the first to speak.

Finally, he said, "Have Riley call me tonight."

A minor victory. At least he wasn't climbing into his Mercedes and heading south.

"I'll be happy to."

She had the distinct feeling she'd won the battle, but not the war. For now, she'd take what she could get. As she hung up the phone, she wondered, would she ever be beyond the reach of the Chicago Holts?

Lily was just getting out of the shower when she heard the back screen door slam. It occurred to her how quickly she'd lapsed from her city ways and begun to leave doors unlocked, screens unsecured—at least during daylight hours. How stupid. She couldn't see the drive from the bathroom window.

Opening the door to the upstairs hall just a crack, she called, "Dad? Riley?"

"It's me, Mom."

Her knees weakened with relief. No more showering with unlocked doors. She wrapped herself in her cotton knit robe and went downstairs. She found Riley at the kitchen table.

"How'd you get home?"

"I walked."

Something seemed off. More than his early arrival. She was getting used to him not looking her in the eye most of the time. It was more than that—the set of his shoulders, a tension that hummed in his muscles. It was as if he was waiting for her to yell at him. Her mother's antennae quivered, then snapped to attention. "Walked? Isn't it too early for you to be off work?"

His gaze rose from the can of Coke he'd taken from the refrigerator. He looked . . . startled.

"What?" she asked, her heart in her throat. What new drama had transpired today?

"Bud said I could leave. Tomorrow's Saturday, he says it's really busy and I should be there early."

"Bud let you go early . . . after getting there late?" She narrowed her eyes. She couldn't get used to calling Clay, Bud. It slid most unnaturally from her tongue. But on the off chance that Riley said something about the marina to Peter, Bud he would remain.

"Yeah." He shrugged and took a drink from the can. "I guess he felt bad about Gramps and all."

*Oh, yeah. And monkeys are going to fly out of my ass any second.* "And you *walked* home." She crossed her arms over her chest.

"It's really not that far." He concentrated on the Coke again.

"Riley."

He jumped to his feet and looked at her with defiance in his eyes. "Jesus Christ, Mom! I got off early. I walked home. Why do you have to make a big deal out of nothing?"

She stared him in the eye for a long moment. He didn't flinch. She'd been down this road before. If something was going on, no amount of pressure was going to force it out of him. Once things reached this point, every word became counterproductive. Making herself take two deep breaths before she spoke, she addressed the only thing that she felt would have any results. "Do not swear at me. I'm not stupid, I know how you and your friends talk to one another. But in front of adults and in mixed company, you'll use some restraint. Am I clear?"

She wanted to say so much more, to unleash the anger that was quickly building up inside. He was lying. She knew it. And she'd bet he knew she knew it.

His jaw relaxed slightly. "Sorry. Can I go take a shower now?"

"Not yet."

His gaze snapped to her again, as if he'd been expecting her to unload on him. But he kept silent.

"I got a call from Grandpa Holt this afternoon."

"Really?"

"Nice try, Riley. I know you called him." She raised a hand to keep him from responding yet. "I don't mind if you talk to your grandparents. But, Riley, hear me now: You are not, under any circumstances to burden"—she chose the word carefully—"them with our problems. Your father has enough to deal with right now. And unless I decide things warrant it, he doesn't need to worry about us right now."

Guilt flashed in his eyes.

She almost felt guilty herself. Bill hadn't even thought of involving Peter.

"Can I go?"

"Is there anything else you want to tell me?"

He licked his lips and looked longingly toward the door. "No."

"Nothing is going on?"

"No."

"Go take your shower."

As he walked out of the kitchen, she heard him mumble something about trusting him.

Her mother's intuition nearly laughed out loud. *No way, buddy. Trust flew out the window with that mouthful of lies you just unloaded on me.*

Clay sat with his elbows on the marina office desk and his head cradled in his hands. The room was dark, dark like his soul. It was late, but he couldn't make himself go home. At least here he could pretend he was a part of this town, not the disassociated outcast he really was. The scene he'd had with Riley this morning played in a never-ending loop in his head.

He'd acted on instinct. There had been no thought behind his violent action. It was now clear he hadn't adjusted to living where threats didn't lie hidden in every shadow, in every whispering sound.

But was it simply his military years that were to blame? Or did it have to do with the emotional trigger Riley set off inside him? When Clay had come to Glens Crossing, he'd done so with a mental promise to let the pain and betrayal of that final summer go. He'd scared himself this afternoon. He knew he'd been looking for shortcomings in the boy, just so he could pinpoint and punish—wound the parent by wounding the child. And he knew it was wrong.

He hated the fear he'd put in the boy's eyes.

He knew he should have followed the kid right away, apologized. But his shame kept him from doing it. An apology would require something in the way of an explanation. How could he explain a life he no longer understood himself?

Had Riley gone home and told his mother Clay had attacked him like a madman? Clay shook his head. If he had, it would have been nothing short of the truth.

Now his conscience was eating him alive. The boy was his responsibility—just like the kid in the church had been.

He pushed away the image that haunted his nights, and got up out of the chair. Self-pity always sickened him, especially when it was his own.

Snatching a set of boat keys from his desk, he got up and headed for the door. It was time to be a better man. He had to look at Riley and see Riley, not an extension of Peter. He had to stop begrudging the kid every time he surprised him with a show of strength or character.

If Riley hadn't gotten home, Lily would have called. But Clay couldn't rest until he knew for certain. He didn't want to see Lily—for more reasons than he could count. Of course, there was the fact that he'd laid out her son, a half-grown *boy,* this morning. But there was more. Something that was much more dangerous than taking down a charging teen. Her return had brought back dark feelings he thought he'd buried with his father. Yet there was something inside him that electrified when she was around, no matter how he tried to deny it. Whether it stemmed from anger or misguided passion left over from their youth, he couldn't say. He wasn't sure he wanted to examine it closely enough to find out.

But he was supposed to be in charge of Riley's work hours and he'd fallen short of that responsibility. He had to know the boy was home and safe.

Right after Lily and Riley finished the dinner dishes, Riley went out and sat on the dock. Neither of them had said much while they ate. The lies that Riley had told sat with them like an unwelcome dinner guest. Lily assured herself that if something terrible had happened at the marina, Clay would have called to report it—if not to her, at least to Steve Clyde. Riley was there under his order, after all.

She was on her way to the basement with a load of laundry when she looked out the kitchen window and didn't see his dark silhouette on the dock. For a split second her stomach dropped to her toes. Just as she started toward the door to check on him, she saw movement by the boathouse. Riley walked back out on the dock and sat at the end again.

Maybe those lies were making him restless.

Lily was still in the basement doing laundry when she heard him come back in. He called down the stairs and said he was going to bed. Then she heard the thump of his footsteps and the squeak of the risers as he went upstairs.

She was tired, too. The hours she'd spent helping clean up the Crossing House put kinks in her shoulders and knives in her back—but did little to make the place look any closer to reopening. She took a couple of Advil and poured herself a glass of wine, then went out to sit by the lake. She stopped at the boathouse to get one of the ancient Adirondack chairs. When she reached for the latch, she realized the door was ajar. Funny, she was certain she latched it when she was finished in here yesterday. If she hadn't, it would have blown wide open in the storm.

Wishing she'd brought a flashlight, she slowly opened the door. She breathed a little easier when nothing shot out of the darkness at her. Once the door was fully open, she reached to the side and flipped on the light. It was one of the yellow kind that isn't supposed to draw bugs. Lily thought that was probably because the darn thing didn't put out enough light for a bug to see from across the yard. She strained to see details in the dimness.

Everything was as she'd left it yesterday—a semi-organized mess.

Maybe Riley had been in here. She made a mental note to ask him—or at least be more aware of his movements. Could he have something stashed out here?

God, she was tired. Tired of the constant vigilance, the continual fight. If only Peter could be more of a partner in raising their troubled son. But Peter needed maturing himself.

Silently, she thanked God they hadn't had more children. Maybe there was a grand plan for life, after all. What had seemed cruel beyond words had turned out to be for the best in the long run. She just didn't have the energy to spread herself any thinner.

The chairs were near the door. She grabbed the one that looked the sturdiest and pulled it out onto the lawn.

It was cool enough that no boaters had ventured out onto the lake tonight. Later in the summer, Friday nights would be filled with the steady putter of idling motors and laughter echoing across the calm water. Lily pulled down the long sleeves of her knit shirt and wished she'd put on a jacket. But she knew it was only a matter of time before the wine took away the chill. She took a long sip as she settled into the chair.

The crickets and frogs were making such a ruckus that she saw running lights before she heard the putter of the boat's motor. Someone had braved the chill after all.

She watched the lights move slowly in her direction. Instead of motoring on down the lake, the boat swung around and headed directly toward her dock.

Lily set her wine glass on the ground and stood.

The boat's engine cut off and it drifted the rest of the way in.

Walking to the shore end of the dock, she stopped and

crossed her arms over her chest. She heard the quiet lap of the water against the boat hull.

"Hello?" She hadn't noticed how totally dark it was out here until now.

A figure jumped out of the boat, onto the dock. "It's not as easy to find this place at night without the light on the flagpole."

"Clay? What are you doing here?" After this morning, he was the last person she expected to see.

He knelt, tying the boat to the anchor rings on the dock. "I just finished working on this inboard and needed to run it."

*Riley. This has to be about Riley.* Maybe now she'd find out what was going on. "That doesn't explain why you're *here.*"

He walked toward her. She was shocked to realize the way he moved felt so familiar, even after all these years, even in the dark. He stopped a few feet away from her. She could now make out his features. He looked so much younger in this light, the toll of the years softened by the darkness. A little quiver unsettled her stomach. He stood before her, youth restored, the boy she loved beyond reason.

*Did love, Lily. Keep it straight. Those days are long gone.*

"I just wanted to make sure Riley made it home safely," he said.

He looked a little edgy, as if ready to sprint back to the boat as soon as she answered. "And why the sudden concern?"

"Not so sudden. I'm responsible for him during work hours. He left on foot; I just want to confirm that he's where he's supposed to be."

She had the same feeling about Clay as she did about Riley. Neither one of them was being totally honest. Odd.

Clay had made it clear he was just waiting for Riley to screw up. "He's here."

"Good." He paused for a bit, then turned and looked over the water. "Kids are a damn nuisance. Ruin your life."

"Spoken like a man who *shouldn't* have children." Peter might have had trouble relating to Riley, but he'd never been deliberately cruel. He'd made the effort every day. He and Riley were just polar opposites, neither able to bridge the gap into understanding. "With that attitude of yours, I'd feel sorry for the kid who had you for a parent." She immediately wished she could recall the words.

Instead of the terse response she expected, Clay chuckled. "Touché."

His laughter caught her off guard. It was a sound she'd tried to erase from her memory. It reached right into the pit of her stomach and flipped her insides upside down.

He fell quiet again, looking up toward the house.

Her breath caught. The light from the distant kitchen window reflected in his eyes, taking Lily back fourteen years, back to a place she had no business going. Oh, but how she wanted to. It had been so long since she'd felt this rush of need. She could feel the increase in her heart rate, her pulse echoed in her ears. God, how could he do this to her without even trying?

He started to take a step toward the dock, but hesitated. "Sorry about the Crossing House," he said. "How's Benny?"

"What?" All that had registered beyond his moving away was the rise and fall of his voice.

"Benny," he repeated. "How is he?"

She was thankful for the darkness; it hid the desire she felt flushed on her cheeks. "He's good. Fully recovered."

Taking a deep breath, she tried to get her mind off of something that would never be. She forced herself to make conversation. "I think he might take the opportunity to do some upgrading when he does the repairs."

"Really? Like what?" He stopped moving toward the lake and stood still, sounding like he really wanted to know.

"Make it more of a family place, separate the dining room from the bar. That kind of thing."

Clay tilted his head, just as she remembered him doing when puzzled. "I didn't know he wanted to change things."

Lily let the comment lie. It was time to say what she should have said this morning. "I should thank you."

"For what?" There was that tilt of the head again.

There was something changed about him— something . . . inviting. She had to remind herself of the cold way he'd said he'd never forget the past.

She said, "Stan Jeffers said you went in and carried Dad out—he was unconscious."

"It wasn't a big deal. The stairs were still intact, just walked in and brought him out."

"Well, it's a big deal to us. We're grateful."

For a moment, Lily listened to the night noises, waiting.

"Guess I'd better be going," he finally said. His voice held a hint that he didn't really want to.

"All right." God, she wanted to ask him to stay—just to talk, to see what had happened to him, to understand why he'd changed. But these were dangerous waters.

He didn't move to leave. In fact, he took a small step closer.

Lily's heart beat loud in her ears. She mimicked his half step. Now she was close enough to hear his breathing. She wondered if he could hear her heart.

His hand came up to touch her cheek. The guarded expression that she'd seen in his eyes since her return had completely disappeared. For the moment, his eyes held the caring, the longing, the spark of hunger that haunted the deepest hours of her nights.

She allowed herself to be drawn into the candid desire in those eyes. Her gaze welded to his.

"What happened to us, Lily?" he asked softly.

This was the Clay she remembered. Her body trembled. She hoped it didn't register in her voice when she said, "I guess we grew up." It was the safest answer she could muster at the moment.

Keeping his hand on her face, he leaned closer and whispered, "I want to be a kid again."

"Oh, God. Me, too." There was no disguising her trembling now.

He inched closer.

She parted her lips. It had been so long since she'd been touched by a man. She hungered for it, the closeness, the connection.

Somewhere in the far reaches of her mind, she heard a phone ringing—or was that her own ears?

Clay's breath brushed her lips before he actually touched her. It was tantalizing, prompting her to reach for him. She wanted—

"Mom!"

Clay jerked away so abruptly that Lily jumped backward. She stumbled slightly, then regained her balance.

"Are you out there?" Riley called from an upstairs window.

"Y—" She cleared her throat. "Yes."

Clay took another step away from her.

"Dad's on the phone."

"Okay. Talk to him for a minute. I'll be right there."

A distance greater than the space between she and Clay rose in the darkness; she could see it in his eyes, in the set of his shoulders. She realized she couldn't go back. They would never be those kids again.

He said, "Go on."

And now she heard that distance in his voice. He was hoarse with arousal, but there was an edge to his tone.

She made herself walk away, her body throbbing with unfulfilled yearning, her heart homesick for what used to be.

Once she heard the creak of the dock, she turned around and asked, "Do you want to tell me what happened with Riley today?"

He stopped, but didn't turn to face her. After a long moment, he said, "No. It's between Riley and me."

As he climbed into the boat, Lily had the oddest feeling that he was *protecting* Riley.

And that just made no sense at all.

*Peter, damn his hide.* Betrayal stung as fresh as if it had happened yesterday. The simple ring of a telephone had cracked like a leather whip, laying open old scars.

Clay had left the marina with the conviction to be a better man. Then he'd seen Lily. For the briefest moment, he had thought he could get past it all, reconnect with her. There could be no doubt, the spark was still there, strong enough to ignite an arsenal. But he'd been foolish to play with such a volatile mix. Again.

Peter's timing couldn't have been better planned. His phone call had brought reality back into sharp focus.

In that brief moment, Clay realized just how vulnerable he was to her. It wasn't just the sexual lure. He'd felt the need in his heart, too. And there was where the danger lurked.

In his effort to be a better man, he'd almost offered himself up for sacrifice. There were things that had changed forever, no matter how he wanted it to be otherwise.

He couldn't fool himself, Riley *was* an extension of Peter—and Lily. Once that child had been born, there was no way to separate the three. Divorce or no divorce, they were a family. You could break the legal ties, but the emotional connections would always remain. And Clay could no more face that, day in and day out, than he could fly.

So, as he broke all of the rules by speeding along the lake in the darkness, he vowed to strive to judge Riley by his own deeds and to banish all fanciful thoughts about a future with Lily.

The past was over. There was no undoing it.

Clay's visit left Lily restless in ways she hadn't experienced in years. A restlessness that she'd nearly forgotten existed. A kind of hollow yearning, like that undefined need when you had begun to explore the opposite sex but had yet to discover lovemaking. You knew you were reaching for something, something fantastic, but had no idea exactly what it was. It was an adolescent longing, something no grown woman with a teenage son should be suffering.

She knew if Riley hadn't called her to the phone, things could have gotten completely out of hand. A part of her grieved the missed opportunity, while her good sense told her to be thankful she'd been saved from herself.

She didn't even attempt to go to bed until after her third glass of wine. A lot of good it did—sleep remained unattainable. She read a couple of chapters in a new novel. As soon as she began to feel drowsy, she turned out the light. The instant she settled her head onto her pillow, her eyes popped open, her mind slammed into high gear, teasing her body over lost prospects.

She flipped and flopped under the sheets, stared at the ceiling, went to the bathroom twice, beat her pillow into lumpy submission, and still sleep eluded her. When she finally drifted off, sometime after four, she was startled back awake by what she would have sworn was Peter's voice calling for help.

It felt like she'd just closed her eyes when her alarm clock went off. After rolling her pillow over her head to shut out the noise, responsibility kicked in and she dragged her weary body out of bed. She stumbled into Riley's room to wake him, only to find the bed empty. She checked the bathroom. No Riley. When she got to the kitchen, she found a note on the table: *Mom, I woke up early and decided to go on to work. I'll call you when I need a ride home.*

Lily looked at the clock. She hadn't overslept; it was half past six. She looked back at the note. It was definitely Riley's scratchy handwriting—no forgery left by a crafty kidnapper.

Something was going on. And she had an idea that Clay knew what it was.

# Chapter 9

Lily's quest to discover the new mystery brewing within her child proved to be much more elusive than she'd imagined. For the first few days, Riley had made himself scarce, as if he were waiting for the axe to fall. It was all she could do not to grab him and shake the truth out of him.

On Tuesday morning, she forced herself to approach Clay on the subject. She hadn't spoken to him since their meeting beside the dock and really didn't want to face him now. It seemed the longer she went without dealing directly with whatever was going to follow that kiss, the harder it was to face it. But, having steeled herself with an extra cup of coffee and more makeup than normal in her morning routine, she followed Riley into the office.

Clay was quick to realize she wanted to speak to him alone and sent Riley out to the boatyard. Once her son was out the door, Clay said, "Need something?"

There was nothing of the longing she'd heard in his voice the other evening. He seemed as aloof as he'd been when she'd come to the marina that first day.

She avoided looking him in the eye when she said, "I was

wondering . . . Riley . . . have you noticed anything . . ." Forcing her gaze to meet his, she finished, "Anything different?" She felt like she was ignoring the pink elephant in the room, but pushed forward with her purpose.

Clay looked as uncomfortable as she felt. He picked up a set of keys from his desk and jangled them in his hand.

"Different good, or different bad?" For a moment, he looked directly at her. It made her even more self-conscious.

She lifted a shoulder and felt utterly stupid. She was asking him to read her son when she hadn't been able to do it herself. "Not bad, really." She paused. "He's been *different* since last—"

"Boy's doing his job."

Apparently, neither of them wanted a reminder of that day—or evening. Should she tell him she knew how wrong that kiss would have been, just get it over with and out in the open? She didn't want him thinking she had any illusions about the two of them.

Before she could decide, he put the keys in his pocket and stepped from behind the desk. He didn't move toward the front door, but toward the one that led directly to the boatyard—away from Lily. "That all?"

He didn't wait for an answer. He left her alone in the office listening to the indistinct babble of a morning talk show from Cecil's old radio on the windowsill.

With his departure, Lily could finally draw a breath without a struggle. But her questions remained like a lingering scent. Was he skittish because of their near-kiss, or because of something that had happened between him and Riley?

She left the marina with no answers, but with a clear sense that whatever had transpired here, Clay and her son had reached some sort of truce.

\* \* \*

Riley surprised her on Wednesday morning by telling her he wanted to walk home from work. She stood there with her mouth open and he quickly added he'd be home before dark. As the sun didn't set until after seven, Lily felt he was giving himself quite a bit of leeway. And he seemed a little too cheerful about it, as if he were looking forward to it. But she decided to allow it. She wanted to be certain that Riley knew she wasn't blind and stupid. Yet she had to be willing to give him a little bit of rope, if only to see if he would hang himself with it.

For the rest of the day, she tried to figure out a way to check up on him, but the idea of dressing in camouflage and shadowing her own son from the woods was just a little too ridiculous.

He arrived home just as the sun was dipping below the tree line, in the best mood she'd seen him in in months. There weren't any telltale signs of trouble, no drug-induced glazed look to his eyes, no hint of smoke—cigarette or weed—on his clothes. Lily had almost been ashamed of herself when she hugged him hello just to get a good sniff.

Still, her mother's intuition said something was going on. There was no easy explanation. He wasn't behaving badly. On the contrary, he was less volatile than he'd been since she and Peter separated. His complaints of mistreatment at work had diminished to the occasional grumble. Although his rising and heading to work before she'd awakened that first morning was a fluke, he did actually set his own alarm. Instead of playing video games every night, he had taken to closing himself in his room and reading a book that he must have found on Peter's old bookshelf.

Recalling the boathouse door had been ajar the day he'd arrived home from work early, Lily had turned the contents of the shed upside down, looking for contraband. Whatever was responsible for Riley's good mood, she felt certain it wasn't drugs.

Her only break in the constant worry about her son were the hard hours she put in at the Crossing House, helping with the cleanup, making suggestions for the planning of the changes.

On Friday she made her final big push.

"Really, Dad, you'll more than make up the difference in the first months. If you expand your business, you'll increase your income, more than offsetting the renovations and increased expenses."

He rubbed his chin and Lily heard the rasp of early morning whiskers. "I don't know—I've held this place without a loan from the bank for more years than I can remember. To go into debt now—"

"The bank wouldn't have approved the loan if it wasn't a sure thing. They see the potential." She attributed his hesitance to his longtime commitment to old-fashioned values. Which were fine, but when a person ran a business, he had to be forward-thinking.

"Why would the bank care?" Faye mumbled as she worked circles around Benny as he stood in the center of the gutted room with the contractors' estimates in his hand. "They'll get their money one way or the other. Either Benny pays, or they take the business."

Reluctantly, Lily turned her attention to Faye, who insisted on nosing in on every conversation. "That's ridiculous. The bank doesn't want to run a pub. They only approve loans when the business is viable."

"Listen to you!" Faye's voice mocked. "You'd think you've been runnin' a business yourself."

"I'm just saying, the bankers—people who *know*—think it's a good idea. You have to be willing to take a few risks—"

"There!" She rounded on Lily and stuck a finger in the air. "You said it. Risk—"

"All right!" Benny raised a hand to his temple. "You're making my head hurt."

"Dad." Lily turned her gaze to him. "This town needs more family places. You'll still have the bar business, your regulars, you'll just be adding to it."

"Well, I have to decide today." He sighed heavily. "The cleanup is nearly done, the contractors can start next week."

"It's a good plan." Lily put an arm around his shoulders and tried to ignore Faye's snort in the background. They had all worked their fingers raw, now tempers were short. They'd begged and pushed, getting contractors to work overtime to get things back up and running. She didn't want to go nose to nose with Faye and get her dad off track. "This town needs—"

"Okay," he said.

Lily blinked. "Really?"

"I'll call the carpenters this afternoon." He raised the papers.

"Oh, Dad!" Lily threw her arms around his neck. "This is going to be great! Everybody in town will come. Business will boom! There are so many things to decide. Colors, furniture . . ."

His thick arms folded around her and he patted her on the back.

Lily closed her eyes, so she didn't have to see Faye's pinched disapproving face over her dad's shoulder.

After doing the final prep work for the contractors on Saturday, they decided to take Sunday completely off to recharge.

Riley went to the Dew Drop with his grandpa for breakfast,

then for a guided tour of the town, as Riley hadn't seen much of it since his arrival. A little male bonding, her dad had called it. Lily had been pleased by her son's willingness to go. Riley had even asked if he could stay in town for the afternoon; there were activities planned at the park to celebrate the Memorial Day weekend. She'd told him she'd meet him on the playground at the big double slide at four o'clock.

After they left, she took her coffee out onto the dock and watched the early fishermen in their low-slung bass boats. The morning sun was behind her, casting her long shadow upon the still water. A fine vapor mist still clung to the surface of the lake, blurring the edges of her silhouetted form. It was going to be a very humid day.

Which brought her to her next thought: What was she going to do with herself? She considered finishing setting up her potter's equipment in the boathouse. But that seemed a waste of precious energy, since she wasn't likely to have time to do any pottery until after the Crossing House was back in business.

Maybe she'd take a walk. She'd been here long enough that curiosity was outweighing reluctance. Had the "old haunts," as Peter had called them, changed much in the past years? If she didn't go today, who knew when she'd have the time?

Settling on a course, she went into the house to put on her tennis shoes and grab a bottle of water.

An hour and twelve mosquito bites later she found herself on the trail that led to The Place. When she and Luke had found it, it was just a narrow deer path. She recalled how her brother had pointed out the tracks, explaining how the animals traveled through the woods on their own version of roads. The path was still easily found; maybe the deer still used it.

As she neared the creek, her footsteps slowed until her forward progress stopped altogether.

"Come on, Lily," she said. "If you can face the fire tower, this should be a piece of cake."

While the fire tower held the most emotionally explosive moments of her adolescent life, this place had witnessed much broader experiences. Almost all of the memories forged here were good. The few that were painful all wrapped around Clay in one way or another—the accident with the fireworks, and their last conversation before he left, the one that ended everything.

Quieting her thoughts, she started walking again.

There was a sharp curve in the path just before The Place. Lily moved with quiet reverence as she made that curve, as if she were approaching hallowed ground. When the rocky outcropping came into view, she was glad she'd been so silent in her approach.

Clay sat on the ground under the ledge, at the very spot of their last meeting here. He was barefoot, with his shoes sitting beside him. He wore jeans and a white buttoned shirt with the tail untucked and the sleeves rolled to his elbows. His feet were planted flat on the ground, his knees drawn up with his arms resting on them, one hand clasping the opposite wrist. His head was down, his hair falling onto his forehead, shielding his eyes. From this angle, he looked so young, so vulnerable. Nothing like the man at the marina. She could almost believe he was still twenty-one.

Suddenly she was eighteen again, her heart made ethereally light by love. Emotions shot through her like lightning. Emotions she never thought she would feel again—the wonder, the unquestioning devotion, the demand for touch, the visceral aching need. Her stomach felt like she'd just taken that first drop on a roller coaster. God, just looking at him made her body heat up with remembered passion. This place magically stripped away the years, giving her a chance to recapture a part of her that she'd so purposefully destroyed. The part that loved unconditionally, wholly— blindly.

He appeared unaware of her presence.

She held her breath and watched, feeling like a Peeping Tom, but unable to help herself. What he would do, secluded and unwatched? Would he show a glimmer of the person she remembered—help her forge another link in the fantasy that she really could go back in time?

For a long while, he remained as still as a startled rabbit, motion frozen in time. Lily fought the urge to step into the clearing, to show herself, allow the thoughts and feelings she'd been fighting for the past week to flow unhindered to the surface. It would be so simple to let the past years, the past pain, slide away, here in this place. But would he feel the same? Or would he meet her with hard eyes and harsh words?

It would be easy for her, much too easy, to take that leap back toward youth. That almost-kiss by the dock had proven that. Too easy, and much too big of a risk. He'd rejected her once and it had nearly killed her.

She took one silent step backward.

His head snapped up, his eyes focused on the exact spot where she stood. Now she was the rabbit held immobile, hoping not to be seen by the wolf.

"Lily?" He said it softly, as if spoken to a dream. The sound of it drove straight to her heart.

She knew she should run while she could. Her reaction

to his calling her name told her she was too weak, too vulnerable.

The tone of his voice said he was as swept back in time as she. With both of them so defenseless against the past . . .

Instead of doing the smart thing, the thing she knew to be best, she followed her heart. She drew a steadying breath and stepped into plain sight.

"Yes." She tensed, waiting.

He surprised her by smiling. That smile made the transformation complete. They *had* traveled back in time. They were young and in love, and nothing else mattered.

The smile must have taken him by surprise, too. He quickly wiped it from his face. But not before Lily had seen true joy in his eyes. It was there for one unguarded second, then gone with a blink.

"I didn't mean to intrude," she said, shifting her weight nervously, but not moving any closer. Would he be angry, thinking she'd been spying—which, of course, she had? "I was just walking. . . ."

For a long moment he simply looked at her, his expression unreadable. He no longer resembled the boy; nor was he the hard-hearted man she'd been dealing with. He stood up and pushed the hair from his face.

She started to back away. She could feel his silence building into a cold wall. He *was* angry. The rock-hard set of his jaw said so.

Then he stopped her by speaking. "This is the first time I've been back here." His gaze moved from her to the ledge overhead and back to her again.

"Me, too." She wasn't going to admit that, it just fell out of her mouth.

"It hasn't changed like I thought it might." He held himself still, as if afraid that any movement would shatter the moment and send shards of the past like shrapnel toward their hearts.

With equal care, she took a step closer. There was a twining of past and present, love and fear, anticipation and dread that she couldn't untangle in her soul. It seemed too dangerous to speak what was on her mind, so she followed his lead.

"Someone has been here," she said. "Someone uses it."

He nodded and gave his head that once-so-familiar tilt that tugged deep inside her. "I hope it's kids."

"Luke said something like that to me once, a long time ago." A long time ago—but it felt like yesterday. "I told him that adults might use it a few times then forget about it. Kids would fight for it."

"And we did." That beautiful smile crept back and Lily's heart surrendered its brief battle to remain free.

She smiled, too. "That you did."

After a moment, during which she could tell he was fighting the memories, he finally said, "I'm willing to share now." He motioned for her to come and sit with him.

She knew she should say no. She should turn right around and walk out of this woods. But her feet moved forward, not in retreat. She purposely sat more than an arm's length away from where he sat, her back against a tree. Any closer and she might give herself away, might reveal to him that she'd never really let him go.

She couldn't stand the silence, the way they patently avoided looking at each other. "How is it that you're not at the marina today? Sunday is a big lake day."

"Cecil couldn't take real retirement. After the first month, he came and asked for Sundays back. He wanted a day when it would be busy and he could catch up with all of the people he used to see. I think his wife was driving him crazy."

"I see." She swatted a fly that was pestering her.

They sat in heavy silence for some time. Reminiscing was one thing, but where were they to go from here? In this place, they could ignore their differences for a short while. But ignoring wouldn't solve anything. If they were ever to find a common ground, which she firmly believed would be in Riley's best interest, it couldn't be done by ignoring the unpleasant.

Might as well really get the ball rolling. "I saw that boy you fired. At Kingston's Market. He's working in the produce section."

He nodded but his expression remained closed. "I knew it'd work out."

Lily's spine stiffened. "Really? It sounded to me like you didn't give a damn about that kid."

"Kevin was an accident waiting to happen at the marina. If I didn't fire him, he was going to end up in the hospital."

"You didn't have to be so mean to him. He seems like a nice kid."

"He is." He looked pointedly at her. "But I'm *not* a nice man—I'm a coldhearted jerk. Everybody knows it."

She looked sharply at him, but he looked away and picked a weed nearby and began to shred it.

The realization hit like a blinding light. He did it so the kid could save face. Kevin wasn't incompetent; Clay was an impossible boss, a bad guy. The juxtaposition of the Clay she knew and the Clay she now saw clicked into sharper focus.

He looked at her and apparently read her mind. Raising a palm, he said, "He was going to get hurt. I had to fire him. He was a lawsuit in the making."

"Whatever you say." She wanted to reach out and place

her palm against his. Good thing she'd put the distance between them, or she might have done it.

"Don't make things what they aren't." There seemed to be a resonance to that statement that went beyond the current topic.

She ignored it. "I suppose you have an equally self-serving reason for paying for Jason McGuire's summer camp?"

He shifted and drew his knees up again, but didn't look at her. "Where'd you hear that?"

"Don't forget who my dad is. Nothing gets by him in this town. Just because the bar's down doesn't mean he's out of touch."

"Sure hope he's back in business soon. Friday nights just aren't the same with bottled beer."

Lily didn't miss the deliberate shift in conversation. She obliged, momentarily glad for a topic that wasn't a minefield; it gave her time to adjust her opinion of Clay, the man. She'd been convinced he was a heartless bastard. And that played well with the version of him she'd created in her memory—the version that made the pain less sharp, that made it easier to pretend she was glad he'd left her. Now she could see, under all of that gruffness lived a very good man. There were questions that begged to be asked, but she didn't want to take a chance and sabotage their conversation.

"Bottled beer will have to do for a while," she said. "It's going to be a few weeks before the Crossing House will be open again. He's doing some major renovations. It's going to be really nice, more upscale."

He looked at her, the way he used to, like he could clearly see deep into her soul, and her heart hit a double-beat. "You just can't get over it, can you?"

"What?" Why did he have to look at her like that?

"Here you are, the richest lady in town"—he waved a hand in the general direction of the lake cottage—"and still you can't get over the fact that you were raised over a bar. Don't you understand? Nobody cared then, nobody cares now."

Anger washed over her in a hot wave. She shot to her feet, unsure which pissed her off more, the fact that he called her rich (which she most definitely was not—at least not anymore) like it was an accusation, or the fact that he presumed to understand what her childhood had been like. He'd been raised in a respected family.

She pointed a finger at him. "Maybe *you* don't understand. You didn't have to grow up over a bar and live in a town where everyone knew your mother deserted her family—ran off with another man without even telling her children goodbye. Just left for the drugstore one day and never came home." Her voice rose as she picked up speed. "You didn't have to go through every day listening to whispers behind your back, having other kids' moms not let them come to your house to play—having people watch to see if you're as big a whore as your mother!"

Lily's mouth snapped closed. Her breath froze in her lungs and her trembling hand covered her mouth. Her eyes stung, but she refused to cry. She'd never said those words to anyone, rarely admitted them to herself. But once they started coming, they were like a runaway train driven by pure emotion.

She turned away.

Clay got up and moved close behind her. Every cell in her body thrummed with his nearness. After a moment, his hands grasped her shoulders and he pulled her back against his chest. For the briefest second she held herself rigid, then she relaxed into him.

"Lily." His breath tickled her ear. "You're not your mother."

Clay didn't know where in his heart those words had come from. For years he'd been convinced that she was exactly that—a woman driven by selfishness, mad for money, abandoning those who loved her for the promise of a better life.

But in the past few days, he'd begun to doubt.

He turned her to face him. He had to see her eyes, see the truth. He'd never had that chance fourteen years ago, had never been able to look into her eyes and ferret out the reason why.

She wouldn't look him in the eye until he put his finger under her chin and forced her. His hand slid to the side of her neck and rested there.

When her eyes met his, an ice pick pierced his heart. Suddenly he didn't care what she believed. The only thing that mattered was the moment—the look of need in her eyes, the softness of her skin under his hands, the wild throb of his pulse in his veins, the pulse that echoed his in the side of her neck. Holding her gaze with his, he was a boy again, that boy he'd been searching for for so long.

He should take his hands off her. But she felt too good, too tempting.

Slowly, he lowered his mouth to hers, his heart hammering like an inexperienced teen's. His lips grazed hers lightly, testing her response.

His mind spun wildly into the past, to the first time he'd wanted to kiss these lips—in the old fire tower, hiding from a horde of teenagers playing some stupid game. It had begun in innocence, but the feelings that swept through him while they'd been isolated on that dark summer night had taken him by surprise. He'd always felt close to Lily, protected her. But this was different. He'd looked into those blue eyes, at those smiling lips and his heart had slammed into high gear. He was in love with her. When it had happened he could never pinpoint, but that was the moment when he'd fully realized it. He loved her and he wanted her—all of her. The shock of sudden and unexpected desire had stopped him in his tracks—that and the fact that she was too young, too innocent.

Now she was neither young nor innocent. And her lips answered his in a way that couldn't be misinterpreted. Her arms slid around his back, her hands knotting in his shirt, and she closed the space between their bodies.

He moved them as one, backing her up against the smooth-barked sycamore.

Then he drew away slightly, still close enough to recapture her kiss. He whispered, "Show me." He held up his scarred right palm.

Her left hand released his shirt. Slowly, as she held his gaze steady with hers, she slid her palm the length of his arm, coming to rest on the back of his hand. She moved his hand, placing it on her collarbone. Kissing him once again, she moved his hand lightly over her body, guiding it steadily downward until it rested on her breast.

Clay pulled away from the kiss just enough to see her eyes. Oh, God in heaven, those were the eyes that haunted his dreams. Blue gone gray with wanting. Lashes half shadowing the iris.

He hovered there, feeling her breath on his lips, drinking in the look in her eyes, and wanted time to stop.

That thought made him realize the danger. He had to stop this now, before it was too late. He drew in a breath and tried to lift his hand from her breast. But she held it firmly against her. He could feel the frantic beating of her heart against his thumb.

"Lily—"

She stifled his words with a kiss.

He made one more halfhearted effort at extricating himself, but when her tongue began to tease his and her hand moved his down her ribs and over the soft curve of her hip, he was lost.

When fabric changed to skin under his touch, he knew he was almost there, to the place that connected the two of them through time and turmoil.

She halted his hand against her thigh for what seemed an eternity and he thought his heart would explode out of his chest. She'd captured his body, his soul, with just one touch.

Then she slid his hand under the hem of her shorts. When he felt the silky smoothness of her inner thigh, the scar on his palm tingled as if electrically charged. When their hands finally reached their destination, he pressed the scar on his palm against the one on her leg.

A quiet yet demanding little moan came from the back of Lily's throat. Her hand left his and pressed against the zipper of his jeans.

Jesus, he was going to come right now if she didn't stop.

Kneeling in front of her, he held her shorts hem high and kissed a circle around the white scar on her leg. When he traced the scar with his tongue, she buried her hands in his hair. Her knees buckled slightly, but she caught herself.

"This brand makes you mine," he said as he looked up at her. "No matter what happens. Always and forever. Mine."

Her knees did buckle then. He steadied her as he stood once again.

Running his hands under her shirt, he peeled it over her head. Her hair fell onto her face in a cinnamon-colored fan.

He pushed it back with both hands as he cradled her head and kissed her again. His tongue explored her mouth; he pushed the strap of her bra from her shoulder and cupped her breast.

The way she clung to him, the way she pressed herself against him, forced the last shreds of reality away. There was nothing in this world but the taste of her, the feel of her skin, the need to make her completely his.

The button popped from her shorts as he tried to undo it. It only served to make him more frantic. Working together, they peeled away her shorts and panties. She kicked them off while they switched their efforts to ridding him of his jeans. He felt her hands trembling as she slid them inside to shove the fabric away. The clothing disappeared as quickly and completely as their hesitancy.

He lifted her and she wrapped her legs around him. Her back was against the tree when he entered her. She threw her head back and he watched the rapid pulse in her beautiful neck as he moved within her. His body demanded more, drowning out the sweet ways of his heart.

He rocked her against the tree. Her eyes closed and her teeth bit down on her lower lip, making him want to do the same. But before he could lower his lips to hers, she moaned, pulling him deeper with her legs. He was lost.

She came and the feel of her body welcoming his was like a remembered dream.

It was over in the brilliant flash of a falling star. They clung together, breathing raggedly.

When he finally felt like he could take a step without collapsing into a puddle, he kicked off his jeans and carried her to the overhanging rock.

He held tightly onto the past, beating the doubt back into

the darkness. He'd had but a taste of what he'd dreamt about for years, he couldn't let go just yet.

Standing her on her own feet, he reached for the plastic garbage bag he'd discovered earlier. She smiled at him when he produced the blanket and spread it with a flick of his wrist.

Then he saw the hesitation bloom in her eyes.

*Don't leave me, baby, not yet.* He pulled her to him and kissed her. At first she tensed and he feared she'd already shut him out. But soon he felt her tentative touch slide under the shirt on his back. He lowered himself to his knees, his lips and tongue tracing a line down her body until he reached the place that made her shiver.

Pulling her down with him, he stretched out on the blanket. Rolling her onto her back, he raised to his knees to get rid of his shirt; he wanted nothing between them.

As he was kneeling, he saw her hand reach for the edge of the blanket to cover herself. He locked one hand around her wrist and she released the fabric. He held her arm firmly on the ground and looked at her.

She actually blushed.

He could hardly believe how beautiful she was—more beautiful as a woman than she'd been as a girl.

Lying next to her, he pulled her against him. She snuggled there, her breath tickling the hollow of his throat. They'd woven a delicate web of illusion and by unspoken agreement, they weren't going to ruin it with talk.

They spent a long while in silence. Then her hands began to caress and explore.

He remained quiet, allowing his body to say what his heart could not. He treated her with the devotion of the twenty-one-year-old he'd been, allowing himself, for a single afternoon, to once again pretend that love was possible.

Despite his sweet intentions, before long he had to fight the need to possess her totally. But her mouth demanded, her nails dug into his back and her legs opened, telling him she needed the possession as much as he.

Just as he came, he heard her cry his name and her fingers dug into his hips. Two into one. The violent clash of spirits and the flawless joining of flesh. It was perfect.

Their bodies remembered, even if they'd forced their minds to forget.

*Chapter 10*

Riley looked through the crowd gathered in the park, disappointment swelling in his chest. He tried to ignore it, deny the feeling altogether. He'd told Mickey he'd meet her at noon by the stationary steam locomotive in the park. It had been twelve twenty-five when Gramps finally dropped him at the limestone-pillar-flanked entrance.

He had thought his grandfather would never finish with the touring and the stories. It wasn't that Riley wasn't interested in hearing about Uncle Luke and Mom as kids, but he was having trouble associating the "Lily" Gramps talked about with the woman who was his mother. With each new story, the picture was becoming clearer. He actually liked hearing Gramps talk; it gave him a totally different view of his mom. However, being late had made him miss Mickey.

Standing in front of the locomotive, he looked at his watch again. Twelve-forty. Either she'd given up or hadn't showed at all. That was probably it. You just couldn't trust a girl.

Last Wednesday he'd gone to that place in the woods on his way home from work. He hadn't let himself hope she'd really be there. It was one thing to hang out in the woods by yourself when you were ditching school, but the first day of summer vacation had to have a whole lot more going on— even in Glens Crossing.

That thought had brought another. What if someone was out here with her? He'd almost turned around and headed back to the road when he heard her singing.

She had been there—and alone. After the first awkward moments when he'd made sure she understood he wasn't looking for her, they'd started talking about the book she'd given him. Before he realized it, the sun was casting long shadows on the ground and gloom was gathering under the trees. He'd had to run all the way home in order to make it before sunset.

"There you are."

He spun around. Mickey stood right behind him with a smile on her face, pale hair and braces winking in the sun. Her eyes were brown, an odd contrast to her hair. They looked like maple syrup in the bright sun. And she had freckles on her nose. He realized this was the first time he'd seen her outside the shade of deep woods.

"Oh, were you looking for me?" he said as offhandedly as he could manage. His chest felt funny, all squeezed and tight. Maybe he was getting sick.

"Yeah, Goofy, I said I'd make a picnic for us. Did you forget?"

He shrugged. She'd started calling him Goofy when he'd called her Mickey Mouse. He pretended it made him mad, but it really didn't. She was sort of cute when she said it.

"I was too late to get a picnic table, everybody and their uncle are out here today. But I found a good shady spot for a blanket. Come on."

Riley followed a few steps behind. It was weird, the way

he'd looked forward to seeing her, but now that he was here, he wasn't sure he wanted to be at all. She was only a stupid girl.

It was just because he didn't know any other kids around here, he told himself. Maybe she could introduce him to some guys and then things would be right again. He sure didn't need all of this creepy uncertainty. He didn't know what was wrong with him. At school, he always knew what he wanted and went after it; other guys looked to him to make decisions. But here, with her, it was all mixed up.

They passed several groups of guys their age and none of them even gave a glance their way. Suddenly Riley was certain Mickey didn't know any boys. Not as friends anyhow. That thought made a fluttery feeling in his stomach. He was her only guy friend.

Mickey walked beyond the picnic tables. She stopped at the edge of the woods that flanked the creek, by a patchwork quilt spread beneath a giant tree. There was an old-fashioned picnic basket on the blanket.

"Where'd you get this stuff, from your grandma?" The second he said it, he wanted to take it back. It sounded nasty. Sometimes he just didn't know what to say to her.

It didn't seem to make her mad. She sat on the quilt Indian-style. "The picnic basket was Granny Fulton's, actually it was her mother's—so it's really old. I found the quilt at a garage sale. Can you believe somebody would sell something like this? It's handmade." She ran her hand over the stitches.

One quilt pretty much looked like another to Riley, but he shook his head and sat down across from her. He didn't think he'd ever met anyone who actually shopped at garage sales. Maybe her family was really poor. Suddenly he felt guilty for her supplying his lunch.

She opened the basket and started pulling stuff out. "I didn't know what you like, so I brought a bunch of different stuff."

She handed him a bottle of water. "Let's see, if you don't want that, I have herbal tea." She paused and looked at him.

"Water's fine." Herbal tea? She did like grandma stuff.

"I have a turkey wrap with alfalfa sprouts . . . a chicken salad sandwich with no-fat mayo on nine-grain bread . . . a soy-cheese and veggie wrap, that's for me, I'm a vegetarian . . . baby carrots and yogurt dip . . . apples . . . grapes . . . and"—she pulled out the last container as if it were the grand finale—"homemade trail mix."

No chips? No brownies? No cupcakes? Nothing out of a crackly bag at all? What kind of picnic was this? This wasn't grandma stuff. It was worse, it was hippie stuff.

"Do you have any regular food in there?" He made a show of peering into the basket.

"This is regular food—at least it should be."

"If you're a vegetarian, what about all of that bats-eat-mosquitoes, snakes-eat-mice stuff? What'll happen to all of the cows and pigs if nobody eats them? The farmers won't feed them anymore. Then you're gonna have a world full of starving cows and skinny pigs."

"Don't be ridiculous. I didn't say nobody should eat meat. I just choose not to. I hardly think the cows of this world are in danger—at least of starving to death."

He chose the turkey wrap and tried to pick the stringy grass off of it when Mickey wasn't looking. He guessed it wasn't too bad.

After they'd eaten and Mickey was packing up the basket, Riley sprawled on his back and looked at the leaves overhead. A fat brown squirrel was jumping from branch to branch, chittering and chattering like it was really mad about something. What would make a squirrel mad? he wondered. *Maybe its parents are getting a divorce.*

"Uh-oh."

"What's the matter?" he asked, without sitting up.

Mickey let out a long breath. "My mom."

Riley shot to a sitting position. How had he gotten so close to Mickey? His head had been right beside her thigh. He slid sideways until there was at least three feet between them. When he looked around, he realized how isolated they were from most all of the other picnickers.

*Oh, crap!* It wasn't hard to read the look on Mickey's mother's face.

"Michaeline!" She lowered her voice as she got closer, so no one but Mickey and Riley and the squirrel could hear. "Do you want the whole town to think you're a tramp, lying around on this blanket with this, this . . . boy?"

Riley was braced for the fight as Mickey set her mother straight, just like she set him straight time and again. But Mickey seemed to get smaller just sitting there. She hung her head so her hair hid her face.

"Sorry." Her voice was the softest he'd ever heard it. "We were just having a pic—"

The mother's ice-blue gaze cut to Riley.

He stood, squared his shoulders and offered his hand. "I'm Riley Holt, ma'am." Now maybe she would yell at him and leave Mickey alone. She could yell at him all day long as far as he was concerned. They hadn't done anything wrong.

Suddenly the mother's head tilted slightly to the side, her mouth formed a relaxed O and her eyes grew wider. It was the same look Riley had seen on people's faces when they heard he was William Holt's grandson.

"Nice to meet you, Riley." She shook his hand in a totally

girly way. Now she was smiling—he guessed it was okay to be a tramp if you did it with a rich kid. "Your mother and I went to school together. Michaeline and I just saw her the other day and said how we should get you children together. How did you two manage to meet all on your own?"

Riley felt, more than saw, Mickey cringe at his feet. She remained sitting, rearranging things in the basket. He said, "Mom dropped me off and we ran into Mick—Michaeline. She introduced us."

"Is your mother still here?" Mrs. Fulton looked around.

"Ah, no. She had to leave."

"I'm sorry to have missed her. Tell her I said hello." She started to walk away, floating this time instead of barreling like a steamroller. "You two behave yourselves."

Riley watched her go, unable to look at Mickey.

"Thanks," she said in an almost imperceptible tone.

He sat back down. "For what? Changing the Wicked Witch of the West into Glenda the Good? I wish I had that power over all adults."

Mickey laughed, sounding like herself again.

Jesus, they were only having a picnic. It's not like they were *doing it* right here in the park. Riley wondered what kind of life Mickey had at home. But he had a pretty good idea.

He wanted to punch Mrs. Fulton right in the mouth.

The return to earth from Lily's sexual high came with a crash. She'd just added one more memory to The Place— and this particular memory was one she almost wished she could erase. She couldn't deny that she'd done what she'd sworn to herself she wouldn't do under any circumstances— allow Clay Winters back into her heart. But, as she lay naked in the woods with her head on his chest, listening to the steady beat of his heart, she couldn't deny it had happened.

She was still trying to decipher the man he was deep inside. Obviously, he wasn't the hard-ass he wanted everyone to think he was. But he was different from the way he used to be—in ways that seemed dark and unfathomable to her. She didn't really *know* him anymore.

They lay in false intimacy—two people separated by time and experience. For a brief moment they'd been able to pretend. But they were adults, with adult lives that were on intersecting, but not in the least similar, paths.

Having sex might have felt good, but it didn't solve any of the issues between them. It just made them more difficult to bring up.

She wished he would say something.

Finally, keeping her head where it was because she didn't want to look him in the eye, she said, "Why did you come back to Glens Crossing?"

He took a deep breath that lifted her head slightly. He settled his hand on her hip. "Looking for the things I lost, I guess."

She didn't understand. He was the one who'd turned away from what he had here without a backward glance. She wanted to ask him to explain, but she wanted to do it with her clothes on.

Taking a quick scan to see if she could locate all of her clothing, she was disappointed. The only article within reach without getting up and moving was her bra, which somehow had become tangled with Clay's boxers.

She decided to brave the question. "I don't understand."

He breathed deeply. "I always felt the most at home here. I guess I'm just trying to recapture the good moments of my childhood."

"And?"

"And you can never go back." A cool edge crept into his voice. "I'm not the same person I used to be."

"None of us are." She tried not to think that what they'd just done had been, for him, a last snatch at youth. "We change with the world around us or we break into a thousand pieces."

He didn't say anything further, so she pressed on. "Tell me about yourself—what you've been up to these past years." She felt like she was being noble, the first to step into dangerous territory.

She felt him shift under her, putting just a bit more space between their bodies. "I was in the service for a long while—overseas."

"Really?" She couldn't help but look at him now; she propped her chin on his chest. "Luke's an Army Ranger."

"I know."

"You two keep in touch?" Why wouldn't Luke have told her that?

"Not really. I've run into him a couple of times."

"Oh." Now that she had a crumb, she was more curious than ever. His being in the service seemed good, safe ground. "What branch of service?"

"Started in regular army. Then I did some specialty work."

"What kind?"

"I could tell you—"

"—but then you'd have to kill me." She laughed. "Luke's used that on me a hundred times." She was feeling more at ease. "Ever married?"

She heard his sharp intake of breath.

It had just fallen out of her mouth, flowing in the same

way it would in a conversation at a class reunion. The question was out there, there was no calling it back.

She had to remind herself, this wasn't just any conversation. Clay wasn't just any man.

"No."

"Ever get close?" The best way to diffuse this was to forge ahead, deal with it like a normal exchange.

"Never."

"No family, then?" God, this was painful. But she'd taken this path, she had to finish it.

"Jesus Christ, no! I can't think of anything worse than having kids. Not in this world. Besides, I wouldn't be any good at it. God spared me that particular misery." He made it sound like he'd been dealt plenty of other miseries, though.

*Well join the club, buddy.* She'd dealt with miseries by the boatload, many of them delivered by Clay's own hand.

He withdrew the arm that was around her and laid his hands on his chest. There was more to his action than physical distance. Lily felt a change come over him.

"You *are* on the pill. . . ."

She felt a little spark of anger; now was a fine time to ask. She certainly didn't see him digging for a condom a few minutes ago. She lied, "Yes, of course."

In truth, she hadn't worried about birth control for years. After trying unsuccessfully to have another child while Riley was a toddler, she'd given up even the thought of birth control.

"Good."

That pretty much dried up her desire for conversing. She was suddenly naked and vulnerable.

"I have to go." She rose and started to gather her clothes,

making every effort not to look at him as he sat up on the blanket.

He didn't try to stop her.

She was nearly dressed when he spoke again. "Lily."

She froze as she was zipping her shorts; there was something very distant in his voice. "Yes?"

"This doesn't change anything. You were right. We're both different."

She didn't know what she expected him to say. She'd been thinking many similar thoughts herself. But his voicing the words stung like lemon juice on a rug burn.

"Do you think I want something from you?" she asked, keeping her tone as cool as his.

"Women always do. Don't try to make things what they aren't. I'm not the same. You're not the same. We can't try to fool ourselves."

A dread chill crept over her. The door that had cracked open briefly, allowing her to think she could understand him, slammed closed. She guessed that was exactly what she had done—fooled herself. Again.

He didn't care. He was interested in getting laid.

He sat there, unconcerned about his own nudity, as she put on her shoes. She didn't know if he watched her, because she kept her eyes turned away from him.

"Well," she said as she started for the path. "Goodbye."

He didn't say anything.

"Clay?" She stopped and turned back around. Even as she did it, she cursed herself for being weak.

"Go home, Lily." His voice was flat, final.

She didn't know if he meant to the cottage on Mill Run Road, or to Chicago. Her pride kept her from asking.

\*    \*    \*

That chill that crept into Lily's belly when Clay had told her not to fool herself spread like frostbite. By the time she got back home, she was actually shivering. She felt light-headed and her stomach had turned sour.

She had deluded herself once again. She'd let her body take charge, and no good was going to come of it. She felt stupid and cheap and alone. If only he'd opened up to her, given her the opportunity to understand. But he'd turned so cold, it was as if *he* had been the wounded one in their last parting. She remembered that argument of fourteen years ago as if it had happened this afternoon:

"Hey," Clay said, as Lily arrived at The Place. He walked over to her and hugged her tightly, then gave her a kiss that made her ears ring. "I'm glad you could come."

Kissing him had yet to settle into routine for Lily. She still couldn't believe it. He loved her. Her. She'd been so used to furtive gestures and her own unfulfilled longing that it was going to take some getting used to. After all this time, thinking friendship was all she could ever hope for, he loved her. He'd loved her for six weeks, three days and sixteen hours. He said he'd loved her for far longer than that, but wanted to wait until she finished high school before he let her know. So she'd started counting from the moment he told her.

No one else knew yet. It was getting harder and harder not to slip in front of Peter. Luckily, Luke was away, he'd enlisted in the army a year ago. Lily doubted she'd have been able to shield her emotions from her brother. He always honed right in on whatever was going on in her mind.

So this summer, instead of four of them, their group had been reduced to three. And their time wasn't as carefree as it once had been. Clay was working at the marina part-time and Lily had a job at Arctic Express, "Frozen treats straight from the North Pole," for the summer. She planned on commuting to Indiana University in the fall—which somehow had suddenly become next week.

"Well, you sounded pretty funny on the phone. Is something wrong?" In fact, her heart had started racing with the call and hadn't slowed since.

"Oh, God, no!" Clay said, taking her hands. "Everything's right. Last night was the most incredible moment of my life. I've wanted us to be together for so long." He paused. "I was just worried, did you . . . are you . . . okay?"

"Clay." She took her hands from his and cupped his face. "I didn't do anything I didn't want to do." She looked down for a moment and her cheeks warmed. "As I recall, it was my idea."

"I just don't want you to have anything to regret. Not now. Not when it's taken us this long to . . . get together."

He was so sweet, just like she knew he would be. Her heart was near to bursting with love for him.

She slipped her arms around his neck and kissed him. He wrapped his arms around her waist and pulled her closer, until her heels lifted off the ground.

"God, I love you," he said against her ear. "I wish I didn't have to leave tomorrow."

She groaned. "Me, too." She'd been dreading it all week as she'd watched Mrs. Holt ready the cottage to close it up for fall.

"I'm going to tell my dad when I get home. I've only got one more year before I'm done at Northwestern. He might as well get used to the idea that I'm going to be coming back here and not going on to law school."

As much as she wanted to jump at the chance to tell

everyone, she reined in her emotions. Douglas Winters was an imposing and formidable man. The only thing more powerful than his wealth was his will. Lily had only met him once. He had done nothing to hide his contempt for this small Indiana town and everyone living here—especially her and Luke. Seems they were an unwanted influence on his son, tarnishing his city polish with their very presence.

She'd heard horror stories for years of Clay's dad's temper. Most of them came from Peter; Clay didn't like to talk about his dad. The man ruled his empire and everyone in it. Any deviation from his dictates led to immediate retribution and threats to disinherit. It was clear, if Clay chose a path other than the one his father had lined up for him, there would be hell to pay.

"Clay, I think you should wait. I mean, there's no reason to get him all worked up."

He looked at her as if she were crazy. "I don't care if he's furious."

Lily noticed he didn't say he didn't care if his dad was *mad,* he'd used the word *furious.* And that just confirmed her fears. "Maybe you can ease him into it over the course of the year. If he cuts you off, you won't be able to finish school."

"I don't care!" His voice rose. "Don't you see? It doesn't matter."

"But if you don't finish school, what will you do?"

"Finishing school isn't more important than us! I'm not going to law school. I'm not joining his firm."

"I'm not saying we're not important. And I've always known you didn't want to be a lawyer. But you're so close to getting your degree. I don't want you to do something you're going to regret in the long run."

He looked at her as if she'd just slapped him in the face.

"Be reasonable, Clay. We've waited this long. It won't hurt to keep it to ourselves a while longer."

"Are you having second thoughts?" There was an edge of accusation in his voice.

"Of course not." She put a hand on his cheek. "I love you. Another year isn't going to change that. Anyone else knowing isn't going to change it. It's not worth throwing everything away right now."

"It's worth it to me." He grabbed her shoulders. "I'm willing to throw everything away for you. Nothing else means anything. I don't care if the bastard cuts me off without a penny."

He was so fixed on his course of action, nothing she said seemed to sink in. "At least wait awhile, test the waters and see how it works out."

"Why are you so anxious for me to wait? If he cuts me off, he's going to do it now or later. Once I tell him, nothing will change that outcome. I've made up my mind."

She pulled away from his grasp. "So that's it—you've made your mind up and nothing else matters?"

"I'm fed up with him running my life. I'm ready to end it."

She tried to soften her approach; he seemed to be sliding further and further down this slippery slope. She didn't want to be the ruination of his life. The day would come when he would undoubtedly resent her for it. "Please. Think about what you're doing."

"I'm taking charge of my life. He's pushed me around long enough. I can't stand it." He buried his hands in his hair and fisted them there. "My God, Lily, you don't know what it's like!"

"You'll be at school. You won't even have to see him. Once you're finished, then you can talk to him. Why are you so bent on destruction?"

"Destruction? Is that how you see it? I see it as devotion—to you. I guess maybe you don't feel the same way."

"Ooooooh!" she made the noise through gritted teeth. "Don't turn this on me! You know how I feel."

"I'm beginning to see that very clearly. 'Don't tell Peter.' 'Don't tell your dad.' Yes, it's all becoming crystal clear."

"You know that's not why I asked you to wait. I'm thinking about you—and your family."

"And you think that once I get past today, I'll come to my senses and step into my dad's future for me—get him to accept you once I'm there."

"I want you to be happy. You don't know what it's like to be separated from a parent forever. I just want what's best for you."

"Well, I guess I'm the best judge of what's best for me."

"Don't do it, Clay. You'll be sorry." She was surprised at the cool, level way she managed to say it. She knew what he'd be throwing away. Although she might not know what it was to have money, she knew very well the value of family.

His head snapped around, his eyes holding all of the fury she'd sensed buried deep inside him. "It's my decision!" His voice vibrated with anger. He jabbed a thumb into his own chest. "I'm the one who'll have to deal with the consequences."

Lily took a step backward. She'd never seen this kind of rage in him. It took her a second to steel herself to go against it. "Oh, really? And I suppose it will in no way affect me. If we're going to be together, we have to make these kinds of decisions together."

"I'm willing to sacrifice everything for us." There was a defensive tone in his anger now. He was daring her to contradict him.

"Well, maybe I'm not." The words fell icy and hard from her lips.

Suddenly his eyes lost their fire and turned deadly cold. "Afraid I'll lose all my money?" His tone was cutting; the angry blackness that had been lurking in his soul spewed out in his words. She knew his father had hurt him. But he looked at her as if she'd do the same.

"You bastard." How could he love her and even think something like that?

She was too furious to argue further. She was going to say things that could never be recalled, things she would regret. So she stood there with her chest heaving and her lips pressed together.

He turned around and walked away.

It seemed impossible to believe then that that would be their last conversation for fourteen years.

She'd tried to get in touch with him, had called his father's house when she got no answer at his school number. Douglas Winters had told her, in a detached and impersonal tone, his son was no longer living there and would not be back. When she asked how she could get in touch with him, Mr. Winters said he had no idea. Then he hung up.

When she'd called Peter and told him what Mr. Winters had said, he didn't have any further details. He said Clay and his dad had had a huge blowup—and now he was gone.

Clay had vowed he loved her—and he turned right around and walked out of her life. Words. Empty, meaningless words.

At least this time there had been no pretense of love. This time he'd been straightforward with her, telling her right up front that there wasn't any foundation for them to stand on.

And she'd given herself to him anyway.

# *Chapter 11*

Lily managed to avoid Clay altogether for the next two weeks. It was as if he were making the same conscious effort she was to ensure their paths didn't cross. But there was something else that captured her attention more than her relationship—or lack of one—with Clay. She should have started her period three days ago. She didn't even feel like she was going to. God in heaven, how had she been so stupid?

She told herself over and over again, she just couldn't be pregnant. Surely the fates couldn't have it in for her that much. She couldn't be. It was impossible.

*Impossible?* a little voice inside called. *Think again.* Possible it was. Pregnant, with the child of a man who was a stranger, who had proven he didn't care—who didn't *want* children.

She was no better than her mother, throwing away the security of her child for the love of a man. She'd satisfied herself and threatened the well-being of everyone who depended on her—Riley, Peter. Her father. What would this town think of him? *Oh, yeah, I know Benny Boudreau, had a whore for a wife and a slut for a daughter.*

All because she couldn't control her love for a man who didn't want her.

Shame heated her cheeks, but she forced away those nasty little voices that were calling her names. She had to take one day at a time, one ordeal at a time.

Tomorrow she'd get a test. She couldn't make any decisions until then. Plus, there were other things worrying her.

Riley was an ever-increasing puzzle. Just when she'd begun to see improvement in his attitude, he'd become increasingly restless. He was short-tempered and withdrawn.

She suspected Clay was making Riley's workdays difficult, misdirecting the frustration that should have been aimed at her. Once, when she'd dropped Riley off at work, she'd caught Clay looking at her from the storage shed door. He quickly retreated inside, making it impossible to read his expression. But his body language shouted, *Stay away.*

If Clay was making Riley's life hell, Riley was remaining tight-lipped about it, refusing to divulge the slightest hint of his troubles. Was Clay using coercion to keep her son from reporting ill treatment? Clay himself had said he'd be a terrible father; this just proved the point. He was too selfish, too vindictive to care for a child.

Carefully stowing all of those nagging problems away in an airtight box, Lily picked up her keys and called Riley downstairs. Tonight was the grand reopening of the Crossing House and Clay had let Riley knock off work early. Which, now that she thought about it, didn't wash with the picture she'd been painting of Riley's misery, or Clay's treatment of him.

"Riley!" she called again.

His head appeared at the top of the stairs. "What?"

"It's time to go." She turned and started toward the door. She heard him thudding down the stairs. Why couldn't teenage boys pick up their feet? Perhaps, she thought, it was because the feet grew first, like puppies', and their legs hadn't grown strong enough to lift the extra weight.

Turning around to wait for him at the door, she sighed and rolled her eyes. "You're *not* wearing that."

He looked down at the black T-shirt that bore a near-obscene logo for one of his favorite bands and raised his palms at his sides. "What's wrong with this? It's cool."

"It may be cool, but you're not wearing it tonight. Your grandfather's gone to a great deal of trouble and expense to upgrade his restaurant. We can't go in there looking like . . . like . . ." She waved him toward the stairs. "Just go change into a shirt with *buttons*."

Riley turned around and muttered something under his breath.

"What did you say?"

"Nothing."

"No. Repeat what you said so I can hear it." That was one of Peter's old tricks, and nothing infuriated her more. He'd get in the last jab under his breath so she couldn't argue any further. Not man enough to say it to her face and deal with the aftermath.

"It was nothing!" He kept his back to her.

"Turn around here and say what you have to say to my face." She took a step in his direction and stopped just short of grabbing him and spinning him around.

Slowly he turned. His face was no longer that of a boy, but a man, with a man's determination. "I said, he doesn't even like it. He did it for *you!*"

"Who did what for me?"

"Gramps. He liked it the way it was—*you* wanted it to be different."

"Why would you think something like that?"

"Because Faye told me." He paused. "He did it so you could be proud of him—of what he does. Gramps told her the new 'pub' was like trying to fit into somebody else's clothes."

She felt like the air had been ripped from her lungs. She forced herself to take a deep trembling breath before she said, "I'm glad you told me." Working to remain calm when her insides had taken flight, she added, "I'll talk to him." She wanted to say more, to justify to Riley why this had been a good business move for his grandfather. But it wouldn't sound any different than the excuses she'd punished him for making over and over again.

"No, Mom. Please. I wasn't supposed to tell." He looked at his feet and, for the first time in the last minutes, looked like the boy he was, young and unsure and confused. "I shouldn't have said anything."

She slipped an arm around his shoulder. "It was the right thing to do and I thank you for sharing it with me. No one will ever know we had this conversation. It—it helps me a lot." She hugged him close. "You make me very proud." She patted his shoulder. "Now go change your shirt so we're not late."

Clay wanted a beer. A draft beer. And he knew, for the first time in weeks, he could get one. But that draft beer had strings attached. He'd have to see Lily. He didn't know if he was strong enough.

At The Place he'd sent her away, and she'd gone. But he might not be so lucky next time. As much as it pissed him off to admit it, had she refused, had she come to him with those not-so-innocent blue eyes and said she was staying, he wouldn't have had the strength to get up and walk away himself.

Just like that, he'd discovered that no matter how he'd tried to convince himself otherwise, he was still vulnerable to her.

Anger at his own weakness thrummed in his veins. He should never have touched her. There had been a single moment when he could have stopped things and he had not. Instead, he'd said the words that had opened the floodgates, then been swept helplessly away.

God, he hated being helpless. His father had tried to make him feel helpless—powerless to do anything except what he dictated. But he'd broken away from his father.

He'd thought he'd broken away from Lily.

It had been a break that he hadn't planned. All those years ago, when they'd had that last argument, he'd been the one to walk away. But it had never been his intention for that to be the end. His anger had overwhelmed his good sense. And that anger had been misguided at her. He knew that now. But the emotional battlefield he'd found himself on with Lily had scared him to death.

It had taken him his entire life to finally get the courage to make a break with his father. Oh, he'd known it was coming, that he wanted a different path. But loving Lily had given him the strength to stand, had made him truly see how awful the life his father wanted for him would be. He was ready to do it—and she had tried to take it all away. At that moment, he'd been so set, so focused, he couldn't see anything beyond the confrontation with his father. Each of Lily's comments hit him like rejection.

He'd walked away, and his life had quickly spiraled out of control in a way he couldn't possibly have foreseen. The opportunity to straighten things out with Lily had been taken from him.

Knowing what he knew now, that her feelings for him

were no more permanent than a Popsicle in the sun, he realized it was the best thing.

But that particular betrayal had branded him deeply. He'd thought he'd locked both Peter and Lily out of his mind, out of his heart.

Once again, he'd been wrong. He'd forged his body and his mind in fire, so that it was like tempered steel. But there was a flaw. An underlying weakness. It had lain hidden for years, just waiting to be tested. Once he saw Lily again, it hadn't taken long for that flaw to crack. And if he didn't guard himself, it would rend him completely in two.

He locked up the marina and climbed into his truck. He started it and sat there for a minute, engine idling, mind racing. He could feel the restlessness building, telling him to leave. That's what he always managed to do, wasn't it—leave a place before the emotional atmosphere got too intense?

While he was in Special Ops, he never remained in one place long enough for things to get personal. It was his job. He *had* to live that way. But deep down, he couldn't deny that life suited him just fine. The life of a nomadic chameleon precluded messy emotional entanglements.

Once he returned to Glens Crossing, he never fell into complete rhythm with this place. He never connected. Now he had to wonder, maybe he never wanted to—without Lily here.

There was no doubt that Lily qualified as a messy emotional entanglement. It wasn't like he could avoid her, there was that kid of hers. Day after day, he and Riley faced off for their own version of tug-of-war. They were both too pigheaded to be the first one dragged through the mud. Clay had no doubt he could win, overpower the kid with his position and his strength. But that just didn't seem fair. The kid was a fighter—which could be a good thing, a sign of strong character. It could also be a pain in the ass. Nevertheless, Clay wanted to see good come of this battle, not beat the independence out of the kid's spirit. If he left now, who knew what kind of situation the kid would end up in?

Shit. This was one fucked-up mess.

Clay put the truck in gear and headed toward the Crossing House. He didn't want to hurt Benny's feelings by ignoring his grand opening. He was man enough to be in a crowded room with Lily for forty minutes without breaking into a million quivering pieces. He owed Benny that. The man had befriended Clay when Clay's own attitude drove most people away. That friendship meant something to him.

One beer and he'd leave. There was bound to be such a crowd, he probably wouldn't even see Lily.

He believed that long enough to drive there and pull into the parking lot. Then he caught himself looking for her Toyota and realized how far gone he was. He circled around the building and pulled back out onto the road, his taste buds crying out in vain for that draft beer.

When Lily walked into the Crossing House, she looked at it with different eyes, her perception altered by a few simple words from her son. Her dad looked as uncomfortable in his new vest and starched apron as he did in his changed surroundings. What had seemed a great new beginning just a few hours ago now looked like a selfish effort to change her father, to hide her past.

Oh, God, was she that shallow? Had that really been her intention all along?

After his initial hesitation, her dad hadn't given a single hint to her that he didn't like the changes. And he didn't give one now. He smiled broadly and waved her closer. As he folded her in a hug, his starched collar chafed her cheek; even the hug didn't feel right.

"Okay, folks," he said loudly with his arm still around her, "time to launch this ship!"

The serving and kitchen help gathered close. Many of the faces were new, as Henry now had a full staff and more servers had been hired. They'd been able to salvage the old walnut bar. It was the only fixture that had been truly irreplaceable. It now gleamed with new finish and a new brass foot rail.

Her father took a split of champagne and tapped it just hard enough to break it on a marble cutting board on the bar. The glass cracked. The contents of the bottle bubbled and foamed. The crowd cheered.

Faye bustled from the kitchen with a huge round tray of tiny paper cups, each containing a splash of champagne. As she delivered a cup to Riley, Lily stiffened. It was only a sip of an alcoholic beverage, but with Riley's recent behavior, she didn't want to give him a green light on such things.

She was just about to say something when Faye said, "Sparkling grape juice for you, junior."

Then Faye shot Lily a look that said, *I'm not stupid.*

Lily grudgingly nodded her thanks.

Riley looked pleased as could be to be included. Faye looked pretty happy herself—until she looked back at Lily again. Apparently all of her smiles were reserved for Riley.

Benny raised his glass, the tiny paper cup looking like a thimble in his beefy hand. "To years of prosperity and good times at the Crossing House!"

"Here, here!" everyone else rumbled in unison.

As Lily drank her sip of champagne, she watched Faye give her dad a kiss on the cheek.

Then the woman was back to business. "All right.

Everyone to work. I'm gonna open that door and I can see through the stained glass there are people waiting outside." She marched over to the door and put her hand on the deadbolt. "Here we go!"

Lily was astounded by the steady flow of bodies through the door. Her self-doubt about pushing her dad into the wrong decision began to wane a bit.

Someone put money in the jukebox, which now played CDs, and music brought the place to life. Lily saw Brownie from the garage, with his wife—Lily poked around in her memory for her name . . . Marianne, that was it—and his Aunt Rose and Uncle Carson. It had been Carson's quarter that started the music. Gosh, Rose and Carson didn't look a day older than when Lily left Glens Crossing. They all four squeezed into one of the new booths near the back. All of them here at five o'clock meant Brownie had closed early.

Sheriff Clyde commandeered three tables and pushed them together for his huge brood. Lily noticed Riley moved to the far side of the dining room from the Clyde family.

There was Karen Kimball and her daughter, Mickey.

Cassie Edmunds came in with what had to be a date. They claimed a couple of bar stools. At least she had a romantic interest other than Clay. That lifted Lily's spirits a tad.

Mildred must have left the Dew Drop in someone else's hands for the dinner hour in order to be here.

The biggest surprise of all was Bea, the Pink Lady from the hospital, and three of her little gray-haired friends. They actually came in and sat at a table in the bar, because the dining room was filled.

Benny was working as furiously as a one-armed paper hanger within minutes. Faye bustled between the kitchen and the dining room. Lily needed to find some way to help.

She found it when Benny called for more clean glasses. The dishwasher was taking too long. So she filled a sink behind the bar and rolled up her sleeves.

The next thing she knew, Faye had her delivering food to the tables. Lily felt completely out of her depth and kept getting the orders mixed up. Time and again, she cast a grudgingly envious glance at Faye, who seemed to be doing sixteen jobs at once without missing a beat.

Lily stopped by Bea's table to say hello and thank her for coming.

"We wouldn't have missed it." She smiled. "Now, where did I put my glasses? I can't read this dessert menu without my glasses." She patted her pockets, then started to dig in her purse.

Lily waited for a few seconds, giving Bea's friends the opportunity to help her, but they had their noses buried in their own menus. "Um, Bea?"

Bea dropped her wallet and a pack of tissues on the table and kept rummaging. "Yes, dear?"

Lily leaned closer and whispered, "They're on top of your head."

Bea's hand fluttered to the top of her head. "Oh, for heaven's sake!" She laughed. "I do that all the time. Thank you."

"Enjoy your dessert," Lily said, then went back to washing glasses at the bar.

As she plunged her hands in the soapy water, she realized she hadn't seen Riley for some time. Craning her neck, she looked into the dining room. A few of the older kids had gathered around the jukebox in the back. She saw Riley there, near the edge of the group of kids, talking to Mickey Fulton.

She felt good about him making a few friends here. And Mickey seemed like a nice, quiet girl.

Several minutes later she caught up with the washing and stretched her aching back muscles.

A flutter of motion at one of the bar tables drew Lily's attention. Bea and her friends were moving chairs and looking around the table and floor. Lily dried her hands and went to see what the problem was.

"Did you check the outside pocket of your purse?" one of the ladies said, with the slightest edge of annoyance.

"Well, of course I checked," Bea said.

"Can I help you with something?" Lily asked.

"Oh, no, I'm sure we'll find them," Bea said.

Two gray heads disappeared under the table. A thin voice called out. "Not down here."

"What are you looking for?" Lily asked.

"My car keys," Bea said.

Lily helped one of the women up from the floor. "Did you go to the ladies' room, by chance?"

"No, I didn't."

"Why, Bea, you did, too. Twice."

"I did?"

The woman leaned closer and lowered her voice. "Too much iced tea, remember?"

"Oh, yes. I do remember. But I didn't take my keys. Why would I have taken them to the ladies' room?"

"Maybe I should go have a look, just to be certain." As Lily walked toward the rear of the restaurant, she had the uneasy feeling that she was being watched. She glanced back at Bea's table. All four ladies were still focused on finding the lost keys.

Once in the tiny restroom, Lily found a set of keys with

a photo frame holding a soccer photo that said *Gramma's Pride* on the counter by the sink.

As she returned to the bar, Lily saw the reason she'd felt watched. There, at the end of the bar, sat Tad Fulton. Any doubt that he'd recognized her when she'd passed him as she entered the Dew Drop a few weeks ago vanished. He knew who she was, all right. But that wasn't joy she saw on his face. It was something much more calculating.

He held her gaze for a moment, then looked into the bubbles in his beer.

"Are those my keys?" Bea's voice startled Lily. "Where on earth did you find them?"

"On the counter." She forced herself to look back at the table of women as she handed the keys to Bea. "They got pushed behind the flowers."

"Thank you, dear." The ladies gathered up and headed out.

Lily smiled, but her gaze quickly moved back to Tad. He had a frown on his face, but now he wasn't looking at her. She followed his gaze. Her stomach knotted. He was watching his daughter and Riley. She really didn't like the way he was scowling at her son.

She had known Tad as long as she could remember. He'd been in Luke's class. Always the hotshot, always the center of attention. Even in grade school, the whole town had been on his bandwagon. Tad had a gift with the basketball. And in Indiana that was a big deal.

And he'd done exactly as everyone had predicted—Indiana's Mr. Basketball his senior year at Glens Crossing High. He'd gone on to play college ball. Occasionally, Lily had caught a Purdue University basketball game on TV. Tad seemed to be more of a benchwarmer than a hot scorer for the Boilermakers. There had been talk by the sportscasters that Tad's limited playing time had more to do with his attitude than his ability. Lily could believe that.

Since she'd been back in town, she'd had a few of the gaps between then and now filled in. Sometime during his junior year at Purdue, he'd knocked up Karen Kimball. Surprisingly, to Lily anyway, he married her. Apparently he'd made sure everyone knew she was the reason he'd given up the NBA. Lily saw that for the convenient excuse it was. Plenty of NBA players had families. But very few benchwarmers were invited into the NBA.

But it was her personal history with him that made Lily's guts churn. She knew she shouldn't be so bitter. After all, it was a lifetime ago. She was now a grown woman with a life completely independent of this town and Tad Fulton. Still, just the sight of him made the sting of humiliation rise in her cheeks and rage roll like a flaming ball in her chest.

That night when she was fourteen and Clay had stopped her from going with him when they'd played slips had been the beginning of her strange and confusing relationship with Tad. Time and again he'd made overtures toward her, showing up at her house, talking for hours, making her believe he really was a nice guy. He'd even kissed her. But it quickly became clear that his relationship with her was something to be kept in the closet, away from the eyes of the rest of Glens Crossing.

Tad had made her feel she was someone to be ashamed of. That shadow had followed her into her adult life. It was stupid and she knew it. But it was a fact.

He turned and looked at her again. She forced herself to hold his gaze. Finally, he slid off the stool and walked out the front door.

Her dad startled her by speaking in her ear, "Damn shame. That boy had talent. He's gone and wasted it."

Lily just nodded, unable to find her voice. Maybe Tad had snatched it when he looked at her. Wouldn't be the first thing he stole from her.


"Good God, Benny, I don't think we can stand this much success," Henry said when he came out of the kitchen, wiping his hands on a towel.

The last customer had left at one. It was now two-thirty. Most of the other help had gone home. Riley was upstairs in his grandfather's apartment watching TV. Just Faye, Henry and Lily remained with her father.

Faye said, "It's just curiosity. Everybody wanted to see the place. It'll settle down by next weekend." She cast a pointed look at Lily. "Then we'll see."

"We need this kind of business," Benny said. "I, for one, hope it keeps up. Can't have the bank coming in here and hauling away the furniture." He said it as a joke, but for Lily, knowing what she now did, it stung.

Lily looked at Henry. "Had lots of compliments on the food tonight. I think the reputation will keep people coming in."

Henry smiled with pride. "Well, we'll see." He yawned and gave his cheek a scratch. "Think I'll be headin' on home."

"Yell up the back stairs for Riley to come down on your way out, will you?" Lily asked.

"Sure thing." He disappeared through the swinging door.

A short time later, when Lily and Riley got in the car, she said, "I saw you talking to Mickey Fulton."

He looked out the window. "Yeah. So?"

"So, I thought it was nice. She seems nice, a little shy, maybe. I'm glad you've met someone your age."

"She's not shy." His gaze snapped around to her. "She's smart. And she has *opinions* about stuff."

"Oh. Opinions. You must have had quite a conversation tonight." Lily was fishing, but she didn't want to cast her line directly at her target and have him shy away.

He shrugged and looked out the window again.

"Well, in any case, I'm glad you met someone."

He grunted. "You know her mom?"

"We went to school together. We weren't friends or anything."

"So, you didn't like her?" There was something in his tone that made it seem like more than a casual question.

"Well, I wouldn't go that far. We didn't really know one another." She wanted to say, *No, I didn't like her, she was silly, superficial and a snob.* "Why?"

He shrugged and looked back out the window. "No reason."

"Maybe we should have Mickey out to swim sometime soon."

"Geez, Mom, I just *talked* to her." He rotated in his seat, giving her as much of his back as the seat belt would allow. "Don't make a big deal out of it."

"Okay, okay."

He didn't look at her again. When they got home, he jumped out of the car and hurried to the house. His plan to avoid her ran into a brick wall when he couldn't get in the locked door.

He held the screen open for her to use her key, with his gaze fixed on the lake. The second the deadbolt slid free, he was in the house and heading up the stairs.

Lily locked the door behind her, then dumped her purse on the kitchen counter. That's when she noticed the basement door was open. A cold stone dropped in her stomach. That door was never left open.

Slowly, with quiet steps, she moved to the open door. The light was on in the basement. She listened for a long moment, but heard nothing but the steady tick of the water softener.

She looked around the kitchen. The back door was dead-bolted. Everything appeared in order. She checked the living room. The TV and stack of old stereo equipment were still there.

Maybe she was overreacting. Maybe the door hadn't been latched and opened on its own—from a breeze or something. Maybe Riley had been down there earlier. It had been light when they left, she wouldn't have noticed the basement light.

But *what if* someone was in the house? She'd just let Riley go upstairs alone.

She took the steps two at a time, flipping on overhead lights as she went, until she reached her son's closed door.

"Riley!" She knocked and opened his door at the same time. His room was empty.

Her body flashed hot and her heart stopped.

The toilet flushed down the hall. Lily spun around just as the door opened and Riley came out. "What?"

She nearly melted into a puddle on the floor with relief. She swallowed and took in a breath to steady her voice. "Did you go in the basement today?" She went on in his room and looked in the closet.

"Hey! Why are you looking through my stuff?" His bare feet slapped the hardwood hall floor as he trotted toward his room.

"I'm not looking through your stuff." Then she turned

and looked at him. "Worried I'll find something I shouldn't?"

He shifted his weight and rolled his eyes. "Yeah. I've got a huge stash of marijuana in my underwear drawer and some LSD in my shoes. God, Mom, really . . ."

"The basement door was open. I just wanted to make sure no one was in the house."

Riley moved to the bed and flopped down. "Maybe we've got ghosts."

"Very funny. Go to sleep."

Just to settle her own mind, she checked all of the closets. Every door and window was locked and intact. The windows in the basement were very narrow and had been painted shut fifty years ago. No one could have come in through them.

She went to shut off the light and close the basement door, the butterflies in her stomach beginning to settle. She flipped the switch, but the fluorescent light over the washer must have been left on. Turning the main switch back on, she went down to shut it off.

After switching the laundry light off, she turned and those butterflies again shot into flight. There on the rug at the bottom of the basement steps was a dark smudge—a footprint heading toward the stairs. It was too big to be Riley's.

Lily frantically scanned for other prints. There was a faint one about a stride away from the first, back toward the coal room.

With a dry mouth, she grabbed a baseball bat that had been stacked with a pile of old sports equipment. The unfinished basement was one huge room. She followed the footprints with a hammering heart. She told herself it was stupid, illogical, to think she'd find someone; the footprints all pointed in the opposite direction. *Yes, but his feet would have been clean by the time he came back.*

The prints stopped at an old wooden door near the antiquated furnace. The coal room. Lily had forgotten about the old coal chute. Peter had told her he used to sneak in and out late at night through there.

"I've called the sheriff!" she shouted at the door, and waited to hear movement on the other side.

Strain as she might, she couldn't hear the slightest scrape of shoe on concrete or gasp of inhaled breath. The dark silence on the other side of the door didn't ease her fear.

Well, there was no way she was going to sleep tonight unless she opened that door. If someone had come in this way, she assured herself, he'd had plenty of time to get back out since she returned.

She put her hand on the old latch and lifted. The sound echoed like a cannon shot in the basement. Lily swung the door wide and jumped backward at the same time. She held the bat high in the air, ready.

For six long heartbeats—she counted them as they pounded in her ears—she waited.

Then she took a step forward and reached in, turning on the light. A porcelain fixture with a single bulb didn't eliminate the shadows from the corners. But as Lily's eyes adjusted, she could see well enough to confirm she was alone.

She lowered the bat and walked into the tiny concrete room. The old iron door that opened to the outside was closed, but not latched. She reached up and tried to slide the latch home. It was rusted in place. She pounded it with the bat a few times, trying to loosen it, but had no luck.

Dammit. No way could she sleep knowing this was open. She went back out into the main basement and closed the door. There was no more than a crude lever latch, no way to lock it. Well, if she couldn't lock it, she was at least going to make sure she heard if someone tried to open it. She grabbed one of the metal shelving units and dragged it, its metal feet squeaking and squalling as they danced over the concrete floor, until it was directly in front of the door. There was enough junk on it that if it fell, she should be able to hear it clear out on the dock.

As she went back upstairs and closed the basement door, she couldn't shake the creeps. She jammed a kitchen chair under the knob. The creeps remained. Someone had been in her house. The question of *why* kept circling like a vulture in her brain.

Maybe Riley *had* been nosing around down there. She sure couldn't call the sheriff and say she found a footprint in her basement. Nothing was disturbed, nothing vandalized.

But now she knew that coal chute was unsecured. She felt as exposed as if she were going to sleep naked outside on the dock.

Instead of sleeping in her room, Lily laid down on the couch, the bat beside her. If that shelf toppled over, she'd be ready. Tomorrow she'd find a way to secure that iron door.

# Chapter 12

The next morning, as the rising sun was angling through the living room window, Lily gave the house a thorough once-over. Nothing was missing, nothing out of place. She'd simply allowed her imagination to run away with her. She felt silly and childish.

Still, that silly, childish behavior had led her to discover the unlatched coal door, she told herself, so it couldn't be all bad.

When she entered her bedroom, everything appeared as it should be. Then, as she approached the dresser, she noticed one of the drawers wasn't fully closed. As that was one of her pet peeves, she was certain it hadn't been that way when she'd left the room the previous day. And, in her frenzied search last night, she'd been looking for an intruder, not something as subtle as a partially open dresser drawer.

Inching closer, she extended a trembling hand to the drawer handle. Slowly, she opened the drawer, her breath held, her flesh crawling with the thought of some stranger touching her personal things. She fully expected to see the contents in disarray, rumpled by frantic hands searching for jewelry or cash.

Her gaze fell on the interior.

Everything, all of her panties and bras, was still neatly folded—seemingly untouched.

Sliding the drawer closed, she looked around the room. The open basement door. An unidentified footprint. Her dresser drawer ajar. There were just too many things out of the ordinary. She felt an insidious mixture of violation and revulsion that made her skin crawl. Someone uninvited had been inside her house.

Then she saw it and her breath froze halfway to her lungs, her heart jolted into a frantic beat. A slanted ray of sunlight struck her pillow, and on that pillow lay a single yellow rose. Her entire body flashed hot.

It hadn't been her imagination. Not at all.

She approached the bed with muted movements, as if the rose were a bird that might be startled into flight. Her vision telescoped. She watched her hand, feeling like it was completely disconnected from her body, reach for it. Her fingers brushed the slightly wilted petals and a chill swept down the length of her arms. She jerked her hand back and walked out of the room, leaving the rose alone in her bed.

As she paced downstairs, thoughts tumbled wildly in her brain. A yellow rose. A symbol of friendship. Who would have left such a thing? Who, that would also know about the coal chute?

The list of possibilities ran quickly through her mind. The caretaker had a key to the front door. He was also seventy-six years old and round as a dumpling; Lily just couldn't see him skinnying in through that two-foot-square ground-level iron door. Not to mention the rose made absolutely no sense in his case.

Peter was still ensconced at the Sheldon Center; she'd called and checked.

On an inspection of the outside of the house, Lily had discovered that the coal chute door was behind a thick evergreen shrub. A passerby would never have noticed it. Someone familiar with this house had found a way in.

Not a passerby. Not Peter. Who, then?

It came to her in a flash of insight that was quickly followed by a wave of irritation. Clay. He would have known. He also knew she wasn't going to be home last night. And after all of his talk about disliking bottled beer on Friday nights, he hadn't even shown up at the Crossing House. Plus, Clay had plenty of reasons to apologize.

Still, she couldn't see him doing it. He hadn't shown himself to be a man to take such a surreptitious route to an apology—or apologize at all for that matter. It just didn't make sense.

But, she asked herself, what about Clay did make sense? He treated the world as his enemy, yet his compassion lived comfortably under that porcupine's exterior: he'd paid for a disabled boy's summer camp, but had not wanted a soul to know he did it; he made a special trip to her house to make certain Riley had arrived safely the day he walked home from work; he looked at her with cold indifference in his eyes, then loved her tenderly and completely—then resorted once again to frosty rejection.

It was as if he didn't trust anyone near his soul, and any threat to the wall he'd built around it was met with quick opposition. That thought brought everything into clear focus. His distance was his shield. She could see it so clearly now. And she knew, no matter how he'd hurt her, he, too, had somewhere, somehow, suffered a hurt as grievous himself.

Maybe he had regrets.

God, if she didn't watch it, she'd have herself feeling sorry for him.

Riley came downstairs and interrupted her thoughts. She fed him breakfast, thankful for the temporary distraction. Then she drove him to work, organizing her plan of confrontation all the way. Clay's truck sat in its regular spot. She looked around; today she *wanted* to see him. She had to look at his face, to see if there was a trace of guilt there.

She hung around for several minutes after Riley got out of the car and walked into the marina office. Since her early rising, the morning had turned gray, the lake choppy with waves from a strong, cool wind. A couple of die-hard Saturday boaters were backing trailers into the water at the launch ramp, optimistic about a better turn in the weather.

Clay didn't emerge. After dismissing the idea of tracking him down, she backed out of her parking space. Maybe she'd have better luck when she picked Riley up.

She went back home. The first thing she did was pick up the rose and throw it in the trash. Once it was out of sight, she tried to put it out of her mind.

As she took her shower, she took mental notes on her body. Were there any symptoms of pregnancy? Her breasts were tender, but that often happened right before her period. What if she was pregnant? Abortion wasn't an option for her. She firmly believed in a woman's right to choose. But that was a choice she wouldn't—couldn't—make. Not after having one child.

She'd managed to put it out of her mind for a couple of days, but now it was eating her alive. She had to know.

Once she had herself put together, she went to buy a pregnancy test. Chances were no one would notice if she bought it in town—and she was a grown woman, after all. But she decided to drive to Macklin, the nearest neighboring town, to buy the test. She remembered a drugstore on the main drag there.

She could always drive to Bedford, but that was over an hour away. No sense in making more of a trip than necessary. It might be fun to see Macklin, an old high school rival town, again. In fact, this little road trip might be just the break she needed—clear her head.

The road between Glens Crossing and Macklin had enough hills and ninety-degree curves to be qualified as a roller coaster, which kept her progress at a snail's pace. So different from the expressways she'd been driving for most of her adult life—roads whose character had been carved away to make way for speed and volume. There was something liberating about having to *maneuver* a road.

The gray underbellies of the clouds lowered. Before she got halfway to Macklin, rain began to fall, along with the temperature. She turned on the windshield wipers and the defogger. Listening to the steady rhythm of the wipers and the thrum of the rain against the body of the car, she almost forgot the reason for her mission.

The sign that warned to reduce speed ahead almost made her laugh. But when she drove into the tiny town, her humor dried up. She passed the two-story brick high school, home of the Macklin Mavericks. The building had been old when Lily was in school, built sometime in the twenties. Now it was abandoned, chained doors and broken windows. A victim of consolidated school districts.

Macklin's business district had never had much beyond a grocery, drugstore, hardware, gas station, a tavern and feed store. But what met Lily was a ghost town. Weeds sprouted from cracks in the grocery's parking lot—which was beside the building, where a fire had destroyed its neighbor years before Lily was born. The drugstore had been converted into an antique store and then had its windows covered in paper when that, too, apparently had gone out of business. The hardware, tavern and feed store still seemed to have a gasp of life left in them.

Lily pulled into one of the parallel parking spaces in front of the hardware; it didn't require much skill, there weren't any other cars parked in that block. A weight settled in her chest. Little towns like this were dying by inches all around the country and nobody noticed the loss. Cities grew, suburbia sprawled and farms were owned by corporations. If Glens Crossing wasn't the county seat, it might have dried up just like Macklin.

There was a real sadness with that thought. How would Lily feel if she'd returned to find Duckwall's Hardware closed, the Dew Drop's windows painted over, the Crossing House boarded up? It surprised her when she realized how much that would hurt.

After sitting there listening to the rain patter on the roof of the car, she put it in gear and did a U-turn in the middle of the street—which was illegal, but there was nobody around to care.

It would take her another hour to get to the next town— and who knew what she'd find there? She decided to head back to Glens Crossing; she didn't want to be gone much longer, just in case Riley was let off work early because of the rain.

Having seen the dying town somehow made Lily more desperate to know if she was pregnant. She didn't know why there seemed to be a connection, but the sight of that deserted street fired the urgency of her quest. She decided to take a chance on Hayman's Drug in Glens Crossing. Old Man Hayman hadn't recognized her when she lived here, she doubted he would now. If there weren't a bunch of people she knew there, maybe she could just pick up the test and slip out unnoticed.

She drove around the square twice before she found a parking place in front of the drugstore; it was raining hard and she didn't have an umbrella.

When she entered the store, she felt like she'd been transported back to her childhood. The only thing that had changed was the date on the magazines in the magazine rack. The same institutional gray tile covered the floor in the three aisles. The lunch counter still had the same gray Formica with a geometric light gray and pink design. It was fronted by the same chrome and vinyl stools. In fact, this stuff was old enough that it had come around and become in vogue again.

Just looking at that counter made her think of tax day when her dad brought her and Molly here for traditional hot fudge sundaes. She wondered if they still had the best sundaes in the world (hand-dipped, not the squirt stuff she'd served at the Arctic Express).

Was Shirley still tending the counter? Until ten-thirty only coffee was served. After that you could order from a limited menu. Lily looked for Shirley of the perpetual blue-black hair. She was disappointed to see a drip coffeemaker on the counter with a slotted box for coins and a sign telling the customers to help themselves—Hayman's Drug operated on the honor system until lunchtime.

The whole scene was all oddly reassuring after seeing the haunting sight of what was left of Macklin. Lily began to feel better.

There were only a couple of other customers in the store. An elderly gentleman was seated in one of the chairs parked next to the pharmacy counter, apparently waiting for a prescription to be filled. A mother with a toddler was trying to select a card while keeping junior from climbing the shelves. Lily didn't recognize either one.

She walked to the feminine hygiene section—and found it right where it had always been, far left aisle, rear section. Glens Crossing wasn't yet ready to sell tampons, douches and vaginal creams right up front.

Lily's gaze raked the tiny section three times before she gave up on finding a pregnancy test. She walked toward the pharmacy counter, which, of course, was raised so if you were under five feet tall, you didn't have a chance of seeing over the top. She wondered if they designed it that way to keep all of those tempting drugs away from childish eyes.

Well, her eyes weren't childish, and they immediately saw where the pregnancy tests were—right there on the back wall behind the pharmacist, next to the Trojans and the LifeStyles. Crap. She was going to have to ask cranky old Mr. Hayman for a test.

She waited for a moment; the pharmacist was on the far side of a tall shelf. Glancing around to see if anyone she knew had slipped into the store, she was startled when someone said, "May I help you?"

Jerking her head around, she was sickened to see not Old Man Hayman, but his grandson, Mark. She would recognize that shock of red-orange hair anywhere. "Um, yes. . . ."

"Lily? Lily Boudreau? I heard you were in town."

"How are you, Mark?"

"Good, good."

"So, you're the pharmacist now." *Just my luck.*

"Yep. Took the store over from Granddad about six years ago." He shook his head. "To tell you the truth, I never thought I'd land back here. Planned on finding a job near Indy when I graduated from Purdue. But Granddad was showing signs of failing health. You know—one thing leads to another, and—well, here I am."

"Yes, I do know," she said wistfully. Then she remembered her manners. "How is Mr. Hayman?"

"Pretty good. Managing better now that he lives in a retirement community in Florida. The winters were really getting hard on him. So, what made you move back?"

"Oh, I'm not here permanently, just for the summer. Staying at Peter's lake house."

Mark smiled. "Just like the old days, huh? I remember Peter always had that big bonfire at the end of summer . . ."

"Yeah, just like the old days. Except now I'm the *mom*."

"How many kids do you have?"

"One. A son. He's working at the marina."

"Oh, I did hear that, now that I think of it."

*Yeah, if you hadn't, you'd be the only one in this town.* She kept her mouth shut and smiled.

"What can I get for you?"

Uh-oh. No way was she asking him for a pregnancy test. "I, uh, got into some poison ivy. What do you suggest is best? I haven't had it since I moved to Chicago. I'm sure there's something better than calamine lotion nowadays."

"Sure thing. What you want is something with cortisone in it. And it doesn't hurt to take a few doses of Benadryl orally along with it. You'll find both at the other end of aisle one."

"Great, thanks." Did he really number the aisles in this place? She glanced overhead. There, suspended from thin nylon line, were three signs: AISLE 1, AISLE 2, AISLE 3. Just like the big chain stores. Lily stifled a chuckle and went to purchase ointment she didn't really need.

When she left Hayman's she was like a child who'd been told she couldn't have something. With each denial, her determination to get what she wanted grew proportionally.

She drove straight to the only other place in town that might have a pregnancy test, Kingston's Market. She'd passed an aisle with health and beauty aids when she did her shopping. She certainly didn't think she'd be needing anything of this nature, so hadn't looked to see exactly what they carried in the way of contraception and such.

She was studying the limited choices and had just spied an at-home pregnancy test (there was only one on the entire shelf) when a voice startled her.

"Hi, Lily."

She spun around to see Cassie Edmunds looking over her shoulder. "Hello." Could Cassie have followed the line of her gaze and known what she was looking for?

If she did, she didn't give any indication. She said, "Had any more run-ins with our buddy Tad?"

Lily thought that an odd question coming from the blue. She shook her head. "Nothing to speak of. Why?"

Cassie shrugged and eyed something on the shelf over Lily's shoulder. "Just wondered. Saw him looking at you funny last night—like something was on his mind."

"Maybe he was just trying to figure out who I was. It has been a long time."

Cassie pressed her lips together and cocked her head to the side, reminding Lily of a bird. "Maybe." Her voice said she was just being agreeable. "Haven't seen you in for the blueberry pancakes yet."

Lily smiled. "I'm gonna make it one of these mornings. Promise." She paused. "So, what did you think of Dad's new place?"

"Real nice. Skeeter, my date, liked the big new TV hanging on the wall. Said it'll make it a good place to watch the game."

"Skeeter—doesn't he work for Brownie at the garage?"

"Yeah, but just until he opens his own place." She sounded almost defensive. "He's going to get one of those Tire Barn franchises."

"Oh, that'll be great." Lily didn't think Skeeter had enough brains to count his money, let alone negotiate a franchise purchase. "He going to locate it here in Glens Crossing?"

"Yeah. But he's waiting—doesn't want to run Brownie out of business. He feels like he owes him, so he's going to wait 'til Brownie's closer to retirement."

Lily nodded. "That's very loyal."

They stood in awkward silence for a moment. Then Lily said, "I just need to grab something here." She reached in the opposite direction of the pregnancy test and grabbed blindly. When she looked at her hand she was gripping a large tube of hemorrhoid cream. "See you around."

Cassie stood there, smothering a chuckle. "'Kay."

When Lily glanced back over her shoulder, Cassie picked up the lone pregnancy test and shielded it behind her purse as she headed toward the checkout.

*Now, there's something to think about. Wonder who's the prospective daddy?*

A nasty little thought snaked into Lily's mind—Cassie had gone out with Clay shortly before . . .

Lily shook her head to rid herself of even the hint of speculation. That scenario would be just too awful for words.

She stashed the tube she'd picked up on the candy shelf and headed out of the store. She'd already purchased one ointment she didn't need, she'd be damned if she was going to get stuck with a lifetime supply of hemorrhoid cream, too.

Now the only available pregnancy test in Glens Crossing sat safely guarded by a carrot-topped pharmacist.

Before she got to her car she stopped and let the cool drops of rain hit her upturned face. There was something infinitely calming about rain.

She'd just have to drive to Bedford to buy a test. But that would have to wait until tomorrow. She told herself it didn't matter; she wasn't going to be any more or less pregnant tomorrow than she was today.

Clay watched as Riley finished gassing up the only customer they'd had all day. Heavy rain started to fall just after he put the gas nozzle in the tank, but Riley didn't hurry. He didn't cut corners. He took care of business.

When he came in, dripping, Clay handed him a towel.

Riley took it. "Thanks."

The easy way he said it took Clay off guard. Over the last few days, the snide comments and snippy remarks had diminished. What had followed was far from friendship; it was more of an uneasy truce. They had been working inside the garage today, Clay showing Riley how to rebuild an engine. Although they'd worked in silence except for Clay's instructions and Riley's occasional question, Clay sensed a change in the atmosphere.

"I don't think we're going to be bothered by any more boaters for a while," Clay said. "Why don't we go down to the Arctic Express and grab a Coney dog and a shake?" The kid deserved a break. He had actually proven himself useful and made the rebuild job go faster. He had a very good mechanical aptitude and was surprisingly quick on the uptake.

Riley froze, his startled eyes peering over the towel that was pressed against his face. "Now?"

He made it sound like Clay had just sentenced him to a long prison term. "Yeah, now. Unless you aren't hungry."

"Uh, no . . . I mean, yes, I'm hungry."

"All right, then." Clay walked out. "Lock the door behind you."

Riley rode in the pickup alongside Clay with the same air of wary confusion he might have shown had he just been kidnapped. Clay let the atmosphere build. Now that he had made this step, he didn't know exactly how to proceed from here. He'd decided to be a better man, to stop picking on the boy simply because he was Peter's son. At first it took lots of tongue-biting and deep breathing, but as they'd worked together this morning, he started to see Riley as a person unto himself. Clay supposed that was, at least in part, because the kid had shown himself to be the complete opposite of Peter in logical thinking and understanding mechanics. Riley was a natural.

They pulled into the nearly empty parking lot at the Arctic Express, directly under the lighted sign shaped like a giant banana split. There wasn't a dining room, just two walk-up windows for ordering and a few picnic tables out front. Since it was pouring, they'd have to eat in the truck.

"A couple of Conies and a chocolate shake do you okay?" Clay asked as he put his hand on the door to open it.

Riley shifted in his seat and reached for his wallet.

"Don't get your money out. My treat."

Riley looked at the windshield wipers as they slapped back and forth. "If you're buying, I'll go get it—I'm already wet, anyhow."

"Deal." Clay handed him a twenty.

Riley jumped out and ran to the window. There was a slight overhang; he pressed himself up against the serving ledge to keep the rain from running down the back of his neck.

When Riley hurried back with a sack and two large cups

in a cardboard carrier, Clay leaned across the seat and popped open the door for him.

"I didn't know if you wanted onions and relish," Riley said as he climbed in. "So I got two with and two without."

"I'll take mine plain, thanks. At my age, onions tend to disagree."

He was surprised when Riley barked out a laugh. "You make it sound like you're a grandpa or something."

Clay watched the water slide down the passenger window behind the boy. He felt like it had been a hundred years since he had been thirteen. "Some days I feel like one," he said. "A great-grandpa."

Riley put a straw through the top of the cup and handed Clay a shake. "Should I cut up your hot dog, or do you think you can gum it okay?"

Immediately the boy cringed slightly. Clay could see that he wanted to recall the words.

"Nah. I put my Poli-Grip in this morning, so I should be all right."

Riley flashed the first genuine smile Clay had seen from him. Then they both unwrapped the Conies and started eating. With their mouths full, no one expected conversation.

After several minutes with silent chewing and avoiding eye contact, Riley said, "Gramps said you knew my mom when she was a kid."

There was much more buried in that single statement than the words conveyed. There were a hundred unasked questions, a thousand curious musings. Clay wasn't sure he was prepared to deal with them. But the kid was making an effort. The least he could do was try to carry on a civil conversation.

"Yeah. Since she was eleven. Actually, I was more friends with your Uncle Luke. He was closer to my age."

Unfortunately, Riley didn't take the Uncle Luke topic switch.

"I can't imagine my mom being a little girl. She's always so . . . so . . . uptight."

Clay thought of the little girl with the bleeding hole in her leg, the way she refused to cry and scream like most girls her age would. "I guess she was always sort of . . . grown up for her age."

Riley chuckled. "That's a nice way of saying grumpy and boring. Was she one of those dorky girls that never thought about anything but being *good* and sucking up to the teachers?"

Clay sensed that it was much more difficult for Riley to behave than it had been for his mother—or his dad, for that matter. He could relate to that; he'd spent most of his life bristling against constraints.

"Well, your mom had a lot of responsibility when she was a kid. She had to take care of lots of things at home. And she looked after her little sister. She didn't have it easy like you do." Clay couldn't keep the slight edge out of his voice. For some reason, Riley's thinking poorly of Lily bothered him.

Riley nodded, and looked out the windshield. "Because her mom ran off and left them." He seemed deep in his own thoughts.

"Yes. But also because of the kind of person she is. She worries about other people. She wants everything to be good for everybody else." He'd said it to make a point to Riley, but he couldn't deny the truth of that statement. Lily, the child, had always been a giver. It was something he'd denied for years. He had convinced himself she'd changed, become selfish and cruel; that was the only way their past made sense.

"She's a worrier, all right."

Clay looked sharply at the boy. "Well, some people have given her plenty to worry about."

Color crept into Riley's cheeks. He looked down at the Coney in his lap and didn't say anything. Clay was glad for the remorse showing in the boy's features, and the fact that he didn't pipe up with a long list of excuses and justifications.

After putting the last bite of sandwich in his mouth, Clay put the truck in reverse and pulled out of the parking spot.

Riley quietly sipped on his milkshake the whole way back to the marina. When they started working on the engine again, he seemed lost in thought.

Clay had plenty of his own thoughts. Why had he felt compelled to defend Lily?

The answer came quickly. He wasn't defending her. He was simply telling the truth. Lily *had* cared—at least when she was a girl. She hadn't stabbed him in the back until she was a woman.

Still, that thought remained as unsettled as a candy wrapper in a windstorm. It skittered and twirled, refusing to take rational shape. Logic said she'd been a gold-digger from the start of that last summer, looking to hook up with a man with money in order to escape her life here—a life that had been shadowed by a mother's desertion and growing up on the wrong side of the tracks. Why else would she shift her affections to Peter so quickly after Clay had been disinherited? Maybe she'd been playing them both all summer long—maybe that's why she insisted they keep their relationship a secret.

But, as much as he wanted to believe that, wanted to cast her in the role of villain and seductress, it just didn't fit with the person he'd known since she was eleven.

At one point after he'd learned of her marriage, he'd

actually gone after her to demand an explanation. An ache swelled in his chest as he recalled that day.

It had been almost eighteen months since he'd seen her. Eighteen months in which his life had been snatched from his control. That time had been stolen, the harm done never to be reversed. But the day had finally come for a reckoning. Clay stood across the street from the Holt Building, waiting with his shoulders hunched against a cool March wind that had kicked up.

Peter and Lily had been easy enough to find. He hadn't wanted to speak to Peter's mother; that would have been too awkward, required far too many explanations. But a quick trip to the library had given him all he needed—more than he wanted to know. All of Chicago's society pages covered the elopement of Peter Holt and a nobody from a small Indiana town. They'd portrayed it as a Cinderella story. It made Clay's stomach turn sour. Only he knew the bitter truth—both he and Peter had been played and reeled in like prize marlin. A marriage certificate had been the ticket out for Lily Boudreau—now residing in the penthouse of the Holt Building instead of a cramped apartment over the local tavern.

Over the past months, Clay had envisioned a thousand different ways this day could unfold. Even now, he hadn't decided exactly what he would say to her, or how he was going to go about it. He wanted the pain of the moment to be as acute for her as her betrayal had been for him. Was he going to march right in and pound on the door, confront her in front of Peter? God, he wanted to see the startled look on her face when she opened the door and saw him for the first time. Or would he wait until tomorrow and corner her when Peter was at work?

He was still debating when Lily and Peter emerged from the building. Peter had a protective hand on the small of her back and Lily was pushing a stroller. *Christ, they had a baby.* Clay felt like he'd been gut-punched. He sagged back against the granite face of the building behind him. A baby. His hands clenched until his nails bit into his palms.

The front of the stroller was draped with a blanket to block the wind—a blue blanket.

Clay stood there, working to even out his breathing as he watched them walk down the street. Even in his worst nightmares he hadn't felt this raw and angry. That baby brought an image crashing home that he'd tried to block out of his mind since he'd learned of Lily's marriage—Lily naked in Peter's arms, writhing under him, digging her nails into *his* back, *his* name breathless on her lips. . . .

Pressing his palms against his temples to squeeze away the image, Clay fought the sting of tears.

He wanted to ruin her. He wanted to tell Peter the truth, that she'd implemented a calculated plan to marry money, that she had been leading them both. He wanted Lily's life destroyed, as his own had been.

He stood there until they were gone from sight.

Not today, he decided. Not while this new wound was still bleeding. A baby. Jesus Christ.

The next day dawned and he still couldn't bring himself to confront Lily. No matter how he cut it, punishing Lily would mean dealing Peter a boatload of pain, too. Clay supposed he should consider himself lucky. He found out about Lily before it was too late. Peter would have to live with her the rest of his life.

The thought that Peter had been deceived gave Clay a reluctant bit of satisfaction. Clay never quite believed Peter made much of an effort to help when Clay's father had abandoned him. Although his situation certainly hadn't been Peter's responsibility, Clay knew *he* never would have left a friend alone in such a desperate situation.

And now, Clay decided, Peter was on his own. Maybe that Cinderella story would all come crashing down. Then again, maybe Peter would never have to see that the woman he'd married was motivated by self-centered greed. Whatever the outcome, it wasn't going to happen at Clay's hand.

Clay left the city, hating himself for not having the strength to drag the truth out into the light.

From that moment, Clay had locked Lily out of his mind. Until a few weeks ago, he'd refused even to think of her— at least when he was awake and in control. His subconscious had had a different attitude altogether.

The very next day, he'd joined the army and his life had taken a turn that led him away from the familiar. He'd lived the past years mostly on foreign soil, far from the memories that haunted his dreams.

Riley said his name. Clay looked up and realized he had slipped completely away from what he was supposed to be doing. He gripped a wrench in his hand so tightly his entire arm was trembling.

The kid looked worried.

"You okay?" Riley asked. "You look like you had a stroke or something."

"Fine. You get that carburetor clean?" Clay seeped slowly back into this world, this time, and noticed the steady drum of rain on the metal roof.

"Yeah, about ten minutes ago. We already put it on. Don't you remember?" Now he looked *really* worried.

Clay forced a laugh. "I guess when you've done this as many times as I have you click over to autopilot."

Riley stood and looked at him for a moment. Then he said, "Can I wash up now? My mom'll be here to get me in a minute."

"Go on. I think I've had it for today, too." He wiped the wrench on a red shop rag.

Riley disappeared into the bathroom.

When Clay turned around, Lily was standing just inside the door. He fumbled the wrench and it clattered onto the concrete floor.

"I didn't mean to startle you," Lily said.

"Damn thing is slick with grease." Clay picked up the wrench and finished wiping it off. "Riley's almost ready to go."

"I came in to talk to you."

"Really?" He raised a brow.

"Don't pull that crap on me. We need to talk. I think we're both far too old for this type of game."

"What the hell are you talking about?"

She crossed her arms over her chest and walked closer to him. Close enough that he could smell her perfume. But it didn't appear that she was wearing it for his benefit. She looked peeved.

"If you wanted to apologize, you should have just called."

"I don't have a clue what you're getting at."

"I'm *getting at* you sneaking into my house last night. Really, Clay, I thought you were more mature than that."

"I haven't been inside that house in yea—"

"Well, someone was. And you and the caretaker are the only two people I can think of familiar enough with that house to sneak in the way you did."

"I didn't do any *sneaking*. If someone broke into your house, you'd better report it to the sheriff." His blood rushed hot. Someone inside Lily's house? The dangerous possibilities set off a cascade of worry.

"I think you know there was no 'break-in.'"

"Now you're talking in circles. Tell me what happened."

The door to the bathroom opened. "Mom? What are you doing in here?"

"I just had a couple of things to discuss with *Bud*. You go on out to the car. I'll be right there."

"I'm supposed to meet some kids at the arcade at six."

Lily's sharp gaze shifted from Clay to Riley. "And when did you ask permission to do that?"

"Sorry. I forgot. They just invited me last night at Gramps's place. Can I go? Please."

Clay said, "The kid did put in a good day's work."

Lily's intense scrutiny swung back to Clay. She made him feel like he was thirteen, too.

"I just thought it might help you decide," he said quietly.

"Come on, Mom. I don't have to work tomorrow."

"Let's talk about it in the car," she said as she put a hand on Riley's shoulder and moved him toward the door. "And you . . ." She turned to Clay once Riley was out the door. "I've got more to say to you. Can you come by my house at seven?"

Clay nodded. She damn well better have more to say to him. He needed to know what happened last night. And he wanted to check out the security of that house himself.

"Just use the front door this time," Lily said, then she disappeared into the gray rainy afternoon.

# Chapter 13

Lily stopped by the Crossing House on her way home. Riley groaned quietly but knew better than to make too much noise. Lily had agreed to let him meet his friends tonight for pizza and to play in the arcade. He wasn't to go anyplace else. When she'd told him she was going to pick him up at nine-thirty, he'd rolled his eyes and huffed an exaggerated sigh, but didn't argue.

"I just want to make sure Gramps doesn't need any extra help tonight," she said as she opened the car door. "The parking lot is already pretty full."

"Please hurry, Mom."

She pulled her jacket hood over her head and got out. The rain had fallen steadily all day and the lot was filled with puddles. She splashed her way to the door.

Once inside, she smiled with satisfaction. The place was nearly as busy as it had been the previous night. Some of the jitters seemed to have settled out of the serving staff. Faye had a smile on her face; that was a good sign. Lily went into the bar to see her dad.

"There's my girl!" he called over the heads of the young men perched on bar stools.

"Hi, Dad. Looks like things are going well."

He smiled broadly. "Couldn't be better." He stepped closer when Lily slipped onto an empty stool. "Faye still isn't convinced, but she'll see. Can I get you anything?"

"Actually, I stopped to see if you needed any more hands tonight."

Faye's voice came from behind Lily. "That's real sweet of you, but I think we've got things under control just fine. Don't we, Benny?"

"That we do." He smiled. "We've gotta learn to do this for ourselves."

Faye walked away, muttering under her breath that some help was more trouble than it was worth. But Lily pretended not to hear.

Cassie Edmunds came in and sat three stools away from Lily. When Benny asked her what he could get for her, she told him she was waiting for someone. Then she added, "A Coke would be nice."

*No beer? Maybe the results of that pregnancy test were positive.*

Lily told her dad goodbye and headed back out into the rain. As she was turning out of the parking lot, Clay's truck turned in. Through the rain-streaked windshield, she thought he looked a little guilty as he waved.

Once they got home and Riley headed up to take a shower, Lily called the bar.

"Dad! Sounds even busier. . . . I just wanted to offer my help again." She hoped she didn't sound as transparent as she felt.

"It's not fair to have you waste a Saturday night here. We'll be fine."

"You're sure?"

"I'll call you if we get into trouble, how's that?"

"Okay. Good luck."

"Thanks, honey."

"Wait, Dad!"

"Still here."

"Um, is Bud there, by any chance?"

She heard glasses clink and longnecks spritz open. "Yeah, sittin' right here next to Cassie. Want to talk to him?"

"No!" She calmed her voice. "No. I just thought I saw him as I was leaving. I'll let you go." Lily hung up before her dad could ask any more questions.

Cassie and a pregnancy test. Cassie and a Coke. Cassie and Clay. It didn't take a nuclear physicist to solve that equation.

Oh, boy.

Lily dropped Riley off at the arcade. He hunched against the rain and ran to the door, then disappeared inside. Lily was a little disappointed; she'd hoped to get a look at these new friends of his. Maybe she'd have more luck when she picked him up.

As she headed home, she drove past the Crossing House, even though it wasn't actually on her way. Clay's truck was still in the parking lot. She glanced at the digital clock on the dashboard: six twenty-five. She hoped he had things all set- tled with *Cassie* (in her mind the name rang out in a jealous and juvenile singsong tone) by seven. She mentally admon- ished herself for such a catty thought. This situation was beyond belief. How could she have allowed herself to be so foolish?

Once back home, she resisted the urge to freshen her makeup and brush her hair. She left her wet tennis shoes on the rug beside the door and didn't bother to go find another pair. She didn't want it to look like she'd given a single thought to her appearance when Clay arrived.

It was dark in the house, but she didn't turn on any lights, not yet. There was something soothing about the gray gloom that surrounded her. She sat on the leather sofa for ten minutes, her bare feet curled underneath her, rehearsing in her mind what she was going to say to Clay.

At six fifty-five, she got up and switched on the lamps and the front porch light.

At seven-ten, she was still sitting by herself.

At seven-twenty, she switched off the porch light. It just seemed too needy, shining all alone out there for somebody who didn't even have the decency to call and say he wasn't coming.

At seven-thirty there was a knock at the door.

Lily considered ignoring it.

Then she decided that was just too petty and got up and opened the door.

Clay stood there, wet hair plastered to his head, jacket and jeans soaked through. "Sorry I'm late. Cassie had trouble with her car and I had to give her a jump."

Lily bit back the nasty comment that threatened to pop out about his already having jumped Cassie, and opened the door wide enough for him to come inside.

"So how is Cassie?" Her tone sounded petulant even to her own ears.

He looked at her with wary confusion on his face. "Fine—I guess."

"She have any *news*?" She drew the last word out.

Clay's brow furrowed. "Not really. I didn't talk to her much."

"Hmmm." Lily couldn't help but pinch her mouth tightly when she made the noise.

"What's going on with you?" Clay asked in a way that almost made Lily believe he didn't have a clue.

"Nothing. I'll just get right to the point, so you can get back to Cassie."

"I don't know where you're getting all of this me and Cassie idea, but you're way off the mark."

She lifted a brow. "Really?" Then she waved a hand in the air before he could reply. "It's none of my business."

Crossing his arms over his chest, he said, "You're right. But just to settle that question in your mind, I don't have anything to do with Cassie. I stopped for a beer. When I was leaving the Crossing House, she was in the lot with the hood up on her car."

Lily put both palms up and shook her head. "You don't owe me any explanation." Inside, her thoughts tumbled. Could she be that far off the mark about his relationship with Cassie? She finally said, "Come on in."

They were still standing on the big rug in front of the door. "Maybe we should talk here. I'll ruin your floor."

"That's fine. I don't think you're going to be too comfortable with what I have to say anyway. No need to get cozy."

He shifted his weight and swiped the wet hair away from his face. "I'm all ears."

His casual tone set her teeth on edge. "After all of that talk about Friday nights and draft beer, you didn't show up at the Crossing House last night. Apparently you found a better way to pass your time."

"And that would have been?"

"Come on, Clay. I know you were here. What I want to know is, why?"

"I thought we'd already covered that subject."

"Not to my satisfaction."

He turned slightly and examined the latch on the door. "It doesn't look to me like this door's been tampered with. Someone come in through the back?"

She crossed her arms over her chest. "You know you didn't."

"Maybe you should just tell me what happened. No one broke in the front door. No one broke in the back door. What makes you think someone was in here at all?"

"Footprints. You weren't careful enough about that coal room."

His gaze sharpened. He stopped looking vaguely amused—an expression Lily had been keeping her hands tucked under her arms to keep herself from smacking off his face—and started looking genuinely concerned. "You *did* call the sheriff?"

"Not necessary. I can think of only three people who know about that coal chute: the caretaker, Peter and you."

"I imagine Peter's parents know it's there."

She flipped her hand in the air. "They also have a key to the front door. Can you see Samantha Holt crawling in through a dirty coal chute if her life depended on it?"

Clay loved Samantha Holt, a woman who'd mothered him after his own mother was gone. The only warm family memories Clay had after his mother died were centered around Peter's mother. But there was no way he could see her in anything but designer sportswear and spotless shoes. "No. No, I can't." He couldn't help but smile.

"So? You still want me to call the sheriff and sic him on you?"

"Lily, believe me, if I had been in your house, you'd never have a clue." He leveled a look at her that made the hair prickle on her neck. "There wouldn't be a trace that a forensics team could find."

Lily fought to conceal the chill that swept over her. She knew there was something cunning and sharp lingering just behind Clay's eyes. But she had no better idea what put it there than she had weeks ago. She shook her head to rid herself of thoughts that were outside her current problem. "Why are you playing this game with me?"

A flinty look hardened his gaze. "I don't play games. That seems to be your forte."

She threw up her hands. "All right, goddammit, that's enough! I'm sick to death of your snide little comments. *You* were the one who deserted *me*."

He took a step closer to her. "Christ! That's a good one. That's not at all how I remember it."

She leaned in, not wanting him to think he was intimidating her. "Just how do you remember it? All of that talk about loving me, wanting it to be forever. It was a load of bullshit. And I was so blind with love, I bought it."

"Blind with love? Or with the desire to put this town behind you? That love transferred pretty quickly to the next available candidate."

"You left. Why should you care who I loved or when I moved on?"

"You knew I was coming back."

A bark of bitter laughter escaped Lily's throat. "It only took you fourteen years—I guess I should have waited."

He grabbed her arm and pulled her so close they were nearly nose to nose. "Things happened. It just took longer than I'd planned to get back. When I did, you were in Chicago, married to Peter." The gold in his eyes sparked with his anger.

Lily jerked her arm free; it was painful enough that she

knew he'd left a bruise. "You disappear without a word—
and blame *me* for not sitting around and waiting—"

"I sent Peter with the message—one you couldn't possibly have misinterpreted."

"Come on! Peter? Peter, who didn't know where you'd
gone?" Lily couldn't keep herself from yelling. She pretended not to see the shocking change that came over Clay's
face. His color faded; the tense way he held his mouth slackened. "Really, Clay, you can come up with something better
than that. At least a letter lost in the mail has the *ring* of
plausibility to it. And besides, if you had a message for me,
why didn't you just pick up the goddamn phone?"

He backed up and slumped against the doorframe. His
eyes lost the sharp focus of anger and fogged with pain and
memory. His hand shook as he rubbed his face. "Oh, God."
He swallowed. "He didn't tell you."

The room suddenly took a spin. Darkness edged her
vision; all she could see was the bleak truth in Clay's face.
There *had* been a message.

Once Lily found the strength to move again, she went to
get Clay a towel, then started a pot of coffee while he dried
off. As the coffee finished dripping, they sat on opposite
ends of the big couch, like strangers in an oncologist's
waiting room; the obvious subject too weighty to undertake,
yet too large to dance around with small talk. By unspoken
agreement, they remained silent until the coffee was in hand.

Lily returned to the kitchen and brought back steaming
mugs.

The rain beat against the roof, the darkness pressed
against the windowpanes and a black ache strained the con-
fines of Lily's heart. She handed Clay his coffee, but

avoided looking him in the eye. When she sat down, she wrapped her cold hands around the mug for warmth.

After a few minutes with nothing but the rhythmic drip of the rain in the downspouts, Clay set down his mug and spoke. He kept his gaze fixed somewhere beyond the rain-streaked window.

"When I went back to Chicago, I did what I'd intended. I told my dad. I'd known it was going to be bad, but, Jesus, Lily, I didn't know a person could be so vile to his own flesh and blood."

Lily closed her eyes so she didn't have to see the pain on Clay's face.

He went on, "I knew he would cut me off. I was prepared to leave school—get a job. But he *exploded*." He hit his fist against his palm to emphasize the word.

Lily opened her eyes and saw Clay was now looking at her.

"I mean, he really lost it. He even took a swing at me with a fireplace poker."

"Oh, my God," Lily whispered. "Did he hurt you?" Douglas Winters was a big man with a bad temper. Lily couldn't imagine what it would have been like to stand before him alone and face his wrath. She also knew, no matter what the man did, the Clay of fourteen years ago wouldn't have raised a hand against him, even in self-defense.

Clay shook his head; his eyes remained glazed with memory. "Once the initial violence passed, he started with the threats and manipulation that I had expected. It went on and on, threats against me, you, your family. And I had no doubt he could carry out each and every one.

"In the end, I threw my car keys at his feet and told him he could take the car, take the money, take his powerful name. I didn't need any of it. I wasn't leaving for you, I was leaving for me.

"As I left I heard him yelling, 'Don't come back. You're as dead to me as your mother.'" Clay gulped in a drink of air. As if the words had starved his body of oxygen. "It didn't take long for me to find out he meant it."

Lily's own breath came in shallow puffs. "What happened?"

"I left Dad's on foot. It was late and I planned to call Peter to come and pick me up sooner or later, but I needed to walk—I needed to run, I needed to fight the wind." His hands clenched into fists. "My God, Lily, I'd never been so angry and so exhilarated at the same time."

The emotion of fourteen years ago was etched so clearly on Clay's face that Lily ached. She hadn't been there for him. He'd taken the biggest and most painful step of his life alone. From the perspective of adulthood, it was so easy to see and understand each of their mistakes. What they say about hindsight was absolutely true. Lily had had no idea of the true depth of his conviction, or his misery under the yoke of his father.

"I was pissed as hell with him," he said. "But I'd finally done it. I was finally free." He rubbed his face with both hands and he paused.

"That freedom lasted all of two hours."

# Chapter 14

As Clay explained the events of that night to Lily, he was quickly transported back in time. He experienced the buzz of emotion in his nerves, could feel the damp night air on his skin, smell the smoky barroom, hear the quick sharp scream that had drawn him into something he wished with all of his being that he'd never begun.

Clay's jacket was wet from the mist. Walking down Rush Street, he passed bar after bar. Finally the moment came when he stopped and walked in one. He only wanted a single scotch. One. No more. But as he finished the first one, the edge began to fade from his agitated rage. He figured a second would even him out enough that he could get to sleep.

He held up his glass and nodded to the bartender.

After he finished the second, he would call Peter.

He sat at the bar in hunched solitude. The trendy nightspot was crowded even on a weeknight. Too crowded for Clay's mood, but he was tired of walking. He was tired of everything. Tomorrow he would call Lily and they could get things straightened out.

He'd have to stay away from her for a while, just to make sure his dad didn't have an excuse to make trouble for her family. But after that . . . they'd be free to start a life together.

His unsettled mood set his body at odds with the scotch he'd consumed. He felt like he had live wires buzzing just under the surface of his skin. Instead of that second scotch further blunting the anger, it seemed to have pumped fresh agitation into his veins.

Better head home before he got any worse.

The pay phone was off to the side of the front door, in a narrow hallway that led to the restrooms. When he started down the hall, he saw a strung-out-looking middle-aged woman leaning against the wall, shouting at someone through the telephone. She didn't miss a beat in her tirade when she shot him a look that would have stopped a linebacker.

He waved an apology and stepped back to the doorway that opened onto the sidewalk. As he dug around in his pocket for change, a sound between a yip and a scream jerked his attention to the street. He stepped out just in time to see a huge hulk of a guy backhand a woman half his size. She slammed against the brick front of the bar, staggering, twisting an ankle and breaking the high heel off her shoe.

Clay shouted, "Hey! Stop!" He walked closer.

The man took a step toward the woman, who covered her head with her arms in anticipation of the next blow.

"Hey!" Clay grabbed the man's shoulder and felt rock-hard muscle under the silk shirt. He ignored the good sense that said he was biting off more than he could chew.

"Get lost, asshole," the man said, but kept his back to Clay.

Clay jerked on the shoulder.

The man spun around with an animallike growl. Clay

saw the flash of a knife blade reflect the blue neon glow of the bar's sign.

"Just leave the lady alone," Clay said, with his palms raised to indicate he didn't want a fight.

"Lady?" The man laughed as he took another step toward Clay. "You better get your eyes checked, sonny. This bitch ain't no lady. You wanna know what else she ain't?"

Clay stood his ground, but didn't answer. He wondered briefly why the woman wasn't taking the opportunity to run for real help.

"This bitch ain't no concern of yours." The knife slashed through the air, close enough that Clay felt the rush of air on his face. "Now you run along and let me take care of my business."

"Can't do it, man." Clay didn't know what made him say it, but it came out. "Just let her go and you and I can go have a drink."

The man's face twisted into a wicked smile. "Why, you're just about the funniest white boy I ever laid eyes on."

The bastard's cocky arrogance, coupled with the whimpers from the woman, pushed Clay's hot button. "And you're just about the *stupidest* I've ever laid eyes on."

The man lunged so quickly, Clay had no chance to dodge. In the blink of an eye, he was locked in a struggle to keep the knife from making deadly contact. Somewhere on the fringes of his awareness he heard the woman screaming again. With that, he simply tried to stay alive until help arrived.

Seconds passed and no one rushed in to help. Clay's desperation grew. His muscles burned. The guy was strong.

Off balance, they fell to the concrete walk. The jarring impact loosened the man's hold on the knife. Clay managed to wrench it from his grasp, but the man kept fighting, trying to turn Clay's hand on himself.

When the siren came to an abrupt halt, Clay barely registered it.

When the officer pulled him away from the man, he was so focused on the struggle that he actually tried to break free, to go after the guy again.

A nightstick to his forearm sent the knife clattering to the sidewalk. Until he heard it hit, he'd forgotten it was still clenched in his hand. The pain from the blow radiated up into his shoulder and into his neck.

He grabbed his bruised arm and yelled through gritted teeth, "Okay! Okay!"

"You have the right to remain silent . . ." The officer's voice sounded gravelly in his ear as he clamped on the hand-cuffs behind his back.

"Wait! It was his knife—he was beating up on that woman!"

"You mean that woman right there?" The officer spun him around to see the woman kneeling next to the man, who didn't look like the scratch on his forearm was going to be anywhere near fatal. She cried and ran her hands over his body, checking for more injuries. Another police officer stood next to them.

She turned to Clay and yelled, "He tried to kill Bubby!"

Clay shouted, "Hey, I tried to help you!"

"You cut Bubby!" She collapsed on the broad shoulder and cried like the guy was drawing his last breath. "Oh, I'm so sorry, baby. It's gonna be all right."

Clay turned to the cop. "It wasn't my knife. He attacked *me*."

The officer pulled him toward the cruiser. "Tell it to the judge."

Clay was shoved in the back of the police car. The door slammed closed. He noticed there were no handles on the inside. When the cop climbed in the front, on the other side of a thick wire mesh, Clay said, "What about the other guy?"

"Robinson'll take care of him."

"Take care of him, as in tend his wound, or arrest the bastard?"

The policeman ignored him. He called a code on his radio, then put the car in gear.

Once through booking at the police station, Clay was put in a holding cell with about twenty other guys from various levels of the lower social strata. He felt totally out of place, and hoped to God it wasn't written all over his face.

Within minutes he drew interest. One guy approached him, trying to push a little relief from his "situation" in the form of pills. Clay didn't want to think how the guy must have smuggled them into the cell. Another, dressed in a cocktail dress and spike heels, asked him for a date. He ignored them both.

He spent a sleepless night, guarding himself from various forms of violation.

At one point, he saw "Bubby" escorted in and, fortunately, locked in a different cell.

In the morning, he called his dad and explained what had happened and asked for him to arrange a lawyer.

There was a long pause on the other end of the line. Clay had begun to wonder if his dad was still there when he said, "That's most unfortunate."

Then the line went dead.

Clay hadn't expected much more. But he had thought that by the time his bail hearing rolled around, his dad would have softened enough to at least send one of his underlings to bail him out.

Standing alone before the bail magistrate, Clay listened to the charges against him. Jesus, they made it sound like he was a real criminal. Since there was a knife involved, they were going to charge him with a felony. Bail was set. When Clay called the bank to get the funds—he'd worked all summer and had just enough to get himself out—he discovered the account, which had been in joint names with his father since Clay was a child, had been closed.

Well, he'd thrown his family's name and power away. Now it was time to pay the price. He decided, no matter what, he'd face it. There was no way he would call his father again.

Lily interrupted his tale. "Why didn't you call me? I would have gotten the money together somehow."

Clay's chuckle held no humor. "Because I knew that's what you'd do. There was no reason to drag you into it. Besides, bail was high—really high. At the time I wondered if my dad had put a bug in the bail magistrate's ear." He waved the thought away and sighed. "I really did think I was going to get out. At first I couldn't even believe they were buying the other guy's story. But the initial hearing took care of that delusion. Then I thought my dad would come around—"

"What about Peter?" Lily asked.

"No money—at least not that kind. I wouldn't let him ask his parents."

"But once you'd figured out you weren't getting bail, you should have called me."

"Lily, I wasn't staying at the Holiday Inn. Telephone calls were difficult to come by. Besides, I didn't want you to know I was in jail. It was all just a stupid mistake."

"Damn right!" She got to her feet. "Not calling was a stupid mistake. A stupid, male-pride-fueled mistake."

He looked up at her. "That's not the part that was the stupid mistake. I'd do that part exactly the same again. It's the arrest that was a mistake."

Lily spun in a frustrated circle. "Jesus, Clay, you'd do it again, knowing that it would be the end of us?"

He grabbed her hand. "Sit back down." When she didn't move he added, "Please."

She stood rigid for a moment, she'd waited fourteen years to hear this; now she wasn't sure she wanted more. The sheer absurdity of the entire fall of events was impossible to believe. But she sat down.

He said, "I told Peter to tell you that I had a fight with my dad and it was going to take a few weeks to get things ironed out."

"That's it? *That's* what you told Peter to tell me?"

"Yeah." He looked at her, apparently surprised by her reaction. "In light of our last conversation, that should have told you to wait. I didn't want to tell Peter more about us, not yet." He paused and laced his hands together between his knees. "So did he?"

Lily blinked, her mind whirling with the reality of what had happened. "Did he what?"

"Tell you."

She closed her eyes and drew in a deep breath. "He told me you'd had a fight with your dad—" she heard Clay's sigh of frustration and finished, "and that you were gone. He didn't know where, but he didn't think you were coming back."

This time Clay was the one on his feet. "Lily, if you're lying to me—"

She looked at him from where she sat on the couch, his

form blurring with the tears that she tried to keep from falling. His accusation should make her fighting mad, but all she felt was tired. Tired and disconnected from her life. "That's what he said. When I called your dad, he said the same. You'd left. No one knew where you were." A little hiccup caught in her throat. She could muster no more than a whisper. "And you didn't come back."

The whispered words hung in the air between them. Her accusation of desertion stabbed like a knife in his heart. He *had* come back. But Lily hadn't waited months, or the years she'd sworn herself to. He came back—and found her married to his best friend.

Lily sat stock-still on the couch as Clay paced around the room. The coffee was cold, but Lily clung to the cup as if it were a lifeline. Clay felt he could use a lifeline, too, but had no idea where to grab. He needed to attack something, but didn't know which way to aim his anger. Peter had let him down. Had it been intentional? Peter hadn't known about Clay's relationship with Lily. But why would he tell her Clay wasn't coming back?

When Clay made his next revolution around the room, his gaze fell once more on Lily. His anger found its target. He moved directly in front of her. She didn't look up at him. She just stared at that damn cold coffee.

"Tell me, were you working us both from the start?" he said with a bitter edge. "Or did you turn to Peter because I was out of money?"

The lethargy that had seemed to have a hold of Lily evaporated. She shot to her feet and slapped him across the face.

It stung, but he welcomed the pain. Physical pain was now. Physical pain was real and easy to understand.

She stood there in front of him, her anger like an electrical charge in the air. He felt it lifting the hair on his arms.

"You don't know anything about how things were for me." She took two deep breaths. "And you don't care."

She started to step around him, but he grabbed her arm. "Then tell me! Tell me why you married Peter. Tell me why you didn't wait."

The look in Clay's eyes stopped Lily cold. She wanted to justify her actions. She wanted him to know she'd done the most logical thing at the time. He'd left her without a word, for God's sake.

But if she bared her soul, it would be her undoing. It would destroy her.

She looked him in the eye and said, "Because you left me. You could have called. You could have written. You didn't care enough to keep what we had. You threw it away."

"Dammit, Lily, I just explained—"

She steeled her heart against the pity she had for both of their situations. "I know now. If I had known then . . ." She raised a shoulder. "But I didn't. All I knew was that you left me. I was hurt. Peter was there to pick up the pieces. Peter gave me the strength to go on."

He let go of her arm and looked to the ceiling. "God, Lily." It was a strangled sound that broke Lily's heart.

"Peter loved me. And I loved him—just not the way I love you." It was as much of herself as she could share, here, now. She waited, waited for him to make a sound, make a move.

Finally, he leaned his forehead against hers. They stood in silence for a few minutes, listening to the rain and the beating of their own hearts. Then his arms slipped around her and he pulled her close.

His shirt was still damp and sent a chill through her as

she pressed against his chest and put her arms around his waist.

Clay said, "You said, you love me—not *loved*."

She nodded, but couldn't say more.

After taking a deep breath, he said, "A wise man once said, 'Youth is wasted on the young.'" He sighed; Lily felt the heat of his exhaled breath in her hair. "I don't know if ours was wasted, but we certainly made a mess of it, didn't we?"

She leaned back and looked into his face. "I don't know about you, but I'm not over the hill just yet."

He smiled, then he kissed her. It was a kiss that spoke of bittersweet memories, of things lost, and maybe, she thought, just a hint of possibility.

When he lifted his face from hers, she said, "You've got to be freezing in those clothes. Maybe you should take them off and I'll put them in the dryer."

"Why, are you trying to get me naked?" He smiled that boyish smile that flipped her heart in her chest.

"I'm just thinking of your health."

He kissed her forehead. Then he said, "Lily, it's taken fourteen years to get to the top of this mountain." He paused. "I don't want to screw it up again."

Against her will, her heart sped up. He spoke of the future, of them being together. After all of these years, the thought scared her to death. What if they did screw it up? What if, once they spent more time together, they discovered the only thing they had in common was mutual lust?

And getting involved with Clay would affect other people. Riley's life was already tumultuous enough. Did she want to force two people who so obviously disliked each other to spend more time together?

She sighed. "I'm not sure what I want. Everything is so complicated."

He cupped her face and smiled down at her. "It always has been, Lily. For you and me, nothing is simple."

Stepping back, he let her go. Then he turned around and walked out into the rainy night.

Lily watched with a lump in her throat as the door closed behind him. She put a hand over her abdomen. Complicated. Maybe more complicated than he knew.

Lily turned out the lights and sat back down on the couch. She wanted to wrap herself in the darkness, have nothing to distract her from her thoughts. She was sure she'd done the right thing guarding herself against Clay. She couldn't tell him everything. But with tonight's revelations, they were discovering new footing with each other. What she had spent years viewing as betrayal turned out to be no more than cruel fate and mischance. It was going to take a while to wrap her mind around that.

She didn't see how they could realistically find their way back to each other. She was a mother first—and Clay didn't want children—especially Riley. The two of them were like male lions fighting for territory.

And if she was pregnant . . .

Then there was Peter. Emotionally fragile Peter, who was waging a battle with himself—alone. A relationship with Clay for her would mean devastation for him.

She tried to keep in mind that what was done was done and nothing would change it. Still, the question nagged: Had Peter deliberately deceived her? If he didn't know she and Clay were involved, he might not have seen the importance of Clay's message. Or perhaps he was protecting her from the pain of knowing their dear friend was in jail.

In this quiet moment, sitting with tears on her cheeks in the dark living room of the lake cottage, Lily resolved that no matter what Peter's motivation, she wasn't going to delve more deeply into his reasons—at least not right now, with both Riley and Peter in such rocky emotional circumstances. The facts were what they were. Nothing would change the past.

Having decided that, she worked to let go of the anger simmering against Peter. She listened to the sounds of the rain, the branches scraping against the house, and the ticking of the clock. By a sheer force of will, she released her resentment, one resistant fiber at a time.

A sad calm settled over her. The past was done. And her future was hers to do with as she would. She just had to make sure the choices she made didn't sacrifice other people's happiness for her own.

The clock struck the hour. Nine. She needed to get herself together and go pick up Riley.

Just as she was about to switch on the lamp, there was a loud thump on the side of the house. The side with the coal chute. She froze and listened for a few seconds. There wasn't anything more.

"A raccoon," she said. It didn't make sense, but it made her feel better. She was glad she'd had Mr. Duncan, the caretaker, secure that door. He'd been there sometime while she was out this morning and left a note on the kitchen table. Then she herself had checked to be sure it couldn't be opened from the outside. So, raccoon or not, nothing was coming in that way.

Turning on the light, she felt better. She put on her shoes, grabbed her purse and keys. Then she opened the front door—and screamed.

Her body shot through with white-hot panic. Before she

could get her breath, the figure outside the screen door called her name.

"Lily! It's all right. It's me."

All of her muscles gave way at the same time. She grabbed the edge of the door to keep from collapsing into a puddle on the floor. "Clay! What are you doing?"

"I came back because I wanted to see if that coal chute was secure."

She finally remembered to breathe. "You could have just called." Pushing open the screen, she stepped out on the porch with him.

"I wanted to make sure myself. I don't like the fact that someone got in here in the first place. Now that you know it wasn't me, I want you to call and file a report with the sheriff."

"It's fine now. The coal chute door is latched. No one can get in."

"But *why* did someone come in in the first place? Nothing was stolen?"

She shook her head. "Maybe I overreacted. Maybe that footprint had been there all along." She wasn't going to tell Clay about the rose. Maybe she would make a report to the sheriff tomorrow, but Clay didn't need to know. She wasn't sure how Riley would react if he got wind of all of Clay's sudden concern.

"I don't like it." He touched her face. "Keep your doors locked. Be aware when you come and go. No one can see this place from the road. You're pretty isolated."

Lily tried to ignore the feelings his caring touch set off and stayed with the safe and the mundane. "I survived the streets of Chicago. I think I can manage Glens Crossing."

"Don't let the quiet atmosphere fool you. Crazies can pop up anywhere."

She pulled the door closed and locked the deadbolt. "See, I have good safety habits, Officer Winters."

"Maybe I should wait here while you pick up Riley."

Lily couldn't imagine how she'd explain Clay sitting in their living room when they got back.

"I mean in the truck, not inside." It was as if he could read her mind, a talent that didn't seem to be dulled by the passage of time.

"I'll be fine. I've been coming and going out here for weeks."

"Yeah, well, last night was the first time someone slipped into your house. Something's changed."

"What do you mean?" She stopped halfway across the porch.

"I don't imagine it's someone who had theft in mind— they didn't take anything. And this house has been sitting empty for a good long time. Why wait until it's occupied to sneak in?"

"Well, maybe that's it. Maybe it's kids that were sneaking in and using this place while it was empty. Maybe they just discovered it's not anymore."

"Maybe." He didn't sound like he thought the idea held water. "A few weeks ago, I was driving by late at night—" At her indrawn breath, he held up a hand to silence her. "A car pulled out of your drive, without its lights on."

Lily decided to take heed of his desire not to discuss what *he'd* been doing driving by that night. "Maybe it was kids on a date, parked. They still do that here, you know."

His eyes showed a flash of memory—pleasant, heated memory this time. "Just the same, keep your eyes and ears open."

She gave him a salute. "Yes, sir. May I go now, sir?"

He didn't appear amused.

"I promise, I'll be careful."

He walked her to her car and opened the door for her. Once she was inside, he stood there for a moment in the rain and just looked at her. Then he tapped a finger on the window and walked to his truck.

The warmth of security filled her chest. After feeling adrift for the past months, Lily had found an anchor. She just hoped it didn't pull her under.

Clay resisted the urge to follow Lily to town and back. He followed her out the drive and turned in the opposite direction. He needed to keep moving. To think. His mind was filled with contradictions. These past few weeks had made it clear that he wasn't over her. Although, even after their conversation tonight, he didn't feel she was justified in marrying Peter so quickly. He couldn't deny, presented as it was, she must have felt deserted. With court delays and the ever-changing court-appointed attorneys, it had taken over a year for Clay to be acquitted of his "crime." If he had known it would take so long, would he have asked her to wait while his future was in complete limbo?

His life had taken a turn. One that led him to capitalize on his anger, his cynicism. Jail had changed him. When he embarked on an army career that led him to deal in the bartering of lies and betrayal on a global basis, he thought he'd found the perfect fit. He deluded himself into thinking he was on the right track for eleven years.

That delusion ended the day he found the dead boy on the altar steps of the ruins of a church in Eastern Europe. For weeks he'd told himself that the boy's risk was minimal, was justified by the amount of information he was able to supply. Clay realized, as he stared down at the thin body and empty eyes, that he'd been hiding from the truth. It was simply a lie he'd been telling himself to ease his conscience.

Filled with self-loathing, he'd buried the orphan in the churchyard. That day, something in him changed. His view of his job shifted. No longer could he justify the evils he himself committed in the name of routing out *greater* evils.

After a week of self-punishment, he decided to make a change. He would see if he could salvage at least a scrap of the person he used to be, before those dying embers were extinguished from his soul forever. He decided to go back to Forrester Lake.

Now that life was long behind him. He needed to sort out his emotions, which had somehow in the last hours become one huge knotted mess. There were so many unanswered questions. He knew why Lily turned to Peter, but not why she'd rushed into marriage. Why had Peter told Lily he wasn't coming back? There wasn't a way he could assemble things in his mind that made sense. He was trying to put the past behind him. Could he do it without those answers?

As he drove the hours of the night away, the realization came that he could not. He was going to find those answers.

# Chapter 15

"You're pretty good at this—for a girl," Riley said as he watched Mickey creep closer to his high game score at Galaga.

"Yeah, well, watch out, 'cause you're about to be toast." She frowned as she concentrated on the arcade game.

Riley watched her face as she played. She didn't get frustrated and bored like the girls he knew in Chicago, who, once they figured out they weren't going to beat him, usually decided it wasn't any fun and quit. But Mickey never gave up. In the past half hour she'd adjusted her strategy to improve her score. And she was right, she was about to catch him. Maybe persistence wasn't such a good thing in a girl. He shifted nervously as he watched. Mickey said she'd never played before tonight; he'd been playing this game forever. He now wished he hadn't admitted that to her.

The quarter ran out, thank goodness, before she caught up with him.

"Wanna play again?" he asked. If she stopped now, his top score would be safe. But he didn't want it to look like he was *afraid* she'd beat him.

She looked at her watch. "No, I have to be home by nine."

"Too bad, you might actually have beat me," he said, feeling relieved that she hadn't and just a little sorry she was leaving. "Is your mom picking you up?"

Mickey shook her head. "I only live three blocks from here. I walked."

The arcade was in an old storefront a block from the courthouse. There were plenty of streetlights outside that reflected the misty drizzle. Her mom was going to make her walk home in the rain?

He followed her over to the table where she'd left her jacket. Standing with his hands in his pockets, he watched her put it on. There was a little argument going on inside his head. He wanted to walk her home. But he didn't want the guys hanging out in the arcade to see him do it. Besides, what if she didn't want him to?

She pulled her hood up over her hair. "Guess I'll see you around." She started for the door.

"Yeah." He lifted his chin and kept his hands in his pockets.

He thought she hesitated just as she was about to open the door, but then she went on out. Watching her through the plate-glass window, he saw her glance at the sky, then lower her head against the breeze.

Riley's feet itched. His hands flexed in his pockets. If he was going to do it, it had to be now. She was almost out of sight.

She disappeared.

He sprinted for the door and trotted after her. He was so intent on catching up, he didn't see the ankle-deep puddle until he was in it. Calling her name, he splashed on through.

Mickey stopped and turned around. "What?"

Catching up, he said, "My mom said girls shouldn't walk alone after dark. She'd be mad if I let you go by yourself."

"Oh." She sounded surprised and a little confused. "I'm really okay. I do it all the time."

Riley shrugged. "It's no big deal. Besides, I'm in enough trouble with my mom right now."

"Okay." She started walking again.

Riley kept his hands out of his pockets as he walked beside her. Occasionally, the back of his hand brushed hers, setting off a weird feeling in his stomach.

After a bit, Mickey said, "Your mom doesn't seem the type to get all crazy mad."

"What?" As Riley had been concentrating on the strange way Mickey's glancing touch was making him feel, her comment caught him totally off guard.

She hesitated as she took two more steps, then said, "Well, it just seems like your mom's not a . . . a . . . yeller."

Riley got the distinct impression that Mickey didn't really want to talk about *his* mom. "She gets mad enough— I guess she doesn't actually go batshit or anything."

"Has . . . does she ever hit you?" The words came slowly and so quietly that Riley almost couldn't hear them.

"No." His heart started to beat faster. "Well, I guess when I was a baby, she smacked my hands and stuff. And I do remember getting paddled once when I was four and ran out into the street."

Mickey shook her head and looked down at her feet. "I don't mean like that."

A ball of anger started to form in the pit of his stomach. He stopped and put a hand on her arm. "Does your mom hit you?"

She didn't look at him, but kept her gaze on her shoes. "No—she yells a lot." After a pause, she added, "She says some really nasty things."

Riley's jaw tightened. "Like what?"

Mickey lifted a shoulder and tried to start walking again, but Riley held her still. "Stuff about my dad." The words came slowly and she kept her gaze on the ground. "Awful stuff. She says she never would have married him if she hadn't been pregnant with me. And she says . . ." There was a catch in her voice. "She says they must have given her the wrong baby at the hospital, because she can't believe she had a daughter as 'unattractive' as me." She rushed on, as if in justification. "But that's only when she's really mad. I know she doesn't mean it."

Riley couldn't imagine hearing such words from his mother. No wonder Mickey seemed to shrink when her mom was around. But worse, he suspected that if Mickey told him this much, there was even more awful stuff she was keeping inside. "What about your dad? Does he hit you?"

Her chin was tucked to her chest and her hair fell over her face. "Not very often."

The answer hung there in the air between them for a long while. Riley worked to breathe it in, to understand. How could anybody hit Mickey? And how could her mother be such a bitch? He wanted to put his fist through something.

Mickey didn't elaborate further, but seemed relieved to have said as much as she did. After a moment, she slipped her hand into his and they walked the rest of the way to her house in silence.

It was a good thing she'd stopped talking, because Riley couldn't concentrate on anything other than her small hand in his. It made him feel big—and protective. It also made him nervous. He didn't look at her as they walked.

She stopped and dropped his hand at the bottom of the steps to her front porch. "Thanks." She made fleeting eye contact, then hurried up the steps and into the house.

Riley watched her with what felt like a hot, heavy rock in the center of his chest. He stood there for a minute, then he turned around and ran back to the arcade. He pushed himself, making his muscles burn and his lungs ache. His feet pounded the wet pavement and with each footfall, he imagined he was stepping on Mickey's mother's face. He'd wanted to tell Mickey that her mother was wrong, she wasn't "unattractive," but the words had stuck in his throat. Now it was too late. Too late to try and ease the pain he saw in Mickey's eyes.

He didn't feel like going back inside the arcade, but it started to rain hard again and it would be twenty minutes before his mom came to get him. He went in. Earlier he'd thought that after Mickey left, he'd try to strike up a conversation with some of the guys hanging out. Now he didn't feel like talking.

Slipping a quarter in the slot, he grabbed the controls of Road Rage. It was a game that suited his mood just fine.

Riley recognized the kid in a black baseball cap playing the next game over. He and his friend had sat at the table next to him and Mickey earlier in the evening at the pizza place. They both looked to be about sixteen.

Riley nodded a greeting, but didn't say more.

"So," the boy in the baseball cap said, "you gettin' any from Blondie?"

Riley's hands froze on the game controls. His body flashed hot with a fresh wave of anger, but he held his tongue. The last thing he wanted was to alienate himself from the only guys he'd managed to talk to since he'd come to town. He cast a cool smile their way and said, "Nah. Just met her."

The other boy walked closer and nudged Riley in the ribs with his elbow. "I told him he was wrong. You look like the type who goes for hot chicks. Blondie there is about as chilly as you can get." He laughed and bobbed his head.

The first boy said, "*You* say. I say, that's one sweet piece of ass."

Riley let go of the controls and spun on him. "Watch it!"

"Dude! Relax. I'm no poacher. Besides, I wouldn't mess with the T-man's daughter. No way."

There was a hidden meaning in the way the guy said "the T-man." Riley fought to keep his hands to himself and asked, "So, what's the deal with her dad?"

A raised-brow look passed between the two boys, as they made fists and knocked knuckles against each other.

"Whoa! Dude, should we tell him about the T-man?" Baseball Cap asked his buddy.

"Seems like a guy with your reputation," the kid put an arm around Riley's shoulders, "might just have a use for T-man."

Riley stood silently waiting, his curiosity about anything and everything pertaining to Mickey's life outweighing his desire to punch this guy in the nose.

Baseball Cap stepped close enough for Riley to hear him whisper, "You need anything—T-man can hook you up." He stepped back and nodded to confirm his statement.

The kid next to Riley added, "Weed. Pills. You want it, he's got it."

Riley was about to tell these guys to go play with themselves, when he realized the full implication of what they were suggesting. Mickey's dad was a dealer. The dad who didn't hit her very often.

He'd just think about this for a while.

Forcing a smile, he said, "Good to know."

\*     \*     \*

Riley was unusually quiet on their way home from the arcade. Lily had to wonder if his night out hadn't gone well. Of course, when she asked, he said everything was fine. She just hoped "fine" wasn't the same kind of fine he'd been experiencing of late—the kind with exploding toilets and sinking boats.

The weather remained miserable. There were few cars on the road, even though it was Saturday night. Lily had to remind herself that Saturday night in Glens Crossing wasn't like Saturday night in the city. By eleven o'clock the stop-and-go lights switched to blinkers and the only drivers left on the road were those under twenty-five.

Just after she turned onto Mill Run Road, she noticed another pair of headlights swing around the corner behind her. She hadn't noticed anyone behind her on the main road. As they traveled, she kept one eye on her rearview mirror. Could Clay have actually been waiting somewhere along the highway for her to return? As much as she'd made a big deal of her independence, the thought that he'd be so concerned about her safety gave her a good deal of comfort.

The road curved. A fat possum darted out from the weeds, its close-set eyes shining lightning-blue, reflecting the headlights.

"Look out!" Riley shouted.

The possum stopped.

Lily slammed on the brake pedal. The antilock brakes shuddered as the tires worked to grip the wet pavement.

"Mom!"

The right front tire bumped over the possum. Lily cringed and her stomach lurched at the thud that resonated through the floorboards. "Oh, God. . . ."

"Mom! You killed it!"

"I didn't mean to!" Every cell in her body was quivering from the adrenaline rush.

Lily let the car coast along for a second, waiting to stop trembling. She pulled in a deep breath and looked in her rearview mirror to see if the possum was still on the road.

The other car's headlights rounded the curve; she saw the red brake lights reflect off the wet pavement. She crept along and got to the far right, leaving enough room for the car to pass on the narrow road.

It didn't. It didn't ride right up on her rear bumper, either. It hung back, matching her decreasing speed. Now that it was closer, she could easily see the headlights were much too low to be Clay's pickup.

The possum disappeared from her mind. Now her attention was fastened on the car behind her. She sped up slightly. At first the car behind her hung back, then gradually matched her speed. Clay had seen a car coming out of her driveway in the wee hours. Now she wished she'd asked for a more specific description.

The turnoff for the lake house was just ahead. Lily quickly decided not to take it.

"Hey, where are you going?" Riley sat up straighter in his seat and looked out the driver's side as they passed the entrance to the lane.

"I forgot I told Gramps we'd stop by on our way home." Lily wanted to go straight to Clay, to have him make good on that protective attitude he'd been laying on her this evening. But that would require too much in the way of explaining to Riley. That particular can of worms needed to be left unopened and on the shelf at the moment.

"Man. Can't you just call him?"

"We won't stay long." Her gaze flicked to the rearview mirror. The headlights paced along behind.

She didn't turn on her signal, and she braked at the last minute before she made the right turn onto the road that connected them back to the highway. But the car behind her had enough distance, it didn't throw him. After a couple of seconds, the headlights turned just behind her.

Lily's heart felt like a fluttering moth at the base of her throat. She had to concentrate on the road because it made several serious curves before it ran into the highway. When she looked back in her mirror, the road behind her was dark.

"What's wrong?" Riley asked.

"Nothing."

"You keep looking in the mirror and you took that corner like Gramps."

Lily managed a chuckle and glanced his way. "Gramps still doesn't like to brake to turn a corner?"

Riley grinned and shook his head.

"Uncle Luke always said he was trying to save his brake pads." She patted his knee. "Maybe I should reconsider letting you ride with him," she teased, glad to have diverted his attention.

At the stop sign at the intersection with the highway, she waited, watching for the headlights to emerge from the last curve. As there was nowhere to pull off the road, let alone turn, she fully expected them to show up.

"Mom?" Riley sounded concerned.

"What?" She kept her eyes on the mirror.

"You can go." Riley pointed to the darkness on their left.

"Yeah." She looked at him and smiled weakly. "I guess that possum still has me shaken up." She made the right turn that led them back toward town.

She kept a rearward watch all of the way to the Crossing House. The mysterious headlights didn't reappear.

The lot was full, so she had to drive around back to find a spot to park her car.

"I'll wait out here," Riley said, when she turned off the car.

"No. You come in with me."

"Geez, Mom. I'm not a baby. I can sit in the car for five minutes."

"Gramps wants to see you." Lily felt completely justified in the little white lie. She didn't want to alarm him, but there was no reason to take unnecessary risks.

Riley cranked up an Olympic-sized sigh and opened his door. They ran to the entrance side by side in the rain.

"Why don't you go say hello to Faye?" Lily said as she headed into the bar.

"I don't know why I can't go on the other side of that stupid wall. It's not like I'm going to order a drink. . . ."

Lily silenced him with a stern look, but deep inside she agreed; she'd thought the same thing when she was a kid. She watched him head toward the kitchen, then she stepped into the bar.

"Hey there, Lily!" her dad called. "I thought I told you we didn't need help."

She smiled and slid onto a bar stool. "I just picked Riley up in town and thought we'd stop for some buffalo wings."

Benny looked so pleased, she felt guilty. She should have known he'd like her and Riley to stop as customers. But she'd been run here by fear. Again, she felt selfish and inconsiderate.

He said, "Go on out and find a table. I'll come and say hi to Riley in a minute."

"Okay." She'd considered telling him about the car following her. But he already had his hands full. There was no reason to worry him. The car was gone. And Lily was going to be on her toes from now on. She was going to do as Clay said, not let her feeling of security in this little town overcome her good sense.

When she stepped into the dining room, she saw Faye talking to Riley near the kitchen door. They were laughing about something. Lily felt a quick stab of jealousy at the way Faye put a motherly hand on his shoulder and the easy way they shared a joke.

Once again, she felt small and petty. She should be glad for the friendship they seemed to be building. She walked toward them. Faye's smile slipped just a bit when she saw her.

Lily nodded. "Faye." She put an arm around Riley. "I think we're going to share a platter of wings." She took a step toward the kitchen. "I'll go tell Henry."

Faye stepped between Lily and the kitchen door. "I'll tell him. You two go find a seat." Her voice was pleasant enough, but there was a glitter of resentment in her eyes.

Lily held her gaze for a moment, wondering if this was the time for a showdown. She had poured hours and hours into this place and she was tired of being treated like a meddling outsider.

She glanced at Riley. He was already walking toward an empty table, out of earshot.

"Coming through!" One of the servers called, headed toward the kitchen with a tray full of dirty dishes.

After a second's hesitation, in which Lily felt Faye was weighing the same question—go teeth, hair and eyeballs? or back down?—Faye turned and pushed the swinging door open. The server followed. The door swung shut.

A mixture of relief and disappointment spun in Lily's chest. The air between her and Faye definitely needed clearing. And Lily was in just the right mood to let loose her frustration. She was tired of the perpetual challenge in the woman's posture, of being treated like an intruder in her father's life.

She walked to the table knowing the battle had only been delayed, not avoided.

Riley didn't complain about the detour, as Lily had anticipated. He talked briefly with his grandfather when Benny took a minute from his work to say hello. But Lily could tell something was bothering him. Normally, she couldn't get the child filled up. Tonight, he barely tasted the heaping platter of wings Henry sent from the kitchen.

Lily spent half of her time wondering what was going on with Riley, and the other half organizing her thoughts to confront Faye. She made a pretense of eating a wing or two, but in the end boxed up most of them to take home.

As they stood to go, Lily said, "I'm going to hit the restroom before we go. I'll met you at the front door."

He nodded and swung his jacket on, then headed toward the door.

Riley stopped near the entrance to the bar. He looked in, thinking he'd wave to Gramps. But Gramps wasn't behind the bar. He was standing off to the side, near the door, talking to the sheriff.

Riley's first thought was that they were talking about him. He leaned his back against the wall, ensuring he couldn't be seen from inside the bar, and listened.

The sheriff said, "I'd appreciate it if you just keep your ears open. Sooner or later, we'll get a clue to work with. I'd just rather it be sooner."

"Will do," Gramps said. "Don't need that poison around our kids."

"Guess it was inevitable, knowing the world we live in. We'd made it this long, I'd hoped . . ."

Riley heard Gramps slap the sheriff on the back. "You'll get him. Gotta nip this in the bud—can't have drugs taking over the high school."

"Oh, it doesn't stop at the high school, Benny. Even the little kids are at risk. Arresting the users doesn't stop it. I need to find out who's dealing."

Dealing? God, did the sheriff think it was him? Just like an adult, always fingering the kids when a grown-up was causing all the trouble. He felt sad for Mickey. His own dad might be a screwed-up alcoholic—but at least he wasn't a drug dealer.

"I'll see if I can pick up anything," Benny said.

"Thanks. I appreciate it."

Riley took a giant sideways step, away from the bar. When the sheriff came out, Riley had his back to him, studying a framed poster of an ancient castle on a rolling green hill.

"Mr. Holt."

Riley turned around. "Sheriff."

"How are things going at the marina?"

Riley smiled and tried to look enthusiastic. "Good. I'm learning a lot."

"Getting on with Bud okay?"

"Okay enough." Riley didn't want anyone to think he *liked* working with Bud. The man was mean—and crazy. Still, sometimes Riley actually found himself looking forward to going to work on the boats. Riley had even caught himself almost liking Bud when they rebuilt that engine today. Sheesh, maybe he was going crazy, too.

The sheriff nodded. "See you around."

"Yeah." Riley shoved his hands in his pockets and watched the man walk out the door. He didn't act like he thought Riley was the one selling drugs; there hadn't been suspicion in his eyes. But why else would he have been talking to Gramps about it?

"Ready?"

Riley jumped at his mother's voice. "Yeah."

"What's the matter?" she asked.

"Nothing."

"You don't look like 'nothing.'"

"I'm just ready to go home."

"All right, then. Let's go." She put a hand on his shoulder and they walked out the door.

Riley had been braced for the fifth degree on the ride home. But his mother seemed preoccupied. She didn't ask a million questions as usual. In fact, she hardly spoke at all. And it seemed to him that she was still looking in the mirrors a lot.

She was even weirder when they got to the house. She was all, "Let me go in first," and "Don't go upstairs until I go with you."

"What's going on?"

"I just think we shouldn't be so complacent—I heard a house on the lake had been broken into. We should be careful."

Riley tilted his head and raised a brow, but didn't say any more. There were houses being robbed all the time in Chicago and his mom never acted this way.

By the time he finally got to his room and had the door closed behind him, he was out of the mood to read more in his book. Everything tonight was just crazy.

His time with Mickey had been fun, but that was nuts, too. All day long, he'd had a strange little buzz of excitement going, like he usually got right before going on a roller coaster. That buzz had shot through the roof when she took his hand as he walked her home. And his guts knotted when he thought about her dad. What was up with that bastard? He hit her. He was a dealer. How could somebody so rotten have such a great daughter?

As Riley laid on his bed in the dark, he flexed his fingers and popped his knuckles. He just wanted to tear something apart.

The telephone rang as Lily was getting into bed. She answered.

There was a moment of silence, then Clay said, "I just wanted to make sure things are okay there."

Lily couldn't suppress a small smile. "We're just fine." She paused. "Thanks for checking."

"All of the doors are locked?"

"Of course."

"You have a phone handy, in case you need to call someone in an emergency?"

Lily wondered, *Are you the someone I should call?* As she had the thought, she realized that would be her first instinct, to call Clay—just as she had when they were young. She licked her lips. "Yes. Right here beside my bed."

There was a long pause. "Do you have my number?"

The question took her by surprise. "Ah, no. Only the marina."

"Get a pencil."

"Just a second." She should tell him to go climb a tree; if she needed help she'd be calling the sheriff. But something inside her ached for the connection, yearned for the touch of his concern.

"Okay," she said, once she was ready to write down the number.

He gave it to her, then he asked, "Does that phone have speed dial?"

"Really, Clay, I think you're overreacting." He'd really be over the top if she told him she thought she was being followed earlier. No doubt he'd be over here watching over her and Riley while they slept. Neither Riley nor Clay needed that kind of relationship right now.

His voice took a harder edge. "Does it?"

"No, I think this phone is as old as Peter." As soon as she said his name, she wished she could recall it.

For a long moment he was quiet. Lily held her breath.

"Just don't take any chances. If you hear a noise . . ."—he hesitated—"call me. I can be there in five minutes."

"All right." A part of her wanted to tell him to come now, don't wait for an emergency. Come and wrap her in the security of his nearness.

"Goodnight, then—and don't screw around if you hear anything."

"Goodnight, Clay. Thanks."

Lily crawled between the cool sheets feeling more lonely than she had in months.

# Chapter 16

On Monday morning Clay noticed a different feel to
Riley's silence. They never spent much of their day talking
to each other. But Riley seemed more distracted than unso-
ciable this morning. Clay considered asking him what was
up, but he knew he'd get the standard, *nothing*. He'd get further by just letting the kid stew for as long as he was inclined
to. If Riley wanted to talk, he'd open his mouth and start
talking. Still, Clay couldn't help but be a little curious.

After Clay had signed for the daily UPS delivery, he
walked out to the dock, where Riley was stocking the ice
cooler. Riley was grabbing the seven-pound bags and slamming them so hard into the freezer, Clay was surprised they
hadn't burst open.

"Hey, easy, there," he said. "You look like you could use
a punching bag."

Riley shot him a narrowed look, then chucked the next
bag into the freezer.

Clay busied himself nearby, pretending to ignore the
crash and bang of the bags landing in the ice chest.

As Riley picked up the last bag, he paused. "Shouldn't

doing the right thing be easy? I mean, it's the *right thing*—a person shouldn't have to get so bent out of shape over it."

Clay's hands stilled in his work, but he didn't look at Riley. "Sometimes doing the right thing is the *hardest* thing."

The last bag landed in the freezer with a thud. "I thought you could tell something was right because it caused the least trouble."

Clay shook his head. "I've found just the opposite. Sometimes to do the right thing makes you put everything at risk."

Sitting on a big rock nearby, Riley looked out over the lake and rubbed his hands on the thighs of his jeans. They were reddened from handling the ice, but Clay was pleased the kid wasn't whining about it.

Riley said, "If someone trashes your friend, isn't it the right thing to stand up for them, set the guy straight—no matter what?"

"I guess, it depends on the 'no matter what.' You can make things worse for your friend by setting up more trouble."

For a long moment, Riley was quiet. Clay busied himself and let the boy think.

"I should have kicked that guy's ass." Riley said it so quietly, Clay wasn't sure he was supposed to hear.

Clay went over and sat beside Riley on the rock. "I guess you have to ask yourself if you betrayed your friend by *not* kicking ass." He paused and felt Riley's gaze shift to him. "If you'd taken that guy on, would it have saved your friend pain, or caused more?"

Riley shot to his feet and lifted his hands in the air. "Geez, I don't know! How am I supposed to know something like that?"

"It's not an easy call for a man to make." At Clay's use of the word "man," Riley's shoulders squared just a bit.

"I just feel like I let—my friend down."

"Was it easy *not* to fight?"

"God, no." Riley's hands fisted at his sides. "I wanted to take a swing at that guy so bad . . ."

"Then my guess is, you did the right thing." He got up and walked back to the office, leaving the boy alone with his thoughts.

He tried to remember life when he was thirteen. He'd met Lily and Luke about that time. The Boudreau kids had begun their relationship with him and Peter as enemies, but once Lily's accident happened, they'd been solid friends—at least until adulthood brought change.

Now he and Lily weren't enemies. They weren't friends. They were estranged lovers looking for some sort of equilibrium, a level place to start. And he felt nearly as confused as Riley.

At nine o'clock Riley was already up in his room reading—reading, not listening to angry music or playing violent video games. The subtle proof that he seemed to be changing for the better made Lily relax enough that her own creativity began to work again.

She settled on the couch with a sketchpad. She had a few new pottery designs floating in her head, and she wanted to commit them to paper before they left her. She was still too nervous to actually try working with clay. While Riley was at work, she'd driven to Bedford and bought a pregnancy test. For the "most accurate results" she had to wait until morning to take it.

She didn't feel pregnant . . . exactly. Some of the symptoms were there, yet it wasn't as she remembered it from the first time. There was no doubt something was going on with her body; she'd never been this late with a period—except when she'd been pregnant with Riley.

Picking up her pencil, she tried to concentrate. Since the Crossing House seemed to be running just fine with no help from her, she had to find some way to fill her days. Maybe she could ask Mr. Duckwall if he would sell a few pottery pieces on consignment at the hardware store.

The first sketch was just beginning to take shape when she heard the crunch of tires on the drive. The windows were open, but even if they hadn't been, she felt confident she would have known someone was there. Since the episode with the yellow rose, she'd been as alert to sounds around the house as a police dog.

She walked to the front door and turned on the porch light. Her tension left her when she saw Clay's truck. For one childish moment, a little skitter of happiness danced around her stomach. It was the same feeling she'd had years ago, always spurred by the mere sight of him. She tried to ignore it and undid the hook that secured the screen door.

As he got out and came up the steps, she saw he had a box in his hands.

"Hi," she said, hating the awkward way she felt with each meeting.

"Hi." His voice was soft and rough at the same time, making that feeling in her stomach take off again. He stood outside, just looking at her through the screen. "Can I come in?"

Lily gave her head a little shake. "Of course." She opened the door. "What do you have there?" she asked, pointing to the box.

"A new phone—with programmable memory."

Smiling she said, "You think I can't remember 911?"

He stepped a little closer. "I don't want you to call 911. I want you to call me."

Lily's breath hitched in her throat. Her mouth went dry. "Don't you think the sheriff is bet—"

He raised his hand and put a thumb over her mouth. "No one can protect you like I can. Let me."

With her heart running like a hamster in a wheel, Lily couldn't ask the question that was on the tip of her tongue: *Because of your training? Or because you care like no one else?*

She took a step backward, trying to get enough air around her to draw a breath. "The only modular plug is upstairs. That line was run later. The kitchen is hardwired."

He started toward the stairs. She just watched him go.

He stopped halfway up. "Gonna show me where, or do I have to find it myself?"

She started after him. "Clay, really, I can plug the thing in myself."

He'd reached the upstairs hall; she was afraid he'd speak loudly enough that Riley would come out of his room. How would she explain this to him?

But Clay didn't say anything. He just waited at the top of the stairs for her to catch up.

Brushing against him as she passed, she headed to the master bedroom. Once they were inside, she closed the door. Riley's room was at the opposite end of the hall, and she heard his stereo playing, but she didn't want to risk him hearing Clay's deep voice and coming to investigate.

At the soft click of the door closing, Clay turned to her with a raised eyebrow.

She ignored it and pointed to the nightstand. "Phone's there, the jack is right behind the table."

Clay picked up the old Trimline phone on the stand and

followed the cord to the wall. He unplugged it and started to neatly wind the cord around the phone. "The new one will need an electrical outlet, too."

"I think it's behind the headboard." She walked over to the bed, making an effort not to make eye contact with Clay. He stepped out of her way and she knelt on the mattress. Pressing her forehead against the wall, she peered in the small space between the headboard and the wall. "There it is. Right in the middle."

She turned to look at him, and was immediately sorry she had. He stood there, frozen in midmotion, the boxed phone in his hands, his eyes locked on her. The expression on his face said he'd forgotten completely about the phone. Lily realized she'd been leaning over, putting her posterior right in his face. Quickly, she spun around and sat on the mattress.

He tore his gaze away, and his cheeks actually reddened. He cleared his throat and opened the box. "We can pull the b . . . bed out—"

"Right." She pulled down on the hem of her shirt. "Right."

Clay ducked his head behind the nightstand and finished unboxing the phone out of her line of sight. Then he put the phone on the table and unwound the electrical cord and transformer. He stood right in front of her. She sat there looking up at him, all thoughts wiped cleanly from her mind by those brown eyes.

After a second, he said, "It'd be easier to move the bed if you weren't on it."

"Oh!" She jumped up as if someone had set off a firecracker under her. She didn't stop moving until there was a good three feet between them. God, how stupid had she looked sitting there staring at him?

Clay moved the bed out and plugged in the transformer.

Lily watched the muscles of his back and shoulders move under the taut fabric of his shirt. When she realized what she was doing, she quickly shifted her gaze to the dresser across the room.

Once he moved the bed back into place, he sat down and picked up the cordless receiver. Then he punched in some numbers. "I already charged it. Now I'm on speed dial. All you have to do is press one." He pressed the number and Lily heard the tones in the receiver he held between them. "It wouldn't hurt to carry this with you, so you have it wherever you are in the house."

"You're kidding, right?"

His gaze held hers. "No, I'm not. When you're in the shower, I want this thing on the floor beside it."

There was something in his tone that told her not to argue. Suddenly she felt like a child, too foolish to know when she was in danger. "All right."

"Come over here and I'll show you a couple of other features."

She moved slowly toward the bed, stopping just in front of him.

"Here's how you set the ring." He pushed a button on the base and then another on the handset. "The volume of the receiver can be changed here." He pressed a series of buttons. "And if you want speakerphone, just press this."

Lily wasn't paying any attention to the numbers or the buttons. She was transfixed by the simple movement of his fingers, the cadence of his voice, the way his hair fell over his forehead as he looked down at the phone in his hand.

It suddenly occurred to her he was waiting for her to say something.

"I'm sorry, what did you say?"

"Speed dial," he repeated. "Want any other numbers pro-grammed in?"

"Um, I guess not." Was it him? Was it her out-of-balance hormones? Was it the fact that she now knew they'd been robbed of the chance at love by a stupid twist of fate? Or was it that they were behind closed bedroom doors together for the first time? Lily didn't know. All she knew was that she could hardly concentrate on putting together a full sen-tence since they came in here.

Clay put the phone in its cradle and reached out for her hand. "Would you please stop looking at me like I'm going to hurt you?"

Lily drew a deep breath. Oh, if he only knew the power he held to inflict hurt. She couldn't deny it, she loved him. She'd never stopped loving him. But they were as far apart now as they had been when she was in Chicago married to Peter and he was sneaking around dangerous territory overseas.

Having denied her feelings for so long, now that he sat here, grasping her hand in his, she could feel herself sliding helplessly into a quagmire of emotion. All she wanted to do was, for a brief moment, be his. To pretend nothing existed outside this room, they had no past and the future was a blank slate waiting to be filled with loving memories.

If she hadn't felt the tear roll down her cheek, she wouldn't have known she was crying.

He kept her hand in his as he stood. He stopped the tear with a finger and his gaze held her as captive as if he'd wrapped her in ropes and chains. She watched with a riot in her soul as he took that tear and put it in his mouth.

"I remember how you taste," he said in a hoarse whisper. "It's like I've held the memory of you on my tongue."

Then he traced his lips along the trail of her tear and

Lily's heart cried out for those memories, too. They came crashing back in a tidal wave, the feel of his skin on hers, the smell of his hair after it had been warmed by the sun, his work-worn hands on her breast, the heat that exploded under his touch.

God, how she wanted to feel that heat again.

His breath tickled her ear as he kissed it and she stood lead-limbed and trembling. She tilted her head to the side as his lips kissed their way down the side of her neck. He kept her hand in his, lacing his fingers through hers.

Lily was frustrated by the space he maintained between their bodies. The only contact was his lips on her neck and a single held hand. She wanted to press herself against him, be absorbed completely by his body, surrender her entire being to him.

He whispered against her skin, "I won't hurt you again." Then he stepped back and dropped her hand.

It took a moment for it to register in her sensually clouded mind that he was heading toward the door. She fully expected him to lock it and return to her. Instead, he opened it and started out of the room.

"You're leaving?" Her voice was little more than a squeak.

He hesitated, but didn't turn back around. Bowing his head slightly, he said, "Yes."

"Why?"

"Because I don't want to hurt you." He looked over his shoulder at her. "We need to take our time."

"Isn't this a little like closing the barn door after the cow is out in the storm?" She couldn't keep the edge out of her voice. Here she stood, possibly pregnant with his child, and he wanted to take things *slowly*.

Letting the door drift back closed, he returned to her,

pulled her into his arms and kissed her. His kiss matched the pent-up passion she was feeling. She let herself be carried away on the sensations he aroused, on the possibility. . . .

He let her go and looked in her eyes. "I don't want to ruin this. It's too fragile, too precious."

Then he turned around and left her trembling with unfulfilled desire.

After a restless night, Lily got up with the sun. She didn't know if her tossing and turning was due to being nervous over taking the pregnancy test this morning, or her jumbled emotions stirred by Clay's visit. He'd said he didn't want to ruin what they had—but Lily still didn't know exactly what that was. They'd made love weeks ago and the walls had risen higher between them. Now he was acting like a super-hero responsible for her safety. After kissing her with enough passion to make her knees weak, he said he wanted to go slowly.

She pushed her hair away from her face and went down the hall and into the bathroom, home pregnancy test in hand. She locked the door and set the box on the sink ledge. For a minute or two, she just stared at it, as if this were a show-down and if she blinked first she was the loser.

Finally, she picked up the box and tore it open. After rereading the instructions, she got down to business. Just before she peed on the stick, she froze. This was it. Once this step was done, she couldn't pretend. She closed her eyes and whispered a prayer.

"Please, God, let it be negative." It seemed ludicrous after spending years on end with just the opposite plea on her lips. Her prayers had been ignored then; but in the long run, God had been right. He couldn't possibly abandon her now.

The ten minutes it took for the results to appear felt like days stacked on end. She'd planned on taking a shower while she waited. She knew better than to stare at the test stick; a watched pregnancy test was much like the proverbial pot of water put on to boil. But she set the tester on the edge of the sink, started pacing the tile floor and found she couldn't stop. As she made another orbit around the room biting on her thumbnail, she looked the white stick surreptitiously out of the corner of her eye, as if it were a coiled snake she didn't want to startle into striking.

Her watch rested on the back of the toilet. She stared at it from two feet away. She could see the minute hand had moved to the four. It was time.

Closing her eyes, she reiterated a prayer that was much too late to do any good, and reached for the test stick. Once it was in hand, she looked to the ceiling first, swallowed and looked at the test in her hand.

The strength went out of her knees and she sat hard on the toilet seat. Negative. It was negative.

# Chapter 17

After indulging in a good stress-relieving cry, Lily fed Riley breakfast. Then she drove him to work. When they pulled into the marina, the office door was closed. Normally, the door remained open during operating hours. There was a hand-printed sign taped to the glass: MARINA CLOSED TODAY, BUD. Underneath that was a business-sized envelope with Riley's name printed on it in huge block letters.

Riley got out and untaped the envelope from the glass. He pulled out a small piece of paper and read it, then turned around and came back to the car. "Guess I have the day off."

"Why didn't he call?" She was already irritable, and Clay's inconsiderate behavior chafed Lily all the more. "We didn't need to drive all the wa—"

"Mom! Relax. The note said he left in the middle of the night and didn't want to wake us."

"The middle of the night? Where did he go?"

Riley shrugged. "Didn't say."

"Hmmm." What could have called him away in the middle of the night? What kind of wee-hours emergency could pop up for a single loner like Clay? Especially one that called him away from the speed dial he'd made such a big deal about just hours ago.

"Did he say when he'd be back?"

"Tomorrow. I'm supposed to come to work at the regular time."

Her frustration rippled again. *Call* me, *not the sheriff.* Really? Good thing she hadn't actually needed to.

Lily pulled out of the parking lot and turned toward town.

Perhaps this day would be a chance for her and Riley to have some relaxed time together. Maybe she could figure out what was going on inside his adolescent head. "I'm hungry," she said. "How about we go to the Dew Drop and have some pancakes?"

Riley looked at her with surprise in his eyes. "You *never* eat pancakes."

"Well, I feel like pancakes this morning. And don't give me 'I already ate,' 'cause I know you can put away three breakfasts before noon and still eat a huge lunch."

Lifting a shoulder and tilting his head, he said, "Okay. Pancakes."

Lily drove into town with her mood as unsettled as a field full of grasshoppers. The relief she'd initially felt at the test results had given way to an odd mix of feelings. Of course, a pregnancy would have really screwed things up for everyone, particularly for Riley. But, her mind countered, perhaps in the long run it might have been for the better; he could have had a sibling to stand by him after she was gone. No matter what anybody said these days, blood was indeed thicker than water. Lily couldn't imagine not having her brother and sister. Even though they lived scattered all over the globe, there was a certain sense of security just knowing they were there.

Also, as she looked at her ex-husband's life, Peter might

have fared better if he'd had a sibling or two to dilute the concentration of parental involvement. Neither Samantha nor Bill could see the fact that their efforts to insulate their only child from pain and disappointment had crippled him. The fact that they controlled most every facet of Peter's life had prevented him from learning to stand on his own. Although motivated by the best of intentions, they had only fostered weakness in their son.

But there were other emotions at work, things deep inside her, things no one else could know. And, as she looked inward, Lily discovered a few startling facts about herself. As she picked apart the fibers of her emotions, she had to admit there was a more selfish reason for this morning's peculiar discontent. Forcing herself to examine it more closely, she found Clay at the center of it. A baby would certainly have brought things to a head between them. All of the secrets would have come crashing out of the closet. And, she realized as she pulled into a parking space in front of the Dew Drop, she was tired of keeping her shoulder against that door to prevent those secrets from spilling out.

There was no way to open that door and not have people get hurt. She guessed that was the epicenter of this emotional earthquake. If she wanted to build some sort of future with Clay, Peter would have to be hurt. If she protected Peter, she had to give up the possibility of an honest relationship with Clay. And, of course, that just swung back around to the question of what was in Riley's best interest.

These were the same demons she'd been wrestling since she saw Clay that first day at the marina. On top of everything else, the guilt associated with her lie of omission was muddling her judgment. It was difficult, not being truthful with Clay, especially over something that could be so life-altering, regardless of the pain he'd caused her in the past.

Inside her head, the battle lines had been drawn, the armies had massed their artillery, diplomacy had been blown out of the water. The only way for this conflict to end was all-out war. And, as in any war, there would be casualties. She just had to make sure her son wasn't one of them.

Already her head throbbed from the mental combat—and the first shot had yet to be fired. She got out of the car and headed into the Dew Drop, hoping a shot of caffeine would help.

Mildred was ringing up a customer at the register when they walked in. "Just take a seat anywhere. Cassie's out sick and I'm shorthanded this morning. Be with you as soon as I can."

"Thanks, Mildred," Lily said as she followed Riley toward a booth halfway to the rear of the restaurant. As she did, all of the patrons at the counter either smiled or nodded in greeting. Even those she didn't know.

It stunned her to realize she'd once again become a part of this place. Or maybe she'd never been truly separated from it. Perhaps she was the one who'd set up barriers. Throughout junior high and high school she'd shied away from making eye contact with those she passed on the street or encountered in the market. It stemmed from those first weeks after her mother had left. Every time she caught someone looking at her, she could hear the thoughts going on in their minds, the accusation and condemnation, the guilt by association. It set up an avalanche of shame that Lily just now had begun to realize might have been manufactured in her own mind.

Riley stopped without warning, and Lily ran right into the back of him. He didn't start moving again with her nudge.

"What's wrong?" she asked the back of his head.

"Hi, Riley," a girl's voice came from the other side of him.

Riley's shoulders tensed. He quickly said, "Hi," and spun around to sit in the booth, putting his back to the girl in the next booth—which, when he moved out of the way and Lily could see, turned out to be Mickey Fulton.

Lily smiled at Mickey and said hello, then looked at Riley, whose face was beet-red. She was just thinking how cute this whole scene was when she realized who was sitting across from Mickey, with his back to her. Tad.

Slowly he turned in his seat, resting one elbow on the back of the booth. He smiled at Lily, but there was something off about that smile. It felt—predatory.

"Hello, Lily Boudreau," he said. "Nice to see you back in town."

She imagined her face matched Riley's. Her heart sped up and her mouth went dry. And that really pissed her off. She was a grown woman. High school was fifteen years ago. She put on what she hoped appeared to be a confident smile and said, "Hello, Tad."

Well, maybe that adolescent shame hadn't *all* been self-inflicted.

Then she added, tilting her head slightly, "Didn't I see you the other night at the Crossing House?"

An unsettled look crossed his face, then he nodded. "You did. You looked so busy, I didn't want to bother you."

"How thoughtful." This just felt all too familiar, Tad deciding just when and where he would acknowledge Lily. She wanted to tell him to go take a flying fuck at the moon, but that was entirely out of the question with the children present.

It occurred to her, as she looked at Mickey's questioning

eyes, that she had only been about a year older than the girl when Tad began to blur the social lines that divided them.

Clay had saved her from herself the first time Tad started playing his games. But, as was the norm, he, and Peter, had gone home to Chicago for the school year. He wasn't around to stop her from her own foolishness.

Lily had spent the years immediately after her mother ran off perfecting the art of being invisible. She didn't cause trouble. She minded her own business. She didn't dress in attention-grabbing fashion. She didn't even make much noise. The less attention she drew, the less likely people were to remember her mother's desertion, and the better things would be for her little sister, Molly. Then, starting the first day of her freshman year in high school, Tad, who was a senior, began to "see" her.

Lily noticed him watching her during lunch in the cafeteria. At first she looked immediately behind her, assuming he was eyeing one of the cool girls. Then, as she carried her tray to the dishwashing room, his gaze followed—he was definitely looking at her. Although he didn't look particularly mad, Lily wondered if he was still miffed about the game of slips. Why else would he be staring at her?

As she walked home from school that day, he pulled his car to the curb and called to her. She ignored him, thinking he was up to no good—which, as it turned out, was right. Instead of going on, he paced her as she walked, asking her things like why she was mad at him, and did she want to go to the Arctic Express for a Coke. He followed her all the way to the Crossing House.

Later that night, he called. She gave him the cold shoulder. It had to be some kind of practical joke—guys like Tad Fulton only went after girls like Amy Whitson and Karen Kimball. Lily didn't even dwell on the same planet.

Although he never followed her home again, he called every night, always when she and Molly were home alone. Luke had a job after football practice at Kingston's Market and didn't usually get home until eight. Tad never called after eight. Of course, Lily didn't see the pattern of concealment at the time.

He was persistent—and charming. Finally she agreed to meet him at the park on her way home from school. Tad didn't have a job; he said his folks said basketball was his job, his ticket to college. As basketball practice was still weeks away, he had time on his hands.

It quickly became a routine, their private after-school meetings in the park. At school, their paths seldom crossed. Except at lunch, where of course he ate with Luke and his senior buddies and Lily ate with the freshmen. She didn't really think much of it, but she should have heeded those first warnings her instincts had given her.

One day, as she and Tad sat side by side on top of a picnic table near the woods, he'd kissed her. It was nice, but nothing like the kisses she'd read about in books. And she certainly didn't get the same chilly ripple on her skin that she had with Clay's *almost*-kiss in the fire tower. But that was different. She and Clay were friends and he would never see her any other way. She'd sworn to herself that she wouldn't ruin things by letting him know how she felt. Tad was treating her like a guy treated a girlfriend.

The day after the kiss, there had been a pep rally at school. As the student body filed into the gym, Lily had spotted Tad talking to Karen Kimball and some of her cheerleader friends. She walked over to him, a stupid smile plastered on her face. Fool that she was, she assumed she and Tad were "together."

When she touched him on the arm and said hi, he barely

turned her way, muttered something that more resembled a grunt than a greeting, and went back to his conversation with the girls in short pleated skirts and red and white pom-poms.

As Lily had walked away, feeling like she'd been gut-punched, she heard Amy ask, "What's with her?" Tad said he didn't have a clue, maybe he'd looked at her in the hall and now she thought they were *friends*.

All of the wonderful things Tad had said to her, all of the dreams Lily had foolishly shared with him, shattered like blown glass against brick. She spent the pep rally locked in a stall in the girls' bathroom and waited there until she was certain that everyone had left the school.

Later that night, Lily was surprised when Tad called. She told him she didn't want to talk to him if he could only speak to her when no one was looking.

She sat silently while he explained away his behavior, apologized profusely, promised it would never happen again. And like a fool, she believed him. He was, after all, very charming.

She stopped believing him after the third time.

Then things got ugly.

Quite often Tad followed her in his car, but now kept a block away, never pulling alongside as he'd done before.

Then one afternoon, needing time alone, Lily went to The Place after school. She'd just settled down with a book when she heard a twig snap and a rustle in the nearby bushes. She shot to her feet and saw Tad step into the clearing.

"What are you doing here?" she asked, her fright adding a sharp edge to her words.

He stopped and looked down at his shoes. "I just wanted to talk to you. You won't take my calls." Then he looked up from under his brows with an innocent smile on his lips and said, "That little sister of yours is impossible to bribe."

"Let's just say she's smarter than I am."

"But she's not as pretty." He took a step closer.

"She's *ten years old*." Lily crossed her arms over her chest and shot him a disgusted look.

He inched nearer. "I can tell she's not going to be as beautiful as you." He reached out with a finger and brushed her cheek.

"Save it, Tad."

"Come on, Lil! Don't be mad. I know I screwed up. I just want things back the way they were."

Anger burst red and hot inside Lily. "Like they were? You mean, you sneaking around with me, then treating me like I'm invisible when other people are around? Kissing me in secret, telling me . . . things . . . then making fun of me with your *friends*?" Now she leaned closer to him and said, just short of a shout, "Is that what you mean, Tad?"

He grabbed her shoulders so quickly she didn't have time to jump back. He jerked her against him and said, "This is what I mean." And he kissed her.

Lily clamped her lips together and was as unresponsive as a person could be.

Tad tried to force his tongue inside her mouth. While Lily was concentrating on fending off that invasion, he shoved her backward against a tree. Her mouth came open with a gasp and his tongue took advantage.

Lily's anger quickly turned in the direction of fear when he pinned her against the tree with his body and pulled her blouse from the waist of her jeans. Then his hands were on her skin.

Anger gave her strength. A growl started in her throat.

She bit down on his tongue. He jumped backward, holding his mouth.

"You keep your hands off of me!"

"Jeeshus!" He looked at his hand for blood and saw some. "You bith me."

"I didn't bite hard. But I'm warning you, you get near me again, and I'll do worse."

A change came over him then. He switched from macho man to wounded little boy. He sat down on the ground and stared at his bloody hand. A thick rope of red-stained saliva ran from his lip. "Don't tell Luk—"

"Save your breath." She tucked in her shirt and picked up her book.

Tad pretty much disappeared from her life after that moment. But occasionally she caught the look, or him staring out his car window when he passed.

She'd never told anyone about her encounters with Tad. She'd been too ashamed—not to mention if Luke found out he'd have kicked Tad's ass to Kalamazoo and back. Wouldn't that have fanned those remaining embers of gossip back into full flame? It had taken years for the last Boudreau family scandal to disappear from the lips of the gossipmongers. Lily had had no desire to start it up again.

Mildred came to their booth and both Riley and Lily ordered pancakes, even though Lily's appetite had taken a nosedive since she saw Tad. But she'd plow through them, she wouldn't let him win, not this time.

Before their food arrived, Tad and Mickey got up. He paused as he passed Lily's table. Instead of behaving as she had in school, she looked at him and held his gaze. Tad was the first to look away.

He put a hand on Mickey's arm and said, "Aren't you going to tell your friend goodbye?"

Lily didn't miss the way the girl flinched when he touched her.

"'Bye, Riley." She looked at Lily. "Mrs. Holt."

Riley grunted and didn't look up.

Lily smiled. "Good to see you again, Mickey."

Tad said, "See you real soon, Lily."

"Goodbye, Tad." Her words carried enough frost that he should get the idea.

They left the café.

Lily said, "Riley Holt, where are your manners? How could you be so rude to such a nice girl?"

"I didn't mean to be rude—to her."

"What's that supposed to mean? You wanted to be rude to Mr. Fulton?" Not that Lily didn't want to do the same.

He shrugged and Lily could see there was a real struggle going on inside her son.

"What is it?" she asked.

"I didn't want to look at him."

"Mickey's dad?"

He nodded and Lily's heart started to race. "Has something happened between you and Mr. Fulton?"

"No." Riley wasn't looking at her at the moment either.

"So—why?"

"I was afraid I'd say something I shouldn't—do something . . ."

"What's going on, Riley?"

"It's just, Mickey is nice—and her parents . . . her parents aren't."

Lily had already seen how Karen bowled over her daughter, but what did Riley know about Tad? Lily had first-

hand experience about how close Tad could come to violence. But he'd been just a kid then.

"Do they hurt her?"

"Mom, don't say anything! It'll make it worse for
Mickey."

Lily was going to ask how he happened to know so much
about Mickey, but there were more important issues at the
moment. "Her mom seems . . ."

"Blind and bossy." Riley finished for her. "She makes
Mickey feel like she's nothing."

For a second, Lily was so taken aback by her son's adult
insight that she couldn't say anything. Then she said, "I'm
sure she just wants Mickey—"

"To be just like her! And Mickey's so much *better* than
her."

Lily was beginning to see Mickey meant something to
Riley, more than a passing acquaintance. "What about her
dad?"

Riley shrugged.

Reaching across the table, she put a hand on his. "Tell
me."

He closed his eyes and shifted in his seat. "She says he
doesn't hit her very often."

"That's what she said?"

He nodded.

Lily fought the urge to run out the door and hunt that bastard down. But good sense grabbed hold. There were all
sorts of ways to interpret a statement like that. Lily didn't
approve of any hitting, but a child's interpretation could be
anything.

She moistened her lips and said, "The best thing you can
do for Mickey is listen. If she says anything else like that, I
want you to tell me."

Riley pulled his hand away and put it in his lap.

"Riley, I mean it. I promise not to make things worse for Mickey."

Keeping his gaze focused on his hands, he nodded.

Just then, Mildred brought the pancakes. Lily went through the motions of spreading butter and topping them with maple syrup, but she couldn't shove down a single bite.

The need for confrontation had gnawed Clay's bones until, in the middle of the night, he finally climbed on his motorcycle and headed north.

He now sat in the brown recliner in the small room at the rehab facility, rubbing his sleep-deprived eyes. The only other furniture was a twin-sized bed, a tiny bedside table made of wood-grain-covered particle board and a lamp that appeared to be a garage sale cast-off. There was no television, no telephone, no carpet. Off-white steel miniblinds covered the window that overlooked an asphalt parking lot with faded yellow space markings. The Sheldon Center was not at all the type of rehab facility in which he'd expect to find Peter Holt, heir to the Holt millions.

When he'd first pulled up to the place, he'd thought Samantha Holt had given him the name of the wrong treatment center. But a telephone call posing as Peter's father had confirmed that Peter was, in fact, a patient here.

As Clay sat there mulling the disparity of economic levels between the hospital and the man, something Lily had said came back to him. She and Peter had to sell the house when they divorced. He'd thought that it was simply to divide up the property, but perhaps it had been from financial need. Why else would the ex-wife of a Holt be driving something as ordinary as a used Toyota?

Peter worked for his father, and there was no doubt his

father had controlled Peter's finances when they were in college. Perhaps he held the purse strings to the family fortune close to his own chest. Peter would be dependent upon whatever salary his father deemed appropriate. And the divorce settlement would have been peanuts.

There was another thing of which Clay had no doubt; Bill and Samantha Holt would never, never subject their only child to alcohol rehab. They would bail him out, cover his tracks and make excuses until they were blue in the face. But they would never outwardly admit that Peter had a problem.

Clay was getting a clearer picture of Lily's current circumstances by the minute.

Footsteps stopped outside the door. The doorknob rattled, and Clay got to his feet. He put on a neutral expression and stood with his hands folded before him.

The door opened.

"Hello, Peter."

Peter, who was halfway through the door, literally jumped backward several inches. "Christ Almighty! Where in the hell did you come from?"

Clay considered it a rhetorical question. "It's been a long time."

Peter closed the door behind him and put on a nervous smile. His gaze shifted from place to place, looking everywhere but at Clay. Edginess tensed the muscles of his face. It was the same look Clay remembered from childhood when he'd been caught in a lie and was frantically looking for a way to slip out of it.

He finally said, "I'm not allowed to have visitors."

Clay gave him a chilly smile. "I won't be here long."

Peter's gray gaze slid like a drop of mercury around the room. "How'd you get in here?"

"I just put a few of my old talents to work. There aren't many places I can't get inside—if I have a mind to."

"Ah"—Peter nodded knowingly—"Luke said you were in some sort of special operations." Now he seemed to be regaining his footing. He continued on as if they'd run into each other on the street. "God, it has been years. Still in the service?"

"No."

The short answer seemed to make Peter more nervous. He stuck his hands in his pants pockets and rocked back on his heels. "What are you up to now, then? Where are you living?"

Clay didn't say anything for a long moment. Very quietly, and with clear meaning, he said, "I'm living in Glens Crossing."

Peter reacted as if Clay had slugged him in the stomach with a sandbag. He actually bent slightly at the middle. When Clay didn't say anything further, Peter's mouth opened and closed a couple of times. Then he recovered a bit. "You must have seen Lily, then."

Clay nodded. "Lily—and the boy."

It appeared as if someone had sucked all of the air out of Peter. He folded in on himself, skin against skin, leaving nothing but a wrinkled, one-dimensional husk. "Oh." He paused and staggered slightly to the side. Then he swallowed dryly. "I see."

Clay shut out the part of him that felt pity for Peter, his lifelong friend, a man whose weakness had been inbred. Clay had driven all night so he could ask the question face to face. "Why? Why did you do it, Peter?"

Suddenly Peter sprang back to his true form, his cheeks flooded with color. He took a step closer and pointed a finger at Clay's chest. "I suppose I could ask you the same question!"

Clay had been prepared for a litany of excuses, for profuse apologies, but not this counterattack. "What are you talking about?"

Peter's jaw set with a determination that Clay didn't recall ever seeing in his friend. "You knew I had feelings for Lily. A whole year before. . . . But you had to be the one. You had to show me up just one more time."

"What feelings? You neve—"

"Bullshit! Don't try to make me believe you hooked up with Lily that summer just out of the blue. And you snuck around about it! You were afraid I'd win, that she'd love *me* more. You always treated her like she was your special property."

Clay struggled to get some kind of bearing on this conversation. He felt like he'd charged up a hill with an automatic rifle to face an enemy and discovered it armed with pinwheels and peashooters. He was fully ready to take on a man, for a man's deceptions, only to find that Peter had reverted to adolescence. "Afraid she'd love you . . ." He pointed to the chair. "Sit down and explain to me exactly what you're talking about."

Peter stared at Clay for a moment, then sat down. Clay sat on the bed and clasped his hands, resting his elbows on his knees.

It took a few seconds, but Peter finally began to talk. "The day Luke left for the army we drove him to the airport, remember?"

Clay nodded.

"And Lily cried all of the way back to Glens Crossing. Everything was changing." He waved a hand in the air to emphasize the point. "And I told you that while you were inside the house and she and I were alone on the dock, I kissed her." Now his gaze honed sharply on Clay. "And you

told me I should back off. She was too young. It might ruin
a friendship she really needed right then. I had a girl in
Chicago . . . you came up with a million reasons."

Clay thought back to that night. He did remember Peter
telling him that he'd kissed Lily—and he also remembered
how vehemently he'd gone after him for it. At the time, he
believed all of those reasons he'd laid out to Peter. It was
only later that he realized that underneath all of those logical
reasons, he was jealous. Lily was his to protect, his to comfort—his to love.

Clay said, "Don't try and tell me you were in love with
Lily. You never mentioned anything about it again. And you
did have *three* girls at Northwestern. You could never keep
yourself to one at a time. You think that's what I wanted for
Lily?"

"Ahh! There it is!" Peter jumped to his feet. "What *you*
wanted for Lily! You always had to play the hero." He raised
his hands in the air. "Well, that time you finally screwed up,
buddy. I"—he thumped his chest—"was *there* for her." Then
he stuck a finger right in Clay's face and said, "You knocked
her up, then left her alone! *I* was the hero when it counted!
While you were off playing spy, I was raising *your* kid."

The room rocked to the side. Clay's heart shot into orbit.
He couldn't seem to pull any air into his lungs. "Riley is
*mine*?"

Peter once again looked like a cornered animal. He tried
to back away, but Clay shot off the bed and grabbed the front
of his shirt.

"Is he?" Clay's voice sounded more animal than human
through his clenched teeth.

Peter licked his lips and closed his eyes. "Oh, God. She
didn't tell you. . . ."

# Chapter 18

Clay let go of Peter's shirt as if it were suddenly contaminated with the plague. In doing so, he shoved Peter backward and Peter landed in the recliner.

Clay stood there, chest heaving, heart racing, staring at Peter for a long moment. He wanted to hit him. He wanted to rant and scream. He wanted to pull out his own hair. But he reined in his fury and finally asked, "You knew from the beginning?"

Peter nodded. "She called looking for you—after you'd . . . you were . . ." He shook his head. "I knew something was up, so I went down to Glens Crossing the next weekend."

"And she told you?"

Peter nodded again.

There was such a hurricane of emotions battering Clay's good sense, he didn't know if he could continue to contain himself. After making two complete circles around the room, he turned on Peter again. "You son of a bitch! You *knew* where I was—why didn't you tell her?"

Peter seemed to gather himself a bit. He stood and faced

Clay. "And what would you have had her do? Sit around Glens Crossing, pregnant and unmarried, waiting for you to get out of jail?" He paused. Then, in a voice Clay had heard Peter's father use time and again, he said, "It was the best thing."

That I-know-better-than-you tone ignited Clay's anger again. He raised his fist, but stopped short of throwing the punch. "Best for who?" His words ground out between clenched teeth.

"Don't get all holier-than-thou on me! Your dad had cut you off. You didn't have a job—you were in *jail,* for chris-sake! Lily needed someone to take care of her right then— not when you finally straightened out your life.

"So I did it. I took care of Lily. I took care of Riley." He straightened his shoulders and took a step back. "We are a *family,* and nothing will undo that."

Those words resonated in Clay's head. He'd thought the same thing the first moment he'd seen Peter and Lily with the baby stroller on that windy Chicago street. He'd thought it again weeks ago. No matter what separated Lily from Peter—divorce papers or a thousand miles—the two of them would always be bound together by that child. *His* child.

Clay blew out a long breath. "Who else knows?"

"That Riley isn't my biological child?" Peter shifted farther away from him. "No one."

"Bill and Samantha?"

"I said no one. Not my parents. Not Benny. Not Luke." He cut through the air with his index finger. "No one."

Clay didn't know if that made it better or worse. It certainly made it more complicated. Who would ever have questioned? He and Lily had been meeting in secret. Peter had been around the entire summer, too.

Peter was talking again. It took a moment for Clay to pull himself back to the conversation. "What?"

"Are you going to tell him?" Peter asked with his arms folded across his chest.

Clay didn't respond.

"It will hurt a lot of people. Especially Riley. You don't even know him—I've been his father since before he was born."

That tipped the scales—and totally pissed Clay off. "What's the matter, Peter? Afraid I'll steal them back?" He turned and walked out of the room.

Riley had gone for a walk. Lily was in the boathouse getting ready to work her new pottery design. She felt somewhat satisfied, thinking she now understood, at least in part, her son's mood of late. It was clear he cared about what happened to Mickey. But she didn't know exactly what she'd do if, at some point in the future, he came to her and said Tad was abusing the girl. That was very, very dangerous ground to walk. A child's interpretation of abuse could be totally skewed—any form of punishment might qualify. But Mickey didn't seem like the kind of child to exaggerate, or embellish a tale just for the attention.

Lily supposed she'd have to start with Karen. Maybe Karen suspected the very same thing and just hadn't been able to get Mickey to confide in her about it. As Lily thought of the way Karen treated her daughter, she couldn't blame Mickey for not sharing anything with her mother.

Maybe it was just teenage talk. Perhaps there wasn't anything of substance behind the words other than an adolescent cry for attention. But if there was a problem, Lily hoped nothing would happen while she and Riley were staying in Glens Crossing that would drag them into the middle of it.

As soon as that thought crossed her mind, Lily was ashamed. If Mickey needed help and had found a friend in Riley, then she should be hoping for exactly the opposite—something to happen while there was someone here she could turn to.

Lily tussled with her conscience as she plugged in the potter's wheel and slapped a blob of wet clay on it. She was just about to turn on the switch when she heard a voice.

"There you are! Been hollerin' and knockin' on the door for ten minutes."

Lily looked up to see Faye standing in the open double door, her red hair like a flaming halo with the backwash of the sun. She was dressed in lime green, with a shoulder bag and sandals of the same color. One hand tightly grasped the strap of the purse slung over her shoulder.

"Sorry, I didn't hear." Lily reached for a towel to wipe her hands. "Is everything all right?" She couldn't imagine what had brought Faye to her door.

"Well, no. It isn't." She tilted her head to the side and added in a conspiratorial tone, "You and I need to have a little heart-to-heart—without your daddy's big ears around."

Lily didn't think she wanted to hear anything Faye had to say; the very sound of the woman's voice put her on edge. But she could hardly shoo her away with flapping arms and loud noises the way she did the wayward geese that tried to nose their way into the boathouse.

"Would you like some coffee?" Lily made a gesture toward the house.

"Listen, now, you don't have to pretend. We both know we don't like each other." Lily opened her mouth out of polite habit to deny it, but Faye held up a hand to stop her. "Doesn't matter. Because we *do* both love your daddy."

"What's wrong with Dad?" Lily's heart sped up a bit.

"The doctor says it's just a warning—"

"What is?" Alarm prickled Lily's skin.

"Well, I'm trying to tell you." She stood there and gave Lily the same silent glare grade school teachers used when someone was talking out of turn. When she finally seemed satisfied that Lily wasn't going to interrupt, she went on. "He's been having this tightness in his chest"—Faye splayed her hand across her heart—"and some pain—"

"Heart attack! Dad's having a heart attack?" Lily headed toward the door. "Where is he?"

"Would you just put your interfering little tushie down on that chair and *listen* to what I have to say?"

Lily stopped and looked at Faye. Her panic subsided somewhat. After that scene at the hospital, Lily knew if Benny was in any danger, Faye would be hanging from the rafters, squawking like a crow.

Lily finally sat down, even though she didn't like the way Faye was talking to her. One battle at a time.

"Okay, tell me what's wrong with Dad."

"As I was trying to say"—she gifted Lily with one more pointed look—"he's been having this tightness in his chest, so I hauled his cranky backside to the doctor today. Oh, he didn't want to go—you know Benny. But I told him if he didn't, I was going to quit and leave him to run that damn *pub* by hisself." She paused, seeming to relish the drawing out of the story.

"The doctor said it was just a warning—called it an 'episode.' Your daddy's been under so much stress lately— with the fire, and now running this new kind of place. Of course, before this he didn't have a lick of debt, but now the bank is holding a big note—so that's weighing on him, too."

"You're trying to say it's *my* fault he's having heart trouble?" Lily asked, coming back to her feet.

"I'm not here to lay blame." She raised a hand, lowered her gaze, and turned her head slightly.

The look on her face told Lily that wasn't exactly true. As long as that blame could be laid at Lily's feet, she was certain it'd make Faye's day to put it there all tied up with a neat purple bow. Lily forced herself to remain quiet until Faye had said her piece. But her body was buzzing with the need to lash out, to defend herself.

Faye went on, "I'm just telling you what's happening. Benny's under a lot of stress, he worries about everybody. He knows if this business fails, Henry is going to be out of work—and we both know Henry's too old and too deaf to find a new job. He's concerned about Riley. . . . All I'm saying is that we all need to make sure we don't give him anything more to worry about right now."

"That's how you see me, someone who just causes Dad worry?"

"Now, don't go putting words in my mouth—"

"But that's it, isn't it? You don't like me taking any of his attention. That's why you've been so nasty to me." Lily found herself practically nose to nose with her. "I'm his *daughter*, for God's sake."

Faye's face hardened; her eyes glittered with anger. "You're his *grown* daughter. You haven't seen fit to show your face around here for years, left him here alone so you could live in the big city with your new rich family." She flung a well-manicured finger to the north. "You think that didn't hurt him?"

"But I always brought him up to see us—"

"Yeah, well, that's just nice." Sarcasm rang in her voice. "Too busy to pop in and see how *his life* is going, just drag him all over creation on the holidays when he wanted nothing more than to be at home.

"You leave here without a thought for him. But once you lose your rich family, here you come, dragging back here with a boy who's in trouble and no plan for your future. And if that wasn't enough to put on your daddy, you have to try and *change* what he is. Now that you're back in town, Benny and the Crossing House aren't good enough. No, you have to push him into changing. Now it's all on him. He has to make it work—or the bank will have everything."

"I never said the Crossing House wasn't good enough! That's not the way it is at all. And the changes in the business are *good*. Dad stands to make a lot more money and this town needed a place like the 'new' Crossing House."

Faye waved a hand in the air to dismiss her argument. "I'm sure we could stand here and chew on this all day—"

Lily stepped forward. "I don't want to 'chew on' it, I want you to finally admit that the changes to the business are *not* the disaster you predicted."

"That's not why I came here."

"Well, as long as you *are* here, let's just get this one point out of the way."

Faye cast a longing look at the lake, as if she were planning an escape. "All right! All right!" She threw her hands in the air. "Business is good." Her hands settled on her hips. "Can we get back to your daddy now?"

"Yes." Lily doused the spark of victory that wanted to ring out in her voice.

"I came to tell you it's time to put your daddy first. He can't keep workin' seven days a week and fretting over everybody's happiness."

"Dad cares about people, *lots* of people, not just me. There's no way you can stop him from worrying about other people."

"I know that! It's just some people are a lot closer to his heart, and that makes the burden of their problems heavier."

Most of what Faye said was true, albeit biased in the telling. Lily hadn't really thought about how it would affect her dad when she looked to him for help with Riley.

She ground her teeth together. The biting reality in Faye's words gnawed into her heart. But Faye was right, she was a grown woman who shouldn't be relying on her father to sort out her troubles.

"What do you want me to do?" Lily tried to sound receptive to suggestions, even though she wanted to knock Faye down on the ground and roll around in the dirt with her for a good round.

"I just want you to be aware — to keep from putting extra concern on his shoulders. I know you feel you need help with Riley, but Benny's raised his kids. He's earned a rest from that part of life."

Looking at things in that context, Lily felt like a failure not only as a daughter but as a mother as well. She'd be damned if she'd let Faye see it. "Maybe he could hire another bartender, shorten his hours, take a day off."

"He's already hired and fired two—nobody runs that bar to suit him. I'm thinkin' employees cause him more stress than they relieve. But he'll find the right combination eventually. We just have to help him all we can until then."

Lily simply nodded. "Did the doctor put him on medication?"

"An aspirin a day. Don't that beat all in this day of advanced medicine?"

"Maybe he should see a specialist. I can take him to Chicago—there's a wonderful heart hospital—"

"There you go again!" Faye threw her hands in the air.

"Runnin' your daddy's life. I think he and Dr. Shelley can decide when and if he needs to see a specialist."

She was turning Lily's good intentions against her. "I just want to make sure he's well cared for."

Faye narrowed her gaze and looked at Lily from the corner of her eye. "So do I, sugar. So do I."

"I'll get cleaned up and go see him." Lily moved to close up the boathouse.

"I think it'd be better if you didn't. He didn't want you to know, said you have way too much on your hands at the moment to be worrying about him."

Lily felt like an interloper. She'd come home only to discover the fabric of her father's life had simply rewoven the hole she'd left. For the briefest second she truly hated Faye. Which just confirmed that Faye was right, she was putting her feelings before her father's.

Apparently Faye had said her piece. She turned and walked back toward the house. As she did, she said, "We just have to help him, without him knowing he's being helped."

Lily stood there, blinking in the sun, until Faye disappeared around the house. She forced the anger away. Faye thought Lily wanted the changes in the Crossing House for her own selfish reasons. Clay had said much the same. She tried to see clearly into her own heart.

The new Crossing House was busy; the town seemed to like the changes. But she had to ask herself, was her dad happier? From what Faye had said, the answer to that was resoundingly clear.

Faye had made her feel like a criminal for wanting to take him to a specialist. Lily just wanted what was best for her dad.

What followed on the heels of that thought made Lily's stomach roll. She was starting down the same road with her dad that Peter's parents had done with Peter and Riley. Thinking she knew the best course, she'd pushed until that path had been followed. But, she thought, her dad seemed happy about the renovations to the Crossing House.

Faye's unbidden voice rose in her head, *He's happy because it pleases you.*

She recalled the defeated way he'd looked that first day when he returned to the Crossing House after the fire. That place was his whole life. He liked it just the way it was—it had been *comfortable* for him.

Now it was a burden.

Shame flushed her cheeks.

Good intentions aside, Lily had to admit, maybe she'd made a mistake.


Riley had just about been ready to give up on the idea that Mickey would show up when she walked into the clearing. He'd been hanging around the place where they'd spent that first day together, reading his book. Well, he was trying to read. But every time he heard a chipmunk in the brush or a bird in the trees, his gaze shot immediately to the path.

"Hi," he said, now not at all certain why he'd been so anxious for her to arrive.

"Hi, Goofy." She walked over to where she kept her blanket stashed. "How come you're not using this?" she asked, as she pulled it from the black garbage bag.

Riley lifted a shoulder. "Forgot about it." Which, of course, wasn't at all true. He just felt like he was trespassing, using her stuff when she wasn't around.

Mickey spent a few minutes getting herself situated, then she said, "You can sit with me, there's plenty of room."

She leaned her back against a tree and opened her book.

Since she wasn't making a big deal about it, Riley got up and moved to the blanket. He laid on his stomach and opened his book to the same page he'd been trying to read for the past half hour. But the same question that had been plaguing him since he got here kept running in circles in his mind: Did Mickey know her dad was a dealer?

He looked at her from the corner of his eye. Her hair hid most of her face as she read. He wished she'd look up so he could see her eyes, just for a minute. It seemed like if a person was carrying that kind of secret, if you looked closely enough you should be able to see it in her eyes.

She kept reading.

Finally, he gave up and closed his book. Rolling onto his back, he looked into the treetops. He laced his fingers over his chest and decided he was just going to have to start asking questions.

He turned his head her way and asked, "Do you eat breakfast with your dad every day?" Of course, he doubted it. Mickey had looked too uncomfortable sitting across from her dad in that booth at the Dew Drop.

She took a minute, looking like she was finishing reading a sentence, then she raised her eyes to meet his. Riley suddenly didn't want to look into her eyes, for secrets or anything else. He looked back into the trees.

"No. I think he's feeling guilty," she said.

Riley's heart sped up, but he didn't look at her. "Guilty? About what?"

Mickey sighed. It was a sound filled with sadness. "I guess because he spends so much time with my brother. I heard Mom saying some stuff about it to him on the phone the other night."

That wasn't the kind of guilt Riley had been anticipating.

Mickey went on, "I don't mind that he spends more time with Drew. Dad and I don't have much to talk about."

Riley could relate to that. He and his dad, although they spent plenty of time together, never seemed to have the same idea about anything. Dad just couldn't understand why Riley questioned all of the rules, wanted an explanation for everything. But it seemed stupid to just follow along because somebody at some point in time decided that was the way it was going to be. A person should think about what he's doing, understand why things work the way they do.

He was getting off track. "What does your dad do—for work, I mean?"

"He's a salesman for Burkhardt Chevrolet. He told me that's how he got such an expensive car. He gets a deal."

"Oh, yeah?" Riley rolled onto his side and propped his head on his hand. "What's he drive?"

Mickey swatted a fly away. "Some Corvette."

How could girls do it? "*Some Corvette,*" like they're all alike and the details didn't matter. "What year?"

She shrugged. "Pretty new. It's black."

Black. Again with the girly particulars.

"Convertible or hard top?" Was he going to have to drag it out one bit at a time? With his buddies, he'd have had everything by now, horsepower, engine size, options—how often it was waxed.

"Convertible."

"Man, I wish my dad drove a car like that."

Mickey asked, "What does your dad drive?"

Riley shook his head. "Boring BMW—just like everybody else."

Mickey laughed. "Like everybody else! I don't think there's even one of those in Glens Crossing."

"Where I come from, they're everywhere. Everybody

drives the same car, everybody wears the same clothes, everybody listens to the same music, everybody goes to the same golf club. It's like they're afraid to be different."

Mickey seemed to think about that for a second. "Hmmm, I don't think I'd like that. I'd probably stick out more there than I do here."

He wanted to assure her she stuck out for all of the right reasons, but he just said, "It's boring. Real boring."

"Well, I think it's boring around here."

"It's not the same kind of boring." Suddenly it all became so clear to him. Why hadn't he seen it before? "There it's the kind of boring that makes you itch, makes you feel like you have to do *something* just to prove to yourself you're not exactly the same as everyone else, just so you know you *can* be different."

"Is that why you blew up the bathroom at your school?" Mickey asked as easily as if she were asking him if he preferred basketball or football.

"It was only the toilets, not the whole bathroom. And how did you know about that?"

"Things get around." She paused, then she asked with a giggle, "Is it true that a teacher was on one of those toilets?"

Riley rolled his eyes. "Don't be ridiculous. Who said that?"

"I don't remember, I heard it somewhere. You can never believe half of what you hear around this town."

That brought Riley's original question rushing back. Did she know her dad sold weed? Or maybe, he thought, that was one of those things that had been growing with each telling—like a teacher on the toilet. How could anybody even believe such a thing? Maybe her dad wasn't a dealer at all.

"How come you're not at the marina?" she asked, pulling him from his current dilemma.

"Marina's closed. Bud had to leave town for something."

"I've got some money, wanna go get ice cream?"

"Sure." He helped her fold the blanket and they headed out on the path that led to Mill Run Road.

About halfway to the Arctic Express, a car passed, then slowed to a stop. Riley watched nervously as its reverse lights came on and it began to back up toward them.

"Oh, brother," Mickey said with disappointment in her voice.

"What?"

"Ryan Thompson and Matt Roberts. Trouble on wheels."

When the car backed alongside of them, Riley saw it was the two guys from the arcade. "Hey," he said, and stepped closer to the passenger door.

"Dude, you need a ride?"

Riley noticed that Mickey hadn't come any nearer to the car. "Nah, thanks. What are you guys up to?"

"We're lookin' to hook up with a little entertainment later tonight. Care to join us?" The one in the passenger seat looked past Riley's shoulder. "But you can't bring her. T-man won't have any of that."

"When and where?" Riley asked.

"We can pick you up."

"I'm gonna be out, I'll just meet you. Where?"

"Well, T-man likes to do his business at the park. Meet us at the gate at eight."

"I'll see what I can do." He stepped away from the car. "Later."

The engine revved a couple of times, then the car peeled away, leaving behind the stink of hot rubber.

"Morons," Mickey said as she waved the smoke away from her face. "What'd they want?"

"Nothin'. I just talked to them the other night after you went home."

She looked into his eyes and touched his arm. "Those guys are up to no good. You'd be better off to stay away from them."

The seriousness and honesty he saw in her eyes made him shift his feet. "No problem."

For the rest of the walk to the Arctic Express, Riley was mulling over how he was going to get out of the house tonight.

# Chapter 19

After Faye left, Lily felt like all of her creativity had been sucked into a red and green whirlwind and carried away. She wrapped the potter's clay in plastic and closed up the boat-house. She'd just gotten out of the shower when she heard Riley come in. She looked at her watch and was surprised to find it was after two.

She'd planned a late lunch due to the fact that Riley had already had two breakfasts. He was in his room when she came out of the bathroom. She called through his door, "Ready for lunch?"

He grunted a positive response; she went to the kitchen and made sandwiches. It was too nice to be inside, so she called Riley down and took lunch on a tray out to the dock. She'd pulled the Adirondack chairs out to the end of the dock, so she could sit in the evenings. Riley rarely joined her.

Just when she was ready to call him again through the open windows, he came out the back door and down the steps.

"It's hot, why are we eating out here?"

"It's not hot. It's a pleasant summer day. The sun on your skin will help build vitamin D."

"Really, Mom . . ." He sounded exasperated, but had a smile on his face.

"Really. It's essential for good bone growth."

"I'd rather eat in the shade."

"Too bad."

He shook his head and sat down.

About halfway through his sandwich he said, "This morning I ran into some of the guys I met at the arcade."

"Really? Out here by the lake?"

He nodded. "They asked me to come to the arcade again tonight."

Lily's first instinct was to say no, absolutely not on a work night. But she knew from experience that only led to a bullheaded confrontation, so she asked a few questions first. "Who are these boys?"

"Ryan and Matt."

"Do they have last names?"

Riley set his jaw and blew out a long breath. "Yes, I'm sure they have last names—I just can't remember what they are."

"How old are they?"

He shrugged. "Dunno. I guess around my age."

Lily didn't like the way he wasn't looking at her when he answered these very basic questions. "I don't know that it's a good idea to get in the habit of going there and hanging out on a weeknight—when you have to work so early the next morning."

"Geez, Mom. It's not like I go to bed before eleven anyhow."

She sat there and pretended to be mulling it over. No way was she letting him out on a weeknight, especially with kids who only had first names and indefinite ages. Although he seemed to be making progress, she just couldn't trust him that far yet.

"Oh, Riley, I don't think so. Maybe you can invite them over here tomorrow night for a cookout. I'll do those baked beans you like." Better to put names and faces together before she let Riley stray too far with them.

He got up out of his chair with a jerk. "Never mind. I knew you wouldn't let me." His footfalls on the dock were so hard on his way back to land that Lily felt them vibrate her chair.

"Yeah," she said under her breath. "I'm a regular killjoy. Ruin everything. Just ask Gramps."

The taciturn teenager Lily expected to be dining with didn't show up. Riley was quiet but polite when he came down for dinner—not at all the brooding, resentful boy she'd anticipated seeing. He even offered to clean up the dishes by himself.

Lily was pleased and allowed herself to bask, ever so briefly, in the warmth of relief. Not everything she had done since she left Chicago had turned to shit. Even if she'd screwed up with her dad, this summer was beginning to do exactly what she'd hoped for her son. His temper had calmed, his mood swings had mellowed and he seemed to be accepting responsibility both at work and at home.

She considered telling him she'd changed her mind about the arcade, but she didn't want to send the wrong message there, either: Behave like a model child for ten minutes and you can immediately get what you couldn't by throwing a fit. She'd just wait and see. If over the next few days his positive attitude continued, she'd grant him extra privileges.

Riley went up to his room early to read, saying he was

almost finished with *The Lord of the Rings*. Lily was impressed—that was one thick novel for a kid who had to be forced at gunpoint to read the novels assigned at school.

After he went upstairs, she went out to sit in one of the chairs on the dock and watch the sky darken. She stretched her legs in front of her, crossing her ankles. Leaning her head against the tall slatted back of the chair, she let herself become hypnotized by the slow and subtle transformation of color as the sun slipped farther below the horizon. By concentrating on the changing sky, she could keep Faye's accusations and decisions about Riley at bay—at least until it became dark. Once full darkness fell, she always had a difficult time ignoring the monsters under the bed.

The heavens took on the magnificent purple of twilight and Lily saw lights come on in the few houses nestled in the trees across the lake. The rosebush at the side of the boathouse perfumed the warm air. Somewhere someone had started a wood fire. She breathed in the scent of summer nights from her youth. Timeless fragrances that instantly drew images of bonfires and lakeshore gatherings, games played by restless teens and the warm security of having Luke and Peter and Clay nearby.

A dog was barking, the sound echoing across the water. Lily felt more at home than she had anywhere in the past fourteen years. And that surprised her.

From the moment she'd married Peter, she'd felt like a visitor, a displaced person taking up residence with a charitable family, a poor relative to be tolerated but never fully expected to fit in. She'd waged an active battle against her sense of dislocation for years. She redecorated the house Peter's parents had bought and were reselling to them, but it didn't make it feel any more her own. She hosted holiday dinners and brought her dad to visit. Still, the feeling lingered behind each opened gift and every dirty dish. Branching out beyond her household, she joined in community activities—of course, they weren't activities Samantha approved of; Lily spent her time working with illiteracy programs and teaching pottery classes to inner city kids. However, nothing gave her the settled peace she was looking for. She hadn't imagined she'd find it right back where she started, in the place she'd so willingly left behind.

She heard a footfall on the dock. Sitting up, she turned in her seat and looked over her shoulder, fully expecting to see Riley.

The broad-shouldered dark silhouette standing at the shore end of the dock was certainly not her son. It was a man. His form was backlit by the soft yellow light from the kitchen window. He wasn't moving, just standing there with his hands in his pockets.

The image of the single rose on her pillow flashed through her mind—a mystery not yet solved.

"Hello?" she said, rising to her feet.

The man walked slowly toward her.

Just when she was ready to start making some real noise, she recognized him.

"Are you trying to give me heart failure?" she said.

Clay didn't say anything, just kept his slow, steady pace toward her. When she saw the tense way he moved, memory came crashing back. He was furious. He rarely lost his temper. Never could she remember hearing him yell, but holding that anger in restraint took all of his strength and it resonated in each and every muscle.

"What's happened?" The words fell from her lips without thought.

He stopped in front of her, but didn't say anything. His

gaze held her as immobile as if he'd had his hands clamped on her shoulders.

"Clay, you're scaring me. What's wrong?" She reached out and put a hand on his arm. He jerked away as if she'd burned him with her touch.

"You weren't ever going to tell me." The words came slowly, as if he had to force each one from his throat.

Lily flashed hot all over. He couldn't know. No one knew. Her own father didn't know. The only one . . .

She closed her eyes and the dock seemed to rock wildly beneath her feet. An iron band clamped around her chest, making it impossible to breathe. The evening grayed more deeply than was natural. Teetering slightly, she grabbed for the closest thing to steady herself—Clay's arm.

This time he didn't pull away, nor did he offer further assistance. Lily clung to the rock-hard muscle in his forearm, wanting nothing more than to dissolve into liquid and flow through the planking of the dock.

She forced her eyes open but couldn't bring herself to look into Clay's. She focused on his chest instead. "You went to see Peter?"

He nodded once.

Lily's heartbeat thundered in her ears. Her mind scrambled wildly for direction. "Why? What good could possibly come of it?"

He did yank his arm away then, ignoring her question and leaving her adrift in a sea of uncertainty. This was the moment she'd never thought would come. Clay had been gone for fourteen years, allowing her to put even the shadow of a possibility of dealing with this scenario out of her mind. And even after she had seen him again, there was little danger. Peter was locked safely in rehab two hundred and fifty miles away. She would be gone from Glens Crossing by the end of the summer. There was no way this should have happened.

But Clay had gone to see Peter. Had there been an ugly confrontation? Or had they discussed things like calm adults, each laying his cards on the table? The strained feel of Clay's muscle under her hand told her it had been an emotional meeting. She wondered if Peter had explained why he'd neglected to give Lily Clay's message, why he hadn't told her where Clay was when he so obviously knew. She desperately wanted the answers. But she didn't want to ask. All she could do was stand in the red cloud of Clay's fury and wait.

He spun around and walked in a tight circle on the dock. His hand massaged the back of his neck as if working out a cramp.

If he didn't say something soon, Lily was going to faint from holding her breath. She wouldn't, she couldn't, be the one to speak next.

On his third tight revolution around a spot on the dock only he could see, he stopped and faced her again. His jaw flexed rhythmically, his mouth was drawn into a tense line. Then he said, "What good could come of it? Considering your current position, I guess that question is reasonable. Weeks and weeks have gone by and you never hinted . . . I guess you're right, what good could it do *you*?"

"What good could it do *anyone*? Right now, I can't see a single shred of good come of it. Can you say you're better off now than you were yesterday?" She paused, but not long enough for him to respond. "No! This has just raised more misery."

He stared hard at her. For a moment she thought he was going to explode into violence. Then she heard him suck in a deep breath and let it out in quivering bursts. "Misery for who?"

"Look at us! Yes, all four of us have been robbed of what should have been. But just maybe we're better off for it."

"Better off!" He barked out a sharp crack of mirthless laughter. "Peter's an alcoholic. The kid is two steps away from getting thrown in jail. You're continually running away—"

"I'm not running away!"

"Really? The way I see it, that's *all* you've done." He let that remark hang in the air for a moment. "You ran away from this town. You ran away from your marriage. You thought you could run away from Riley's troubles. You're trying to run away from your past by changing your dad." He paused, then said with darkness in his voice, "But worst of all, you ran away from your faith in me—in what we had together."

"Ohhh, that's not fair," she said in a low tone. "You were gone! I had to make a decision, and I had to make it quickly. I did what I thought was best—it turns out it *was* best. You were in jail. I couldn't stay here and cause Dad and Molly more embarrassment. Just what would you have had me do?"

He shook his head and moved closer. "I'm not talking about *then*." He pointed a finger behind him. "I'm talking about *now*." He jerked his finger in front of him and pointed at the ground. "This summer. Here, in Glens Crossing. You've lied to me every day since you came back by keeping this from me. Even after you knew I didn't leave you of my own free will."

"Oh, my God! When do you think I should have told you? The first day at the marina? Or maybe after Riley repeatedly cried himself to sleep because of your harsh treatment? Or perhaps after you made love to me, then treated me like I carried a contagious disease for two weeks after?"

"Stop looking for excuses."

"I don't need excuses. I have valid, concrete, legitimate *reasons*." She punctuated each word by slapping the back of one hand against the palm of the other. "And none of them have anything to do with running away. Riley is in a terrible place right now, trying to see his way through some really difficult times. He loves Peter as his father. Should I upset his entire world, just so you're in on the biological reality of his being?

"And what about Peter? He's in such a precarious emotional state right now. Riley is his son, in every way but one. Riley is Bill and Samantha's only grandchild. And Dad? Do you know what dragging all of this out now will do to him?

"And, honestly, up until this moment, I thought *you* were better off not knowing. You can barely stand to be in the same room as Riley. You don't even want children." She stopped and drew a breath. "No one knows, Clay. No one has to know. It's better left alone. I made that decision a long time ago. It's too late to undo it."

He advanced on her, anger glittering in his eyes. "It's never too late for the truth!"

Lily felt what was left of her world crumble beneath her feet. She barely found the breath to form the words, "Are you going to tell him?"

"Funny," Clay said, in a tone that held absolutely no humor, "Peter asked the same question."

Standing her ground, she made herself press on. "Are you?"

"I haven't made up my mind yet."

Lily felt a touch of relief. At least he wasn't going to bull into the house this very minute, shouting it as he ran up the stairs.

"Where is he?" Clay asked.

That relief evaporated. "Why?"

"Don't sound so scared. I said I haven't made up my mind."

She swallowed. "He's in his room."

He stood there for a minute and Lily futilely searched for the right words to make him see reason.

He said, "I thought you and I had a second chance." His hard gaze held her until she nearly flinched. "I couldn't have been more wrong."

He turned around and stalked back toward land.

It took all of her willpower to not go after him. Pleading would do no good. He'd been blindsided. Why wouldn't he be angry? She needed time to formulate an approach that would ensure a positive outcome.

She'd been so certain it was best for Clay not to know. She'd made that decision after she saw what a changed man he was; she'd done it alone—and maybe that wasn't fair. Maybe Clay had the right to know, whether he wanted to be a parent or not.

She still couldn't understand why Peter had told him. Was it in a fit of one-upsmanship? Had he even considered the fallout it would cause—not just with Riley, but with Bill and Samantha? She and Peter had decided long ago that *no one* would ever know. Peter's name was on the birth certificate; there was no way for anyone to discover otherwise.

She felt like throwing herself in the lake. There was no way she and Clay could get beyond this. But an even greater concern was her son—their son. If Clay insisted on telling him, how would Riley react?

Well, she just couldn't let that happen. She had to make Clay see.

Her first instinct was to go to her dad. He'd be disappointed in her not being honest with him from the beginning, but . . .

Faye's accusations came crashing back.

Things were one huge mess—but she was going to have to find her way through on her own.

Lily sat in the darkness, listening to the gentle lap of the water against the deck pilings. She took herself back in time, to the moment when she'd made the decision that set the course for her life—for Riley's life.

At the time, Peter's motivations seemed noble and born of love. She tried to recall exactly how things had progressed that fall.

She had waited two weeks after her fight with Clay. By then her anger had cooled. If Clay was ever going to get over it, his anger should have calmed too. She called him at the apartment he shared with Peter. A stranger answered the phone. There had been a lot of noise in the background, like a party. She asked for Clay. The stranger had told her Clay had left school. Then she'd asked for Peter, but Peter had gone to the liquor store.

After hanging up the phone, Lily had gone to the bathroom and thrown up. Clay had left school. But he hadn't made any effort to contact her.

Over the next week, her nausea came more regularly. She was late enough with her period that she was fairly certain she was pregnant. The more she tried not to think about it, the more it dominated her thoughts. Panic inched ever closer, threatening to take over altogether.

Finally, she tried to reach Clay through his dad. In such

an impersonal tone that it seemed he was discussing a stranger, Douglas Winters confirmed that his son was gone. He had no idea where, nor did he care to know. When Lily pushed, Mr. Winters said that Clay would not be returning— ever. Then he told her not to call again and hung up the phone.

Panic did overtake her then, covering her like a flaming blanket. Clay was gone. She was pregnant. What was she going to do?

Three days later she finally spoke to Peter, hoping against hope that he knew where Clay had gone. When Peter confirmed that Clay had indeed moved out of the apartment, she couldn't keep a choked sob from escaping. When he pressed for answers, she took the Douglas Winters approach and hung up the phone.

Peter showed up in Glens Crossing the next weekend. He was concerned and attentive, making her see what a good friend she had in him. Saturday night he took her to Arctic Express for a hamburger. On the way home, she had to have him stop the car so she could throw up in the bushes. His concern had been like salve to a stinging burn. He took care of her, and later that night she confided in him that she was pregnant.

Peter wasn't in the least judgmental. He held her while she cried, murmuring reassuring things over and over, until she began to feel she might have the strength to withstand what lay ahead.

She loved him for his friendship. She loved him for his lack of condemnation. But most of all, she loved him because he cared enough to let his own life slide by while he helped settle hers.

He missed the next week of school, refusing to leave her to deal with this on her own. During those days, she and

Peter sat out at his parents' lake house, talking the time away. She got a strong sense that Peter truly cared for her—not just as a friend. But that just made things too complicated to even think about, so she tried to ignore the closeness that was growing between them.

Late in that week, she told him she'd made a decision. She was leaving Glens Crossing. She'd go someplace where no one knew her and find a job, start a life. No one here had to know about the baby. Her family had already endured one scandal. She didn't want to be the source of more pain for her father. And the embarrassment to Molly would be horrible. Plus, Molly wanted to be a doctor—and to do that, she was going to need a scholarship. Many of those scholarships were awarded by local people. Lily couldn't risk staying here and interfering with Molly's chances.

Immediately Peter said he had a much better solution. He admitted he was in love with her and asked her to marry him.

She refused with tears in her eyes. She told him that she *did* love him—but she wasn't *in love* with him. And there was no way she could ask him to settle for that. But Peter hadn't been the least deterred. He'd been persistent with his arguments and persuasions. By the next Monday, he had nearly convinced her that they could make a life together, could be a family.

Lily had begun to see that maybe *loving* someone was enough. Being "in love" hadn't held her parents' marriage together—hadn't kept Clay by her side. Maybe the quiet kind of love was safest and the strongest.

Peter had never once suggested she abort the pregnancy. And for that she would be ever grateful. It's not that she hadn't considered it. She had. It was something that had gone around and around in her head for days on end. She was mad as hell at Clay. She was furious with herself. But this baby was innocent. The pros and cons had warred in her heart until she thought she'd lose her mind. But, in the end, Peter had saved her from having to make that choice.

She didn't know if she could ever forgive him for not telling her where Clay was that fall. Had she known, she would have turned Peter down and waited for Clay. Then would Riley have been better off?

At this point, she could only speculate. But she felt in her heart, even though he was going through some difficult times now, Riley had a better start than he would have had being born to a single mother and a father in jail.

At nine o'clock, she decided to take a hot shower to try to ease some of her tension. As she went into the bathroom, she saw Riley's light was already out. So much for all that talk about not going to bed until eleven.

The heat and steam did little to chase the knots out of her muscles. The more she tried not to think about the things Clay had said, the louder they resonated in her head. She pushed away the hurtful words he'd flung at her, grasping on to the main reason for her concern, the single thing she had a modicum of control over. How was she going to make sure he didn't tell Riley?

She assured herself, had Clay been bound to behave recklessly, he'd have insisted on seeing Riley right away, laying the truth out before the child without a thought for his wellbeing. He hadn't done that. And the longer she could hold him off, the better her chances were of making him understand why it was so much better to leave things alone.

There was a part of her that felt sorry for Clay's loss, for all he had missed. But fate had dealt them a crappy hand,

and she had to play her cards to the best advantage for her child. Clay would see that.

Her skin was reddened from the hot water when she toweled off. Before she reached the bedroom door, the telephone rang. The shrill sound coming from her robe pocket made her jump. She quickly pulled it out and answered it before it woke Riley.

"Hello." She went into her bedroom and closed the door.

"I thought you said Riley was in his room," Clay said sharply.

She was in no mood to go another round with him tonight. Her voice was as tight as her shoulders when she said, "He is."

"Go look."

"Really, Clay—"

"Do it. I'll wait." Something in his tone made her relent. It wasn't anger, it was something much closer to dread.

"All right."

She put the phone down on the bed and went to Riley's door. After knocking softly, she eased it open. There was her son, right where he should be, under the sheets, curled on his side with his face to the wall. She went back to the phone.

"I just looked in. He's there."

There was a pause. "He's not there. I just saw him."

"Dammit, Clay, I said he's there. Goodnight!" She punched the off button.

After a second, she started to doubt herself. She'd just go take another look. It was ridiculous, but she'd rest better being certain. Here Clay was, hours into fatherhood, and already rocking the boat.

She looked into Riley's room again, this time turning on the hall light and opening the door wide enough to let it fall across his bed.

He was so still.

She stepped into the room. When she laid her hand on his shoulder, a spear of ice-cold fear shot through her. It wasn't Riley, it was pillows. The oldest teenage trick in the book.

She ran back to her bedroom. She had to call Clay, find out where he'd seen him.

Before she could pick up the phone again, it rang. "Riley?"

"I figured you'd check again. You're one damn stubborn woman."

"Where is he?"

"I'll bring him home."

"No—"

He hung up.

Lily's heart lodged in her throat.

Would Riley come along? Or would he put up a fight?

And might Clay deem this the proper opportunity to spill his guts?

She threw on some clothes, then began to pace the front porch.

# Chapter 20

An hour passed. Riley couldn't have been that far from home. Something terrible was happening, and all Lily could do was pace around on her front porch with a death grip on the cordless phone.

As the hour-and-a-half mark approached, Lily saw headlights coming up the drive. She hurried down the steps and met Clay's truck in front of the house, squinting against the glare of the headlights.

The passenger door opened before the truck stopped rolling. Riley got out. He slammed the door and stalked around the truck, right past her and up the porch steps.

As he passed, Lily got the definite scent of marijuana.

"Riley!"

He went inside and the screen door snapped shut behind him.

Suddenly she wished this had been a case of simple disobedience, of leaving the house without permission. It made her heart ache and her temper snap to realize Riley had been out breaking the law. All of his progress had been a figment of her longing imagination.

In a red cloud of anger and frustration, Lily started after him.

Clay must have sprung from the truck like a big cat, because before she made it to the steps, he clamped a hand on her arm. "Don't."

She jerked her arm to free herself, but he held tight. "Let me go."

He didn't release her. "Just wait a minute—"

Setting her jaw and dragging in a deep breath of dread, she turned and asked him, "Did you tell him?"

There was a flash in Clay's eyes that told her she'd wounded him. "No."

"Then where in the hell have you two been?"

"It took me a while to find him. When I did . . ." He looked over her shoulder toward the house.

"I smelled it on him. Where was he?" The relief valve on her anger was leaking. Her voice rose to a near shout. "And where did he *get* the stuff?"

"Hey!" He let go of her arm. "Don't look at me like *I'm* responsible! I just found the kid."

Lily closed her eyes and ordered herself to calm down. Opening them, she tried to coax civility into her voice. "Where was he?"

"In the park, in a car with a couple of older kids. That's why it took me so long to find him, they'd parked behind a thick stand of shrubs."

"An hour and a half? The park's not that big!"

"When I reached in and hauled him out of the back seat of the car, his buddies started the engine and took off. Once I got him to stop swinging at me, we spent some time discussing—actually I talked, he sulked—how some people who say they're your friends, aren't. How some people can't be trusted, no matter how close you think you are."

Lily wanted to slap him. Instead, she turned around and walked to the front door.

"Don't do it, Lily."

"Do what?" she asked without turning around.

"He's the one who's in the wrong. *He* should come to you."

"Well, thank you, *Dr. Phil*," she said as she turned to face him. "I suppose you're just full of parental advice, now that you know."

"Knowing changed everything."

She stepped closer to him. "Knowing changes *nothing!*" The last word came from between clenched teeth and she slashed her index finger through the air for emphasis. "Mind your own damn business." She punctuated each word with a poke in his chest.

Leaning down into her face, he said, "If I decide to make it so, that boy *is* my business."

"Don't you lord that threat over me. And don't act like you're suddenly full of concern for Riley. If you really cared about him, you wouldn't threaten to use him as a tool to hurt me."

She spun around and stormed up the steps. Once inside, she closed the door and threw the deadbolt, as if she could lock all of her uncertainties out in the dark night along with Clay Winters.

Leaning against the door, she waited to hear his truck start. Several minutes passed and it remained eerily silent outside. She turned out the living room light and eased to the window. Looking out, she saw Clay sitting in his truck with the door open, his wrists on top of the steering wheel, his face lowered onto his outstretched arms.

She knew her hostility only served to inflame the situation between them. She'd have to deal with him sooner or later, and do it in a fashion that ensured he wouldn't hurt her son. She certainly didn't want to goad him into telling Riley the truth simply to spite her.

However, her immediate problem was dealing with Riley's most recent fall from grace. Clay was just going to have to wait his own damn turn.

After locking the back door and closing the first-floor windows, Lily headed upstairs. She went to Riley's closed bedroom door and stopped with her hand raised to knock.

Listening carefully, she heard a sniffle. She bit her lower lip.

Maybe it *would* be more productive to wait, see what Riley would do if she didn't insist on having it out right here and now.

She always felt like she had to meet these things head-on, deal immediately, let him know exactly how he'd screwed up and what the consequences were.

*Yeah, and so far that's produced stellar results.*

It really pissed her off to think Clay might actually have a valid point.

She turned around and walked slowly to her bedroom, feeling drained and defeated. Everything she'd been doing—with her dad, with Riley, and obviously with Peter—seemed to have been wrong. Every effort had made things worse. She only hoped she could manage better in dealing with Clay and the whole paternity issue. God, if she didn't . . .

And there was still the nagging worry that the pregnancy test had been wrong. She still hadn't started her period.

She laid down on her bed with her clothes on, leaving the bedroom door open in case Riley tried to sneak back out.

How had her relationship with her son been reduced to that of jailer?

It took all of her willpower not to get up and walk down that hallway.

Lily dreamed she was in the fire tower.

The legendary ghost played a hauntingly sad melody on his fiddle, endlessly searching for the spirit of his lover. The strains wrapped around her, lifted her up until she hovered near the stars.

Suddenly Clay was there beside her, wrapped in the starry night. They tumbled back to earth together, locked in a kiss.

They spent the rest of the night in the tower, making love with their young bodies, promising devotion with their inexperienced hearts.

The pink sky of dawn awakened them. And with the new day, Clay was different, distant—a stranger. When Lily turned around from gathering her clothes, he was gone. Other than the faint scent of his cologne clinging to her skin, he'd left no trace of his presence.

A hollow ache started in her chest. Suddenly she was cold, so very cold.

Then, as she looked out over the rolling woodlands, she spotted smoke. She tried to use her cell phone to call the fire department, but the battery was dead.

Riley was playing somewhere out in the woods. She called his name, only to be answered by a fading echo. She yelled for Clay, but got no response.

She had to get her son to safety before the fire overtook the whole forest. Spinning around, her heart thundering in her chest, fear gripping her insides, she started for the stairs. When she looked down the long zigzag of steps, her head spun wildly, her eyes lost focus and she faltered. The distance between her and the ground seemed to grow.

Grabbing the rail, she forced herself to start down. It was hard to keep her balance; her depth perception seemed askew, each step impossible to gauge. Several times she stumbled, catching herself just before she pitched over the rail into empty space. Even as she forced her limbs to move faster, she seemed to be losing ground.

Taking one panicked look over her shoulder, she saw hungry yellow flames consuming the trees, the area of the fire spreading as quickly as spilled paint.

As she took the next step, it fell away from under her foot. She threw her weight backward, saving herself from a long fall. But as she watched, each tread between her and the ground so very far below crumbled and fell away.

Having no other option, she ran back to the observation deck. She cupped her hands around her mouth and screamed her son's name.

"Mom!" A hand was shaking her. "Mom! Wake up!"

With an indrawn gasp, she sat up.

Riley stood beside the bed looking frightened.

"I'm okay," she said thickly, pushing her hair away from her face. "Just a dream." He straightened and she realized he was dressed. "What time is it?"

"Six-thirty. Do I have to go to work today?"

Her world began to come back into focus—with all of its current problems. "Yes. But that's all you'll be doing."

"Bud—I don't want to see him. He was so . . . so—"

"Bud is *not* the problem. This is your own doing. In fact, you're very lucky it was Bud and not Sheriff Clyde who found you last night."

His lips pressed together, his spine stiffened. Lily prepared herself for the excuses and the promises to do better.

Instead, he sat on the bed beside her, his back collapsing

like a rag doll's. He buried his face in his hands. He looked too weary to be thirteen, too defeated to have lived such a short life.

Lily fisted her own hands to keep from reaching out and comforting him.

"I know I shouldn't have gone. But I had to . . ." He sighed.

"Why?"

The question seemed to surprise him. "Huh?"

"Why did you *have* to go out?"

"You wouldn't understand."

"Unless you explain it to me, I won't."

"I just had to. I wasn't smoking pot."

"I know it's hard to make new friends. But you *know* the rules. I can't tell you how disappointed I am right now." She paused and looked him in the eye. "And I don't think those boys are the kind of friends you need. You should be a better judge of character. Consider yourself grounded."

"For how long?"

"Indefinitely—maybe for the rest of your natural life." She rubbed her forehead. "Just go eat breakfast and I'll be down to drive you to work."

He left the room, his shoulders slumped, his walk not much more than a shuffle.

Lily didn't want to see Clay any more than Riley did. She couldn't hide from him, either. The immediate shock of discovering he was a father had surely worn off enough for him to begin to see things rationally. Riley's antics last night might just be enough to scare him off permanently. What man in his right mind would take on this kind of worry if he didn't have to?

She went into the bathroom to wash her face and discovered she'd finally started her period.

\*     \*     \*

Lily decided to take the confirmation that she wasn't pregnant as the first step in a positive change in the tide of events. And the next step was to treat Clay as if he were on the same team instead of the enemy. Because the way things stood right now, he was exactly that.

She walked Riley into the marina office, feeling the strain of the situation every bit as much as her son.

Clay wasn't anywhere to be seen.

Riley pointed to the back. "Sometimes he's in the shop when I get here."

"Go see and bring him back here."

With the dreaded gait usually reserved for that final walk to execution, he disappeared through the rear door. A minute later Clay stepped into the office. Riley hung in the doorway behind him.

During the drive there, Lily had tried to reinforce how fortunate Riley had been that Bud had been the one to find him. Now it was time for him to step up. "Riley," she prompted.

He returned to her side and straightened his sagging shoulders. After licking his lips and a couple of false starts, he said, "I appreciate what you're doing for me. I'm sorry I was so much trouble last night."

Lily nudged him with her elbow.

Swallowing hard, he then added, "I understand if you have to report this to the sheriff."

For a long moment, Clay stood there with his arms crossed and an unreadable expression on his face. Lily wanted to smack him for making Riley squirm, but kept her mouth shut and her hands to herself.

Finally he said, "I said my piece last night. You know how I feel about honoring obligations."

Lily felt Riley's brave facade begin to crumble. Her

instincts were to rush in and list a dozen reasons why it would be better if Clay didn't speak to the sheriff about this. Suddenly she realized that maybe, just maybe, she hadn't intervened in the past only because Peter's parents had done it for her. This was her first *real* test.

She waited in silence with her insides squirming.

Riley forced himself to look Clay in the eye and said, "I understand."

Lily's heart broke with pride. Her son might still be screwing up, but at least he was beginning to take a little responsibility.

After a second, Riley asked, "Should I start on that Chris-Craft now?"

"Go on."

Lily couldn't begin to gauge what was going on behind Clay's neutral expression.

Once Riley was out of earshot, he asked, "Did he come to you?"

"Yes. He didn't say much, just that he felt like he needed to meet those boys. I know he's lonely here, but I explained, as I'm sure you did, that those boys aren't going to be good for him."

Clay nodded. "Anything else?"

"He said he wasn't smoking. I know bet—"

"I don't think he was."

Lily narrowed her eyes and tilted her head. "What makes you think that?"

"He wasn't acting stupid—in the silly sense, of course he was stupid for being there—and his eyes were clear." Before Lily could grab that and run with it, he said, "That doesn't mean he wasn't *going* to."

Lily started to tremble, suddenly afraid to take a misstep that would lead Riley to a place where she'd no longer have a chance of recalling him. "I've seen what addiction can do—I'm scared to death he's going to follow Peter." The statement was fueled by anxiety, had she not been so frightened her good sense would have stopped it at her lips. It was too late.

She saw Clay's eyes change.

"Since Riley *isn't* related to Peter, you don't need to worry about heredity working against him." His tone was cold, but not hostile. "I think you're underestimating him."

"Hey, Bud!" Riley called. "Need a hand here."

Clay started toward the door.

She said, "I'll be on the dock tonight after eleven. If you can't make it I—"

"I'll be there." He disappeared through the door.

As she drove away from the marina, Lily found a certain measure of comfort in having Clay involved with Riley. Even with the possibility of Clay telling the sheriff, she was glad he'd gotten involved last night. It felt good to have another adult directly involved, someone to, at the very least, argue with her over the best approach. After months and months, finally, she wasn't completely alone in this battle.

Not wanting to be alone, Lily went to the Dew Drop. When she entered, she recognized many of the faces, even some she hadn't known before she moved away.

She took a seat at the counter. Mildred appeared promptly with her pad and pencil. "Hot enough for you out there?"

Lily had been so preoccupied with Riley and Clay that she'd barely registered the weather. In the interest of conversation, she nodded. "Going to be a humid one."

"Thank goodness for air-conditioning. What can I get you?"

"Eggs, over easy, and toast, please."

Mildred turned over the cup that sat upside down on a saucer in front of Lily and filled it with coffee. "Have it in a jiffy."

Lily sipped the coffee, thinking how much better it tasted here.

Several people wished her good morning as they walked by her seat. For some reason, it seemed easier to think about her problems in the folds of the familiar, surrounded by people who knew who she was, who knew her family.

Lily thought about her conversation this morning with Clay. He'd said she was underestimating Riley. What exactly did he mean by that? Underestimating his potential for trouble? Underestimating his powers of manipulation? Underestimating his character?

Mildred brought her breakfast. As she set it on the counter, she said, "So, did you hear about all of the excitement last night?"

Lily's stomach fell like a stone. If there was a marijuana bust, she was going to be sick. She shook her head.

"You'll notice Cassie isn't here . . ."

Looking around, Lily nodded.

"Well, she and Skeeter Johnson were making to elope last night, when Cassie's ex comes barreling up to her house and knocks Skeeter out cold. Had to call the EMS."

It was such a relief that her son wasn't the subject of the town gossip that she leaned closer, prompting Mildred to continue.

"Seems all the sudden her ex wants her back, baby and all—"

"Cassie's pregnant?" Lily tried to look surprised.

Mildred nodded. "She hadn't been keeping it much of a secret."

"So Skeeter's the father . . ."

"She never said, but looks that way." She wiped her hands on her apron and her forehead creased with concern. "Don't know what prompted that ex of hers to come back here."

Lily recovered her manners and tried to stop looking like a sponge ready to absorb all of the dirty details. Suddenly she realized that gossip wasn't always malicious; sometimes people used it to simply communicate. It was obvious Mildred was worried about Cassie.

As Mildred walked away, Lily asked, "So did they elope?"

"Nope. Cassie always was a fool when it came to that no-good husband of hers. She left with him." She paused and patted the counter. "Poor Skeeter."

"Yeah, poor Skeeter," Lily echoed—and really meant it.

The temperature didn't fall much with the setting of the sun. The night air clung to Lily's skin, making her want to jump in the lake just for a few moments of relief. She'd dug an old electric fan out of the upstairs closet and set it up in Riley's room when he'd gone to bed at ten. When she checked him before coming outside, he was sprawled on top of the sheets, snoring softly.

She stood at the edge of the dock, with her bare toes curled over the end of the planks, and drew in several deep breaths. She was not going to blow this by falling into a confrontation with Clay. Although she'd already begun to see things that way, she had to make him see that they were on the same side.

Throughout the evening there had been numerous boats

on the lake. A night like this was perfect for boating; bright moonlight, calm waters, and oppressive humidity. She remembered the nights when she, Luke, Peter and Clay had taken the Holts' boat out late at night with the excuse that they needed to cool off. They'd go to the middle of the lake and cut the motor, then stretch out on the seats and look for constellations. During those nights, the conversation was easy, the mood subdued—it had been perfect.

Now it was late, after eleven, and the lake had quieted. Lily's mood was anything but subdued. As there wasn't a breath of air moving, the water was as smooth as glass, reflecting the moon and stars overhead. Lily searched for the Big Dipper on the water.

Over the stillness of the night, she heard a boat motor idling closer.

The time had come.

Clay was silent as he shut off the motor. Lily grabbed a line and tied the bow while he secured the stern. Once that was done, they simply stood there and looked at each other for a long moment.

"I brought out some wine. Would you like some?" she asked, gesturing toward the side-by-side chairs at the end of the dock.

He nodded once and moved toward one of the chairs, but he didn't sit.

Lily's tank top clung uncomfortably before he arrived; her nervousness now made it worse. Wishing for a breeze, she poured the wine and handed him a glass. Hoping he would follow her lead, she sat down and took a long sip.

He didn't sit, but braced his feet apart, as if readying himself for an assault.

"Clay, please sit down. We have a lot to discuss. I don't want to fight."

Moving with reluctance, he did. Rolling the glass between his palms, he sat quietly for several minutes. Lily let him.

Finally, he said, "Did you know how Peter felt about me—I mean, back then?"

The question was so far from what she expected, it took her a moment to respond. "The envy?"

He nodded, keeping his gaze fixed on the water. "Jealousy. Resentment."

She could tell, by the very way he said the words, the fact that Peter had viewed him in such a light throughout their childhood friendship hurt him deeply.

Lily exhaled a long breath. "A little." She moistened her lips. "I saw flashes of it when we were kids." It struck her that they'd been no more than "kids" when she and Peter married. "After we were married, it got worse." She hesitated. "He'd said all of the right things beforehand, but when it came down to living them . . ."

"Did he take it out on Riley?" There was an edge to his voice.

"Never!" How could he think she would have stayed with him for twelve years if that had been the case? "I have to give Peter that; no matter what the state of unrest between him and me, he *always* loved Riley. That was the only way I got him into rehab—it was for Riley. He wanted to be a good father, set a good example."

She heard Clay's deep breath and felt compelled to say more. "I believe Peter *wanted* to be over it—the doubt, the resentment. And for a while, I think he managed pretty well. But when we tried to have more children and discovered Peter was sterile, that seemed to push him over the edge. Nothing I did broke his free fall. He always feared that I loved you more. His sterility was just one more comparison where he felt he fell short."

She sighed. "As time went on, I think the jealousy was eating him alive. It changed him."

Lily's simple words resonated in Clay's head. Without graphic description, without complaint, she'd made him see how much she'd been hurt, how she'd suffered. She had faced a difficult situation and tried to make the best possible life for her son—their son.

He said, "I imagine the fact that Peter kept a secret was a big factor in his struggle. He never did have the strength to live with secrets."

Lily looked at him, her blue eyes catching the moonlight. "I suppose so. Although at the time I had no idea just how many secrets he held."

"Peter accused me of being selfish, said if I had known about the baby I would have asked you to wait for me—no matter what the consequences for you."

"Clay—" She looked ready to explain herself, but he cut her off.

"He was right."

Lily shook her head, her soft hair falling over her cheeks.

"He was. The moment I found out you were married, I wanted to kill him. I never even considered you had a reason so . . . so strong. And if you'd come to me in jail and told me about the baby, I would have insisted you go home and wait for me. I know I would have. Even though I'd been disowned by my own father and sat in the Cook County Jail, I wouldn't have seen anything beyond us being together. I wouldn't have understood how difficult it would have been for you, for your family."

Looking at Lily now, he saw her cheeks were wet with tears. He steeled himself against them and forged ahead.

"What I can't understand is why you couldn't trust me with the truth once you saw there might be a future for us."

Her shuddering breath told him she was fighting to retain control. "I wasn't sure we *had* a chance until the day you left the phone—things had been so . . . so . . . up and down. Then you went to see Peter and it was too late." She paused. "I suppose, to be perfectly honest, I don't really know if I would have told you—at least not yet. Not until I could see how things were going to go between us—and between you and Riley.

"It wasn't because I wanted to hurt you, but because I don't want to hurt Riley. He's thirteen years old. His emotions and perceptions are all skewed. This is not the time to spring a thing like this on him."

"When—"

She held up a hand. "Please, let me get this out."

Clay slid back in his chair and waited.

After a couple of sniffles, she went on. "Peter is in rehab right now, only because he wants to be a better father to Riley. Frankly, I think that's the only motivation he'll ever be able to find. If I take that away from him, it's like I'm slapping him in the face for his devotion to my son for the past thirteen years. I owe him—"

"What about what you owe Riley? And me?" Clay edged to the corner of his seat.

This time Lily wasn't able to hold in her tears. She cried quietly, covering her face with her hands. "Don't you see? It's not about anything *but* what's best for Riley. I'm his mother. What I want, what would make *me* happiest, isn't an issue. What I owe you has to take a back seat. I have to provide a stable home for him, guide him through his troubles . . ."

"I can help you."

"Oh, Clay." It was hardly more than a rush of breath. "I want that. But I can't see that telling Riley you're his father right now will do anything except throw gasoline on the fire I'm trying to put out."

He clenched his hands tightly around the wine glass. How could doing the right thing and stepping up, taking responsibility for his own child, be viewed as selfish and destructive?

Setting the wine glass on the dock, he got up. "I think you're wrong."

He knelt on the dock and untied the bow line, then got in the boat to untie the stern. When he looked up, Lily was standing right beside the boat, looking down at him. Her face was wet with tears and moisture glistened in her eyes. "At least don't tell him without letting me know first. Please." The last word was lost in a sob.

Dammit. He hated the pain she'd suffered. Mostly because, in every way, it had been because of him. He reached up and grabbed her hand, pulling her into the boat with him.

He caught her securely in his arms and held her close to his chest. The look in those teary eyes—startled, yet wanting—made his heart trip a little faster.

"I'm sorry," he said softly.

She shook her head and buried her face against his chest. Her arms went around his middle. His shirt became wet with her tears. He let her have a good cry—something that he'd bet his life she'd been denying herself for fourteen years.

After a few minutes, he felt her become still and her breathing even out. He cupped her face in his hands and made her look at him. His thumbs brushed away the tracks of her tears and he kissed her lightly.

She smiled and said, "I've seen a change in Riley—

because of you. He respects you. You two are already on your way to building a relationship—I won't take that away from you. I promise. I—I just ask that we approach this carefully, together."

He kissed her forehead. "You're an amazing woman." He sighed and pulled her close. "He's *my* son." The words made his chest squeeze tight. Would he ever get used to it? "I don't want to lose you both again. I want to be a part of his life. Whether I do that as 'Bud' or his father—I'll leave up to you. Just don't lock me out."

She closed her eyes briefly. "Thank you."

He pressed another kiss to her forehead and let her go.

She climbed out of the boat and untied the stern line, tossing it inside the boat as he started the motor.

As he pulled away from the dock, she looked so fragile, so young, standing there in her shorts and tank top. If he could recall the past, he'd do it in a minute, save her from the pain, set things right between them, live their lives as they should have been.

How could loving someone cause so much misery?

# Chapter 21

Clay kept Riley in his line of sight all morning. The more he studied his son, the less settled he became about a course of action. Their relationship was still rocky, filled with uncertainty and verbal sparring. But it was changing, evolving. Even though Riley had resisted when Clay intervened in the park, the boy had finally calmed down and listened to what he had to say. And that made Clay realize how dangerous talking to teenagers could be—what if you finally got them to listen and then led them in the wrong direction? Or drove them to do something simply to spite you? It seemed especially dangerous with a child as confused as Riley.

This morning Clay had the distinct impression that Riley wanted to talk about something. There had been a couple of moments when he almost opened up, but at the last minute had backed away. Clay acted as if he didn't notice the subtle signs that said something was going on. It was much easier to catch a squirrel when the squirrel thought you weren't interested.

As Clay watched the boy work in the shop, it struck him that over the past weeks he'd learned to read Riley's moods—the finer moods, not the in-your-face attitude he flashed so much those first days.

When it was time to take their lunch break on the dock, the squirrel hopped right up beside Clay and offered a nut.

"What happens when a dad knocks his kid around? Is he arrested?"

This topic took Clay so off guard, he just sat there for a second, chewing his sandwich much longer than necessary while he tried to decipher the reason for this question. Lily had been adamant that Peter never abused Riley.

"Well, I guess that depends on the circumstances—law-wise. Personally, I think anybody who hurts a child should be beaten to a pulp."

Riley gave an easy grin at that, relieving a bit of Clay's worry that he was the child in question.

Clay felt like he owed him a better answer, so he went on, "Parental abuse is a sticky subject these days—very serious. A person needs proof to raise such allegations. The child is removed from the home—"

"Sent away? Like foster care?" Riley asked.

Clay nodded. "Most likely. Then there's an investigation. It's really hard to prove, because most of the time, the child won't tell on the parent. They think it's all their fault to begin with."

Riley shifted his weight and ate in silence for a bit. Then he said, grinning, "You'd kick their ass, huh?"

Clay laughed. Then he said, "Got anybody in particular in mind?"

He could see Riley retreat from the question.

"A kid I know in Chicago . . ."

"I see."

"I'd better get back to work," Riley said, picking up his lunch trash as he got to his feet.

Clay let him go, deciding to broach this subject again, as soon as the opportunity availed itself. Whoever was getting knocked around by his dad, it was really bugging Riley.

Riley was ticked when his mom said they had to stop at Kingston's Market on their way home after work. He was sweaty and in a bad mood. All he wanted was a shower and to be left alone.

"Come on in with me," Lily said as she grabbed her purse and opened the car door.

"I'll wait."

"I need you to pick out snacks and cereal."

*Yeah, right.* She didn't even trust him to sit in the parking lot for fifteen minutes without a babysitter.

At least Kingston's was air-conditioned. He got out and followed her inside.

While his mom was sniffing and squeezing peaches in the produce section, Riley hung back, trying to look like he had a reason to be in the store. He picked up a foil bag of cinnamon-flavored bagel chips and tossed them slowly from hand to hand. When he looked up again, he saw Mickey just outside the plate-glass window, heading into the store with her dad and brother.

"Mom, I'm going to go say hi to Mickey." He put the bagel chips back.

After his mom nodded approval, he started toward the front of the store.

He wasn't sure how he was going to get her attention. He sure didn't want to talk to her in front of her dad—not after seeing him in the park the other night.

As it turned out, Mickey saw him as soon as she came through the door. She walked away from her dad. Neither Mr. Fulton nor her brother seemed to notice she'd left them.

She met Riley halfway, in front of the aisle that held the cereal and crackers.

"Hi," she said. "You here by yourself?" She looked around his shoulder.

"Nah, I'm helping my mom. She's sniffing peaches." He jerked a thumb over his shoulder, pointing to the produce section.

Mickey laughed. "Is that anything like sniffing glue?"

He didn't think she'd be making that kind of joke if she knew what her dad was up to. He forced a chuckle.

Mickey pushed her hair back behind her shoulder. That's when he saw it. A greenish bruise on her collarbone—about the size of a thumb. She seemed to notice he was staring and quickly pulled her hair back over it.

"Your dad do that?" he asked, his stomach tying itself in a knot.

Her gaze fell to the floor and she seemed to retreat within herself, much as he'd seen her do when in her mother's presence. "It's nothing."

"It looks like he grabbed you. Bet it's worse in the back." He reached a hand out.

Taking a tiny step away from him, she said, "It's okay. I just got mouthy, that's all."

"Did you tell your mom?"

She shook her head. "Really, it was my fault. Besides, he's dropping us off at home after dinner. I probably won't see him for a while."

Over her shoulder, Riley saw Mr. Fulton and Drew coming toward them. Mr. Fulton had his arm around Drew's shoulders. "Mickey," he called.

Riley watched her eyes as she took two steps backward. The message she was sending was clear; she didn't want him to make a scene. She was scared.

So he just stood there, like a big dope, digging his fingernails into his palms.

She blinked what might have been a *thanks,* then said, "'Bye," very softly, and walked away.

Riley stared at her long blond hair as she left him. His eyes were stinging. He wanted to stop her. But he was a coward. He just stood there and watched her go with her dad—who didn't hurt her very often, but apparently had found occasion to just recently.

Grinding his teeth together in impotent fury, he turned around and ran right into his mom.

"Where's Mickey? I wanted to say hi."

He pried his tight lips apart enough to let out a few syllables. "With her dad. Back there." He pointed toward the butcher's counter.

"What's the matter? Did something happen?" His mom had that just-let-me-at-'em look on her face.

Angry look or not, Riley knew his mother couldn't do anything to help Mickey. If she talked to Mickey's mom, that was just going to make both of Mickey's parents mad. If her dad put a bruise on her for being "mouthy," he'd really let her have it if he thought she was telling other people about it.

"No. Nothing happened."

Just then the Fultons came back to the front of the store. Riley stared hard at Mr. Fulton, trying to say, *I know what you did, you bastard,* with his eyes.

But Mr. Fulton didn't pay the slightest attention to him. Instead, he walked up really close to Riley's mom. "Hello, Lily."

There was something really slimy about the way he said his mom's name. And he was standing way too close to her. It made Riley's hands itch with the need to push him away.

"Tad." She tried to back up a little bit, but bumped into the end-cap on the aisle.

"I've been thinking," he said, very softly. "Seems like since you're staying in town, you and I should reacquaint ourselves. How about dinner?"

Riley saw his mom's back straighten. She quit leaning away from him. "I don't think that's a good idea, Tad." She added more quietly, "I'm not interested in your games." Then she stepped around him.

For a split second Riley thought Mr. Fulton was going to come after her. He watched and waited for him to make a move—Riley would *have* to step in then. But the guy stopped himself and just glared at her back.

As she passed Mickey, Mom said, "Hi, there, Mickey. How's your summer going?"

It was impossible to keep up with the change. One minute his mom sounded like she was spitting nails, the next she was nice to Mickey. At least she didn't hold Mickey's creepy dad against her.

Mickey smiled nervously. "Good. Thanks, Mrs. Holt."

"That invitation to come out and swim still stands."

Tad stepped closer to his daughter. "I don't think that's a good idea, Lily." He mimicked the disgusted tone Riley's mom had just used on him.

Lily shot him a dirty look, then smiled at Mickey and walked to the checkout.

Riley wanted to ask if they could just take Mickey home with them—no way did he want her to have to leave here with that big jerk. But his mom couldn't do anything; adults have to have *proof* before they can help a kid.

Of course, if it actually happened that someone did something to help, there was the possibility that they might take

Mickey away, send her to a foster home. She might never even come back to Glens Crossing.

Proof wasn't going to do Mickey much good.

As Lily loaded her groceries into her trunk, she noticed Tad and his children coming out of the store. Once she was in the car, she looked over and saw them—all three—climb into a Corvette parked defensively at the very edge of the lot.

"Put your seat belt on," she said to Riley, keeping an eye on the Fultons in the rearview mirror.

"It's on. Geez, Mom. What's with you? I always put it on."

She looked at her son and smiled. "Good. There's a law, you know."

He looked at her like she'd lost her marbles. "Yeah, I know."

She started the car and pulled out of the parking space.

While she was waiting for traffic to clear so she could pull out of the lot, she saw Tad's black Corvette pull up behind her. Both of those kids were squashed into a single seat, no seat belt. What was Karen thinking, allowing him to cart her kids around like that?

Lily turned left onto the highway. When she glanced in the rearview mirror again, Tad's car swung into the lane behind her. It was still light, but the clouds had moved in, making it darker than normal. He'd switched his headlights on.

A chill ran down the back of Lily's neck. Those were the headlights that had been following her on Mill Run Road the other night—low and blue-white in their brightness.

The realization that followed made her stomach lurch.

As soon as she got home, she went upstairs to her underwear drawer. She dumped the entire contents out onto her bed and sorted through them. A black lace thong was missing. She knew it had been in the drawer, because when she unpacked she discovered it stuck inside another pair of dark panties. She remembered because she hadn't intended to bring it.

"I oughta take that thorny yellow rose and shove it up his ass."

Tomorrow, she'd call the sheriff and file a complaint. Lot of good it would do—unless the sheriff got a warrant to search Tad's house for her missing panties. She actually had to laugh at the thought. Still, it couldn't hurt to have the sheriff keeping an eye out around her place. That slick black Corvette had no business anywhere near the lake house.

She gathered up the entire pile of underthings and took them down and threw them in the washing machine.


Later that night, the telephone rang. Riley made no effort to answer it; nobody but his dad called him here. He was surprised when his mom brought the cordless phone to him in his room.

She said quietly, as she handed it to him, "It's Mickey."

His stomach felt like it bounced off a trampoline as he took the phone.

"Hello?"

Mickey sounded like she'd been holding her breath. "Hi."

"What's up?" he said, just like she called every day.

"Nothing. I just felt like talking to someone who doesn't have the same last name as me."

She was trying to make her voice light, but Riley could tell she was a little hoarse. Had she been crying?

"Well, I guess you called the right number, then." He

tried to sound more cheery than he felt. When she didn't say anything else right away, he said, "I finished the book."

"You did?" Now her voice sounded really happy, not fake happy. "Did you like it?"

"Yeah." Riley found that once they started talking about the story, it was hard to stop. They talked about the characters, and who did something that was totally stupid, and how cool it would be if there were wizards and elves. They decided if anyplace had such creatures, it would be the place by the creek where she liked to read.

He was surprised when his mom came upstairs and peeked in his room. She pointed to his clock.

How did it get to be ten? He nodded and shooed her away so he could say goodbye in private.

Riley fell asleep wishing with all of his heart that he held special powers, like Gandalf, the wizard. Then he'd take care of Mr. Fulton.

For most of the next day, Riley stewed over ways to make Mr. Fulton pay. He must have been screwing up at work, because Bud kept asking him if he was all right and sticking close by. It was almost like the first weeks Riley had worked here. Except now it felt like Bud's attention was because he was concerned, not because he was watching and waiting for Riley to mess up so he could yell at him.

It struck Riley then, he didn't know exactly how it happened, or when things changed, but he didn't hate Bud anymore. Didn't love the guy, either. But he didn't spend every night dreading coming here the next day.

It was getting on toward the end of the workday. Riley was cleaning the grease off his hands in the restroom. He looked at himself in the mirror and decided it was time to act. He was going to tell Bud. Bud was a guy—a big guy—

a crazy guy. He could kick the T-man's ass. If Mickey's dad knew somebody would come after him if he hurt his daughter, maybe he'd think twice about it.

He finished washing his hands and splashed cold water on his face. If he got out there right now, he'd have a few minutes before his mom showed up.

He was working what he was going to say out in his mind as he neared the back door of the office. What he saw when he looked through that door made him freeze in place.

Bud stood very close to Riley's mom, his hands on her face. Lily reached up and put her hands on top of his, but not to pull them away. They just looked at each other for a long time.

Then he kissed her. Oh, my God, Bud was kissing his mother!

Riley wanted to scream. Wanted to yell. Wanted to kick Bud's ass.

Instead, he turned around and kicked the steel door that was partially open between the shop and the office. It crashed against the shop wall and flew back toward him. He kicked it again.

Then he walked into the office, right past his mom and Bud. They'd jumped apart, both looking like they'd just been caught doing something dirty—which they had.

Walking straight to the car, he got in and slammed the door.

When his mom came out and got in the car, she said, "Riley, things aren't always what they seem. . . . There are a lot of things you don't understand yet—"

Riley cut her off. "Don't bother. I have eyes." She could just save the lame *explanation*. Funny, when he offered an explanation, his mom always called it an *excuse*.

"Riley. It's not—"

"It's not? Oh, you mean you weren't really kissing him?" He crossed his arms over his chest and stared out the windshield. "Take me home."

"I can see we're going to have to wait until later to talk about this." She started the car and headed home.

"Way later."

When they pulled in the driveway, he asked, "Does Dad know?"

"Know what?"

"That you've hooked up with Bud?"

"We haven't 'hooked up.'"

"Looked that way to me." He got out of the car and slammed the door. He knew the house would be locked, so he walked back toward the road so he didn't have to talk to her while he waited for her to unlock it.

For five minutes, he paced the gravel drive. Things had been going okay at the marina. Why did Bud have to screw everything up by kissing his mother?

Riley stomped back to the house and went inside. He headed straight for his room. He heard her moving around in the kitchen.

"I don't want dinner," he yelled, and ran up the stairs two at a time. Before he went to his room and slammed the door, he snagged the cordless phone from his mom's room.

After a few minutes, he could breathe again. Mickey's number was on the caller ID. He dialed it. If someone else picked it up, he was going to hang up.

Luckily, she answered.

# Chapter 22

Lily sat at the kitchen table, a turkey sandwich untouched before her. The television droned on in the living room. She'd turned it on because she couldn't stand the silence.

She told herself Riley was young and rash, and he would come around in time. But she didn't know that she would ever manage to sew all of the pieces that made her a whole woman into one piece of fabric.

She got up and threw the sandwich away, then went to take a shower. Riley's door was closed but she saw his shadow pass in the space between the door and floor. He was pacing. Nothing she did now would have a positive outcome, so she went into the bathroom and closed the door. Just as she got in the shower, she realized she hadn't picked up the cordless and brought it in with her.

She was wrapping herself in a towel when she heard the phone ring. She yelled through the door, "Riley, can you get that?"

It continued to ring.

"Errr." She hurried down the hall to her room and picked it up.

"Mrs. Holt, this is Mickey, can I speak to Riley, please?"

"Sure." She carried the phone to his door. She knocked, then opened it. "Mick—"

The room was empty.

"Oh, shit." Lily went to the top of the stairs and called his name. Securing the towel with her free hand, she ran down the stairs.

She was alone. She remembered the phone in her hand.

"Mickey, he's not here."

She started to punch the off button when she heard Mickey say, "Oh, no!"

Lily brought the phone back to her ear. "What? Why did you say that?"

The girl hesitated.

"Mickey, please tell me. Riley was very upset—"

"I know. . . . I . . . I think he might have gone after my dad."

"What?" Lily tried to gather her thoughts; why would Riley go after Tad?

"I had," she sniffled, "a bruise—Riley was mad be—"

"Oh, God! I have to hang up. Stay right where you are." Lily disconnected and hit number one on speed dial.

Clay's phone rang five times. Lily was ready to give up when he answered.

"We have to find Riley. Mickey said she thinks he went after Tad. I don't know where he lives."

"What do you mean, 'went after Tad'?"

"He thinks he hurt Mickey. Clay, I know Tad is capable of violence. We have to find Riley!"

"I know where he lives. I'm on my way, meet me at the end of your drive."

Lily threw the phone on the bed and grabbed a pair of shorts and a T-shirt. She dressed as she hopped down the stairs. Two steps from the bottom, her foot slipped and she bounced on her backside the rest of the way down. Her wet hair fell over her face. She shoved it out of the way and slipped on her tennis shoes.

She ran out into the night.

Clay stopped so quickly at the end of her drive that his tires squealed. Lily had the door open before the truck came to a full stop. She was barely in her seat when he hit the gas again, the thrust slamming her door shut.

"Should I have called the sheriff?" Lily asked.

"No. We just need to stop him before he does something stupid." He ran a hand through his hair. "I knew something was up with him—all of those questions."

"What questions?"

"He wanted to know what could be done if someone abused their child. But he didn't seem so crazy as to go after a full-grown man on his own." He pounded the steering wheel.

"He wants to hurt Tad—because he hurt Mickey."

Clay shook his head. "He thinks he can take on a grown man?"

The way he said it made Lily want to throw up. She cranked her window down all the way and let the humid air blow on her face. It wasn't much help, but it kept the dry heaves away.

They took a corner too fast. The truck slid sideways. Lily watched a utility pole hurtling in their direction. Clay worked the steering wheel and straightened the truck. A loud thud made Lily flinch. The driver's-side mirror came flying through Clay's open window, narrowly missing his head. It landed with a clank in the space behind the seat.

"It won't do any good if you kill us before we get to him!"

He started to brake. "There, that's Tad's house."

There were no lights on inside.

"His car's not there."

"Dammit!" Clay shouted. Then he asked, "If *you* didn't know where Tad lived, would Riley?"

Panic bloomed anew in Lily's chest. "God, I don't know! I guess he could have asked Mickey—or looked it up in the phone book."

"I'm going to take a quick run around the house, just to be sure." He was gone before she could say anything.

He was gone long enough that Lily thought something had happened to him. The little house was surrounded by tall shrubbery, making it difficult to see anything. She was halfway out of the truck when he came trotting back into sight.

"Nothing," he said as they climbed back inside.

"Maybe we should call Mickey and see if she knows anything else."

"Good idea. Bring your cell phone?"

"Shit!"

He started the truck and swung it in a U-turn. "We can stop at a pay phone. The Shell station—"

He stopped talking so abruptly that Lily thought something had happened to him. Before she could ask what was wrong, he said, "The park. I have a hunch they're at the park."

"A hunch? We're supposed to go on a *hunch*?"

"My hunches are usually right."

"Usually?"

"Got any better suggestions?"

The only other course of action she could think of was to

call the sheriff. He wouldn't have any better idea where to find Riley and Tad than she did.

She said, "No. Hurry!"

Clay slowed the truck when he entered the park gates. Then he turned off the headlights. It was pitch-dark; the park closed at sunset and had no lighting.

"What are you doing? We can't see," Lily said.

"If our eyes don't get used to ambient light, we won't ever be able to see anything outside the headlight beams. I doubt they're faced off in the middle of the road."

"Can't you go faster?"

"I'm driving by feel—"

"Let me out; I can walk faster."

"Just a—"

"Look! Tad's car."

There it sat, long, low and sleek, looking like a panther awaiting prey.

Clay shut off the engine and let the truck coast until they were near the Corvette. "I don't want them to hear us coming."

"Why the hell not? Let's scare the bastard off!" Lily's voice was a squeal.

"I don't think Tad's the kind of guy you want to put between a rock and a hard place." He reached over and grabbed the back of Lily's neck and applied pressure to get her to look at him. "We have to be quiet. If you can't do that, you wait right here."

"Why?"

"I've said it before, Lily. I think you underestimate your son. I think he came here to get Mickey's father *away* from her."

"What do you mean?"

"I need to get out there." He let her go and opened his door carefully. "Can you come quietly?"

She nodded.

He nodded back and they crept out of the truck. Lily left her door open—she understood.

They moved swiftly and silently, Lily following Clay's lead. They headed toward the stand of shrubbery where he'd found Riley a couple of nights ago. It was about thirty yards from where Tad's Corvette sat, in the darkest corner of the playground near the woods.

He heard voices and stopped, holding up a hand to signal Lily. The voices weren't raised; they were normal conversational tones. That helped solidify his gut feeling—Riley had something more inventive in mind than hitting the guy over the head with a baseball bat.

*God, I hope I'm right.*

He could tell Lily was getting antsy beside him. He drew her along with him, moving sideways until they were just a little closer to Riley and Tad, but had a couple of tall white pines to hide behind.

Once concealed, Lily whispered, "Why are we waiting? Let's get Riley out of here." She actually inched toward them.

Clay held her still, but kept his eyes on Tad.

Then it happened. Tad drew something from his pocket and handed it to Riley.

Clay clamped a hand over Lily's mouth when he heard her sharp intake of breath. "Just watch." He tried to infuse as much calm confidence in his voice as he could, but Lily's muscles were like stone under his touch. Her panicked gaze flickered to him, then back to Riley.

She was going to bolt. He tightened his hold.

Just as he felt Lily's teeth on his fingers, the sheriff came out of the woods and a couple of deputies rushed from the direction of the parking lot, guns drawn, a handheld spotlight on Riley and Tad.

Clay pulled his hand away just as Lily was about to take a huge chunk out of his ring finger. She turned on him and said in a hissing whisper, "Why did you wait? Now it's too late."

Tad grabbed Riley and held the boy in front of him as a shield. Riley tried to struggle, but Tad jerked his forearm across the boy's windpipe. Riley's strangled yelp drew Lily's attention.

She scrabbled forward just as Clay was reaching to hold her in place. His fingers slipped from her arm and she was gone. She sprang from behind the trees and ran toward her son.

Shit! Clay pressed more deeply into the shadows. He was the only one in a position to do anything to free Riley.

From all of the shouting, Tad must be threatening to have a weapon. Even if he didn't, these lawmen weren't trained to shoot a handgun at a moving target holding a hostage in the dark. None of them would risk the shot.

He couldn't let Tad get to his car with Riley.

Clay listened carefully to the rise and fall of agitated voices across the playground, timing his dash into the woods to his best advantage. God in heaven, he never dreamt he'd ever again need the skills he'd honed so finely. But he thanked his maker for all of the hard-learned lessons.

Tad wasn't thinking clearly. He was backing away from the sheriff, but not away from the tree line.

Waiting for the moment when Tad moved into his range, Clay quietly stepped out of the woods. In two silent strides he was close enough. He hit Tad on the back of the neck and the man fell like a deflated balloon.

Riley fell forward, away from Tad.

Lily was with him by the time he hit the ground.

Sheriff Clyde handcuffed Tad, then searched him. "No weapon. Plenty of cash and . . . oooh, lookee here, I bet he doesn't have a prescription for these." He handed a baggie of pills over to his deputy.

He nodded to Clay, then turned to Riley. "You know, son, I can't understand why you'd put yourself in this position—"

Lily looked up at him, fear on her face. "Please, Steve, he—"

Riley was struggling to free himself from his mother's grip. "Did it work? Will he go to jail now?"

"I imagine he'll plead guilty," the sheriff said. "If not, you may have to testify. But, yeah, one way or the other, he's going to jail."

Clay could see Lily mentally connecting the dots. She got to her feet and grabbed Riley's shoulders, giving him a shake. "You did this on purpose?"

Sheriff Clyde looked at Lily. "I apologize for letting your son come into harm's way. I moved as soon as he called me and told me what he was up to, but this situation was fully in play by the time I arrived."

Riley looked at his mom, standing tall and proud as he explained about the kids at the arcade. "They called him T-man, but I knew who he was, even before I saw him the other night." His gaze shifted to Tad and his lips tightened. "He won't be hitting any girls now."

The sheriff put a hand on Riley's shoulder. "No, he won't. Not only was he dealing, he was doing it in a public park. Law has special provisions for that—he's in *big* trouble." Then he paused. "And you, Mr. Holt, are forbidden from pulling this kind of stunt again. It could have turned out very differently." His gaze carried the weight of what might have happened.

"Yes, sir."

Clay noticed Riley looked the sheriff square in the eye when he said it.

Clay kept himself to the fringes of the activity while Tad regained consciousness and was escorted to a police cruiser for his trip to the county jail. He wanted to step into the light, tell Riley that he was proud of him, but held back.

When Tad was taken away by one of the deputies, the sheriff offered Lily and Riley a ride home. Lily looked over her shoulder at Clay.

He nodded and took a small step backward.

She turned to the sheriff and Riley, who was talking to the sheriff a mile a minute, gesturing with his hands.

Clay headed toward his truck with a strange unsettled feeling in his soul. He'd been a part of this evening—yet he remained an outsider. He'd felt the gut-wrenching panic of a parent when he realized Riley was in danger; he'd fallen back on old instincts to save his son. Now that his tiny part in this drama was done, he no longer fit into the picture.

"Hey!"

He turned at Lily's shout.

She and Riley were hurrying after him. "Don't leave us stranded here."

He waited in silence, keeping all of the joy he felt at seeing them run after him buried beneath his Bud Winters exterior. When they climbed into his truck, Lily sat in between him and Riley. For a brief second, Clay was able to pretend they were an ordinary family.

The kid was still pumped from the excitement. So pumped he apparently forgot he was mad at Clay for kissing his mom. "Man, that was so cool, how you just hit the guy and he went down." Out of the corner of his eye, Clay saw Riley lean forward and look around his mom.

Clay just gave Riley a nod. He didn't want to encourage any questions about where he'd acquired such talents.

Lily must have sensed it and diverted the conversation. "If it hadn't been for Bud, I would have blown this whole thing. He had confidence that you knew what you were doing."

"Bud?" Riley seemed shocked.

"Yes, *Bud*."

Then Riley leaned forward and looked around Lily again. "You knew Tad was dealing?"

Clay glanced at his son, who seemed much older than he'd been just this afternoon. "I'd heard a few things to make me wonder. But I didn't *know* until you took off after him tonight. I knew you were too smart to just call him out and have a fistfight."

At that, Riley settled back in his seat and fell quiet.

When they stopped in front of the lake house, Clay put the truck in park, but didn't shut off the engine. Riley opened the door and jumped out immediately, then waited for Lily.

She hesitated.

Clay nudged her with his elbow and tilted his head toward Riley. She slid across the seat and got out. After seeing they were safely on the porch, Clay put the truck in reverse and started backing out of the driveway.

A shout stopped him. Riley ran up to the side of the truck. He paused, as if he had second thoughts, then said, "Thanks."

Clay kept his smile tempered and nodded. "Go take care of your mother. She was really scared."

Riley started back to the house, then he called, "Better get that side mirror fixed. Sheriff'll be after you."

Clay waved and backed out of the drive, onto Mill Run Road.

This evening he'd choked down a horrible cocktail of fear, confusion and impotence. But there was one thing that had become resoundingly clear. He loved his son.

# Chapter 23

A week after that awful night in the park, Lily breathed a sigh of relief when Sheriff Clyde called to tell them that Tad had pled guilty—there would be no need for Riley to testify.

There was another reason for her spirits to lighten: Clay and Riley had worked side by side all week long and things were as normal as they ever were between the two of them. The fact that Clay believed in Riley seemed to have offset the fact that he'd kissed Riley's mother.

When Lily picked Riley up at work, she told him of the sheriff's call. He seemed glad, yet she could see he was a little disappointed not to be going into a courtroom and pointing his finger at Tad Fulton.

She then told him that his grandmother had called earlier in the day. "She wants you to come to Chicago for the Fourth of July."

Riley was quiet for a moment. Then he shook his head slowly. "I can't leave Bud here on the Fourth by himself. That's the busiest day of the year. He needs me."

Lily was so stunned, she had to work to keep her mind on the line of conversation. "Your grandparents really miss you."

"Maybe I could go another weekend—one that won't be so busy for Bud."

After a moment, she said, "I think that's a very mature decision."

"Well, I have an obligation."

She smiled at him and drove out of the parking lot. Whether Riley knew it or not, she could see that he respected Clay. The positive influence Clay was having on her son's character was showing more every day.

"You know," she said, "Bud's real name is Clay. Clay Winters." She paused to see how the topic settled.

"Hmmm." At least he didn't turn his back to her.

"He was a good friend of your dad's when they were kids."

Riley turned suspicious eyes her way. "And what about you?"

"He was my friend, too. He and Dad and Uncle Luke and I spent summers together."

"I'd never kiss *my friend's* wife."

She sighed softly. "That's where things get complicated. First of all, your dad and I aren't married anymore—and no matter how much you wish for it, we won't be again. Your dad and I just aren't good for one another."

"How can you say that? Remember how much fun we had when we went to the beach?"

"Of course there were good times. And I don't expect you to understand all of our reasons, but if your dad and I stayed married, I'm afraid he would never have gotten help for his drinking."

"But he is! And he's getting better."

She nodded. "He is. But it's not me that he's working to get better for—it's you. No matter if we live together or in different houses, your dad will always love you, and you'll always be able to do the things you want with him."

"Yeah, yeah, I've heard it before."

"Yes, I've said it all before, but I don't really think you've heard it."

"So what? You want to marry Bud now?"

"I don't want to be married to anybody, not right now anyway. I have to find a job, a new place to live. . . ." She glanced at him; his face wasn't pinched and angry like she'd feared. "I'm going to want to see Clay, spend time with him—he's my friend, Riley. Like Mickey is yours."

"Yeah, but I don't kiss Mickey!"

Lily turned her gaze his way and let it linger. He looked away and his ears turned bright red. She said, "But maybe someday you'll want to."

He did turn his back to her then. And that was just fine. She'd opened a dialogue, hopefully in terms he could relate to. This was a beginning—a very good beginning.

The next day when Lily arrived to pick Riley up from work, he and Clay were standing out in front of the office. They appeared to be engaged in a serious discussion. Riley made no move to come to the car, so Lily shut off the engine and waited. She wasn't close enough to hear what they were saying. Neither of them looked angry. Suddenly she realized that they looked that way less and less often.

Clay handed Riley an envelope and shook his hand. Then headed back inside the office, giving Lily a casual wave.

Riley got in the car. Lily waited for him to explain, but he didn't.

"So?" she finally asked. "What was that about?"

He lifted a shoulder and held up the envelope. "He gave me a check."

"For what?"

"My pay. He said I've covered the cost of the repairs to Mr. Willit's boat. He paid me for the hours this week that were beyond that amount."

"Oh." Lily tried to make the single word sound neutral.

"He said he called Sheriff Clyde. I don't have to come back anymore."

"I see. That's good, isn't it?" This would be the litmus test to truly gauge how things were between Riley and Clay. She nearly held her breath as she waited for him to respond.

"I told him I couldn't leave him without help for the Fourth, so if it's all right with you, I'm going to stay on."

"Well, the Fourth is just next week. . . ."

"He might need me to work a little longer than that. Is it okay?"

"I suppose." Lily had to press her lips together to keep her happiness from bubbling out of her mouth. Maybe there was a possibility that the three of them could be a family in the future.

After a minute, he asked, "Do you think Bud would mind if Mickey came to see the fireworks from the marina dock? We won't have any work to do then, everybody will be watching."

Lily tilted her head and raised a brow. "You'll have to ask Bud."

The old Riley would have asked her to talk to Bud about it.

He pressed his lips together the way he did when he really wanted something. "I will. Tomorrow."

\* \* \*

At eight o'clock in the evening on the Fourth of July, Lily picked up Mickey at her house. They then swung by the Crossing House to get Benny and Faye—who, by some miracle of modern witchcraft, had convinced Benny to leave the bar in the hands of the newly hired bartender for a couple of hours.

Faye had hold of Benny's arm, literally dragging him to the car. He was still grousing when he closed the door.

"Dad," Lily said, "if this guy is sighted and breathing he can handle the bar while the entire town is occupied watching fireworks. You'll be back here before it gets busy."

Her comment was met with an indecipherable grumble.

Lily caught Faye's eyes in the rearview mirror. Faye gave her a playful wink and Lily smiled in return. Theirs was a relationship made of milk chocolate: Too much heat or handling and it would melt into a gloppy mess. But they were slowly finding a balance that would preserve its integrity.

When they reached the marina, there were so many boats anchored for the fireworks that it looked like you could cross the lake by stepping from one boat to the next.

Riley raced up to meet them.

"I've got us all set up," he said to Mickey, pointing to a blanket spread on the grassy hill overlooking the parking lot. "I thought it would be too crowded for all of us to cram onto the dock." He looked over his shoulder at Clay, who walked up right then. "Bud said that spot on the hill is the best."

Riley and Mickey said a quick goodbye and headed up the hill.

"Too crowded, huh?" Faye chuckled. "I think the love-bug has taken a big bite out of that boy."

Lily smiled as she watched the two kids sit down next to each other on the blanket. Wouldn't it be wonderful if love could remain as innocent and uncomplicated as it was for thirteen-year-olds? She wished she could go back in time, to that first romantic summer with Clay, and revel in the certainty that love was all that mattered, love could easily conquer any challenge—as long as you had faith in each other.

But it was going to take more than faith to hold her life together now. It was going to take work.

With one last happy wave from the kids, Clay, Lily, Faye and Benny headed out on the dock. About halfway to the end there was a bench. Faye stopped and sat down.

"I think Benny and I'll be more comfortable on this bench than dangling our feet in the water out there. You go on."

Benny sat next to Faye and she threaded her arm through his.

He said, "I hope this thing gets going. I need to get back."

As Lily walked away, she heard Faye trying to coax him into enjoying himself. And for the first time, resentment didn't well up in Lily's throat.

She took Clay's hand as they strolled to the end of the dock. "Seems nobody wants a crowd tonight."

Clay smiled, then glanced at the kids on the hill. "Did she say anything about her dad?"

They sat down on the dock. Lily took her sandals off and plunked her feet in the water. She shook her head. "She's talked to Riley some, nothing to me—not that I'd expect it. Poor kid; Riley says her mom won't talk about him at all."

Lily had decided not to tell Clay that she'd deduced that Tad was the one who had been in her house and following her. Tad had dirtied enough of their summer.

"Good thing she has a friend, then," Clay said.

"Yeah." She leaned closer and rested her cheek on his shoulder. "Me, too."

He whispered, "Good thing you have Riley—or good thing you have me for a friend?"

She laughed and sat back up. "Both."

For a long while they sat there, close enough to feel each other's body heat but not touching. It grew dark, Lily could only see the running lights on the boats now. A few boaters had sparklers that flared occasionally in the night.

She grew so relaxed, absorbing Clay's nearness, listening to the mix of conversations coming across the water, that her body felt like it was made of butter.

When the first test rocket went off, she jumped.

Clay leaned close to her ear. "Remember our first Fourth?"

A little chill followed his voice, tumbling down her body. "How could I forget? I have the scar to remind me."

He slid his hand up her thigh and softly stroked his fingers under the edge of her shorts. "The best thing about fireworks is that they come after dark."

She laughed quietly. "That and the fact nobody is watching the people on the ground. . . ." Leaning closer, she kissed him.

The explosion of the first brilliant shower of sparks in the sky mimicked the flash of radiance that burst in Lily's heart. She didn't know exactly where she and Clay were headed, and had vowed not to worry herself thinking about it. She just wanted to enjoy their time together and see if they had enough to build a solid future.

"I found a place to rent, yesterday."

"You're going to stay?" He sat up straighter.

"Don't sound so surprised. I told you I wouldn't take Riley away from you again. He's made a friend here. I don't want him back at Carrigan Park—and a little distance between him and Samantha and Bill has proven to be good for him."

She adjusted herself so she could look him in the eye. The wonder and excitement she saw there broke her heart. Oh, how he'd been cheated. Well, no more. "I know the time isn't right just yet, but soon we'll need to tell Riley the truth. He already looks up to you for so much, you're already filling the role of father in so many ways. We can't ruin it with a lie."

Clay swallowed dryly and rested his forehead against hers. He didn't say anything for a long while. In a moment, his hand cupped her cheek and he kissed her. The kiss was laced with everything there was between them: friendship, regret, passion, loss, anticipation and unending love. When he released her from it, her heart was light and her body humming with possibilities.

He pulled her close to his side and she rested her head on his shoulder. The fireworks exploded overhead with pops and crackles, showers of brilliance and color.

Fireworks had brought Clay to her in the first place. And now, for the first time in fourteen years, she watched the breathtaking display with happiness in her soul, unbound by regret, looking squarely at a future. She was finally content, secure; no longer a nomad living in someone else's world. She was where she should be, in Glens Crossing with her son and Clay by her side.

# About the Author

In her first career, Susan Crandall was a dental hygienist. However, her love of reading soon expanded to a love for writing, so she left her gentle tools of torture behind and began to pen novels. After spending several years in the big city (Chicago), she returned to the Indiana town where she grew up. There, she and her husband live with their two children and an eighty-pound "labsky" (half black lab, half husky).

Susan loves to hear from her readers. Write to: P.O. Box 1092, Noblesville, IN 46060. E-mail: szcrandall@insightbb.com. Or visit her Web site at www.SusanCrandall.net.